The Stars Fell on Alabama

Eva Tirey

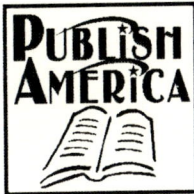

PUBLISH
AMERICA

PublishAmerica
Baltimore

First printing

At the specific preference of the author, PublishAmerica allowed this work to remain exactly as the author intended, verbatim, without editorial input.

ISBN: 1-4241-2345-3
PUBLISHED BY PUBLISHAMERICA, LLLP
www.publishamerica.com
Baltimore

Printed in the United States of America

To my husband, Carlos, who inspired me to write and supported me with his never-ending patience and love.

and

With heartfelt gratitude and thanks to all our Veterans and the dedicated women and men in uniform presently guarding our country's freedom.

Acknowledgements

I am honored and blessed to have had the opportunity to serve my country as a member of the Women's Army Corps. A majority of this novel is based on my journal that I recorded while I was stationed at Fort McClellan, Alabama, and Fort McPherson, Georgia.

If you don't go after what you want,
You'll never have it.

Chapter 1

The early morning sky had darkened to a shell gray and light sprinkling of rain dotted the clean windshield of the Pontiac Chieftain. The last strains of the Platters' hit, "Only You" played softly on the radio. Behind the wheel of the convertible, Elaine Terry was thankful the top was raised. Tiny glistening drops of water inched down the glass in slow motion.

Suddenly, a bolt of jagged lightning ripped the sky apart loosening a crack of thunder that vibrated throughout the car's interior like a shot from a cannon. The heavens burst open drenching the vehicle in the heavy downpour. Pelting raindrops drummed on the leather top, bouncing vigorously off the red hood.

"A future in the Women's Army Corps means being part of a young active world," a feminine voice said on the radio as a military march played quietly in the background. "A chance to travel to places that you have only dreamed about. Meet friends with interests like yours. You'll wear smartly tailored uniforms that are distinctive symbols of the worthwhile, important job you are doing. Each year receive a full month paid vacation. For more information about an exciting and rewarding career in the Women's Army Corps, contact your local US Army Recruiting Center located at five zero one North Main Street in downtown Madisonville. To receive a free color brochure, please telephone Taylor one, six one three two. Again that number is TA one dash six-one—three two."

She reached over and clicked off the radio. For several weeks, she had been listening to the enlistment advertisement as she drove to work. The Recruiting Center's phone number was now as familiar as her home number.

Last month her mama announced her intention of marrying the next-door neighbor, Grant Winston. She realized there was no way she could continue to live at home after the wedding. The way Mr. Winston looked at her gave her the creeps. Each time he got near her, she felt his penetrating gaze

7

stripping her clothing from her body right down to her birthday suit. Unfortunately, it wasn't something she could discuss with her mama, as she didn't want her hurt in any way.

When she had mentioned it was time for her to get a small-furnished apartment and live on her own, her mama had practically gone into hysterics. Mama had protested long and loud, putting her foot down. She told her that they would be moving into Mr. Winston's large four-bedroom home, and that she would have a room of her own. In their small two-bedroom house, she now shared a bedroom with Mama. Two of her three brothers, Bobbie and Gene occupied the other room. Her older brother, Jackson was in the Army over seas.

Soon after Mama's announcement, she had written to Jackson about the WAC advertisement and asked his opinion. He had replied saying it was an excellent idea, informing her of the benefits of the GI Bill to attend college.

Saturdays' mail brought *Greetings from Uncle Sam*, for Gene to report to Fort Knox for induction in three weeks. It gave Elaine the courage to pick up the phone and call the US Army Recruiting Office. She spoke with Sergeant Matar and asked that a brochure be mailed to her office at Western Kentucky Coal Company where she worked in the Research Department.

The following Tuesday, Suzie, the company's receptionist buzzed her office. The secretary's voice sounded over the intercom, "Elaine, please pick up the hand set."

"Yes?" she spoke into the receiver.

"There is a gorgeous—drop dead—good looking man in uniform here to see you," Suzie whispered in a breathy voice.

"I'll be right out," she answered, replacing the phone on its cradle

Seated in the reception area was a man in his mid thirties in an Army uniform. As she entered, the sergeant came to his feet and strode toward her. Compared with her brothers, he was not tall but neither was he short. He stood straight, his shoulders back; his very presence was powerfully impressive. But the thing that struck her most about him was his dark complexion. With the proper attire, he could pass for a sheik right out of an old Rudolph Valentino picture show. In her mind, she imagined him dressed in a pair of skintight pants above shinny, black, knee high boots, a blousy, silk shirt, topped with a voluptuous swirling red cape, and a white turban wound around his blue, black hair. Suzie had not exaggerated his looks. He was one handsome man.

"Miss Terry, I am Sergeant Matar," he extended his hand. "We spoke on the phone. It is a pleasure to meet you. I hope you do not mind my dropping by like this. My office is a few blocks north of here."

"Not at all." She placed her hand in his.

The fingers that wrapped around her sun tanned ones were extremely dark. He spoke perfect English, but he definitely was not from anywhere near Madisonville.

"Please have a seat." She withdrew her hand and indicated the couch where a military hat with a visor rested on top of a brown leather case. The sergeant picked up the bag with the hat and sat down again. He placed the hat on the space beside him and balanced the brief case on his knees.

She sat on the opposite end of the long sofa, his hat between them.

He extracted a large manila packet from his case and passed it to her.

"Have you been in this area long?" she asked, taking the envelope he held out to her.

"Actually, no. Would you believe I was born and raised in New York? My parents emigrated from Pakistan but we are of Arabian and Persian descendants. I scarcely know anyone in the six months I have been in Madisonville."

"That explains your mastery of the English language." She had been correct about him resembling a sheik. "I guess compared to New York this town is just a speck on the map. Although, the sign outside our city limits boasts that *Madisonville is the best town on Earth,* it hasn't much to offer in the way of entertainment—two theaters, a drive in movie and a roller rink. Also, our recently acquired WKTG radio station, where I heard the advertisement about the Women's Army Corps. Of course, we do have a dozen churches, of which not one is Catholic."

"Well, I am not Catholic so that is not a problem," he said, his grin widening, white teeth flashing against his dark skin.

"I really must get back to work," she replied, rising from the couch.

The sergeant rose lithely to his feet, picked up his hat and briefcase, and extended a well-manicured hand. "If you have any questions, please phone me or come by the recruiting office. The address and number are on the brochure."

"Thank you for bringing the papers," she said, slowly placing her hand in his.

"My pleasure," he replied. His handshake was firm but gentle.

As he released her hand, her boss, Mr. Pfeiffer walked through the area.

He nodded and smiled at them, and then he proceeded through the lobby and down the hall to his office.

Darn, now Mr. Pfeiffer would have another guy to tease her about.

Later in the afternoon, Mr. Pfeiffer entered her office and from the wide grin on his face she expected she was in for a bit of heckling. He didn't disappoint her.

Elaine took his teasing, good-natured as usual. She didn't explain who Sgt. Matar was or why he had come to see her. It was going to be difficult to tell him if she decided to enlist. Almost as tough as it would be to inform her mama.

She had worked five years for Mr. Pfeiffer. If not for him, she probably would not finished high school. No, she was not looking forward to breaking the news to him…if she enlisted.

On Saturday morning, she entered the US Army Recruiting Office letting the glass door swing shut behind her.

Sgt. Matar rose from his desk, coming forward to greet her.

"This is a pleasant surprise," he said, releasing her hand.

"I want to talk to you about enlisting," she blurted.

"What made you decide?" he asked, motioning her to the chair beside his desk.

"I liked what I read in the brochure. After thinking it over, I believe it's a great opportunity for me." She sat on the edge of the seat gazing up at him.

"Are you sure this is what you want to do?" asked the sergeant, lowering himself in his large chair.

"Yes, I'm sure." She hadn't any other choice with Mama's up coming marriage, other than to get married, and at the moment, she had not a single prospect. Basically, she would be escaping from an unpleasant situation. To put it plainly, she was running away from home.

"There are some written tests and forms to be filled out." The sergeant leaned back in his chair, his hands resting on the desktop in a prayerful mode. "Did you want to enlist today?"

"Yes, the quicker—the better."

One hour and thirty minutes later, she had filled out the necessary paperwork and completed the written tests.

"Congratulations," he said. "You did excellent on all the exams. How does the 28th of September sound for a departing date?"

"That soon?"

"I could extend it for another week," he said, studying his desk calendar.

"No. That's fine."

"You'll travel by Greyhound Bus to Ft. Knox. I'll pick you up that morning or you can meet me at the bus station. Whichever you prefer."

"I'd rather you drive me," she replied, without hesitation.

He nodded. "A WAC will meet and escort you to the induction center for your physical exam. Once you pass that and you are sworn in, you'll fly to Birmingham, Alabama and then by car to Ft. McClellan. There you'll attend a mandatory Basic Military Training Program." He handed her a small manila envelope. "This is a list of the personal items you will need to bring with you. Everything else will be supplied during your training. Please follow the list carefully. Do not bring items that are not on it as they will be taken and stored until your eight weeks of basic training is completed. Any questions or comments?"

"I've never flown," she blurted.

"Does that frighten you?"

"No, it's exciting. I am looking forward to flying."

"I like your attitude. I predict you will make an excellent WAC."

"I'll do my best."

He walked her out to the lot where her car was parked. She had enjoyed riding with the top down on this warm sunny morning. Puffy white clouds floated in an aqua sky, and a light breeze rustled the turning leaves on the nearby trees.

"Nice convertible," he said, opening the door for her.

"My brother's first new car," she explained. She slid under the wheel and leaned forward to open the glove compartment for her scarf. "It's an on going battle to keep the interior clean," she said, tying the red cloth snuggly beneath her chin.

"I can imagine," he said, his black eyes resting on the white, leather upholstery. "Looks like you are doing an excellent job." He closed the driver's door firmly.

"Well, I can't take all the credit, my kid brother, Bobbie, helps me. He washes the outside and I take care of the interior."

"After you finish your basic training and are assigned to a permanent station, you are allowed to have a vehicle on post."

"Thanks, I'll keep that in mind," she said, putting the key in the ignition with a slightly trembling hand. The engine purred like a kitten in neutral, she shifted to reverse and mashed on the gas; the twin exhausts imitated a lion's roar until she applied the brakes and eased the car into drive. As she left the parking lot, she caught Sgt. Matar's reflection in the rear view mirror.

He waved, a wide grin spread across his face, his teeth white against his dark skin.

"Mama," she said, hanging the moist dishtowel across the stove bar. "I have something to tell you and I don't quite know how to say it. Sit down while I get Gene and Bobbie in here so I can tell you all at the same time."

Her mama's black brows came together in a frown as she sat down at the kitchen table.

A few minutes later, Elaine re-entered the room followed by her two brothers.

"I hope this won't take long," grumbled Gene, her younger brother by two years. A tall lanky young man with blond hair the same shade as hers. "CW is giving us a ride to the picture show," he continued, lowering his body leisurely onto the chair at the end of the table.

Bobbie, the taller of the two boys with wide shoulders for a fourteen-year old, had dark hair and eyes like their mama. He picked up a chair beside the table, turned it around, awkwardly straddled it and folded his arms over the chair back.

Elaine remained standing, facing them. She clenched her hands, her nails digging into her damp palms.

"You've met the guy you want to marry," guessed Bobbie, guffawing and beaming at her.

"No," she replied, laughing with him. "Its nothing like that." She looked around the table from one family member to the next; the three of them had identical expressions on their faces.

Confusion.

"You guys know how I've always wanted to go to college—"

"I know, honey," her mama interrupted. "It was a pity that you had to turn down the scholarship when you graduated from high school."

"I didn't have any other choice." She shrugged. "It only paid the tuition. I didn't have the money to purchase my books and pay for room and board, too. Besides, I was needed at home to help out with our living expenses.

"Well, my dream is going to come true," she said in a rush. "I have enlisted in the Women's Army Corps and at the end of two years I can use the GI Bill to attend college."

Gene shot up from his chair, turning it over. "It's a joke, right?" he asked, picking up the chair and placing it upright.

"Enlisting? Enlisting in the Army?" her mama said bewilderedly.

"It's no joke," she said, looking from Gene to her mama. "I've enlisted in the WAC."

"It's the worst thing I've ever heard. How can you do this to me, Elaine? Don't I have enough to worry me with your brother leaving next month?" The tears marked moist, crooked lines down her cheeks.

"For the love of Pete," piped up Bobbie, "Mom, she's over eighteen. It's her life."

"Shhh," she soothed. "Please, Mama. Don't cry." Elaine sat down beside her. "This is something I have to do."

"It's hard to let go," mama said, still crying. She blotted her mama's tears with the paper napkin Gene handed her.

A loud beeping horn sounded out in the street.

"There's CW," said Gene. "I have to go, Sis. We'll talk later. Come on, Bobbie."

The two brothers beat a hasty retreat from the kitchen.

She ran her hands soothingly up and down her mama's back until the sobs became sniffles. Her mama looked up with red, puffy, troubled eyes. For a moment Elaine feared she might tear up again.

"Have you told Mr. Pfeiffer yet?"

"No, I haven't," she said, dabbing at the remaining moisture on mama's face. "I am not looking forward to it either. Under the circumstances, a few tears are permissible. If you hadn't stopped crying when you did, I would have joined you."

"If you feel like that, why in the world did you enlist"? Her mama's brows came together in a frown.

"Granny always said that there are times in our lives we have to make sacrifices to fulfill our dreams. I don't think two years of my life is too much for something I really want. Do you?"

"I guess not—when you put it that way. Does she know?"

"Huh-uh, but I know she'll understand. Don't get up, Mama. I want to show you the WAC brochure. Just wait 'til you see the gorgeous pictures of the post. The headquarters are Spanish architecture, white stucco buildings with red tile roofs. And I'm going to fly down there." She hugged her mama, stood, and turned toward the exit. "Ft. McClellan isn't that far away. You can visit me," she said over her shoulder as she left the kitchen.

Sometimes in life, a person's gotta do
What a person's gotta do.

Chapter 2

Elaine sat in her office staring at the daily calendar on her desk. The page read Friday, September 21, 1956, her last day of work. She gazed around the room where she had worked the last four years after graduating high school.

When she had gotten up enough courage to tell Mr. Pfeiffer of her enlistment and give two weeks notice, he had insisted she spend the last week with her family. The days had passed in a flurry of activity. Her assistant, Jewel Long's transition to head of the department had gone smoothly.

She cleaned off the desktop and placed the paperweight Mr. Pfeiffer had given her two years ago on top of the box containing her personal items. She ran a finger across the lettering on the marble rectangle; *A cluttered desk is a sign of genius.*

The intercom buzzed. "Elaine, Mr. Pfeiffer wants you to come down to the cafeteria before you leave," said Suzie.

Elaine picked up the small carton from the desk and walked to the door. There she paused—turned—glanced around the room before pressing the light switch. She closed the door firmly behind her.

She entered the darkened room. Suddenly, bright lights flicked on.

"Surprise," everyone shouted.

Elaine looked at the familiar faces crowding near her. All the company employees from the mail boys up had gathered to say good-bye.

She singled out Mrs. Mac, a petite, well-groomed lady in her early sixties. "You promised not to do this," she accused, placing the box on a nearby table.

"I guess it slipped my mind." Mrs. Mac's blue eyes twinkled, and she swept a hand to the side of her short, silver hair. Everyone laughed. She was the office manager and the oldest employee there, but she had a mind as sharp as a hatpin.

The executive dining table boasted plates stacked with fancy cut sandwiches, veggie dips, cheese wedges, and relish dishes. Not one paper napkin, plate or cup in sight. Instead, a pile of company monogrammed, linen napkins, china plates, and crystal-etched glasses were grouped at the head of the table. In the center, a large cake, decorated in yellow. *Good Luck, Elaine. We will miss you.*

After they cut the cake, Mr. Pfeiffer presented her with a black and gold Waterman pen and pencil engraved with her name.

"I expect you to write me often," he said.

"I promise," she replied, replacing the cover on the box.

Mrs. Mac handed her a small ring with keys attached and a card. "We thought you might find use for these." She brought her attention to Billie and Roger, the boys from the mailroom carrying in two pieces each of blue Samsonite luggage.

Her nose stung with the threat of tears. She blinked back the moisture pooling in her eyes and began thanking everyone.

At the close of the party, her boss instructed the mail boys to load the luggage in her car.

"I meant what I said about writing," said Mr. Pfeiffer, "and you better write your mom, too. I can just imagine her calling up your commanding officer to find out why you didn't write when she thought she should have a letter from you and didn't get one."

"I surely hope not," she replied. Elaine was still embarrassed at Mama's calling to find out if she had left for home after a recent employee's bridal shower. She had learned from Mr. Pfeiffer that her mama had been doing it ever since she started working for the company.

The last of the employees drifted out.

"We better leave before the phone starts ringing," he said, chuckling.

On Thursday, Elaine chose the medium size piece of luggage. She checked off each item from the allowed list as she placed it inside the suitcase. Four pair cotton panties... Next she opened the blue cosmetic bag and checked off—one bar of soap—one-bottle shampoo—one-card hairpins—one dozen curlers. She drew a line through the optional hair dryer, as she did not own one. The last item was an electric iron. Sgt. Matar had advised not to bring one but to purchase it at the WAC PX, a small store near the barracks. Besides the things on the list, it was suggested to bring two skirts and three blouses. In the cosmetic case above the tray she placed her white Bible and the new, two-year journal given her by Granny. Together they had decided to call it the *Dreamcatcher*. Lifting out the tray, she added a small makeup bag, a package of stationery, stamps and the pencil given her by Mister Pfeiffer plus a package of ink cartridges for the pen that she placed in her purse.

It had been difficult persuading her mama not to come to the bus station to see her off. She did not want to leave in tears, and she certainly did not want the sergeant to think her a *crybaby*.

The following morning, dressed in a blue-gray suit, she awaited the arrival of Sgt. Matar on the front porch with her two pieces of luggage. She adjusted the white lace jabot neck of her blouse for the third time and picked up her purse from the porch swing. At seven thirty on the dot, a military vehicle turned into the driveway.

"Good morning," said Sgt. Matar, getting out of the car.

She returned his greeting in a steady voice while her heart seemed to be thumping wildly, threatening to jump out of her chest.

The sergeant stowed her luggage in the rear of the automobile and closed the trunk. After settling Elaine in the passenger's seat, he got behind the wheel. "Are you nervous?" he turned, gazing at her.

"Excited," she responded.

The ten-minute ride to the bus station was driven in silence. Only one bus was in the terminal, a *Louisville* designation sign on the front.

"That's your bus," he said, pulling into the parking lot.

He checked her baggage and handed her the tickets along with a large manila envelope. They stepped to the side of the vehicle to let the original passengers re-board the bus.

Sgt. Matar turned to her. "Corporal Vance will meet you at the bus depot in Louisville. You can't miss her; she will be holding a large sign that reads *Fort Knox.*" He smiled and extended his right hand. "I'll be following your progress through basic training and your special schooling. Good luck, Elaine."

She climbed the steps with slightly shaking knees. Gratefully, she sank down on the first empty seat. The drumming of her heart began to slow, and the tremors that shook her body subsided.

By the time the bus passed Central City and some smaller towns, she had begun to relax.

Several hours later, the Greyhound stopped in Elizabethtown just long enough for her to visit the ladies room and grab an egg salad sandwich at the lunch counter.

At one thirty in the afternoon, the vehicle pulled into the Louisville Bus Depot. As soon as Elaine stepped from the bus, she saw a young woman in uniform like the one in the brochure. She was holding a Ft. Knox sign. She smiled and waved to the attractive auburn haired corporal.

The WAC waved, folded the sign, and placed it under her arm. She skirted around the passengers leaving the bus to where Elaine waited for her luggage.

"You must be Elaine Terry." She extended a gloved hand. "I'm Cpl. Vance, your driver."

Elaine watched from the passenger window as the corporal expertly maneuvered through the heavy flow of traffic leading out of the city. Some drivers more impatient than others began honking their horns as the lines of cars ahead slowed to a snail's pace and stopped. Soon, they began to move again.

The post entrance was attractively landscaped; various blooming flowers surrounded the low, whitewashed buildings. Elaine noticed several groups of guys in uniform but no women.

As they drove, Cpl. Vance pointed out some of the structures, including the Battalion Headquarters. In front on a small knoll, short, flowering shrubs spelled out the letters of the Fourth Armored Division.

The car slowed at a long building with a sign depicting it as the US Army Induction Center and parked in the back lot. After entering through the double doors, she and the corporal walked down the wide corridor with doors on each side. At the end of the hall, a sandy-haired soldier sat just inside the open door. His nameplate on the desk read, Sgt. Markham.

Greeting them, he took Elaine's envelope, removed one paper, and handed it to Cpl. Vance. "Take Miss Terry for her physical, the first door on your right."

In the examining room, she met Cpl. Hodges, a nurse in a light green hospital uniform, who handed her a folded white gown and directed her to a small dressing room.

The skimpy gown didn't exactly protect her modesty. Elaine shivered and clutched the closures together as she walked back to the examining room.

"Let's get your weight and height," the corporal indicated a large scale. The nurse noted the figures on a clipboard. Next she took Elaine's blood pressure and a sample of blood out of her pricked middle finger

Cpl. Hodges opened a drawer and took out a small stainless steel apparatus. "This speculum is inserted in the vagina enabling the doctor to examine a female internally. The whole procedure is painless, but you may experience some discomfort."

Elaine's hands began to perspire and her breath lodged in her throat.

The door opened, and a tall gentleman entered dressed in the same light green-colored hospital uniform as the nurse. A stethoscope dangled around his neck.

Her heart skipped a beat then drummed frantically in her ears above the thunderously thumping of her heart.

"Elaine, this is Capt. Belmar," the nurse said. "He will be doing the internal examination."

"Hello, Elaine, I know this is awkward for you but if you follow my instructions, I'll try to make it as quick as possible. The most important thing is for you to relax."

The doctor listened to her heart and lungs before the nurse assisted her in lying down on the narrow, padded table. Cpl. Hodges guided Elaine's bare feet in two cold metal holders at the end of the examining table. She referred to them as *stirrups*. They certainly didn't resemble any of the ones on the saddles she had sat on.

The nurse covered her with a sheet and pushed the backless gown up to her waist beneath the covering.

"Please bend your knees," she said. "Now scoot your back side down the table. That's it, just a tad more." Then she smeared some kind of gooey salve on her most private part. Next she inserted the instrument she had referred to as a speculum.

Elaine flinched. It was like ice, and her heart beat out a frantic rhythm inside her chest. When Capt. Belmar placed one of his gloved hands high on her stomach, she jumped, and she shut her eyes tight.

"Just relax, I want hurt you," he said softly.

He inserted his hand inside the instrument touching her internally. Elaine cringed and gripped the sides of the table harder; she bit down on her lower lip. She couldn't breathe. Her heart pounded so loudly she wondered if the doctor could hear it, too.

They had lied; it not only hurt, it was the most humiliating, embarrassing experience she had ever suffered.

"The hymen is intact," he said to the nurse.

Then he was patting her arm. "Okay. You can open your eyes now. You did very well. Good luck in the service, Miss Terry." He removed his rubber gloves and disposed of them in a waste receptacle before leaving the room.

While she got dressed, Nurse Hodges explained that all the girls entering the service were given the internal exam to insure that none were pregnant.

"For Pete's sake, I could have told him that and saved myself a lot of pain and embarrassment. Capt. Belmar shouldn't tell his patients that it doesn't hurt since it is plain he has never had the exam."

Cpl. Hodges cackled, slapping her thighs.

"Can you honestly tell me that it didn't hurt when you had the exam?" she asked, buttoning her blouse.

"Yes, I can," replied the giggling corporal, "but I had been married, and I've heard that there is less discomfort for a previously married woman. The good news is that you won't have to have the exam again for the next two years. The bad news is when you complete your ETS or leave the service, you will be re-examined."

"Thanks for the information." Elaine rolled her eyes toward the ceiling. "Maybe I'll just stay in the service for the rest of my life."

"Oh, I forgot to mention, that every time you re-enlist, you get another physical, too," she said, laughing.

"My recruiting sergeant totally forgot to mention the exam to me, too."

"Didn't he tell you that you would have to pass a physical before you could be inducted?"

"Sure, he told me that. But he didn't mention anything about me being spread nude on a table and a guy poking around inside me. It must have completely slipped his mind."

"I can understand his lack of information." The nurse construed. "After all, it is a delicate subject to discuss with a pretty young girl. Had you had a female recruiter, it would have all been explained to you."

"It's a little late now."

"Oh, come on now. It wasn't all that bad."

"That's easy for you to say. You weren't the one staked out naked at his mercy like a victim of an Indian torture."

"I don't think that part of the female means anything more than any other part of the body to a doctor. They've seen so many, they are immune." She giggled.

"In that case I should have been screaming bloody murder," she kidded, slipping on her shoes.

"If you don't mind my asking, how did you manage to stay a virgin?"

The heat burned Elaine's face, she couldn't respond.

"Sorry, I asked. I was just curious," said Cpl. Hodges. "It's rare at your age. Not many girls come through here that are still virgins." She handed her an envelope. "Good luck, Elaine."

Cpl. Vance was waiting outside and she was whisked down the hall to another office. The corporal knocked, opened the door, motioned her inside, and closed the door before leaving.

The brass plaque on the large desk read, Maj. J. C. Andrews. Cpl. Vance had warned her that the last part of her physical was with the shrink and not to let him *rattle her cage*, whatever that meant. His nose was eagle-sized, his gray hair and beard reminded her of her grandfather.

Maj. Andrews began the interview by asking her about her home life and why she wanted to become a member of the Women's Army Corps.

She answered omitting the information about Mr. Winston and her mama's pending marriage.

He made a note on her chart. "How do you feel about the opposite sex? Do you like men?"

"I guess they are okay. I get along fine with my three brothers."

"Do you have a special boyfriend?" His brows rose in question, his eyes captured hers.

"No," she answered, short and sweet.

"Why not?" His eyes never left hers.

"I guess because my three strapping brothers scares away any guy who becomes interested in me."

"Too much over protection." The major laughed heartily, picked up a rubber stamp, marked her file, placed it in the manila envelope, and handed it to her. "Miss Terry report back to the main waiting room. Congratulations and good luck."

Elaine roamed the waiting room until she located Cpl. Vance seated next to three women in civilian clothes. The corporal raised a gloved hand, motioning her to join them.

She introduced Norma Chase, a tall blue-eyed red head, and Lydia Bryant, brown haired with whiskey colored eyes. Both girls were from the Louisville area. The third female, Gayle Butler was from Sweetbrier, Kentucky. She appeared too young to qualify, cute with shoulder length curly, sandy hair and large brown eyes.

"This way ladies," said Cpl. Vance. They trooped out of the waiting room and across the hall into a large room; a vast American Flag covered one entire wall. A low, metal railing separated them from a WAC in dress uniform standing behind a podium. The officer was introduced as Major Jameson. She explained what was expected of them as members in the Women's Army Corps.

"Ladies, place your right hand above your heart and face the flag while Major Jameson swears you in."

In a matter of minutes she and the girls pledged their oath of allegiance and became privates in the Women's Army Corps. She was now Pvt.E-1 Elaine Terry, WA8214716 of the US Army.

Cpl. Vance led them out to the parking lot, and they loaded into the station wagon. Chattering like chipmunks, they asked the driver numerous questions enroot to the airstrip.

GI grits and GI gravy,
Gee, I wish I'd joined the Navy.

Chapter 3

"That's what we are flying in?" asked Norma, after getting a peek at the small twin-engine plane on the runway. "I don't much care for the, *blinkin'* size of it."

"You're in the army now, private. You don't have a choice," retorted Cpl. Vance.

They boarded the plane with Norma still grumbling about the tiny plane. Cpl. Vance finished buckling them in and gave each of them a stick of gum.

"Enjoy it," she said. "Once you are in uniform you won't be allowed to chew gum on duty."

A good-looking guy with dark hair ducked his head and entered the plane followed by a short, ruddy-faced soldier.

"Here is your pilot, Capt. Bonelli, and his assistant, Sergeant Doyle," said Corporal Vance, and she introduced them all around. "They are all yours, Captain. Good luck, girls." She executed a salute and stepped through the exit.

"Welcome aboard, ladies," said the captain, "Before we take off, Sergeant Doyle will explain the rules of flying to you." He moved to the front of the plane and took his seat before the control panel.

"I see y'all gotcha gum. Chew it so yore ears won't clog up," said Sgt. Doyle. "Stay in yore seats at all times. Once we get air born y'all can loosen yore belts but keep'em buckled."

He picked up an orange sleeveless jacket from the floor. "This here is a life jacket. Not that y'all will be needin' it but here's how it works." He quickly put it on, buckled the straps and then removed it. "Also the bottom of yore seats are floats should y'all have to use'em."

Gayle gasped. Elaine looked over at her. The young woman had paled, her freckles stood out like the spots on an over ripe banana. Like her, this was Gayle's first flight, too.

Sergeant Doyle stepped to the cockpit and strapped himself in next to the captain. Shortly, they were rolling slowly down the runway. As they picked up speed, the plane shook and groaned, with so much noise she was sure it would break apart before they left the ground. Her gum didn't seem to be working. The faster she chewed, the louder the roaring of the engines became in her ears. She squelched her eyes tight and held on to the armrest. Soon, the noise faded to a dull humming, and occasionally the small plane jerked and bounced up and down like someone dribbling a basketball. She opened her eyes, gazing out the window at the clouds floating by like giant cones of cotton candy. Moments later, the plane was above the snow banks and all around the sky was a pale aqua as far as her eyes could see.

With nothing to look at outside the plane, she focused her eyes on the interior where Sgt. Doyle was making his way down the aisle holding to the leather straps hanging from the ceiling of the plane. A corrugated carton with a rope attached was slung over one shoulder. He reached into the box, and he handed out a bottle of pop and a package of peanut butter crackers to each of the girls as he passed between the seats.

Elaine fished an empty wrapper from her pocket and got rid of her gum. With the first bite of the tiny sandwich, she experienced a loud *pop* in her ears.

"We're crossing the Tennessee border," Sgt. Doyle shouted over the roar of the engines. "If y'all look out the windows on yore left is the Tennessee River. There it is below us."

Elaine pressed her face against the small window gazing at what appeared to be a long, dirty, blue ribbon. The plane descended following along above the ragged string until it ended in a large body of water.

"Yore looking at Wheeler Lake and just beyond is the town of Decatur, Alabama. It's fifty miles north of our destination, the Birmingham Municipal Airport. Better buckle yore seat belts. We'll be landing soon."

A short time later, they were bouncing down the runway. Any minute, she was sure her stomach would heave up its contents before the plane reached the end of the airstrip.

She was grateful for Sgt. Doyle's support as she exited the plane on spaghetti-like legs.

A very sharp Private First Class Lyons in dress uniform met the plane, escorted them to a military van, and introduced them to the two girls in the vehicle. Dolores Kramer, a blue eyed blonde from Atlanta, Georgia, and Helen Rizzo from Baton Rouge, Louisiana, olive skin, black hair and dark eyes.

They got under way as soon as their luggage was stored on the roof rack. Their driver explained that she was conveying them to the Reception Center where they would be housed for approximately one week. While at the center, their clothing would be issued, visit the dental and medical facilities, and be given inoculations.

"Oh no," they all groaned in unison at the mention of shots.

"How far is it to Ft. McClellan?" asked Dolores.

"Roughly about fifty miles, an hour's drive. We should arrive around 1730 hours, just in time for chow," replied the PFC.

"What is 1730 hours?" piped up Norma.

"That's military time for five thirty. I bet you all are getting hungry."

"You betcha," said Lydia, the other girls chiming in to agree with her.

An hour later, the girls' talking ceased as the vehicle slowed and entered the post through the Summerall Gate. Elaine craned her neck to read the "Welcome to Ft. McClellan" sign above the guardhouse. They passed several buildings of Spanish style architecture. The white stucco blockhouses with red barrel tiled roofs resembled the ones in the recruiting brochure. Neatly trimmed surrounding grounds were landscaped with evergreen shrubs, trees and colorful blooming flowers.

The car continued for a few blocks and the driver turned into a large parking area next to an enormously long, low building with a sign above that designated it as the Post Exchange.

"This is the PX, you can purchase just about anything here as in any department store. One end is the commissary which is a big grocery store."

She circled the lot and drove back the way they had entered stopping to point out the bowling alley, theater, and library. Next they slowed to go around a large circle with a huge flag on a tall pole in the middle.

"To your left is the Post Headquarters. The Spanish architectural style of the building makes it unique. Our post is located on forty-five thousand acres in the foothills of the Appalachian Mountains. The Blue Ridge Mountains surrounds us to the southwest and Choccolocco Mountains on the southeast.

"Across the street is Rock Bridge, a favorite spot of all the camera bugs."

Elaine could see why, it was made entirely from large colored stones. A lone weeping willow trailed branches into the small stream running under the bridge. Many bright flowering shrubs banked the side of the entrance facing the road.

"The Spanish architecture of Post Headquarters and that bridge makes our post the military showplace of the Third US Army," said the PFC, proudly.

Driving a little farther, the driver circled a small hill and slowed the car. "The cream-colored building up there is the Hilltop Service Club. That's where you will attend the *Cinderella Night* held in your honor after you graduate from basic training. If time allowed, I would take you all up and show you around, but we don't want to be late for chow."

Elaine caught a glimpse of a series of windows lining the front of the semi-circle structure beneath a dome-like roof.

The car snaked around and up another hill, and PFC Lyons called their attention to a beautiful chapel beneath a cluster of tall pine trees. "The WAC Chapel holds a Catholic Mass and Protestant service each Sunday."

On Galloway Road, their guide pointed out two three-storied, block buildings. "That's the WAC Headquarters and next to it is the Clerical School. Some of you may be enrolled there after completion of your basic training. The long low building across the street with all the windows is the Headquarters Mess Hall where the students and HQ personnel eat."

As they eased slowly down a small incline she pointed out a large one floor building on the right. "Mess Hall Number One where all of you will eat your meals while in basic training. It has the capacity to feed four hundred trainees at one sitting."

PFC Lyons stopped the van at a crosswalk to let a group of girls pass. They were all dressed alike in shapeless brown and white-stripped dresses, and each girl wore a light tan cap on her head.

"Gosh, what ugly dresses," groaned Norma.

"Those are new recruits," said PFC Lyons. "That's what all of you will be wearing through most of your basic training. I know they are not the height of fashion, but they are comfortable and the upkeep is easy. Wash and wear. You'll appreciate those exercise dresses when you start having to wash, starch, and iron the summer cotton dresses. On your left is my Company A. Below that is Company B and behind it is our destination, the Reception Center."

The vehicle continued down the hill and made a left at the intersection and then drove a short distance and made another left into a gravel parking lot bordered by a several huge pines.

"To your right is the Fourteenth Army Band building. And here is your new home for the next week," she said, indicating the cream-colored block structure directly in front of the car.

Each girl toted her luggage down the long, wide, walkway to the center of the three stories high barracks. They entered through the center double glass

25

doors into a large open area. Behind a high counter to their left stood a girl wearing a shapeless tan and white-stripped dress.

"Stack your suitcases inside the Day Room and have a seat." The PFC indicated a room off to the right of the vestibule. Then she turned and approached the girl behind the counter.

Elaine's eyes swept the spacious room as she stepped inside and put down her bags. It resembled a huge living room with sofas and chairs attractively arranged in-groups. A polished upright piano occupied the far end.

PFC Lyons appeared in the archway. "Each of you must sign in with the date and time on the log sheet at the desk. Use the military time 1745 hours."

After Elaine signed the book, she returned to the Day Room and sat down.

Presently, a short black haired WAC entered and PFC Lyons introduced her as Sgt. Levy before taking her leave.

She judged the sergeant to be in her late forties. Her eyes were dark like her own mama's and she immediately classified her as the *motherly* type; at least she hoped so.

"Ladies, please line up in a double file." Sgt. Levy turned with military precision and beckoned them to follow.

She walked beside Gayle as they trailed the sergeant out of the building and down the walkway. At the corner of the structure, they turned left and continued past the end of B Company and crossed the street to the steps leading to the mess hall.

In single file, they entered the long building through heavy double glass doors. The space where the food was served resembled the cafeteria in her high school, only on a much grander scale. The balance of the room contained what appeared to be a hundred small tables with four brown, folding chairs to each table. No more than a dozen girls sat scattered around the dining area.

Elaine approached a stack of metal sectional trays and automatically picked up the top one, and then selected her silverware wrapped in a paper napkin from the bin along side the trays. She placed her tray on the metal cylinders and rolled it in front of steaming pans of food. Behind each food choice, stood a girl in a stripped dress wielding a large serving spoon.

The menu consisted of southern fried chicken, green peas, mashed potatoes with gravy, sliced bread, fruit Jell-O and a small carton of milk.

High up on the wall behind the food counter, a large sign caught Elaine's attention. TAKE ALL YOU CAN EAT, AND EAT ALL YOU TAKE. Printed below in smaller letters, Seating Capacity 400.

"Tonight you may sit at any table as the mess hour is almost over. Tomorrow when you come through the line with your platoon each of you will go to the far end of the room and fill the tables from the back," instructed Sgt. Levy. "And I hope you all read the sign on the wall. It means exactly what it says."

"Yes, ma'am," replied a couple of the girls.

"I am not an officer. You will respond with a simple yes, or yes, sergeant."

After all the girls had eaten, the sergeant instructed where to stack their trays and the soiled silverware in the appropriate container.

Behind Sgt. Levy, in a double file, they trooped back to the Dayroom. After collecting their luggage, they ascended the stairs to the second floor, continued down the long hallway, and paused before a set of glass doors.

"This is the latrine—"

"What's a *latrine*?" interrupted Norma.

"A bathroom," responded the sergeant. At the end of the hall she stopped in front of ceiling high, green, double doors the width of the corridor. She opened one door and held it for them to pass into an enormous rectangular room.

"This is called a *bay*, you will be housed here for the next week," said the sergeant, allowing the door to swing closed behind her.

A series of windows ran along two sides of the room. The walls below the windows were a pale green color and the space above painted light beige. Highly polished dark green asphalt tiles covered the entire floor. Many small, narrow beds were arranged in four rows with two aisles separating them. Along side the head of each bed stood an upright green locker and a low metal locker at the foot.

"Place your luggage down beside an empty bunk," directed, Sgt. Levy, "and follow me."

Elaine put her suitcase and cosmetic bag next to a cot that held a bare mattress and trailed along with the rest of the girls behind the sergeant.

To the right of the hallway outside the bay, they entered the latrine. Opposite the shower stalls were a row of sinks beneath a long mirrored wall. At the far end of the room were enclosed individual toilets.

"Ladies, you are expected to leave the latrine as clean as you find it," explained Sgt. Levy as they exited the room.

The next door opened into a large laundry room, complete with washing machines, dryers, sinks, ironing boards and a clothesline that crisscrossed one end of the room. Across the hall opposite the laundry, they stepped into a small kitchen. Besides the usual cupboards, stove, sink and refrigerator, a single round table with four metal folding chairs sat in front of the door that opened out to a balcony the length of the room.

In the hallway outside the kitchen, Sgt. Levy pointed to doors on each side. "These rooms are occupied by the cadre."

"What's a *cadre?*" spoke up Norma.

"Myself and the noncommissioned officers of the company are referred to as cadre. All of you will be addressed as privates, trainees, or recruits until you finish your basic training."

They followed the sergeant back down the corridor to their own bay. She directed them to unpack their luggage, put their clothes on the hangers inside their steel locker, and stow the rest along with their cosmetic bag in the footlocker. After they finished that task, they were asked to line up with their empty suitcases at the far end of the bay where they passed through the single green door to an iron staircase. Their shoes resounded on the metal steps behind Sgt. Levy down two flights of stairs to the Supply Department where they were introduced to Sgt. Waite. She gave each of them receipts for their luggage and issued a set of white linens, a pillow and brown wool blanket to each girl. Before returning to their bay, they were shown the mailroom and mail-slot to drop their letters to be posted when it was closed.

Back in the bay, Sgt. Levy demonstrated the proper way to make up the small cots.

"The lights will be turned off at 2200 hours, that's ten P.M. civilian time. You must be in your bunks for bed check and no talking after lights out. Good night, ladies," she said and left the room.

After a warm shower, Elaine sat on her footlocker in her pajamas and wrote to her mama. She briefly described her first plane ride and what she had seen so far of the barracks. As she started a second page, the lights flickered. A moment later they completely went out. Quickly, she put her letter and writing supplies in her footlocker and hopped into bed.

Some of the girls continued to talk until a recruit from the other side of the bay said, "Shhh no talking after lights out."

She lay in her bunk with her eyes open thinking about the events of the day when someone came down the aisle with a flashlight. The scope of the light shifted back and forth between the beds. She closed her eyes when it neared her area.

Elaine sighed. What a long exciting day it had been except for the internal exam. Yuck!

Her eyes snapped open and she sat up. She had forgotten to write in her journal about her first day in the military. She crept out of bed, raised the top of her footlocker and fumbled around inside until her fingers came in contact with a familiar leather binder and her pen. Barefoot, she padded down the aisle to the green doors outlined by the red exit light above. On tiptoe, she stretched up peering through the small glass window. The lights were on in the hall; it was empty. She pushed the heavy door open enough to squeeze through. It closed with a loud swish-like suction. In the latrine she put down the toilet seat cover on a commode and sat with the turquoise leather book resting on her lap. Opening it to the first page, Elaine ran her hand across the smooth, blank paper before uncapping her pen. At the top of the sheet she wrote the date.

> September 28, 1956
> Dear Dreamcatcher,
> This is my first day in the military. I can't say as a WAC for I don't feel like I can be called that as yet. I had my first really humiliating experience. An internal exam. I also had an exciting plane ride so I guess that kind of makes up for the other. I think I am going to like it here. The food is good and plentiful. My bed could be a little softer but it beats sleeping on the floor.
> We are housed in a large room called a bay, and the bathroom is referred to as a latrine.
> At ten o'clock—oops I mean 2200 hours (that's military time) the lights are turned out and we have bed check. Which is where I am supposed to be now. I promise to write more tomorrow night...

No more primpin' in a looking glass,
Shine them shoes and polish that brass.

Chapter 4

The next morning bright overhead florescent lights blinked on at five A.M. For a moment Elaine forgot where she was. She sat up and glanced across the bay toward the windows. It was black as pitch outside.

"Rise and shine, ladies." Sgt. Levy opened the double doors and engaged the doorstop. "Put on your sneakers and be ready to line up outside at 0600 hours."

"Does that mean we don't wear nothin' but our sneakers?" piped up Norma.

"No, dummy," someone yelled, along with numerous giggles and snickers around the room.

Elaine dressed in a black skirt and white, batiste blouse and put on her new white sneakers. In the bathroom she cleaned her teeth before removing the curlers from her hair. She brushed her long honey blond hair, flipped it under into a stylish pageboy and fluffed her bangs up letting them curl across her forehead. The last thing she did was wash her hands after using the toilet.

In the mess hall, she ate a hearty breakfast of scrambled eggs, bacon, toast, juice and milk. She and the five new girls returned to the barracks and Sgt. Levy accompanied them on a tour of the ground floor. The entrance where they had entered the building yesterday was referred to as the Charge of Quarters area. CQ for short.

"Remember, ladies, you are not allowed outside the building without the supervision of a cadre member except when walking back from the mess hall," warned Sgt. Levy.

"Gee, it's almost like being in a reform school," complained Norma.

Was she speaking from experience?

After she returned from lunch, on her bed, she found a small, brown wrapped packet. On her footlocker was a manila colored stencil of her name and serial number on top of a folded green duffel bag. There were identical packages and bags on all the beds and footlockers. Quickly, she stripped off the wrapping of the packet. Two metal tags on a long beaded chain and a folded printed-paper fell into her hands. She read the information on her tag aloud. "Terry, Elaine N., WA8214716, T56, Baptist." Unfolding the note, she glanced at the large printed message. *YOU WILL WEAR YOUR DOG TAGS AT ALL TIMES.*

"Privates, listen up." Sgt. Levy came through the door carrying a small carton. "On your bed are your dog tags. They will be worn at all times. Come to the front of the bay and pick up a permanent marker."

Elaine returned to her footlocker and used the stencil and black marker to put her name and serial number on the bag as the sergeant directed. Except for the civilian clothes in the metal locker, she marked all her possessions, including her bras and panties with the initial of her last name and the last four digits of her serial number.

The following morning after breakfast, or chow as Elaine was learning to call the meals, the loudspeaker blared: "All trainees desiring to attend church—assemble in the Day Room at 1030 hours."

She dressed in the suit she had worn when she enlisted; she carried her white Bible and descended the stairs to the appointed place. More than a dozen girls were already seated around the room. Sgt. Levy entered and asked them to line up outside on the walkway in a double row. The number of girls totaled fifteen; the sergeant partnered one of the girls and led them up the hill toward the WAC Chapel.

Elaine walked beside Gayle the short two and half blocks. The sanctuary was almost full and they sat on the back pews. Attending the service were a number of guys in military and civilian clothes.

Upon returning to the barracks, Gayle remarked to the girls that had stayed behind about all the cute guys in attendance.

"Damn, just my luck not to go to church today," swore Norma.

From her language and attitude, Elaine doubted if she had ever spent any time inside a church.

After the noon meal, she sat on her footlocker and finished the letter to her mama. She described the post, the mess hall, and the service at the WAC Chapel.

In the afternoon, four more recruits arrived before chow. A tall country girl from South Dakota, Mae Honsberg was of German decent. June Trell, another friendly girl from South Dakota accompanied Mae. The third girl, Lucy Simmons, a pretty black-haired Texan. And the fourth girl was Donna

Tinker, resembling a thirteen year old, her first time away from her home in Iowa and already homesick.

Monday morning, after chow each girl in the platoon carried a folded duffel bag and boarded the military bus in the lot at the end of the barracks. A short ten-minute ride brought them to their destination, the post's Main Supply Depot. The huge building resembled an enormous department store with numerous shelves of shoes, undergarments, and racks of clothing, and more.

One section contained a series of cubicles, each occupied by a lady equipped with a tape measure. Sgt. Levy instructed them to strip down to their underclothing and then line up four deep in front of the small partitions. Elaine's measurements were put on a clothing allotment form and given to her. After she got dressed, she stood before a long counter carrying her duffel bag.

The first item handed to her was the ugly exercise suits. Two tan and white stripped, button down the waist seersucker dresses with matching shorts. They apparently came in only one size—too large. As she moved down the counter and received her clothing, she stored it in her bag. And last but not least, a girdle. They were informed that they would wear it with their dress uniform.

A loud protest went up among the girls.

She had never owned a girdle and she was not looking forward to being squashed inside it. The garment resembled a pair of elastic panties with a skirt in front and garter straps hanging from it with a snap crotch. She stared at the foreign looking object in her hand, shook her head and dropped it on top of the clothing inside her bag.

Next she went to the fitting booth. She emptied the contents of the duffel bag onto a large table before removing her skirt and blouse. All of her skirts and pants had to be altered to fit her twenty one-inch waist.

Elaine repacked the bag as Sgt. Levy instructed putting the shoes in the bottom and the heavy clothing next with the lighter weight garments on top.

After the trainees had received their clothing, the girls re-boarded the bus and returned to the Reception Company just in time for lunch.

In the afternoon, she marked a total of fifty-four items. She had never received so much clothing before at one time. It was like several birthdays and Christmases all rolled into one.

Following chow, Sgt. Levy announced that they would be standing Reveille in the morning and she instructed them on how to salute. The right hand with the thumb tucked under the fingers brought to the edge of the brow, holding it in position until the bugle stopped playing. After the sergeant left the bay, Elaine went to the latrine and practiced saluting in the mirror.

As soon as the lights went on the next morning, she rolled out of her bunk and dressed in the uniform of the day—an ugly stripped PT dress. After buttoning the bodice, she crossed the skirt and secured it on the left side. She and all the girls disliked it, and they referred to it as the *kitchen maids* uniform.

She had just finished tying her sneakers when an unfamiliar voice sounded over the loudspeakers.

"Second Platoon—fall out and don't forget to wear your cap."

Elaine grabbed her hat and followed the girls to the back of the bay down the metal steps. In the front of the building, they lined up facing the barracks next to the first platoon.

"Stand at attention, heads up, hands at your sides," barked Sgt. Owens, facing them.

Sgt. Levy and Sgt. Hood reported their platoons all accounted for.

A bugle blared over the outside loudspeaker, and Elaine stood tall and proudly saluted like she had practiced.

"Order arms." The First Sergeant bellowed, at the completion of the horn's notes. "Right face—forward march."

At the command, the front line of the first platoon stepped out followed by the second and third line with the second platoon repeating the process. They bobbled to the mess hall trying to keep in step.

After breakfast, the platoon boarded the bus at the end of the building. Their destination was the US Noble Army Hospital where they disembarked and lined up for inoculations.

Along with the rest of her platoon, Elaine was given a series of injections. The last shot was a tetanus that brought tears to her eyes. It was like getting kicked in the shoulder by her brother, Jackson's old shotgun. Some of the girls actually cried from the pain. Then it was back to the mess hall for lunch.

Following noon chow, they returned to the bus. Their objective was the Army Dental Facility to have their teeth checked and appointments for cleaning and any dental work needed. Elaine only required a cleaning and was given an appointment for the following week.

At 1645 hours, the platoon was ordered to fallout in front of the building. They repeated the ceremony from the morning. The bugler played a different tune called *Taps*, and this observance was called Retreat. After the order arms command, the two platoons marched to the mess hall.

Wednesday, October 3, 1956
Dear Dreamcatcher,

After morning chow, each of the girls in my platoon was given twenty dollars to spend at the PX. The store is located in a long block building beyond Company C. It is stocked with everything from cosmetics, small appliances, under clothing, towels, stationery to chips and candy bars.

I used twelve dollars of my money to purchase a GE steam iron. I also selected a portfolio of stationery with the WAC Flag bearers in the foreground on a pale, aqua blue paper because it will look nice with my Waterman pen that writes with turquoise ink...

Thursday, October 4, 1956

This morning my platoon went into the nearby town of Anniston to purchase dress shoes. We weren't given much of a choice in style, as the shoes had to be plain brown dress pumps. Each girl was given a box of brown shoe wax with her purchase...

Friday, October 5, 1956

After chow, we returned to the Main Supply Depot to pick up our altered clothing.

In the afternoon, we were given a set of brass to wear on the collars of our uniforms. We were instructed to place the US on the right collar with our leather nametag beneath and the Pallas Athene insignia on the left side. Included with our insignias was a can of Brasso that has an unpleasant odor. The liquid is beige, but when it is rubbed on the brass and buffed, it turns the cleaning cloth black. We were told that in order to keep the brass shining, it would be necessary to clean it each evening. I can see it will be an on-going job just like keeping the interior leather upholstery of the Pontiac convertible clean.

Tonight our platoon had its first GI party. There were no guests, no music, no sodas or food. Just a lot of cleaning of the latrine, waxing, and buffing the bay.

It was also the evening we had our first fire drill at 2200 hours after lights out. We were instructed to take the blanket from our bed to wrap around our shoulders. Wouldn't you know it? Norma wasn't wearing anything under her blanket. She was lucky that none of the cadre noticed...

Sunday, October 7, 1956
I wore my dress uniform with the new brown pumps to the WAC Chapel this morning. It was the first time I felt like a real WAC. Almost a hundred percent of the platoon went to church. I guess all of the girls were anxious to get out of the barracks. Of course, the fact that they had heard about the cute guys that had attended the previous service might have had something to do with the number of girls that lined up for church...

Monday, October 8, 1956
Today, we were issued our orders for Basic Military Training. I was assigned to the Third Platoon in Company B, along with my new friends.
A letter from mama brought the news of her marriage to be held on Saturday. It will be a simple affair...

The following days gradually settled into a general routine. Elaine got up at 0500 hours; stood Reveille then marched to the mess hall. Each evening she fell out for Retreat before going to chow.

At the end of the third day she went down to the Supply Department to collect her baggage and pick up empty hangers for her uniforms. By the time *lights out* rolled around at 2200 hours, Elaine was packed and ready to go.

The next morning, immediately following chow, Sgt. Levy entered the bay. "Rip up your bunks and turn the linens into the Supply Department. Be sure to get your signed copy of the DA Form 137, Installation Clearance Certificate."

Elaine made four trips before she completed the transfer of her possessions to Company B. Her sleeping quarters were identical to the one she had occupied at the Reception Center. The pastel painted walls were spotless, strong odors of lemon polish, and paste wax lingered in the large open room.

The bunks were assigned in alphabetical order. Tinker occupied the bed to her left, Texas on her right with June across the aisle. Mae was over in the first aisle near the back of the bay.

After lunch the Company B officers and cadre were introduced to the Third Platoon. Their platoon sergeant, Sp. Costello, a young, pretty, brown-eyed blonde didn't look to be much older than some of the trainees. Their Platoon Officer, the sharp looking, Lt. Pustarfi wore a dress uniform so well pressed, it appeared that she never sat down while wearing it. Her straight, dark hair was cut extremely short, and her eyes resembled black beads against an olive complexion. The lieutenant's age was hard to judge, maybe late thirties. A very tall, Capt. Manning in her early forties greeted them in a coarse, jovial voice. Curly lashes outlined her large brown eyes in a smiling face framed by strawberry red hair. Last, the First Sergeant, Master Sergeant Holland, in her late forties, with auburn hair and sooty lashed eyes. On a whole they all seemed friendly and genuinely interested in the welfare of the trainees.

At the conclusion of Capt. Manning's welcoming speech, the officers and cadre left the bay except for Sp. Costello.

"There will be an inspection tomorrow morning at 0800 hours," she announced before exiting the room.

"Oh, no," moaned the entire platoon.

Following the evening chow, Elaine found a three-page directive on her bed. She sat down on her footlocker and began to read the bold black print. DO NOT SMOKE IN BED.

"Attention." Sp. Costello entered the bay, and summoned the platoon to the front of the room.

"The Company B Information Directive on your bunk should be read and kept for future reference. It should help answer a number of your questions. After all of you have read the pamphlet; we will discuss it following the inspection tomorrow morning. At that time I will answer any questions you have concerning the directive. One thing it does not mention is merits and demerits. During the inspection, your Platoon Officer, Lt. Pustarfi, will pass down each aisle and inspect the area. She will be observing your person as well. Those things she finds pleasing, she will award one merit, such as a well-made bunk or nicely shined shoes. Any item not in order, she will give a demerit or a gig as it is sometimes called. Receive a number of merits and you will be rewarded—too many gigs and you will find yourself doing extra duty. Don't overlook the stairwell outside the back of the bay; that is also your responsibility."

After the platoon sergeant left the bay, Elaine finished reading the publication. At 2100 hours she exchanged her dress for shorts and a T-shirt and joined her squad in the latrine to begin cleaning.

A total of twelve sparkling white sinks lined one wall below a long continuous mirror. Eight gleaming tiled shower stalls on the opposite side; across the end of the room were six enclosed sanitized toilets. She took a swipe at the tall, polished mirror that reached from the floor to the top of the entrance door. For the life of her, she couldn't figure out how thirty girls could shower each evening with only eight stalls. Then she noticed the Shower Schedule posted next to the exit.

Squad One 2000 to 2015 hours   Squad Two 2015 to 2030 hours
Squad Three 2030 to 2045 hours   Squad Four 2045 to 2100 hours

Below the schedule, posted in large letters, a notation: NO ONE WILL OCCUPY THE LATRINE FROM 2130 HOURS TO 2200 HOURS IN ORDER FOR THE LATRINE DETAIL TO CLEAN.

With the latrine cleaned to satisfaction, the squad returned to the bay. A large electric buffer was in use on the dark, green marble looking tile. After the floor was buffed to a glossy shine, the girls took turns sliding down the polished aisle in their sock feet.

The following morning, at 0800 hours, the platoon dressed in the ugly exercise suits and awaited their inspection.

"Attention." Sp. Costello opened the bay door. The girls scrambled to stand rigid next to their footlockers.

Lt. Pustarfi entered the room followed by their platoon sergeant.

Elaine strained to hear what was being said as the lieutenant passed down the first aisle, the clicking of her heels echoing on the tiled floor. At last, the officer entered her section. She watched from the corner of her eye as Lt. Pustarfi flipped a quarter above Pvt. Snyder's bunk, and the blanket sagged with the weight of the coin. The lieutenant grasped the cuff of the blanket and jerked.

"Pvt. Snyder, one demerit—your blanket is not tight."

Then the lieutenant strolled smartly into her area. Elaine's lips quirked slightly at the ring of the twenty-five cent piece on the floor beside her cot.

"Nicely made bunk." Lt. Pustarfi turned to address Sp. Costello. "Award one merit to Pvt. Terry."

She slowly let out her breath as the quarter also bounced off her friend, Tinker's bunk. The young girl had been all thumbs when it came to making her bed. She had demonstrated several times the correct way to make the blanket tight until the private mastered it.

Across the aisle, the officer entered Pvt. Well's area and ripped up the bunk without testing it with a coin.

"Sloppy—one demerit."

After the lieutenant left the bay, Sp. Costello gave the command, "As you were," before leaving the room.

The noise was deafening with everyone talking at once comparing their merits and complaining about their gigs. The loud speaker could hardly be heard.

"Third Platoon, fall out in front of the building."

She walked rapidly down the stairs to the outside to take her place in line with the platoon.

"Platoon—attention," said Sp. Costello. "The WAC Training Battalion conducts a formal parade to celebrate each platoons graduation from basic training. We are going to observe a parade in honor of our company's First Platoon."

Elaine's platoon marched behind the second platoon up Galloway Road, past Mess Hall Number One and the Headquarters Mess Hall. They continued up the hill beyond the WAC Chapel and the Clerical School to a huge open area that resembled a large football field. It appeared to have a goal post. Her first assumption was wrong. Between the two tall posts was a Ft. McClellan Parade Field sign. One section of the parade ground held a wooden platform where more than a dozen women were seated. Most of them were in uniform with a few in civilian clothes.

As soon as the platoons assembled on the field, the Fourteenth Women's Army Corps Band sounded a drum roll for the start of the parade. She tapped her toes to the music as the First Platoon proudly stepped to the tempo in their freshly, starched summer dresses. By comparison, Elaine felt unattractive in her drab, ugly PT dress.

After the completion of the observance, her platoon trooped back to the barracks with an added spring in their step.

Monday, 15 October 1956
Dear Dreamcatcher,
My first day of Basic Training was a big disappointment for my platoon and myself to learn that we would be wearing the ugly exercise suits every day.
Our first class was physical training. We did the calisthenics on the wide walkway in front of the barracks.

The routine was strenuous and I worked up a sweat. I learned that I possess muscles that I didn't even know existed and that every one of them is bone sore.

After our PT class we marched to the PX building. Our classrooms are on the second and third floors above the store. The first thing we learned was how to tell military time and how to write military dates. After midnight which is 2400 hours, the time begins with 0100 hours to noon, 1200 hours and then comes 1300 hours and so on. It really simplifies telling time with no AM or PM to cause confusion. In writing the date, day of the month is placed in front of the month's name followed by the year.

My bunk is calling to my aching body and me...

Tuesday, 16 October 1956

We started the morning with our physical training class. I never realized that I was in such bad shape. The exercises were grueling, and there is not a part of me that isn't sore.

In the classroom we studied the chain of command and watched training films. I was surprised to learn that we have to salute an officer's automobile when an officer occupies it. There is a special tag on the front of the car that designates it belonging to an officer...

Wednesday, 17 October 1956

Our calisthenics instructor is still trying to kill us each morning with those strenuous PT exercises. Every muscle in my body aches.

In class today we discussed the different types of jobs held by the enlisted women. We were given a barrage of tests with multiple-choice answers to determine our MOS. That stands for military occupational specialty. The result will determine where we go for further instruction after we complete basic training...

Thursday, 18 October 1956

Finally, I was able to do the vigorous exercises this morning with a minimal amount of pain.

We had only one other class the rest of the day. Studies of the General Orders, which has to be memorized, like Bible verses. The instructor even referred to them as our Bible. They are a cinch for me as I have always done well quoting my Bible...

Friday, 19 October 1956
We got a reprieve—no PT class this morning. We reviewed for a test covering the material we have been studying. After lunch we took a written test. I am happy the extra hours of studying paid off. Mae and I were the only ones to score one hundred percent on the exam.

After chow, we cleaned the bay for inspection in the morning. We were given the *good news* to expect to stand inspection each Saturday for the completion of our basic training. Some of the platoon's response was explosive. Norma's burned my ears...

The following days melted one into the other, each reflecting a similar pattern to the previous. Elaine rose at 0500 hours—stood Reveille at 0600—went to military classes and returned to the barracks for Retreat at 1700 hours—bed check at 2200 hours. And a GI party every Friday night.

In her third week of training, Elaine was appointed one of the four Section Leaders. The fact that she held the record for the most merits in the platoon might have been advantageous.

Monday, 05 November 1956
Dear Dreamcatcher,
This was truly a "Blue Monday." My platoon had KP and it was raining. KP stands for Kitchen Police. And in this instance, Police means to clean as when we are told to *police up the area.* I served in the food line until chow was over and then I cleaned the tables and washed the eating utensils.

It was 2030 hours before I returned to the barracks thoroughly exhausted with just enough time to shower and fall in bed before lights out. Thank heaven I will only have to pull KP one other time...

Tuesday, 6 November 1956

There were three incidents today. First my platoon started close order drill classes. We learned to count cadence in German, Spanish and Japanese. I was honored and thrilled when chosen to drill the platoon to and from the parade field. With this entrusted and coveted responsibility my self-esteem and confidence climbed to an all time high.

The second happening had to do with Pvt. Becke. She was removed from the company as being unfit for a member of the WAC. She prefers girls to guys. Pvt. Becke has red hair cut in a boy's style. I only knew her in passing since she was in the first Section Leader's squad on the other side of the bay. While growing up I had heard of *dirty old men* referred to as *queers* that molested little boys. It never occurred to me that a woman could act intimately with another female.

On a brighter note, we had our pictures taken, and I wore my dress hat…

Wednesday, 7 November 1956

In our second period class, WAC Battalion Commander, Major Sullivan, visited our group to deliver a lecture on homosexuality. Women who take other females for lovers are called Lesbians. She told us if anyone fit that description, she should go to her platoon sergeant and tell her. The major's speech had everyone eyeing each other suspiciously…

Did that mean there could be more like Pvt. Becke among us? And what other unsettling situations were ahead for her?

Hung my stockings on the line,
Now they ain't no longer mine.

Chapter 5

That Friday, instead of the regular PT exercises, Elaine's platoon started a self-defense class with a Judo Instructor, Cpl. Yamada. After watching a training film, the petite corporal demonstrated the movements using different girls from the platoon as her *victim*. At the end of the class, she announced, "We will put some of the things we learned today in practice on Monday."

"Will we have guys to practice on?" asked Norma, hopefully.

All the trainees laughed including Cpl. Yamada.

"Unfortunately not," she replied.

"Ahhh," chimed the girls disappointedly in unison.

> Friday, 9 November 1956
>
> Dear Dreamcatcher,
>
> We lost another platoon member. Not from her being a *homo* but because she was in love with a priest from her hometown. Pvt. Quantell, a soft-spoken girl in Pvt. Harryman's section is said to be mentally disturbed. She is convinced that the priest loves her and will give up his vocation for her. It is rumored that she had a footlocker full of love letters she had written to the priest since enlisting. I don't understand how she passed the psychiatric exam.
>
> On a brighter note, everyone was given a Third Army patch for the jacket of the dress uniform. It's a blue circle with a small red ring around it and a big white A in the middle. I helped Tinker sew her patch because she kept stabbing her fingers. On Tuesday, I have CQ Duty with her as my Runner...

Tuesday, 13 November 1956

In the afternoon, Sp. Costello gave me the news that I had been selected to carry the Company B banner in the upcoming parade on Saturday. Referred to as a guidon, the small flag has a pale green background with the head of Pallas Athene and a big letter 'B' in gold. In drill class this next week I will be practicing the guidon positions. I am very excited and honored to have the privilege of carrying the banner and at the same time anxious that I don't mess up by stumbling when I jog across the field to post. This will be a test of my patience and persistence not to mention my daily prayers.

I am writing this while on CQ Duty. Earlier, the Duty Officer came to inspect the company. It was our Platoon Officer, Lt. Pustarfi. When she entered the area, I called attention—saluted her and reported the company all-present. She signed the CQ book and I saluted her again before she left the barracks...

Friday evening after chow, she stopped to read the Duty Roster posted outside the Orderly Room. The door was slightly ajar.

"Do you think Terry is ready for the parade?" asked Lt. Pustarfi.

Someone in the Orderly Room laughed. "Did you know some of the other recruits call her Private Merit?" The voice belonged to Sp. Costello.

"No, but to my knowledge in the four weeks she has been here she has accumulated more merits than any trainee in the history of this company has in eight weeks. Also the night Terry was on CQ Duty was the first time a recruit had properly reported the company without my assistance," said Lt. Pustarfi.

"She is a perfectionist, but there is one thing about her that puzzles me. What does she do with her damp towel after her shower? I have yet to find one on the rail of her bunk and her person is clean—"

Pvt. Geer approached and Elaine smiled before doing an about face and moving rapidly toward the staircase.

Friday, 16 November 1956

Dear Dreamcatcher,

All of our classes this week have been on Field Maneuvers. Next week, we will be going on bivouac to a

Field Training Area. We are also doing close order drill practice for the parade. I feel a satisfied sense of achievement when it is my turn to give the marching commands and drill the platoon.

After chow this evening, our platoon reported to the Supply Department for field gear. I was issued a helmet, mess kit, rain poncho, sleeping bag and a piece of canvas called a shelter half.

While checking the duty roster outside the Orderly Room, I accidentally overhead an amusing conversation between my platoon sergeant and Lt. Pustarfi...

Saturday morning, Elaine slipped the heavily starched dress over her head, careful not to muss her hair. After buttoning her uniform, she squared her garrison cap on her head, and then tugged it precisely to the right angle above her brow. Next, she pulled on a pair of tan, cotton gloves.

Earlier in the morning during inspection Elaine had collected three more merits. One for her carefully pressed uniform that she and the entire platoon had taken off immediately after the officer and platoon sergeant left the bay. The dresses now hung on the outside of their clothes lockers, with the girls sitting on their footlockers until the hour of the parade.

"Third Platoon, fall out," announced Sp. Costello over the loud speaker above the bay entrance.

She quickly ascended the stairs with a steady thrumming to her heartbeat and a gentle roaring in her ears.

Sp. Costello waited at the entrance and handed her the company guidon. "Any last minute questions?"

"None," she replied, curling her fingers around the staff and taking her position in the ranks.

"Platoon—right face—forward march—count cadence—count," commanded their platoon sergeant.

The platoon's voices rang out in unison. "Sound off. One two—sound off again three four. Sound off. One two, sound off again—three four. Bring it on up. One up—two up—three up—four up. Bring it on down now. One two—three four."

Bright Alabama sunlight glinted on the Pallas Athene and US brass insignias pinned to the privates' lapels as they marched onto the parade ground.

Uniformed training instructors who'd worked diligently the past eight weeks to turn raw recruits into disciplined WACs waited in the bleachers across the field next to the proud parents and invited guests.

At the Company Commander's signal, Elaine jogged down the field next to Company A to take her post. Soon the troops were massed across the field from the bleachers to the reviewing stand, with the colors in the center. The Stars and Stripes rippled next to the WAC colors. An officer quickstepped to the center of the field and faced the company platoons.

The WAC Band marched into position and sounded a drum roll to begin the ceremonies.

"Bring your troops to At-tenn-shun!" One after another, the Company Commanders echoed the adjutant's bellowed order. The air reverberated with shouted commands.

Elaine's pulse accelerated in a quick steady cadence as the ritual announcements rang out signaling the flag bearers to step forward.

When the reviewing party arrived and the colors passed in review, she imitated the Company Commander's order with the guidon to bring the platoons to attention. The Guidon whipped up, the green and gold pennant waved and snapped in the breeze.

At the conclusion of the ceremonies, she marched back to Company B with mixed emotions. Elaine's deep sense of achievement as a member of the corps filled her with loyalty and patriotism. A respected admiration and allegiance to the nation she proudly represented became eternally etched in her mind and heart.

Later that afternoon, Sp. Costello came to the bay carrying several metal posts. She asked them to clear a large space near the entrance. The specialist showed them how to fit four of the shelter halves together to form a tent. Before leaving, she instructed them on what clothing to pack in their duffel bags for the field trip.

On Monday immediately after chow, Elaine dressed in her field attire of helmet, boots and fatigues. She strapped on her backpack, boarded the military bus with her platoon. In a short time they arrived at their destination. The vast field area behind a single strand of barbed wire had nothing but trees and bushes in the way of landscape. Their first instructions were to dig a long narrow ditch in one section. Many of the girls voiced their objections when they learned that it was to be used for a latrine. Next the platoon began to put up their tents according to the practice session they had observed back in the barracks.

Sp. Costello walked through the area and inspected each structure. "Now," she said, "dig a small trench around the perimeter of your tents."

"What's it for?" asked Norma

"Does anyone know why you were told to dig around your tent?" asked Sp. Costello.

Pvt. Harryman rolled her eyes. "It's for a nature call in the middle of the night, what else?"

"Yeah," agreed Pvt. Greer, "each tent will have its own private latrine." Several of the girls laughed.

"Was everyone sleeping during the field training film?" asked an annoyed, Sp. Costello.

"It's to keep the tent floor dry in case of rain," said Elaine.

"I knew that," said Pvt. Harryman.

At mess, the platoon assembled in the dining area for their packs of K-rations. Each package held condensed food in tubes like toothpaste, round crackers, and a small bag of M & M's for desert. Many of the girls complained that they would starve unless they got some solid food. It wasn't a gourmet meal, but filling and the taste wasn't bad, even though the food flavors were mixed.

Following chow, Elaine's platoon marched to the obstacle course. Several times, they ran through a series of old automobile tires laid out in a pattern touching each other like two-dozen chocolate donuts. Next the girls marched double time to where several knotted rope ladders were attached to an eight-foot wall. They were instructed to climb to the top and drop to the other side. In single file each of the trainees jogged down an incline, grabbed a rope and swung across the shallow, wide water filled trench. Two privates landed in the water drenching their boots.

If not for those grueling, tortuous physical training classes, Elaine could have easily been one of the girls in the muddy ditch water.

After standing retreat, the platoon gathered in the appointed chow line. This time, each trainee was handed a larger container. It was not K-rations but something called C-rations, a meal in small tins. Opening the cans was tricky using the tiny can opener attached to the spoon handle in her mess kit. Her dinner consisted of lima beans and ham, more hard crackers and peaches from a can.

At 2200 hours, she was glad to crawl into her sleeping bag, but why did it feel like her helmet was still on her head?

The following morning after Reveille and chow, the platoon marched to another section that held tables and benches where each girl was issued an

M-1 rifle. Before going to the firing range, they were instructed on how to disassemble, clean and reassemble their gun. On several occasions, Elaine had fired her brother's rifle; however, it had been smaller and only fired a single shot before reloading. Many of the girls shrieked each time they pressed the trigger. After practicing with the rifles, moving targets and a bull's eye was used for testing their accuracy.

Elaine scored a hit with each firing, earning a sharpshooter score on the stationary target.

In the afternoon, the trainees moved to an area with a hollowed out dry gully enclosed in three strands of barbed wire. Wearing a backpack and carrying her M-1, Elaine slithered along under the wire to the end of the deep trench while bullets whizzed overhead. Following evening chow, they went on an exhausting mile long march in full combat gear toting their rifles. Exhausted at the conclusion of the night march, she returned to her tent, removed her helmet and backpack, and crawled into her sleeping bag fully clothed.

The third morning, after another meal of K-rations, the platoon participated in war games. As a squad leader, Elaine led her group through various difficult maneuvers to capture the enemy's flag. She was thoroughly enjoying the military games until it began to rain in the afternoon and she had to don a poncho that made her sweat despite the cool temperature. Retreat was cancelled because of the inclement weather. They ate their C-rations inside their tents where they remained for the rest of the evening before snuggling into their sleeping bags.

Rain continued to fall, setting up a syncopated rhythm on the tent combined with the large drops falling from the trees overhead. Wind whipped against the canvas, and the thunder rumbled and rolled like many tanks, shaking the ground beneath their sleeping bags.

The next morning the rain stopped, but the sky was still dark with heavy gray clouds. After eating their K-rations, the platoon did calisthenics before going to CPR and first aid classes in the main tent.

As the morning advanced, the sun inched its way out from among the layers of cotton clouds. The air cleared and became fragrant with the fresh washed scent of trees and grass.

After a lunch of K-rations, the platoon marched to an area containing a square block building without windows. They each were given a canister mask and instructed on its use. With the mask in place, they entered the small building one at a time.

Elaine walked up to Sp. Costello who wore a mask inside the gas chamber. As previously instructed, she took a deep breath before removing her protective mask, quickly rattled off her name, rank and serial number before rushing out of the building. It was difficult for her to breathe. She wheezed and coughed. Her nose, throat and exposed skin burned and her eyes teared for several minutes after washing her face using water from her canteen.

This was one exercise practice that she was happy to have completed. Elaine compared it second to her internal exam as one of her worst experiences. Surely, during her enlistment, she would never have to use a protective mask. She certainly hoped not.

By mid afternoon the promise of sunshine quickly faded and the sky darkened considerably. Foul weather appeared evident.

To the delight of the trainees, the mess hall sent out a complete turkey dinner with all the trimmings to celebrate Thanksgiving. At last, some solid foods. Following the meal, they were given instructions to break camp and pack to return to Company B because a heavy storm was headed in their direction.

Back in her company latrine, the shower was heavenly to her after using her helmet shell for bathing in the field. She soaped up a second time to wash off the caked dirt.

While it rained and stormed all day Friday, the platoon cleaned their equipment. After chow each girl toted her field gear down to the Supply Department and lined up in front of the counter.

"I'm going to miss my helmet," said Elaine.

"You would, you and your hats," responded Mae.

"Well, there's one thing I won't miss and that's my sleeping bag," said Pvt. Tinker, standing in front of her. "That ground was mighty hard. I am grateful to be back in the barracks to have a hot shower and sleep in my bunk. And I would not forget the good food of our mess hall."

"Yeah, that's for sure," the girls agreed in unison.

That afternoon, she washed her dirty clothes and cleaned her muddy boots.

The following morning it was still raining, and the parade was cancelled.

On Monday, the uniform of the day was dress uniform with raincoats because of the threat of rain. The platoon marched to the parade ground for a group picture. Two rows of the reviewing stand was used for the privates to stand on with the first row of trainees on the ground behind the bench that seated, Sp. Costello, Lt. Pustarfi, Capt. Manning, and Master Sergeant Holland.

Only four days until graduation. Where had the time gone? There had been times when Elaine wasn't sure her patience and perseverance would carry her through the grueling assignments and exercises during her training, especially the field maneuvers. Now that it was ending, a curtain of melancholy hung over her. The shared comradeship, the closeness of her fellow platoon members had become like one big family. Many of her friends would be leaving to scatter all over the states, including her. Everyone was anxious to learn where she would be going for the eight additional weeks of special schooling, such as clerical, medical or cooking school before being assigned to a permanent post.

On Monday, Elaine and her entire platoon reviewed and studied for their finale exams on the following day.

After the test scores were posted, she and Mae were given the news that they had been selected for Flag Duty. This honor was awarded to those trainees who achieved high scores on the tests. Two trainees from each company made up the six-member squad of the Flag Detail that put up and took down the huge flag at WAC Headquarters.

The next morning at 0530 hours, the privileged trainees and their platoon sergeants marched up the hill to the flagpole at WAC Circle. After hooking up the flag, it took all six girls pulling on the rope to raise the heavy flag to the top of the pole. No single word described what Elaine experienced as Reveille sounded at 0600 hours, and she stepped back and lifted her hand proudly to salute the Stars and Stripes rippling above. Breathless and weak-kneed, she lowered her hand feeling like she had just run a race in a hundred-degree temperature carrying a rifle and field pack. She thought on the colors of the flag as she marched with the group back to the WAC Training Battalion. Red for valor, white for hope and blue for loyalty. The extra time that Elaine had spent studying and all the hard work had paid off. This elation and thrill of patriotism was something she would remember her entire life.

Prior to the parade, the platoon stood a Command Inspection conducted by Lt. Colonel Lathrope. Elaine was so pleased she knew the general order asked by her and received three merits during the inspection.

A smile twitched Elaine's lips as Sp. Costello passed a hand over the dry towel on the bar at the end of her bunk.

In the parade that followed, she was honored once again to carry the company guidon.

Thursday, 6 December 1956

Dear Dreamcatcher,

This was my big day. We were the three hundred and forty-ninth class to graduate from the Military Basic Training Program. I had a perfect inspection. Again, I was privileged to carry the guidon in the parade. It was stupendous—with out a doubt—one of life's perfect days. Certainly a day that I would never forget, and I am hopeful there will be many more like it. But there were a lot of tears, too, after we were given our assignments for our special schools. My friends, Mae and June are going up to Clerical School with me. But we will be saying good-bye to Tinker and Texas who are assigned to Ft. Lee, Virginia.

Just in time, we got our individual photographs to exchange with our friends.

To celebrate our graduation, we were all given Post Liberty Passes to attend the *Cinderella Night* at the Hilltop Service Club tomorrow evening…

In the afternoon, Mae and Elaine dressed in their taupe uniforms. Together, they walked up the hill to the service club.

"This will be my first time to attend a dance without an escort," remarked Mae.

"Sp. Costello said the guys usually outnumber the girls at these affairs."

"That's a comfort," responded Mae.

The many windowed, round cream-colored front of the building stood out from the ornamental shrubs and colorful blooming flowers that was part of the surrounding landscape. From the covered porch entrance, they entered through the tall glass-paneled quadruple doors that opened into a large vestibule and beyond that a huge ballroom. They peeked inside the dark room before going down the long hall past the restrooms just outside the ballroom. The music room held an upright piano in front of a mirrored wall with numerous sofas and chairs arranged in groups. Next-door was an unoccupied smaller room with rows of comfortable chairs and several sofas in front of a large TV. Half way down the hall stood a high counter with a large *GAME EQUIPMENT* sign on the wall behind it. Directly across the wide corridor, a small, carved wood *Game Room* plaque was placed over the closed door. It contained metal folding chairs arranged around card tables and others with high glossed red and black-checkered tops. This room was also vacant. Farther along the corridor, they came to another closed door bearing a *Writing Room* sign.

Elaine opened the door, flicking on the light.

"This is nice," Mae moved past her into the unoccupied room, gazing around. Two walls contained rows of bulging bookcases. One section was designated for writing with desks and writing materials arranged neatly on the tops.

Another set of restrooms brought the hallway to a dead end. The girls walked back to the vestibule of the front entrance where they entered the empty ballroom. Their heels clicked briskly across the parquet floor to a pair of opened French doors, and they stepped into a long, screened patio. Glass top tables dotted the area that had white, wrought iron chairs padded with blue seats drawn up beneath them. Weaving around the tables, the girls approached a second set of French doors.

She followed Mae through the doors into a large room containing a soda fountain bar with stools. Several smaller tables like the ones in the patio with chairs were arranged around the edge of a small, dance floor. A colorful Wurlitzer jukebox stood opposite the soda counter with blinking lights. Next to it was a pair of swinging Dutch doors. Curious, they strolled over to peek over the tops. Their gaze slid over a long room containing four pool tables, two shuffleboards and several other game tables with a ping-pong table at the far end. Most of the tables were occupied with guys and gals.

They returned to the soda fountain, purchased cold drinks, and sat at one of the small tables.

"Okay, Elaine," said Mae, "it's time you had some hands on practice."

"What," she asked totally bewildered, "are you talking about?"

"The art of flirting. That gorgeous guy sitting alone by the door is a perfect subject for experimentation." But as Elaine began to turn her head, Mae hissed, "Don't turn around for Pete's sake!"

"How can I see if I don't look?" she pointed out as she turned.

His hair was longer than most GI's and wavy, combed back from a wide forehead. It was a deep, rich brown that showed glints of red. His eyes beneath arched brows, even with the distance across the room, she caught the depth of dark brown. He wore a dress uniform with corporal stripes on the left sleeve beneath a round Third Army patch.

"I have never flirted in my life." Elaine swung her head back around.

"It's high time you started. All you have to do is walk slowly past his table, make eye contact, count to ten, drop your lashes and stroll to the jukebox and pretend to look for a selection."

"I could no more do that than I can fly backward, and I sure as heck can't fly forward."

"If you do I'll polish your shoes for a week."

" Mae, I just couldn't."

"Oh, come on. Don't be a chicken," said Mae. "It's a piece of cake."

Elaine stood looking blindly at the selection names on the jukebox. This had to be the craziest dare she had ever taken.

"What song do you favor?" The deep drawl came from behind near her ear.

She whirled around, her breath catching as she gazed into a pair of rich brown eyes. He wasn't as tall as her brothers but he had broad shoulders that nicely filled out his uniform.

"D 4," she said with the straightest face she could manage.

Without looking at the title of the tune, the corporal slotted a coin in the holder and punched the D and 4 buttons.

"Kris Brummel," he said, extending his hand. "Is this your first time at the club? I don't recall seeing you here before."

"Elaine Terry." She placed her hand in his. "Yes, this is my first Post Liberty."

"Pleased to meet you, Elaine. Then you must have just completed basic training?" He stayed lightly holding her hand.

The 45 record slid onto the turntable and the first notes of the music sounded.

"This is the number you played for me," she said.

Kris still held her hand, his fingers comfortably laced with hers.

"I guess we better dance." He inclined his head toward the dance floor. His fingers tightened around her hand, and he drew her to the parquet floor before she could object.

"I don't believe I know this piece," he said, as they began to sway to the tempo. "How's it called?"

"Brown Eyed Handsome Man." Heat blossomed within her and a rush of color warmed her cheeks as she tried to repress the laughter that bubbled in her throat.

His lips split into a delightful smile. He waggled his eyebrows and chuckled softly.

Elaine couldn't hold the laughter any longer, and she began to laugh, too.

The words to the music described him to a T. Still smiling they glided around the small dance floor until the song ended.

"Come and meet my friend, Mae Honsberg," she invited.

Mae grinned widely as she introduced her to Kris, and they spoke a few words in German.

Kris and Mae did most of the talking while she sipped her soda and listened. She learned that after his Christmas leave he was going to Germany, his first time there as he was born in Michigan. When it was time for them to return to their barracks, Cpl. Brummel walked them to the veranda. He halted at the end of the carpeted floor and turned to face them.

"Are you both coming back tonight for the dance?" he asked.

"Most definitely. The *Cinderella Night* is in our honor," replied Mae.

"Save me a dance, Cinderella," he said, looking at Elaine. His lips spiit into a teasing grin.

"Sure, you bet" she replied.

As they walked away, Mae held her hand over her mouth. Out of earshot of the corporal, she removed it and hooted with laughter. "You said that on purpose," she accused.

"What?"

"Bet," she said.

They giggled all the way back to the barracks.

Far away, buglers play.
Sounding taps at the end of the day.
Gone the sun, night has come, day is done.

Chapter 6

Following the evening chow, the platoon reported to the Supply Department to pick up their luggage. In a matter of minutes, the bunks in the bay were littered with civilian clothes as the girls searched for outfits to wear to the Cinderella dance.

Elaine changed twice before deciding on her maroon corduroy skirt and matching weskit with a long sleeved, pink blouse.

Many of the platoon members op-ed to wear their taupe dress uniforms.

As they entered the Hilltop Club, each girl was given a dance card with a short pencil attached by a gold tasseled cord. In the corridor she paused and held her card against the wall, penciling in Kris Brummel for the first and last dance.

"What are you doing?" asked Mae, looking over her shoulder.

"Saving a dance for Cpl. Brummel."

"Don't you mean *two dances*?" teased Mae.

Before they reached the ballroom doors, guys surrounded them asking to sign their dance cards. To her surprise, Elaine's card was returned with a name scribbled on each line.

As if sensing someone watching her, she glanced across the room. Elaine's eyes instantly gravitated to Kris Brummel coming toward her with his long, loose-limbered stride. He was wearing his dress uniform and he wasn't smiling. He came to a stop in front of her, his admiring gaze sliding over her in a way that caused her to blush.

"I guess I'm too late to claim a dance," he said, indicating the filled card in her hand.

"Yes, you are," she agreed. "Unless your name is Kris Brummel." She held the card out to him. "I keep my promises."

His lips turned up in a broad smile that made his brown eyes twinkle. "This is I my lucky night to claim two dances with the prettiest girl at the ball."

"Thank you." The heat of another blush stole over her face.

A PFC rushed up. "May I have a dance—"

"Sorry, fella," said Kris, dangling Elaine's full card in front of him. "Better luck next time. I just got the last dance."

The guy frowned and turned away.

She looked around for Mae who was headed for the soda fountain on the arm of a tall, auburn haired corporal.

"How about a soda before the dance starts?" Kris asked, following her gaze.

Moments later, carrying two drinks out to the crowded patio, he deftly maneuvered around the occupied tables to an empty one next to the wall. He sat the drinks on the table and pulled out a chair for her.

Kris asked her questions about basic training, what school she would be attending and where she was from. Just like all the girls, Elaine felt her state was the best, and she described Kentucky in detail for him. They continued to sip their drinks and chat until the music started in the ballroom.

I believe this is my dance." The corners of his lips spread wide into a smile. Kris scooted his chair back from the table and stood. He held her chair, and then offered his arm.

At the edge of the dance floor, she slipped into his arms. She was conscious of the strength in his arms catching her waist, of the firm clasp of his fingers on hers. Closing her eyes, she flowed with the music as his graceful strides carried them across the floor. She felt as if she were floating. All too soon the melody ended, and Kris relinquished her to her next dance partner.

She barely had time to think after that as partner after partner came to claim his dance.

For the rest of the dances, she was conscious of Cpl. Brummel's eyes following her around the dance floor. He didn't partner any other girl until he came to claim the last dance of the evening.

The music was slow and romantic, an old fashioned tune, "After the Ball."

Kris walked with them to Company B.

"You should have given him your address," admonished Mae, after the corporal bid them good night and left.

Elaine related the story about an incident when her brother had given her address to a buddy overseas. How after writing to her a few months he began writing her love letters and hinting at marriage saying that he planned to visit her on his next leave.

"I am not about to get into another situation like that," she concluded.

"But he is so cute," said Mae.

"Perhaps you should have given him *your* address," she teased.

"He's too short for me."

"I don't think a person's physical appearance should interfere with one's feelings."

"I have always been conscious of my height," replied Mae.

The following morning after chow, Sp. Costello entered the bay and walked down the aisles speaking with each girl. When the specialist was within earshot, Elaine removed her towel from the bar on her bunk and folded it.

"Tinker," she said in an elevated voice, "did you know that you could dry faster with a wet washcloth than with a dry towel?"

"No, fooling?" said her friend, pausing in the packing of her suitcase.

"It's true. I grew up in the country without running water, Mama taught my three brothers and me to use our washcloth to dry. It saved on laundering so many towels. You should try it sometime."

"I think I much prefer my nice fluffy towel," replied Pvt. Tinker. She returned to her packing.

"Pvt. Terry," said Sp. Costello, stopping in front of her. "It's been a pleasure to have you in my platoon. I know you will do well at the Clerical School." She gazed down at the white towel in Elaine's hands, nodded her head and smiled.

"Thank you, Sp. Costello. I'll do my best." She returned the woman's smile.

The platoon sergeant continued down the aisle speaking with Privates Tinker and Wells. At the bay door she turned to address the platoon. "All of you going up to Blueberry Hill need to start boarding the bus in back of Company B. Check your area carefully before leaving."

"Why is it referred to as Blueberry Hill?" asked Norma. "Is that the name of the street where the school is located?"

"No." A smile quirked the corners of Sp. Costello's mouth. "The school is on WAC Circle. Blueberry Hill is a nickname given to the hill the school and Headquarters are located on by some previous graduates. I think it has something to do with the words of the hit song by that name." The door swing closed behind her with a soft swish as Sp. Costello exited the bay.

Norma sung off key a few words of the song and stopped. "Dang. I don't get it," the private said, screwing up her face and frowning. "I don't find anything thrilling about attending Clerical School when I had my heart set on going to a different post."

First, Elaine loaded her luggage and duffel bag in the bus. She carried her uniforms on hangers and draped them over an empty seat. It was a short ride up the hill past the WAC Chapel to the school.

The front entrance to the school resembled that of Company B except for the CQ desk and the Day Room. They were in reverse order of those in the basic training company.

Her sleeping quarters were in a bay on the third floor. The enormous room was divided into cubicles formed by metal clothes lockers with the familiar footlocker at the end of the bunk. To her surprise, they were told to fill the room like they had at the mess hall by taking the empty bunk next to the last occupied bed. The first half of the bay was filled and the three areas of the second half were taken. Mae put her luggage in the first empty cubicle with her in the following one and June across the aisle.

She began unpacking her duffel bag and arranging her footlocker as a group of girls from Hawaii came down the aisle. A petite girl took the bunk next to hers and introduced herself as Delores Pao. Elaine in turn introduced her to Mae and June.

"If they are Mae and June, you must be April," Delores said, before Elaine could give her own name.

"No," she said, and laughed. "My name is Elaine, but I was born in April."

"I think April suits you better," said Delores.

"Yes," agreed Mae, "then we could be called *The Three Months of Bay Three.*"

"Come meet my friends. We all graduated from Company A," said Delores.

"Shirley, Emily, Daisy, Consuelo, and Maria." She introduced them, "and this is April, Mae and June."

All of the Hawaiian girls were petite with shoulder length black hair and dark eyes. Delores was the shortest of the group.

"Do any of you know how to dance rock and roll?" asked Emily.

"Mae is the expert dancer," said Elaine.

"You teach me, and I will teach you the hula," suggested Emily.

"I would like to learn, too," she said. "Would you teach me also?"

"I will," offered Delores, "if you change your name to April."

"I couldn't do that, but you may call me April. It will be my official nickname. Okay?"

"Deal," replied Delores, a big smile lighting her face

> Friday, 07 December 1956
> Dear Dreamcatcher,
> We moved up to Clerical School. The building resembles Company B with our sleeping quarters on the third floor. Classrooms are on the first two floors. Our class hours are 0800 hours to 1600 hours Monday through Friday. We stand Reveille and Retreat but no inspections.
> I was greatly disappointed to learn we would not march in any parades except for the school graduation ceremonies.
> We were all given Post Liberty Passes.
> I have made some new friends, six girls from Hawaii. One of them, Delores Pao is a petite four feet and ten inches. I kind of like the nickname she gave me. Now she has Mae and June referring to me as April along with a number of the other girls…

Following chow the next morning, Elaine picked up her stationery box and headed downstairs to the day room. There was no place to write in her cubicle except on the footlocker and it wasn't too comfortable.

"Wait up," called Mae. "Where are you going?"

"To the Day Room to write some letters."

"I'll walk down with you. I'm on my way to the WAC PX."

Mae walked with her to the archway entrance. "Looks like you won't be writing in there. All the desks are taken."

She looked inside at the full room. Not even one vacant chair. She shook her head. "I think I'll walk up to the service club and take advantage of their facilities," she said.

"Go to the PX with me first, and I'll come with you to the club," offered Mae.

"On one condition. No more flirting lessons."

"I promise." Mae held up both hands in surrender and laughed.

At the store, they split up. She went in one direction and Mae to the back of the shop. She looked over the merchandise but she didn't make any purchase. Mae approached empty handed.

"I was just looking to see if they had gotten any new items," said Mae.

The club writing room was empty. They had their pick of the desks. Mae sat by the wall near the door and picked up some of the service club stationery. "I might as well write a letter to my folks."

Elaine chose a place across the room beside a window. She opened her writing box and took out the two letters. Half way down the first page, she glanced up from the letter she had started to Mr. Pfeiffer. A dark complexioned PFC walked through the open door. As he approached her, he ran his hand through his short black hair. His eyes were gorgeous, a liquid midnight black framed with long thick lashes.

"Hello." He came boldly up to the desk and held out his hand. "Oswaldo Del Valle. Everyone calls me CQ." He spoke with a heavy Spanish accent, and he had a pleasant, genuine smile.

"Pvt. Elaine Terry." She placed her small hand in his brown one. "They call me April," she added, returning his smile.

"I work here in the club on my off duty hours, I'm in charge of the game equipment."

"Yes, I noticed you behind the equipment counter when I came in."

"Do you like to write?" He indicated the partially written letter on the desktop.

"I enjoy writing to my family and friends, and I have two brothers in the army that I write to often."

"Do you know Spanish?"

"Very little. My high school Spanish teacher was sent to Korea in the beginning of the semester."

"I need someone to help a few hours a week, assisting with letter writing. Our volunteer is no longer here. She got transferred." His *is* came out sounding like *ees*.

"I am not sure I understand. What kind of letters?" she asked.

"We have a lot of Spanish soldiers like myself that correspond with English speaking girls. You would be helping them correct their letters to be readable. It would be only an hour from 1830 hours to 1930 hours on Wednesday or Thursday. Could you do these?"

"But I don't speak Spanish."

"It ees not necessary that you know Spanish, although it would be helpful. What do you say?"

"I, ah…." she tried to think of another excuse.

"I tell you what. You help me improve my English and I teach you words in Spanish."

"Okay, amigo. I'll do it." For the life of her she didn't know why she agreed to his request. "I would like to learn Spanish. I think it's a beautiful language. You ask me, could you do these. Don't say *these*—it's pronounced this, very soft. And you said our volunteer ees no longer here. Use *is* not *ees*." She emphasized the word.

CQ repeated the words several times.

"That's perfect," she said. "You owe me two words."

His lips split in a wide smile. "*Tus ojos son bellos.*"

"That is more than two words. I know *tus* is your. I don't know the rest."

"*Tus ojos son bellos*," he repeated. "Your eyes are beautiful."

Her lips formed a silent O. "Thank you," she said, her face growing warm.

"See you Wednesday at 1830 hours."

She nodded as he walked away. He stopped at the desk where Mae sat and spoke to her before leaving the room.

Mae hurried over to where she still sat at the desk.

"What was that all about? I heard him say he would see you Wednesday. Don't tell me—it's what I'm thinking?"

She quickly related their conversation. "I can't believe I agreed to his request. It must have been his eyes. Don't you think he has gorgeous eyes?"

"I didn't notice. I had better come with you to keep you out of trouble."

"Really, who has the flirty eyes?" she teased.

"Are you forgetting Kris Brummel?"

No, she hadn't forgotten him, but what could she say?

Joined the WAC to wear my brass.
Now all I do is march to class.

Chapter 7

On Monday morning, after chow, Elaine and Mae walked down one flight of stairs to their first class in Clerical School. Each of the thirty-six students sat behind a typewriter dressed alike in tan shirtwaists worn with taupe skirts. Ike jackets and lace up granny shoes completed their dress code. The instructor, Specialist Faxon, a tall attractive blond, introduced herself and had each private stand and state her name and where she was from.

The first half of the period was typing and then they switched to speedwriting. After the noon chow, they changed classrooms where they stayed for the remainder of the day learning about security clearances.

After class she and Mae went to the WAC PX and each bought two long sleeved shirtwaists preventing the need of laundry in the middle of the week.

Following the evening chow, the girls rushed to change into their civvies for going out.

"I can't wait to go on leave and bring back the clothes I have stored at my mama's house." Elaine opened her civilian locker and took out two hangers. They contained blouses, one pink and one white. "I don't have much of a choice to wear with my skirts."

"Me, too," agreed Mae, slamming her locker door.

"Would you like another selection?" June crossed the space between their footlockers and tossed a pale, aqua blouse on Elaine's bunk. "It doesn't fit me anymore."

"Would I ever? Thanks. It's lovely," she said, holding it in front of her. She quickly slipped it on, buttoning the nylon blouse, and smoothing down the high lace collar beneath her chin.

"It looks better on you than it did on me and it makes your eyes look blue, too," observed June, before returning to her cubicle.

"That's your color." Mae whistled and waggled her eyebrows.

Elaine checked her watch as she and Mae entered the service club. She was a half-hour early. But that was okay; she had letters of her own to answer.

She stopped at the Equipment Counter to greet CQ.

"Only one guy to help tonight," he informed her.

Mae pulled a book from the shelf and sat at a card table beneath the row of books. Elaine chose the same desk she had on her previous visit, where she had a view of anyone entering the room.

Cordero Rodrigues leaned one shoulder against the wall just inside the door, thumbs hooked in his belt loops. His eyes swept around the nearly empty writing room.

Only two girls occupied the small room. One sat at a card table reading, attractive—but not the beauty CQ had described to him. His eyes gravitated to the girl seated at the desk by the window. From the distance he couldn't tell the color of her eyes downcast, concentration on her writing. The overhead light only allowed a hint of a lush mouth and finely molded cheekbones, but it was enough to make him want to see more. His gaze dipped lower, following the honey-gold hair where it fell across her shoulders, shimmering like silk against the aqua blue of her blouse. The front of the desk kept him from seeing all of her but what he could see aroused an urgent need to view the rest.

Cordero pushed away from the wall, his thumbs loosening their grip and sliding unnoticed to his sides. He must have made a noise; she looked up, pushed her chair back, and stepped away from the desk.

Boldly, he surveyed her form as he walked toward her. He started with her ankles, which were the cutest turned ankles he had ever seen. Then his eyes moved slowly up her body to study the shape of her hips, and her tiny waist then up to the swell of her breasts, not stopping until he reached her face. He liked what he saw. Aqua marine eyes surrounded by thick lashes, her complexion like peaches and cream with pink slightly parted lips.

She was a looker all right. Del Valle had got that right—nothing short of a beauty. He pursed his lips in a silent whistle.

Elaine glanced up from the page; a tall broad shouldered guy walked toward her, his eyes never looking away. She stood and stared back at him, aware of the sheer physical power of his body and his ability to make her feel fragile. There was a devilish sparkle in his ebony black eyes that brought her inner senses to alert. He radiated a confident masculinity and an air of danger that was deeply disturbing.

"Good evening," he said, coming to a halt mere inches from where she waited beside the desk. The savage quality about his dark good looks frightened her even while it attracted her, charging the air with a tension she'd never felt before.

"Hi,' she said breathlessly.

"Cordero Rodrigues," he said and stuck out his hand. His musical Spanish drawl skittered along her spine.

Almost reluctantly she accepted his gesture. The hand he extended was dark bronze with neatly clipped nails. He wrapped his fingers around hers in a firm grip that sent sparks shooting up her arm. She pulled her hand away as if her skin had been burned, which was exactly how it felt. Had he noticed it, too? If so, he gave no outward sign.

"Do you need help with writing a letter?"

"I might." His lips curled into a dangerous grin.

"Please be seated." She indicated the chair beside the desk, sat down, and picked up writing materials. "What is the name of your girl?" she asked, her pencil paused over a notepad.

"I don't know. We haven't been introduced yet. What's your name?"

She gave him a puzzled look that quickly changed to embarrassment.

"I'm terribly sorry—how rude of me not to introduce myself. April Terry, this is my first assignment," she said. Why had she not given him her real name? Was it because he had confused her?

"Abril." He rolled the name off his tongue giving it a musical quality.

"It's April," she corrected him; "it's spelled with a *p* like the month."

"Yes, I know, but in Spanish it's *Abril* with a *b*."

"Actually, it is a nickname. My real name is Elaine." She paused, "Am I to assume that you're not here to write a letter?"

He arched a black brow, a slow grin forming on his lips. He threw back his head and laughed as he rose, stretched his long legs, running a negligent hand through his coal black hair.

It was all the answer she needed.

"I don't find this the least bit amusing," she said, pushing back her chair abruptly and standing.

"I apologize for teasing you," he said, his laughter quickly dying.

She nodded but did not respond verbally.

"I'm not here to write a letter. I just wanted to invite you to play pool with me and my buddy," he confessed with a broad grin.

"I don't play pool," she said icily. "But my fried, Mae is an excellent player. Why not invite her?" She indicated the table where Mae was seated across the room observing them.

"She can come, too. I can teach you. It's easy to learn."

"No thank you," she said coolly. "I have an appointment to help a GI with a letter."

"That's me." He laughed again. "But I don't want to write a letter. I want you to play pool with me and my friend."

"You don't understand," she said, wishing her voice didn't sound so shaky. "I'm not interested."

"I see," he said. His mouth twitched at the corner. "So in other words, I'm wasting my time, am I?"

"Yes."

He rubbed the side of his nose, whether to scratch an itch or hide his grin, she wasn't sure.

"Well, I guess it's my time to waste."

"Suit yourself, but don't infringe on mine."

"Ah...come on—you'll have fun, I promise." He made a useless gesture with his hand.

"I can't. I volunteered for this job. I have to be here for the next—"she glanced at her watch— "forty five minutes and those are my intentions. Am I making myself clear?" She raised her chin a notch and looked him square in the eyes.

A look of wicked amusement reflected in the inky depths of his eyes, his left brow elevated to a questioning arch and when he gazed at her as he was doing now, heat spread up through her body warming her cheeks.

"Absolutely." He inclined his head. "I'll try to remember that," he said, his grin deepening the creases of his lean cheeks.

"Please excuse me," she said, stepping away from the desk. Not waiting for his reply, she quickly crossed the room and marched through the open door. Her step quickened, desperate to put as much distance between him and her as possible. He seemed friendly enough, but she instinctively felt he was also dangerous. In what way, she was not sure.

In the hall, CQ was striding towards her. She paused and waited for him to reach her.

"Abril, I was just coming to tell you Pvt. Torres is on Guard Duty, and he won't be coming tonight. I should have let you know sooner but the counter got busy. So sorry you wasted your time."

"It's okay. I had letters of my own to write. There is a guy named Cordero that came in claiming he was the one I was to help with a letter. I didn't believe him. He was giving me a lot of double talk."

"I am sorry that ees—is my fault. I mentioned that the club had a new WAC volunteer when he stopped at the counter to check out equipment. If he is bothering you, I'll be glad to speak to him."

"That won't be necessary. I put him in his place. My friend Mae is with me."

"Pvt. Torres ees—is coming next week. Can you be here?" he asked.

"Sure, I'll be here. I'm glad to lend a hand."

"Thanks, do you know the word for *hand* in Spanish?"

"No," she shook her head.

"*Mano—tus manos son bellas.* You have beautiful hands." He grinned at her and winked.

"*Muchas gracias,*" she said, returning his smile.

"*De nada,*" he replied. He turned and walked back down the corridor.

She returned to the writing room to find Cordero sitting at the table casually talking with Mae.

Cordero glanced up as Abril entered the room. By the looks on her face, she had found out he had lied about being the person she was expecting. From where he sat, he watched her walk by, the easy rhythm of her hips so graceful as she moved past him. The black demure skirt she wore that reached just below her knees did nothing to disguise the luscious curve of her bottom. She ignored him and went to the desk where she had been sitting when he first saw her. Hastily, she began gathering up the writing materials when a pencil rolled off the desk. He quickly got up to retrieve it.

"I believe this is yours," he said, holding it out to her. He allowed a hint of a smile to play over his lips.

"Thank you." She reached for the pencil, her cool fingers brushing his for a split second. He felt the shock of her touch race through his body.

"Look, I apologize for teasing you. I'm sorry."

"You said that before," she said frostily. "I call it a barefaced lie."

"Hey, you two. Break it up. Let's go play pool," said Mae as she joined them around the desk.

"You know I've never played pool." Abril gave her friend an intense look. This was one difficult girl. About as stubborn as two mules pulling in opposite directions.

"My motto is, you shouldn't judge something before you've even tried it." He grinned at her.

A quick laugh escaped her. "That slogan could get you into a great deal of trouble."

"So it has," he confessed ruefully.

"I haven't played pool since I enlisted. Come on. It'll be fun," Mae pleaded.

"I promise it's a lot more fun than writing letters," he assured her.

"Please," Mae said, flicking her eyelashes in rapid succession.

The shadow of a smile touched one corner of Abril's mouth. "I can see that I'm out numbered."

In the game room she and Mae were introduced as Abril and Mae to his friend Richard Sheets.

"It's April," she corrected him.

Richard was a little taller than Mae's five feet nine inches, probably around five feet—ten, a couple of inches short of Cordero's height. His eyes were a summer, sky blue and his short, light brown, sun streaked hair glistened beneath the overhead lights. Handsome—clean-cut—Joe College type of guy. Fine manners, and he spoke very properly without the use of slang.

With the three of them instructing her, April caught on well enough that she and her partner, Cordero, won two out of the three games played.

"Cord, bring drinks for all of us." Richard handed him a five-dollar bill. "What will you girls have?"

"*Coke*," said Mae.

"Thanks, *Nehi* grape for me." April named her favorite drink.

Mae excused herself to go to the restroom, leaving her alone at the table with Richard.

"Do you like to dance?'

"Yes, I do. We have some girls in our barracks from Hawaii and they are teaching Mae and myself to hula, and in turn, we are giving them rock and roll lessons. Mae is a terrific dancer."

"There is a dance here Saturday night. I would be pleased if you would accompany me."

"No, I can't, but thanks for asking. I plan to attend, and I'll save a dance for you."

She was glad Mae wasn't at the table. He should have asked her to go with him. If he was disappointed, he didn't say anything more as Cordero returned with four *Cokes* and Richard excused himself to go wash his hands.

"Sorry." Cordero sent her a look of apology, "no grape." He deposited the soft drinks on the tabletop before sitting next to her. "Will you be coming to the dance Saturday night?"

"Mae and I plan to attend."

"I could get a friend's car and pick you both up."

"No, thanks." She shook her head. "It's only a short walk from Clerical School."

"Look, I can understand how you might feel about not trusting me, but I can keep my hands to myself. Shoot, I'll treat you like I do my kid-sister if that'll make you more comfortable."

"Thanks for the offer. I've always wanted another brother, but I'll walk anyway."

Mae returned to the table to hear her refusal.

"Save a dance for me," he said, including Mae with a glance.

Richard strolled back and picked up his drink. "There is a nice show on TV if anyone is interested?"

She looked at her watch and then at Mae. "I think I had better leave, I have to be back at the barracks by 2200 hours, and I have things to do before the lights go out."

"Is that every night?" asked Richard.

"No, just school nights and Sunday," Mae informed him. "We are allowed out until midnight on Fridays and Saturdays."

Later after they left the service club, Elaine chatted with Mae as they walked to the Clerical School.

"What did you think of Richard?"

"Nice, very mannerly and handsome in a quiet way. He's the kind of guy that every mother would love for her daughter to bring home," said Mae.

"I thought so, too," she agreed.

"Why did you refuse to let Cordero pick you up for the dance?"

"I've never been alone with a man in a car. I have the feeling he is not the type that my mama or brothers would approve of me going out with." She and Mae stopped at the curb to check the traffic before crossing the street.

"From what you have told me, they never approved of any man."

"You got that right." She giggled then became serious. "There is something about him, the way he speaks, and the wicked look in his eyes that makes a statement that he doesn't care if anyone likes him or not. He has *dangerous* written all over him."

"You've got to admit that was a sly way he made your acquaintance."

"Yes, but he lied. And you know how I feel when someone lies to me."

"You have to agree it was in a teasing manner—no harm done."

"I hope you're right. Still, something about him disturbs me."

"I think you disturbed him more, the way he was flirting with you."

"Huh...you call that flirting. I call it arrogance!"

"When the two of you first met, the sparks were flying. I thought you were going to fight."

"I did feel like smacking his face," she confessed.

"You know what that's a sign of when a man makes you want to hit him, don't you."

"No, I don't," Elaine said, and jerked open the Clerical School door.

"It means you like him," Mae continued, following her inside. They signed the CQ book and headed down the hallway toward the staircase. "I could sure tell he liked you, the way he was eating you up with those devilish black eyes."

"I don't think I should go to the dance." She paused, turned and faced Mae at the bottom of the stairs.

"Don't be silly. What could happen in a room full of people? Besides if he gets out of hand, I can always practice my Judo on him," said Mae, making a few hand motions.

They strolled through the bay doors laughing uproariously.

> Friday, 14 December 1956
> Dear Dreamcatcher,
> I put in for my Christmas leave, seven days. I think that is more than enough time to have to put up with my stepfather's insulting, leering stares...

April checked her appearance in the latrine mirror before leaving the room. She adjusted her maroon weskit at the waist.

She and Mae arrived at the Hilltop Club to find Cordero waiting outside the front entrance. He stood with his shoulder against the wall, his feet crossed at the ankles in a lazy stance. He was dressed in a dark blue suit with a white dress shirt opened at the neck, no tie. His ebony hair, still damp from a shower, gleamed under the porch lights as he pushed away from the wall. The predatory grace of his movements was evident in his relaxed stride as he met them at the top of the single step.

"I thought you weren't coming," he said.

She glanced at her watch. "We are five minutes early by my time."

He shrugged without replying, gave her a little half salute, took both their arms, and walked between them to the ballroom. They crossed the floor to a spot near the bandstand where Richard waited with three *Cokes* and a grape *Nehi* on the table. Richard stood and exchanged greetings with them, and then he pulled out a chair for Mae.

Cordero held April's chair and then took the seat next to her.

Richard wore a light blue sport coat over a white silk dress shirt with dark blue slacks. He sported a blue-stripped tie, the only guy in the room wearing one except for the men in uniform.

On stage the WAC Band tuned their instruments for the first dance number. She glanced around the crowded room. All the tables were in use and some couples stood around the edge of the floor.

"I play the bongo drums with the Spanish Band," said Cordero. "We are practicing tomorrow afternoon for the dance on Saturday. Would you like to come listen to us rehearse?"

Abril hesitated for a moment before she said, "Yes, I would like that." She looked up at him with the most unusual eyes. Eyes he had thought to be a light shade of blue. They were golden with flecks of green that sparkled when she smiled.

The familiar notes of "Unchained Melody" flowed across the room.

Cordero pushed away from the table, clasped Abril's hand and pulled her up to him. He lifted her hand to his shoulder. Her skin was warm and silky beneath his fingertips.

"Dance with me," he said and gave in to the need to hold her. He wrapped an arm around her waist tucking her against him. To have her so close, overwhelmed him. Dancing with her tonight was one of the few pleasures in his life. Keeping his hands off her was going to be sheer torture. He never should have made that promise. She didn't feel like his sister, and he sure as hell wasn't her brother. He had made a lot of errors but that vow to treat her like a kid-sister had to be his biggest mistake.

If you don't ask,
The answer's always going to be no.

Chapter 8

A guy tapped Cordero's shoulder, and he glanced behind him and said something in Spanish. The soldier shrugged and turned away. His voice murmured in her ear as they continued dancing, but April didn't understand the Spanish he whispered to her. The music ended, and he returned her to the table, where Richard was pulling out a chair for Mae.

"Don't sit down," Richard drawled, catching her by the hand before she could be seated as the band began their rendition of "Young Love."

It didn't take long for her to realize that a guy who was an accomplished dancer partnered her. Clearly he loved dancing. He was smooth, by far the best partner she had ever danced with. It was so easy dancing with him. It felt almost like second nature to fit her steps to his lead and to follow the graceful twirling pattern he established on the ballroom floor.

"Where did you learn to dance so well?"

"I went to a great many sorority dances in college and before that I escorted my two sisters to parties." He gave her a brilliant grin as he whirled her about the floor beneath the soft overhead lights. "You don't do so bad yourself. I saw you at the Cinderella dance last week."

"I don't recall seeing either you or Cordero."

"That's because I couldn't get near you, and my buddy had Guard Duty that night."

"What subject did you major in at college?" she asked, changing the conversation.

"*Girls,*" he replied, grinning from ear to ear.

"You're not being serious."

"Very. My parents decided I was wasting my time and their money, and I didn't go back after the third semester. As soon as I quit school, I was drafted," he informed her.

"Do you regret leaving?"

"Not really. Mostly I miss my car I had in college."

"What happened to it?"

"I loaned it to a friend and she wrecked it."

"Oh, how unfortunate. I hope no one was injured."

"Just my car. My parents are giving me another one for Christmas."

Before she could reply, his shoulder was tapped and he released her to another partner.

After the dance was over, the guys walked Mae and her to the Clerical School. At the entrance Cordero said goodnight, and before leaving, he touched his lips to the palm of her hand and closed her fingers over the warm spot.

"I expected him to kiss you goodnight," remarked Mae as they climbed the first flight of stairs to their sleeping quarters.

"I hardly know him. How could I allow him to kiss me? He took me by surprise when he kissed my hand. I actually thought he meant to shake my hand."

"You must be kidding." She hooted. "The way he looked at you and his eyes followed you around the room all evening when you danced with other men. Except for the one time he danced with me, I never saw him partner another girl."

April wanted to confide in Mae that she had never been kissed but that would have invited even more teasing.

On Sunday afternoon, she and Mae walked up to the Hilltop Service Club. Only a few of the rooms were occupied. Most everyone was crowded into the music room where the Spanish Band played. Every chair was occupied, they stood just inside the door until two guys got up, and offered their seats. The band members were gathered around the piano where a black guy played. CQ played a shining trumpet while Cordero kept the beat with his bongo drums to "Why Do Fools Fall In Love." Another Spanish GI strummed a guitar and a pintsized guy energetically shook the maracas. The music ended and Cordero came to where she sat. He leaned down and kissed her cheek.

"Don't do that," she said, pulling away from him.

He straightened his shoulders before replying. "It's just a Spanish custom of greeting." He smiled.

"I reserve that custom for my immediate family members," she quipped.

"I believe I qualify," he responded. "Didn't I promise to look out for you in a brotherly way—like an older brother?" He was still smiling; a rueful curving of a very masculine mouth that matched the amusement in his wicked eyes.

71

"So you did," she admitted.

"Do you like our music?"

"Yes, it sounded like a recording."

"Come meet the guys in the band and tell them what you said." He took her hand and led her to where the other members milled around the piano.

"CQ, you know with the trumpet, Jorge is our piano player. He is originally from the Dominican Republic. Torres plays the guitar, he is Cuban, and Chico shakes a mean set of maracas. He is Puerto Rican like CQ and myself."

After they exchanged greetings with her, she complimented them on their playing.

"What would you like us to play for you?" asked Jorge.

"La Paloma."

"Good choice," said Jorge. He seated himself at the piano and began to play. The rest of the members picked up their instruments and joined in.

She returned to her chair and Richard entered the room. As there weren't any vacant seats, he walked over and perched on her chair arm.

"Do you like to dance to Spanish music?" He leaned over and said in a low voice.

"I've never danced to Spanish music," she whispered in confession.

"I do." He laughed softly. "It will be my pleasure to teach you."

After the band finished rehearsing, she went with Richard to the poolroom while Cordero went to check out the pool sticks. She placed her purse on the last vacant table and looked around for Mae. They needed her to play doubles. Where had she gone?

"Cordero and I are taking our Christmas leave at the same time. He is going to help me drive my car back after he sees his girl friend in New York," said Richard.

"Why don't you purchase one here in Alabama?" she asked, and completely ignored the news about Cordero's girlfriend.

"The model I want is not readily available everywhere. It would have to be ordered and delivered which would take time."

"What make and color do you plan to select?"

"I shall let that be a surprise."

"Where have you been," she asked as Mae joined them.

"Watching TV."

"Did Cordero tell you how we met?" asked Richard. He picked up the triangle and began racking the pool balls.

"No, he never mentioned it." Just like he never said anything about having a girl in New York.

"We went through basic training together at Ft. Dix. One night we were at a party. Everyone was drinking and this guy we had just met got real crazy because I danced with his girlfriend. He pulled a knife and came at me. Cordero—"

"Rich, don't tell them that," said Cordero, walking up behind him.

Richard turned and Cordero handed him one of the two pool sticks he carried.

She would have liked to hear the rest of the story but from the stern look on Cordero's face, he wasn't going to allow Richard to complete the tale.

"What made you enlist in the Army, April?" asked Richard.

"Several reasons. I wanted to finish my education using the GI Bill, and I already had two brothers in the service."

"I bet you left a boyfriend behind," teased Richard. "Or perhaps more than one?"

"No boyfriends. My brothers were very protective of me, never letting me go out alone. Being of similar ages, we went places with a group of friends. I want to keep it that way and not get involved with any one person. I prefer a no-strings-attached friendship." She lifted her chin, meeting Cordero's gaze straight on.

"We won last," said Cordero. "I'll take the first shot." He lined up the cue ball and fired it at the racked balls. It hit with a loud crack that sent the balls scattering in all directions.

"Good break," said Mae, taking her shot, pocketing the number four ball. She missed her next endeavor.

They lost all three games to Mae and Richard.

"What happened, Cord?" teased Richard. "You didn't seem to have your mind on the game."

"Maybe he was daydreaming about going on leave to New York," she said sweetly.

"Could be," agreed Richard, catching her gaze, giving her a meaningful look.

Soon after the last pool game, she and Mae left to go to the mess hall.

"You are awfully quiet," said Mae as they passed the WAC Chapel. "Did I miss something when I went to watch TV?"

"You might say that," she replied.

"Well, tell me, and what was that about New York and that *no-strings-friendship* all about?"

73

"Richard told me that his parents are giving him a new car for Christmas, and he and Cordero are going on leave together and driving it back. That is, after Cordero first goes to see his girlfriend in New York."

"Sounds like he's in the wrong branch of service with a girl in every port." Mae waggled her brows.

"Well, I am not about to let myself get hurt by him. Can you blame me?"

"I've been in love a few times. There is something you should know. You don't always choose whom you fall in love with or who loves you. Sometimes it just happens without our intentions."

"Thanks for the advice. I'll keep it in mind," she said as she fished out her ID, and they entered the mess hall.

After chow, they went to the barracks, refreshed themselves and changed clothing. April wore the aqua blouse that June had given her with her blue-gray suit skirt.

In the service club that evening, she and Mae sat below the bandstand where the Spanish Band played. The members had changed into white dress shirts and dark trousers topped with red sashes. A few couples danced scattered around the floor. Almost immediately, Richard joined them, looking sharp in a two-piece gray suit worn with a black patterned tie.

"We match," he said, studying April's gray skirt "Are you ready for your first Spanish dance lesson?"

"I don't think so," she said, shaking her head.

"I insist." He scooted back her chair, took her arm, and steered her to a cleared corner of the floor away from the dancing couples. He pulled her into his arms. "Follow my lead." He patiently showed her the intricate steps. "Don't look at me, relax—you are too stiff. Get loose. Let your body move with the music."

With a firm hand at her waist he guided her to the rhythm of the swaying music, smoothly adapting the length of his steps to hers with ease that wove them together.

The music was pleasant and upbeat. He expertly swung her through a series of complex steps, and she followed him with smooth grace.

Soon she relaxed, keeping her eyes on him as she concentrated on the steps of the dance. She spun and shifted. Her mouth curved in laughter as she gracefully ducked beneath Richard's arm and twirled away again.

They stayed on the floor after the music ended and waited for the next number.

Later when the band took a break, Richard returned her to the table where Cordero met them.

"Let's go get a soda," he said, attempting to kiss her on the cheek.

She moved and he kissed her ear.

They waited in line for their drinks and carried them out to the patio. She didn't talk, just sat sipping her soda and watching his face. He was frowning slightly.

"I thought you told me that you didn't dance to Spanish music."

"I don't," she said. "Richard was teaching me."

"I hope that's the only thing he is teaching you. Let's see what you learned." He stood and pulled her up with him. He put his hand on the small of her back and guided her through the French doors to the small dance floor in front of the soda counter.

"Don't you have to go back and play with the band?"

"They can get along without me." He shrugged, slotting a coin into the jukebox and punching two buttons.

He was not the expert dance partner like Richard, but his voice compensated for his lack of skill as he sang the words in Spanish to "*La Paloma.*"

Richard interrupted their dance. "Jorge said he needs you with the band to play the last number."

The three of them returned to the ballroom.

After the song ended, Cordero put away his drums and rejoined her at the table with Mae and Richard. "How about some TV?" he asked, taking a seat next to her.

"It's late. I have to go to the barracks."

"Me, too," said Mae.

Richard and Cordero walked with them to the bus stop at the top of WAC Circle. They paused to say good night.

"I have Thursday afternoons off, if you want to go to a movie," said Cordero.

"I can't. I have classes until 1630 hours and then I have to meet Pvt. Torres at 1900 hours at the club to help him with a letter."

"Then I'll see you at the service club," he said.

The following evening April walked up to the club alone, since Mae had a date with the guy she met at the dance on Sunday. On her way to the writing room, she stopped to say hello to CQ.

She had the room to herself, and she sat at her usual desk. Cordero came in and gave her his customary greeting with a kiss on the cheek.

"I'll be in the pool room," he said and left.

A few minutes later, Pvt. Torres entered and seated himself at a vacant desk.

"It is most kind of you to help me with my letter," he said, slowly choosing his words.

"You speak English very well," she complimented him.

"I try but I can not write correctly."

"Tell me about your girl friend."

"Her name is Nancy Strand," he said. He pulled out his wallet and flipped it open. "She has blue eyes and brown hair."

She glanced at the photo of a pretty girl in her late teens or early twenties. "She is lovely. How did you meet?"

"She lived on the post where I took my basic training. Her father is a drill sergeant at Ft. Dix."

"Cordero and Richard completed basic training there. Did you know them before you were assigned to this post?"

"Nah, it's a pretty big post."

"Let's get started. You write what you want to say, I'll correct your grammar and spelling, and then you can recopy it."

While Pvt. Torres was rewriting his letter, she looked up seeing Cordero sitting across the room with a book in his hand. He winked and smiled; she returned his smile. She had not noticed when he entered the room.

"Thanks again for your help," said Pvt. Torres, sealing his letter. He nodded to Cordero as he left the room.

She stood as Cordero came toward her, and she began to straighten the desktop. "Are you checking up on me?" she asked, teasingly.

"Yeah, something like that." He ran his fingers across her journal lying on the desktop next to a box of stationery.

"What's this book?" He picked it up and opened the top cover. "*Dreamcatcher?*"

"My journal." She plucked it from his hands.

He frowned, raising a questioning black brow.

"It's like a diary," she explained.

"Is there anything about me written in it?"

"Uh—huh," she murmured, nodding her head affirmative. "You are mentioned in my journal."

"Can I read it?" He reached to take it back.

"No, it's personal." She clutched it against her chest with both hands.

"Do you write about Richard, too?"

"I write my thoughts and feelings about the things that occur each day," she replied, without giving him a direct answer. "Have you seen Mae?" she asked, slyly changing the subject.

"Yeah, earlier she was watching TV with some guy. Do you want to watch some TV?"

"I'd rather play pool."

"Weren't you the girl that didn't want to learn to play pool a while ago?" he teased her.

"Haven't you heard? It's a lady's prerogative to change her mind."

"Tell me about it."

All the tables were in use, but they found a vacant shuffleboard. Richard joined them to play the winner. She had a sneaky suspicion Cordero let her win, as he was not all that fond of the game.

At last, they got a pool table, the three of them playing, the odd one playing the winner. Cordero won the first game, and then he lost to her with a technicality when he scratched. Richard won the last play.

They both walked her to the barracks. At the door, Richard reminded her, "Wear something colorful tomorrow night. I'm bringing my camera with color film to take pictures to show my parents when I go home on Christmas leave."

April twirled around before the full-length mirror in the latrine to check the seams of her stockings. She wore her favorite aqua blue and lilac print with a rolled white collar that dipped to a V in the back. Mae opened the door as her skirts settled back over the two crinolines beneath the gathered skirt.

"Wow! Where did that dress come from?"

"In this afternoon's mail. Mama thought I might like something pretty for the holidays. I hadn't told her I was coming to see her because I wanted it to be a surprise. I called her a little while ago to let her know I got the dress and that I would be coming to visit."

"You're going to knock some guy's eyes out tonight."

"You think so? Richard is bringing his camera to take some color pictures to show his folks back home. I wish you were going to be at the club tonight."

"I've got a train to catch. Wouldn't you know it? Just my luck to meet someone I really like and he is going on leave, too." She shook her head. "Have a Merry Christmas and try not to let your step-father annoy you too, much."

"Okay." She touched Mae's arm lightly. "You take care and have a safe trip."

After walking down the steps to the CQ area with Mae, she returned to the bay to look for Sybil, a cute blue eyed blonde with dimples. She had invited her to go to the club to meet Richard.

In the music room of the club, she posed Sybil and Richard on a loveseat. He gave her a sour look and refused to smile in spite of her coaching. Two other guys from Richard's company crowded into the photo he was taking of CQ and her at CQ's request. Jerry, their company's tall mail clerk, and another guy called Larsen stood next to her for the picture. She wasn't sure if it was his first or last name, but he was one handsome GI with red hair and sky-blue eyes that reminded her of a dear friend back in high school.

After Richard finished the roll of film, the four of them went to play pool until it was time for her to return to her barracks.

"How are you getting to the station?' asked Richard.

"A friend of mine is Post Driver tonight. I'm getting a ride with her as she has to meet the bus to pick up some new recruits."

The guys walked her and Sybil to the Clerical School barracks.

Cordero said a quiet good-bye to her, turning her palm up and pressing a kiss in the center then closed her fingers over the warm spot where his lips had touched. "Don't lose it and don't forget me."

"See you next year." Richard surprisingly gave her a hug and quickly kissed her cheek.

She walked thoughtfully up the steps to her cubicle. What kind of game was Cordero playing with her? He was going to see his girlfriend in New York and yet he was treating her like she was special.

If you don't step forward,
You're always in the same place.

Chapter 9

Saturday, 22 December 1956
Dear Dreamcatcher,

I left Anniston at 2315 hours last night, and I arrived in Madisonville this morning at daybreak. Mama had left the door unlocked and I went in quietly. I had seen the house from the street, but I had never been inside. I was able to locate the guestroom from her description of the layout of the house, and I slipped right into bed.

Mama let me sleep until almost noon. She kept saying how happy she was to see me.

My grandmother came down from the hills to spend the holidays. She looks so fragile I was almost afraid to hug her.

Bobbie has grown like a weed. He is now the taller of my brothers.

The house is large and very nice, but because of my stepfather I don't feel welcome here. I guess the military is my home now...

Tuesday, 25 December 1956
Today was Christmas. It didn't seem like it; the weather wouldn't co-operate. It didn't snow a single flake.

We spent a quiet day. I gave Mama the eight by ten color photo of me in uniform with some money. I also gave money to Bobbie, as I had no idea what to buy for a fourteen-year-old.

Mama gave me a dusty rose dress with a matching jacket that she sewed and a store bought pink nylon blouse. Bobbie's present to me was a Spanish record album. Mom must have told him that I have become fascinated with Spanish music.

Gene called from Ft. Leonard Wood, and I spoke briefly with him. After he graduates from basic training, he said they were hinting at sending him to Alaska for further training.

In the afternoon, Mr. Winston and Bobbie went out to deliver some gifts to his brother's family. At last, I had some time alone with Mama. I told her about my friends Mae and June and Delores nicknaming me April. She was amused by the story. I also discussed my unusual relationship with Cordero and Richard. How they seem to be an extension of my brothers the way they watch out for me. Surprisingly, she said almost the same as Mae had about not being in control of whom we fall in love with or who might love us. I told her not to worry, Cordero had a girl friend in New York. Then she asked about Richard. I replied that I could never be anything but his friend that he was too much like a brother. Also that he had only indicated friendship toward me. She reminded me that it was the quiet ones I should watch out for...

Sunday, 30 December 1956

These days passed so quickly. It seems that I just arrived and now I am getting ready to leave.

I went through my belongings and crammed my luggage. I put all my 45 albums in my overnight case. I am taking my record player back with me. After I finished packing and closed my suitcases, there were no reminders of me left in the room...

April spun around in her cubical, the full skirt of the blue taffeta dress twirled out above her ankles.

"What do you think, Mae? Is my skirt too long?" She asked.

"It's perfect—just right for dancing," replied Mae.

"That's a relief. I was not looking forward to shortening the hem on—"

"Private Terry has a visitor in the lobby." The PA system drowned out the rest of her words.

"The guys must be back," she said, removing her jacket and hanging it in her locker. She slipped off her heels and replaced them with a pair of flats before hurrying toward the stairs.

Cordero was leaning against the doorjamb of the Day Room. He smiled when he caught sight of her. His eyes glittered like glass; they raked over her and his smile disappeared.

"Hi," she said breathlessly, coming to a halt in front of him. "Happy New Year."

He didn't return her greeting. Instead, he pushed away from the wall, placing his hands on her shoulders, and spinning her around.

"You look very beautiful. Are you going out?"

"No." She shook her head. "I was just trying the dress on when the CQ announced that I had a visitor."

"Were you expecting someone?" asked Cordero.

"Happy New Year," said Richard, as he breezed into the CQ area. He hustled over and gave April a peck on the cheek. "You look marvelous. Are you going somewhere?"

"No." Her eyes slid from him to Cordero. "I knew you guys were coming so I dressed up." She flashed them an innocent smile.

Cordero's right brow arched up as he gave her a look that said he didn't believe her for a moment.

"Cord, look at her eyes," Richard exclaimed. "They are the shade of blue just like I said."

"What's this about my eyes being blue?" she asked.

"We were having a disagreement about the color. He said green—"

"Gold with green specks," Cordero cut in correcting him.

"And I said they were blue just like the dress you're wearing," continued Richard. He grinned from ear to ear.

"I hate to disappoint you"—she gave Richard an apologetic look—"but my eyes are not blue. My military record lists their color as hazel. Someone once told me they were topaz, and that is the reason they change colors like a chameleon to match the color of my clothing."

"You could have fooled me. I was sure they were blue," Richard said, looking closely at her eyes. "Come see my car."

Parked out front in the school lot was a shinny new '57 Chevy Bel Air. It was turquoise blue with fins on the back and a white top.

"It's a beauty, Richard. Congratulations." She reached through the open window of the passenger door and ran her hand down the smooth white leather seat back. "Nice—I like the color combination."

"Would you like to go for a spin?" asked Richard.

"Sure," she agreed.

"Do you want to drive," offered Richard, opening the driver's door.

"No, thanks," she said, taking a step back.

He closed the door and rounded the car of the passenger's side, but Cordero was already helping her into the rear seat. He swept a ditty bag into the far corner and sat beside her.

Richard closed the door, came around, and slid behind the wheel. He backed out of the lot and drove around WAC Circle onto Galloway Road and through the check gate to Lee's Drive-in restaurant across the street from the post entrance.

"How about a burger or something?" asked Richard, turning his head, and looking over his shoulder. "We just got back on post and missed chow."

"Thanks, I've had lunch. You guys go ahead and eat."

Richard placed an order for two burgers and two chocolate shakes through the speaker on the stand next to the driver's side of the car.

Cordero picked up her right hand and dropped a small, white box on her palm.

"What's this?"

"Something I got in New York. Consider it a late Christmas gift."

A pair of earrings nestled inside the black velvet container. They were in the shape of a small cut out silver heart; a bird in flight across the lower half of each heart sparkled with six turquoise stones on the wings and one for the eye.

"How precious! They are lovely. Thank you."

"I think maybe Rich was right. Your eyes are blue." Cordero picked up an earring and held it next to her eyes before he clipped it on her ear.

"It's only the reflection of my dress," she assured him.

A skimpily clad carhop whizzed out on skates, coming to a graceful stop and balancing the tray while Richard raised the window a few inches to accommodate it. The server rolled away, and Richard passed a burger and shake back to Cordero.

Richard opened the glove compartment and grasped a large envelope. He turned sideways in the seat and handed it to her.

"These are for you. I had copies made of the pictures I took before our Christmas leave."

"Thanks." She slid back the flap and took out the photos one at a time. "Oh, these are good. They are the first color pictures I've ever had of myself."

April continued looking at the snapshots while the guys finished eating. She held up a photograph of Richard and Sybil. "This is a nice picture of my friend, but you look like you just ate a green persimmon. You do have a nice smile when you use it."

He wrinkled his nose and shook his head simultaneously as he drove out of the restaurant lot.

"These are great." She returned the pictures to the envelope. "I can't wait to show them to Mae."

A few minutes later Richard pulled into a parking space in front of the Clerical School.

"Anytime you want to use my car, let me know," he said.

"Thanks," she responded. She exited and Cordero walked with her to the entrance.

She turned to face Cordero at the door. "Thank you," she touched a finger to an earring. "I'm sorry I don't have a gift for you. I wasn't expecting you to bring these."

"My mother picked them out. Rich gave her one of the pictures of you and me. She said you were very pretty and she called you *Chica*. It means little one. Do you mind if I call you that, too? You are always correcting the way I pronounce Abril?"

They reached the front door and Cordero stepped to the side of the entrance. He leaned with his back against the wall next to the door, his feet crossed at the ankles.

"It's okay. As I told you my real name is Elaine." April related the story of how she got her nickname.

The car horn sounded. He glanced toward where the Chevy was parked and waved to Richard.

"Some of the girls in basic training called me *Little Bit*, because I was the smallest one in my platoon. With the girls from Hawaii here, I'm not the shortest one anymore."

"I bet you don't weigh ninety pounds soaking wet."

"Ninety-five," she informed him.

The horn honked again.

"You better go. Richard is getting impatient."

"Yeah," he said, pushing away from the wall. "I'll call you."

"Thanks again for the earrings. It was nice of you to think of me while you were away. I'm glad you returned safely."

Wednesday, 02 January 1957

Dear Dreamcatcher,

It was back to classes for me today. We reviewed the work we were doing before our Christmas leave.

Cordero called and told me about a special Third Army Show at the Hilltop Service Club tomorrow night. He said he and Richard would pick me up...

Thursday, 03 January 1957

Tonight I invited Carol, an attractive brown-eyed blonde, from my typing class to go with me to the show and meet Richard.

Mae had a date with Walt, a guy she met before we went on leave. They were at the show, too.

Cordero mentioned that the Spanish Band is engaged for the dance tomorrow night. I tried to maneuver Richard into inviting Carol without any success. I know she likes him, especially his new car. She kept telling him how much she would love to drive it...

Thursday evening, she picked up her purse and strolled gaily down the aisle to the last cubicle.

"Wow." exclaimed Louise as she entered her space. Her big brown eyes sparkled. "That's a beautiful outfit. I've never seen material like that. It changes from silver to turquoise when you move." She fingered one of the jacket cuffs.

"Thanks. We may as well go down and wait in the Day Room for our ride."

Richard was talking to the cute girl behind the desk; she walked up and whisked him over to where Louise stood. She made the introductions and they went out to his car.

In the ballroom of the Hilltop Club, her eyes were drawn to the bandstand where the five-piece band was already playing. The members wore the familiar white dress shirts and black slacks topped with red sashes.

Richard escorted them across the parquet floor to a table near the stage. Cordero looked up and caught her gaze. She smiled and waved to him. He returned her smile with a broad wink as he beat out the rhythm on his twin bongo drums. An unfamiliar guy sat at the baby grand.

She eyed his broad shoulders that strained beneath a crisp starched shirt, the two top buttons opened, exposing a glimpse of bronze skin. From where she sat she could not discern the color of his eyes with his head bowed, his attention on the keys.

Richard whisked Louise out onto the floor to a *merengue* beat.

Jerry, the mail clerk from the 30th Chemical Company, claimed her for the first dance.

"Cord better keep both eyes on you tonight. As they say in Alabama, you look *spiffy*," he teased. He grinned and gave her a mischievous wink.

"I didn't know you were an Alabamian," she teased him back.

"Oh, I'm not. I'm from Oklahoma but when in Rome…" He shrugged, letting his voice trail away.

"Thank you for the compliment. It's the dress."

"I could say something, but I best shut up before I put my big foot in my mouth." He chuckled, making his freckles more prominent.

She laughed with him as he returned her to the table. Richard and Louise joined them. They switched partners for the next number, a *mambo*.

"What do you think of Louise?" she asked, breathlessly.

"She is nice—she doesn't dance like you," he said

"I guess I need more practice to master the Spanish dance steps."

"I meant it as a compliment. She tries to lead. You are a much better partner."

"Well, just *look* who taught me. You are a terrific instructor, not to mention very encouraging." He was one of the most pleasant guys she had ever met. His blue eyes flirted— his smile was continuous, and the best partner she had ever danced with.

"I love to dance, and I enjoy learning new steps. Speaking of *new*, who is the guy at the piano? What happened to Jorge?"

"Jorge was transferred to Germany. That's his replacement, Alberto Montoya.

"I don't recall ever seeing him before."

"He is in the first platoon with Cordero and myself. Montoya just recently returned from an emergency leave. Mostly, he stays in the barracks studying for some classes he's enrolled in at a local college. He is also the company barber, he cuts most the guys hair including mine." Richard ran a hand casually over his sandy locks.

"Sounds like Montoya is very motivated."

"Why all the interest in him?"

"Just curious."

Forty-five minutes and ten dances later, the band took a break and Cordero joined them at the table. She introduced him to Louise.

"How was our playing?" he asked.

"Terrific! You guys sounded fantastic. I see the band has a new piano player. Where's he from?"

"South America," said Cordero.

"Ecuador," supplied Richard as he assisted Louise from her chair.

"I've never met anyone from Ecuador. How about an introduction?" she asked, glancing up at Montoya sitting motionless at the piano.

"Nah, I don't think so. He is a real *stiff shirt*. You wouldn't like him."

She barely refrained from laughing. She knew Cordero referred to a *stuffed shirt*.

"Where did Rich and your friend go?"

"Her name is Louise. Richard mentioned getting something to drink before you joined us."

"I better give him a hand," he said, rising from his seat. "You want grape soda?"

"Thanks, that would be nice."

As soon as he disappeared through the French doors, April ascended the steps to the bandstand. The new guy ran his fingers lazily over the black and ivory keys.

"Hello," she said.

He stood giving her a view of his broad chest and his muscled forearms revealed by the rolled up sleeves of his dress shirt. His exposed face, neck and arms were a deep bronze.

"Would you please play, 'Smoke Gets in Your Eyes' for me?"

The guy glanced down at her; her breath caught in her throat. He wasn't handsome in the traditional sense of the word, but his face was one that made a lasting impression. He had a dark, brooding air about him—and a hint of arrogance that made him appear stuck up. Deep-set eyes, the color of rich chocolate beneath heavy, black brows. A straight proud nose along with a sensuous mouth and a full lower lip created a suggestion of fierce authority.

For a long moment their eyes caught until he broke eye contact, dropping his gaze back to the piano keys.

"No." The shortness of his answer took her by surprise.

Her head snapped back to look up at him, while her mouth hung aghast.

Cordero had him pegged right. The guy had a chip on his shoulder the size of a tree trunk.

86

"Well, thanks a lot," she murmured sarcastically.

She was not accustomed to being ignored. Piqued by his lack of attention, she spun on her heel and stalked off the platform. Louise and the guys were sipping soft drinks as April sat down at the table. Cordero stood handing her a grape soda. Without a word he returned to the bandstand.

"Let's dance," said Richard, as the band's first notes of "I'll Remember" sounded after their break.

With a nod of assent she rose to her feet, moved out onto the floor and into his arms.

"I see you met Montoya."

"Not really. I asked him to play a song for me. Either he didn't know the music or he is just plain rude. I didn't even get a chance to tell him my name."

"And what name would that be? I heard Cordero calling you Chica instead of April."

"If you must know, April is a nickname. My name is Elaine. He calls me Chica because it means little."

"Do you mind if I call you Chica, too?"

"I don't mind." She shrugged. "But what I do mind is that I invited my friend to meet you, and you have danced more times with me."

"Who's counting?" he quipped, a smirk tilting one corner of his wide mouth. "What will you do? Fix me up with an ugly, fat girl?"

"That's not a bad idea," she came back at him. "I just might. You haven't liked any of the pretty ones that I have introduced to you."

For the next hour, she smiled, laughed, and danced every number. She was aware the entire time of Montoya's heavy lidded gaze following her around the floor. Several times she looked up suddenly and caught him staring at her. His eyes slid over her—came back and held hers captive. Chocolate brown eyes that appeared to be shrouded in deep, dark secrets.

As soon as the Spanish band stopped playing, the ballroom emptied quickly. While Cordero put away his drums, she waited at the table with Louise and Richard. She glanced up at the platform. The piano bench was empty. Montoya had left without her noticing.

Never want what's impossible,
You'll always be disappointed.

Chapter 10

Inside the 30th Chemical barracks, Montoya lay in his lumpy bunk. He rolled onto his back and stared up at the ceiling, letting his mind drift. Once again his thoughts turned to a pair of topaz eyes flecked with green sparkles, golden tipped lashes, and hair the color of rich honey. He turned and pillowed his head on his arm, suddenly uncomfortable by the sexual drive that swept over him.

At the oddest times through out the entire day, he had found his mind swamped with images and sensations from the night before of his mystery girl. Was the attraction real or simply his imagination? He was anxious to see her again. Patience had never been one of his strong assets. Perhaps it came from being the youngest son in a family of nine children. Or it was a flaw in his character. What others saw as arrogance he deemed as impatience to have his own way.

Last night at the service club, their gazes had locked. He had gotten a good look at her, and he had felt a jolt to the depth of his soul. The potent, undeniable intense desire had turned his blood to liquid fire. And when she spoke to him, her eyes had held his, and it was as if he were drowning. Like a numbskull when he could not understand what she said, he had become tongue-tied. All his English had flown out the window. The only word he could utter was *no*. He couldn't explain his sudden loss of speech, not even to himself. High color had stained her cheeks, and when she had spoken again, her tone of voice conveyed her anger, and the stubborn tilt to her chin as she stalked away had almost made him smile in reaction.

Without conscious thought, his eyes had followed her to the table where she sat with another girl and one of the band members, and a soldier from his company. His gaze had settled on her, lingering as he took in her lovely features and tantalizing curves.

What would it be like to know her touch? She was not meant to be his, but still he yearned to know her touch on his skin.

What was wrong with him? He was fantasizing about a woman he'd just met. Whatever she was looking for, a future with him wasn't it. He knew that without asking. They did not speak the same language and did not belong to the same culture. Allowing this feeling of attraction to grow would cause him nothing but grief.

He closed his eyes and buried his head deeper in his pillow as the familiar *Taps* at midnight sounded in the distance bringing the day to a close.

> Sunday, 06 January 1957
> Dear Dreamcatcher,
> Cordero didn't call me all day. I think he became annoyed with me because I tried to talk to the new piano player. Last night was the first time he bid me good night without kissing my cheek. So this evening after chow, I went with Mae to the Flick. One of my favorite comedians, Donald O'Connor starred in *Anything Goes*, one of his best films. We both laughed 'til we cried.
> When Mae and I returned to our quarters, the CQ handed me four messages, one from Richard and three from Cordero, "Urgent, please phone me at #2016." It was late, and I still have a *thing* about calling a guy so I didn't return any of the calls...

Pvt. Rodas held the front door open as she and Mae returned from chow.

"I'm sure glad to see you, Pvt. Terry. You have a phone call. This same guy has been calling you every ten minutes for the past hour. He refuses to give his name or leave a message. I told him you were at the mess hall."

"Thank you, Pvt. Rodas," she said. She walked to the CQ desk, picked up the black receiver, "Pvt. Terry speaking."

"Where the hell have you been?" came a familiar voice over the wire.

"Watch your language—you know I don't approve of rough talk. I was at the mess hall."

"I was asking about last night. Richard and I searched the entire post for you."

"Apparently, you didn't try the Flick," she said, sweetly.

There was a silence on the line. "Did you go alone?"

"I went with Mae."

"Why didn't you tell me that you wanted to go to the movies? I would have taken you."

"Sometimes I want to be with my other friends."

"Didn't you get my messages? Why didn't you return my phone calls?"

"As I told you," she elevated her voice slightly, "where I was raised—nice girls do not call boys on the telephone,"

"Couldn't you have made an exception? I was concerned about you."

"No, and I don't like this third degree. Don't expect me to ever call you. Good night." She quickly returned the receiver to its cradle before he could answer.

> Tuesday, 8 January 1957
> Dear Dreamcatcher,
> I guess Cordero is still peeved with me. He hasn't called me in two days.
> It turned cooler during the night and snowed. This morning was cold and a light dusting of white remains on the ground. We were excused from standing Reveille, and we were told that the banks and government agencies in town along with the schools were closed. Imagine that! At home nothing closed when we had three feet of snow...

The following evening, after chow, she exchanged her uniform for a pencil, slim skirt of turquoise blue corduroy with a matching jacket. She slipped on a pair of beige pumps and picked up a purse the same color.

After waiting ten minutes at the bus stop, she decided to walk to the service club. As she cut through the club parking lot, Del Valle was getting out of a blue Pontiac near the front entrance. She followed him into the building and down the hall to the check out counter. He turned over the closed sign on the counter top as she walked up behind him.

"I thought that was you I saw across the parking lot as I parked my car. You will be glad to know that tonight you'll be helping someone write that you know."

"Who?"

"Chico from the band."

"Great. That will make it easier to assist him."

"The band is rehearsing in the music room tonight for the dance on Saturday. What do you think of Jorge's replacement?"

"I'd rather not say." Heat rose to her cheeks, and she turned to leave.

"Wait. What's wrong? I noticed you with Montoya on the bandstand between breaks."

"If you must know, I think he is one of the most arrogant, rude persons that I've ever tried to speak to."

"We must not be talking about the same man. Montoya is one of the nicest guys you would ever want to meet."

"Then it must have been me that he didn't like on sight. I asked him to play a song and he dismissed me with a curt *no*."

"I think I get what happened," said CQ, passing a hand across his chin. "It was his lack of English."

"Why didn't he say so instead of being rude and ignoring me?"

"He is shy and it embarrasses him when he's not able to understand your language. When you speak to him you must speak slowly."

"I doubt that I'll be speaking to him again. Cordero is against me being friends with him."

"I think you will. He is someone worth getting to know. When you finish helping Chico, why not come along with him and listen to the band rehearse. I want you to hear a song that we have translated the words to Spanish."

"Okay, I'll be in the writing room. I have some letters of my own to answer," she said over her shoulder as she started down the hall.

Abril was sitting at the same desk the night he had first laid eyes on her. From the moment he'd entered the doorway, Cordero tried not to look at her breasts. He couldn't help being physically conscious of her. She had a serenity about her that he had found appealing. He had tried to concentrate on that and her unusual eyes to keep his mind off other aspects of her.

Tonight his gaze was drawn to her hands on the desktop. She held a black and gold pen, her fingers long and slender, graceful in their movements as she slowly slid her hand back and forth across the paper. The overhead light cast shimmering golden streaks in her hair; her lips the color of ripe peaches. She was the prettiest girl that had ever looked twice at him, and he had managed to screw up and make her mad.

On Richard's advice, him being the expert when it came to girls, he hadn't called her in two days. Now he was afraid she would tell him to get lost, that she never wanted to see him again.

She must have sensed his gaze for her eyes lifted meeting his. They reflected the same turquoise color as her jacket. He gave her a crooked smile. The corner of her mouth turned up in acknowledgment before her eyes lowered to the paper in front of her. Hell, the girl bewitched him. He didn't like admitting the truth. She was so beautiful, so soft, and so feminine. It was becoming a torment not to touch her. He felt tied up in knots inside, every time he saw her, and he wanted to take her into his arms and make wild passionate love to her.

He knew that was impossible, and yet he couldn't seem to stay away from her.

If she had any idea of the fantasies he was thinking, she wouldn't gaze at him with those wide innocent eyes. Was she still angry with him? She had returned his smile, but then she was always smiling.

Only one way to find out. He shouldered away from the door and moved toward her.

"Hi," he said. He picked up a chair from another nearby desk, turned it around, and put it down in front of her desk. Cordero straddled it and draped his arms across the back.

"Hello," she acknowledged him and continued to write. Her greeting wasn't as warm as it usually was.

He waited until she finished the page, folded it and placed it inside an envelope. He cleared his throat.

She folded her hands on the desk and then she looked up at him. "Did you want something—help with writing a letter?" Her voice was cool, and she wasn't smiling.

"Nah, I called your school and the CQ told me you were out. I remembered you came here on Wednesdays."

"I'm going to help Chico write a letter."

"Chico's okay. He plays with our band."

"Yes, I know. I've met him and the other members except for the new piano player."

He ignored her reference to the newest member of the group.

"The guys are meeting in the music room tonight to practice. Would you come with Chico when he finishes his letter to listen to us rehearse?"

She looked down at her hands, and then she nibbled on her lower lip as if it would help her make the right decision.

"All right," she finally said. "If you want me to."

An hour later, while Chico addressed the envelope, April put away the surplus service club stationery in the large box on the shelf against the wall.

"I think Elizabeth is a lucky girl to have a friend like you," she said, returning to pick up her own writing materials from the desk. She flicked the light off as they left the room.

April entered the music room with Chico and stopped inside the doorway while he strolled to the piano placed at an angle. He continued past the piano to a low table and picked up a set of colorful maracas.

CQ was talking with the piano player blocking her view of him. A member of the group was on either side of the piano. Cordero flashed her a grin and motioned for her to come to the front. Her eyes settled on the back of Richard's head in the front row. All the seats were taken except for the one on his right side. She made her way down between the chairs to the vacant seat. Richard removed a blue jacket from the armchair; she sat down and found herself just a few feet from the end of the piano bench. She had a good view of Montoya as CQ moved away to pick up his trumpet. He raised the horn to his lips, began to play and the group joined him.

"Where were you the other night?" whispered Richard, leaning toward her.

"I've already been through all that with Cordero," she whispered back.

"He started drinking like crazy and cussing a blue streak when he couldn't find you."

"Shhh—I want to listen to the music."

She found herself studying Montoya's hands as he played. They were proportioned, shapely hands with neatly trimmed nails and long fingers. Granny had always said one could learn much about a person by their hands. There was an undeniable appeal about the sight of a guy's clean hands framed by white shirt cuffs, and his deep bronze skin appeared even darker next to the whiteness of the cloth.

Montoya's gaze lifted, as if he sensed himself being appraised. April found herself entrapped by eyes the color of dark chocolate. He flashed her a slow smile exposing a deep dimple in his right cheek.

She'd been able to do nothing but smile in return. He might be arrogant and rude as she had labeled him from their first encounter, but his smile was full of mischief and his eyes held hidden secrets.

Having the sensation of someone staring at her, she let her eyes stray to the left of the piano. She glimpsed Cordero's shapely etched aristocratic Spanish face; black eyes met hers and instantly flared. She studied him for some indication of what he was thinking. If he was angry because he had caught her staring at Montoya, that was his problem. He still owed her an apology for the other night. Besides, she hadn't come to listen to the band because he invited her. It had been to see Montoya again.

She ignored Cordero's intense glares and continued to watch Montoya, his snow-white shirt more brilliant against his dark swarthy skin. He must have inherited his coloring from the Spaniards.

In between numbers, Chico said something to him that must have been funny for he laughed so vibrantly, richly deep. Spanish men had such lovely voices, warm, rich with a musical rhythmic sound.

One thought led to another until she found herself thinking fanciful thoughts of black lace mantillas, Spanish guitars, bullfights and vaqueros.

The music ended and CQ told the guys to take a ten-minute break. Richard and Cordero exited the room together.

She took the few steps to the piano where Montoya sat alone; the tops of his lean bronzed hands sprinkled lightly with fine black hair rested on the piano keys.

"Hello, we haven't been formally introduced. My name is—"

"I know"—He leaned forward, unfolding his lengthy frame and stood. — "You are April," he said interrupting her. He stuck out his hand.

She accepted his gesture and placed her small hand in his large one. His grip was strong, firm, and yet gentle. Her skin prickled and her stomach seemed to drop. At his soft, Spanish drawl, she felt her cheeks warm, and she couldn't tear her eyes away from the steady gaze that held hers. With the tip of her tongue, she moistened her suddenly dry lips, her eyes swept over him compulsively gathering details. He was close to six feet with a hard muscular build. She was amazed at herself for noticing since she was not the type to ogle a guy's body. She never had before, but then she had never experienced such a fierce attraction to any man.

"Elaine Terry," she finished. "April is a nickname my friends call me."

"Alberto Montoya. Everyone in the military refers to me as Montoya." Instead of releasing her hand, he held onto it with a gentle firmness. He flashed her a half smile. His mouth was beautiful, especially when he smiled.

"What else do you know about me?" she asked, smiling in return, tugging her hand out of his strong grip.

"Are you—searching for compliments?" His mouth tilted in a smile, accenting his full bottom lip, his speech slow and calculated.

"You didn't answer my question," she charged.

"Are you truly interested?" he countered.

"Just curious," she quipped.

"That could be fatal," he said, slowly, solemnly.

"I beg your pardon?" she said, allowing a frown to crease her forehead.

"Curiosity—I heard it was fatal to a cat." A teasing smile played across his mouth.

"I've never been compared to a cat before. Is that supposed to be a compliment or should I be insulted?"

"Neither," he returned quickly. "Just my dull sense of humor."

"For someone who is supposed to have a shy knowledge of English—I find it rather interesting."

"I am in the process—of trying to master your language. It is not easy and in order to participate in a conversation such as this, I first have to translate your English into my own language before replying. My Spanish-English dictionary would be helpful."

"I must say you have a fairly good handle on it already."

He frowned, a wrinkle marring his smooth forehead. "Please explain what you mean by *handle.*"

"I should have said grasp or understanding. I'm from the hills of Kentucky—I don't always use the King's English," she drawled, allowing a faint tinge of the south to honey her tone.

"Thank you for explaining it to me. I owe you an apology for the other night."

"Not at all." She shook her head. "I fully understand, and if any apology is necessary, I should beg your pardon for thinking and saying rude things about you."

"Yes—Del Valle told me what you said." He managed a half smile.

"And he told me how badly I had misjudged you."

"Can we start over?" he asked. "Tell me again the name of the song—you wanted me to play."

"Cherry Pink?"

"No." He shook his head. "I am sure that was not it—the title had more words. Something about *eyes.*"

"You're right," she replied, laughing. "I changed my mind."

"What was the name of the other song?" he asked again, insistently.

"Smoke Gets in Your Eyes," she enunciated each word slowly.

"Yes—I know it. It is a favorite of everyone." He was speaking slowly, groping for the right words almost as though he was trying to find his way along an unfamiliar route as he translated her foreign tongue to his own language before responding to her.

"It will be my pleasure to play—the songs for you as soon as our break is over."

Anything more he might have said was interrupted as Cordero came up behind her and took her arm.

"Let's go sit out on the patio," he said, dragging her away with him.

As soon as they were out of hearing range of Montoya, she turned on him. "That was rude, you might have invited your friend for a cold drink with us."

"Montoya's no friend of mine. I don't know why you bothered with him. He's a nobody. He don't even speak good English."

"I could say the same about you. When he talked to me, I understood him quite well."

"The question is—did he understand you?" he said, a smirk tilting one corner of his mouth.

"I'm sure he did. He responded to my questions."

"I wasn't referring to what you said to him but the way you were smiling and flirting."

"That's not true. I was merely being friendly." Flirting was certainly not part of her character in spite of Mae's attempts to instruct her on its finer points.

"Chica, you better be careful around guys like him. You don't know how Spanish men are. They can't be trusted. Often, they get the wrong idea when a pretty girl gets friendly," he warned.

"Really? I didn't notice anything wrong with how he acted and spoke to me."

"I'm warning you—stay away from him."

"I can take care of myself," she said angrily, twisting out of his grip.

In mid step, she stopped and faced him. She raised her chin in a spurt of defiance. "I've changed my mind. I don't want anything to drink. I am going back to my barracks."

"I can't leave to walk you to your school. Wait another hour and I will go with you."

"That's not necessary. I came alone. I can return by myself."

"You have no business walking by yourself at night."

"It wouldn't be the first time. Beside, it's only a ten minute walk to my quarters."

"I'm sure your brothers wouldn't approve of you being alone in the dark."

"Okay," she sighed. "I'll stay."

He took her arm again and they went to join Richard on the patio. He sat at a table that held three soft drinks.

Cordero took a sip of his soda. He passed a hand over his eyes, and then he rubbed the back of his neck. "Man, my head hurts like the devil."

"I don't wonder," said Richard. "It's your fault for drinking so much for these past two nights."

April stood, moving around behind Cordero. "Let me see if I can help you. Where does it hurt?"

He placed her hands on either side of his head. She rubbed his temples, rotating her fingertips in slow circles. Firmly, she stroked back and forth across his forehead several times before moving her fingers down to knead the corded muscles in his neck and shoulders. His tension showed in the knots she rubbed.

Cordero made a rough sound of appreciation. "That feels great. Where did you learn this?"

"From my grandmother. I use to massage my brothers after they had been breaking horses."

"You've got magic fingers. I wish you didn't have to stop, but I have to go finish rehearsing with the band," he said, rising from his chair.

The first number they played was "Cherry Pink," followed by "Smoke Gets in Your Eyes."

During the following hour she caught Montoya's eyes on her. He seemed to frequently be watching her with more than a passing interest in his soft brown eyes. Often, he made the pretense of glancing around the room, but she noticed that his gaze returned to her in a rapid but thorough sweep over the music room. He was interested, but he was clever enough not to show it. She was also aware of Cordero's moody glare as he sat on a stool thumping his drums.

Cordero was noticeably silent as Richard drove to her barracks after rehearsal. Did his lack of conversation imply that he was angry with her for talking to Montoya? Issuing a polite good night, he left her at the front door of the Clerical School.

The following day after evening chow, Cordero phoned. He told her that he would pick her up in an hour. She exchanged her uniform for a cranberry-colored pinwale corduroy slim skirt with matching jacket over a pink blouse. She had just slipped on a pair of black flats when the CQ announced she had two visitors.

Richard made a pretense of looking for someone behind her. "What—no girl friend for me?"

"Sorry, I couldn't find an ugly, fat girl who wanted to meet you," she said, trying to hold back her giggles.

Richard laughed and she laughed with him.

"What's so funny?" asked Cordero.

They laughed harder.

Inside the car Cordero took Abril's hand and placed it on his forehead. "My head is killing me."

She moved farther back on the seat to make more room for him. He scooted toward her and turned his back. Her first touch sent shivers down to his calves. Her hands were surprisingly strong but gentle. He closed his eyes to savor each movement of her fingers on his skin.

"Feel good?" she asked.

"Yeah." God, it was good. Her voice was soft and warm and her lightly pressing fingertips were sheer magic, even though his head wasn't aching at all. He caught his breath.

"Did I hurt you?" she asked, instantly removing her hand.

With a short laugh, he shook his head. "It feels great."

Cordero couldn't tell her the truth; it had caused him another kind of pain. A smoldering heat began in his groin. He couldn't remember ever wanting a woman like this, craving the feel, scent, and taste of her with every fiber of his being.

And he was supposed to treat her like a *sister*?

Fear is often the unseen,
Turn on the light and it vanishes.

Chapter 11

On Saturday afternoon, she came down to the CQ desk in response to a phone call. It was Cordero.

"Chica, I'll pick you up at 1930 hours. I have to be at the club early."

"Okay," she said, "I'll be ready." She replaced the black handset in its cradle, and she thanked the CQ before going back upstairs.

After the evening chow, she dressed in a blue flowered dress with a short jacket in her favorite blue. She went down the hall to the latrine to check her appearance in the full-length mirror.

Mae was at the sink washing her face; her eyes were red and swollen. She wiped her eyes with a paper towel.

"What is it, Mae?" she asked, moving forward to place a consoling hand on her friend's shoulder.

"Walt got his orders for Germany. He leaves this Friday." Mae sniffed and blew her nose.

"I'm so sorry," she said.

"Careful," Mae said, moving away from her. "Don't get your dress wet. Is that a new outfit?"

"Uh-uh. It's one I brought back from Kentucky. Will you and Walt be at the dance?"

"Wouldn't miss it. Why are you dressed so early?"

"Cordero is picking me up in a few minutes because he has to be there for some last minute practice or something."

"Oh, that's right. I forgot the Spanish Band is playing tonight."

Later in the service club ballroom, the first number the band played was "Cherry Pink and Apple Blossom White."

"I guess I'll have to dance with you since you didn't bring a fat, ugly girl for me," Richard said, pulling her into his arms.

"There seems to be a shortage of fat, ugly girls these days," she responded, teasingly. They laughed as he swung her close to the bandstand. She glanced up at the platform; Montoya inclined his head and smiled. She returned the gesture.

"What do you think you're doing?" Richard must have caught the smile she gave Montoya.

"Dancing," she replied, innocently, smiling up at him. The heat that enveloped her face told its own story.

"You know what I meant." He gave her a raised—eyebrow look. "Cordero is jealous enough as it is."

"He has nothing to be jealous about since we are only friends."

"I don't think he knows that."

"If you recall when I started hanging out with you guys, I made a point of telling the both of you that I didn't want any involvement, just your friendship. I haven't done or said anything to encourage a different relationship between us. Have I?" She gave him a meaningful glance.

"We can't always control our emotions." Richard looked away not meeting her eyes.

The music ended and he returned her to the table before she could question him further.

Cordero came down from the platform to dance the last tune with her, "My Prayer."

She gazed up to the bandstand as she listened to the group singing the words in Spanish, all except Montoya. He cast her a dimpled grin before turning back to the piano.

> Monday, 14 January 1957
> Dear Dreamcatcher,
> This afternoon, in my S2 class I was given a large envelope. It contained photos that the post photographer took of my instructor, Sp. Faxon and me in the classroom.
> Cordero called me this evening to ask if I was going to the club tomorrow night. He remarked how he didn't like for me to volunteer my help writing letters with the guys.
> Before he hung up, he mentioned picking me up on Friday after evening chow...

On Saturday after lunch Cordero phoned. He asked if he could come by and pick her up. He never said why he didn't show up last night. He must have called from somewhere closer than his barracks as she had barely adjusted her rust colored tweed dress over the crinolines before the CQ announced she had a visitor.

She entered the foyer where Cordero lounged against the CQ counter dressed in a black sports jacket over a pale blue shirt with matching slacks of the same black fabric as his coat.

April signed out and walked with him to the front of the building where the car was parked. It was empty.

"Where is Richard?" she asked.

"Guard Duty."

He stuck the key in the ignition and turned it. The engine purred and he backed slowly from the lot.

Inside the club, Cordero steered her past the ballroom and through the French doors to the soda counter. The music from the ballroom floated through the open doors.

Cordero picked up their drinks, carried them out to the patio, and selected an empty table by the wall. He sipped his soda, his eyes studying her above the glass.

"Do you mind if we skip the dance, tonight? I don't feel much like dancing."

"Okay," she agreed. "Besides, one of my dance partners isn't here."

He laughed and placed his drink back on the table. From his jacket he brought out a slender, gleaming object and laid it on the table. It looked like a silver handled pocketknife.

"Remember when I said I would look out for you. I want you to know I meant it. If any man bothers you, he'll answer to me." He picked up the knife, thumbed a clasp on one side, and flicked a long, stiletto blade in place.

"Cordero." She drew back nearly upsetting her soda. "Please put that away. It's dangerous to be carrying that around with you."

He laughed. "You mean for the other guy." he said, closing the thin, silver knife.

He opened and closed the spring-hinged, razor-sharp knife a couple of times before slipping it back in his jacket.

"Nobody messes with this Rican."

"I wish you wouldn't carry that knife."

"Does it frighten you?"

"Only that I am concerned that you think you need it. Have you ever had to use it on the post?"

"Not yet, but I might," he said. Cordero inclined his head and raised one black brow.

"Do me a favor. Don't pull that knife out in my presence again."

"Sorry, I didn't mean to scare you."

"Why don't we play some pool?" April asked, deftly changing the subject.

"Nah, let's just sit and enjoy the music." He leaned back and closed his eyes.

She picked up her drink and began to create a pattern of wet circles on the glass top table while she studied him. What kind of a guy was she hanging around with? Not one that her brothers would approve, she was sure of that.

The music stopped and he opened his eyes and stood. "Sorry," he apologized. "I'm not good company tonight. I'd better take you back to your barracks."

They drove the short distance to the Clerical School in silence. He pulled the Chevy into the parking lot of the school complex. Instead of exiting the car, he pillowed his head on his arms around the wheel.

"Is your head bothering you?"

"Not really," he said, raising his head and straightening up. "I have something to tell you."

"I hope it's nothing to do with that knife."

"Nah." He laughed. "It's nothing like that. I quit the band."

"What ever for? You played so well, and I love the music you guys play. Why would you quit?"

"I just did." He shrugged. "Let it go at that."

He walked with her to the door, took her hands, and stood looking down at her for a long moment. "Good night, Chica," he said, and he walked back toward the car.

She turned and watched him drive out of the lot. The automobile moved forward and stopped before reaching the street. It made a sharp left and she stared after the vehicle until the red glow from the taillights vanished down the hill.

What was going on? Was he having a problem at work in his company? Why did he think he needed a knife?

It's not always easy to make the right choice,
When you don't want to accept the truth.

Chapter 12

Monday, 21 January 1957
Dear Dreamcatcher,
This was a *Blue Monday*, it rained all day and if it gets any colder it could snow. I wouldn't mind, as there was none in Kentucky at Christmas.

In class we learned to type Morning Reports. I can't say I like them, as they must be letter perfect. If a mistake is made the entire report must be retyped.

Our entire afternoon period was used for typing Deposition Form 96, not all that exciting...

Wednesday, 23 January 1957
Today's class work was fun. We practiced doing Company Rosters and Company Bulletins. We had to make up our own bulletins and some of the girls got real creative and typed hilarious compositions.

Because of the cold and rain, I didn't go to the service club tonight...

Thursday evening April and Cordero went to the movies to see one of her favorite actresses, Susan Hayward in *Demetrius and the Gladiators* with Victor Mature. It was just the two of them as Richard was on CQ Duty.

After the movie they got in Richard's car and drove over to Lee's Restaurant.

"What will you have?" he asked.

"Nothing for me. I'm not hungry."

"How about a soft drink?"

"All right."

After he placed their order through the speaker, he got out to fish his wallet from his back pocket.

"Here." He handed it across the seat to her. "Pay the waitress when she brings my food. I want to wash my hands."

Several minutes passed before a cute young carhop rolled up on skates and hung a tray on the window. April opened the leather billfold and paid the server. A card fell out on the seat as she placed the change in the wallet. She picked it up. It was Cordero's drivers' license, and she noticed his birthday was the second of May. The year was 1938. He was eighteen not twenty-four years of age like he had told her that he and Richard were the same age. He was a teenager. Actually, he seemed like the older of the two. She let out the breath she had been holding relieved that she had never treated him like anyone but a brother. Suppose she had let him kiss her. She would have felt like a *cradle robber*.

Later Cordero walked her to the Clerical School door. "I'm sorry the picture made you cry. I'll not take you to another sad picture. I never want to see you cry again."

"I liked the movie. It's good to cry once in awhile."

He shook his head, negatively. "I don't understand you."

She could have told him that makes two of us, because she didn't understand him either.

In her room while April was getting ready for bed, she discovered that one of her earrings was missing from the pair given her by Cordero.

> Friday, 25 January 1957
> Dear Dreamcatcher,
> Only one more month of school before I graduate. I'm enjoying the classes. I almost feel like I'm back in high school. I hope my new post will be nice and Mae and I get sent to the same place. A very slim chance of that. This is a beautiful post but I want to leave. My feelings are becoming confused now that I know Cordero's true age. Also, I find myself attracted to Montoya...

"We better get our purses and go down stairs, the guys will be here any minute."

"Just how did you persuade Cordero to go to the dance with the Spanish Band playing?" Mae held the mirrored latrine doors open allowing her to pass through without crushing the bouffant skirt of her blue dress.

"Easy. When he asked what I was doing tonight, I said you and I were going to the dance at the service club. He replied that he and Richard would pick us up."

"And he agreed just like that?"

"Well, he didn't look too happy, but he didn't give me an argument."

The final notes of "Blueberry Hill" faded away as they strolled into the ballroom. Before the foursome reached their table the band launched into their rendition of "Cherry Pink and Apple Blossom White." She glanced up at the platform.

Montoya's eyes met hers. He smiled and nodded his head as if to say, *this is for you.*

She smiled and inclined her head in a gesture of recognition.

Cordero must have caught the communication between them because after seating her, he said not to anyone in particular, "It's been a tough week. I don't want to dance. I'll be in the poolroom. Let me know when you are ready to leave." With that he stalked from the ballroom.

Mae stood to dance with Richard and shot her a knowing look with raised brows.

For the rest of the dance set, Richard alternated dancing with her and Mae.

"How about some soft drinks?" asked Richard as he pulled out Mae's chair.

"A *Coke*," Mae responded.

"Nothing for me, thanks," she said.

As soon as Richard was out of hearing range, Mae leaned forward to speak above the noise of the room. "Are you and Cordero having a spat?"

"You heard what he said. He wanted to play pool." She shrugged her shoulders. "I wanted to dance."

"If he's playing pool, he has an awfully long cue stick."

"What did you say about a cue stick?"

"I said," she raised her voice a notch. "Cordero would need a very long stick to play from where he's standing holding up the wall next to the French doors."

She steeled herself from turning her head to look across the dance floor to the doors. "He must have gotten tired of playing or he couldn't get a table."

"He's been standing there for the last three songs. I'm surprised you didn't see him. He hasn't taken his eyes off you."

Richard approached with three bottles of *Coke* and a grape *Nehi.*

"Richard, I didn't want anything," she reminded him.

"Force of habit." He laughed and set the drinks on the table.

With Richard sitting next to her, the view of the French doors was partially blocked. By tilting her head she was able to get a glimpse of Cordero. He was leaning against the wall just like Mae said. His arms were folded across his chest, as though he'd been lounging there a good long time. He was frowning intently in her direction.

Someone walked up beside Richard and her view of Cordero was totally obscured.

"Care if I join you?" asked Larsen, stopping beside their table.

"Okay by me," said Richard. "Have a *Coke*. We seem to have an extra one."

"Thanks. Don't mind if I do," said Larsen, taking the bottle from his hand and sliding into a vacant chair.

"Larsen, what state are you from," she asked.

"Texas, ma'am," he drawled.

"That explains it," she said.

"Explains what, ma'am?"

"The reason that I've never seen you at one of these dances with a date. Isn't it said that a cowboy never lets anything come between him and his horse except his saddle?" She bit her lower lip trying to keep a straight face, but when Mae started to giggle and Richard guffawed, she lost her cool and laughed along with them. Larsen hooted the loudest.

For the next hour April danced most of the numbers with Larsen except for a few dances she consented to guys that came to the table between numbers asking for the next dance. Several times she glanced up at the platform to catch Montoya watching her. She avoided looking in Cordero's direction altogether.

The band played her favorite song again for their last number. Richard settled a hand on her waist and drew her gently into his arms among the swirling drifts of couples below the bandstand.

"Do you like Montoya?"

"Richard!" she gasped at the unexpected question, nearly stepping on his toes. It would have served him right. "I don't really know him well enough to comment."

"Are you going to go out with him?" Another surprise.

"Do you think I should?' She threw back at him.

"No," he said quickly. "You didn't answer my question."

"I told you. I hardly know the guy. We've only spoken a few words, and besides, he hasn't asked me for a date."

"He will. I've seen the way his eyes followed you around the room tonight."

The music ended and they returned to the table.

Cordero was sitting in her chair sipping her grape drink. He pulled a sour face. "How can you drink this stuff? It tastes like sweetened water."

She ignored his comment, picked up her purse and followed Mae and Richard out to the parking lot.

Cordero was extremely quiet on the drive to the Clerical School.

Tuesday, 29 January 1957
Dear Dreamcatcher,
I got a telephone call in the evening after chow. I assumed it was Cordero. It was Del Valle calling to ask if I would fill in for him at the Equipment Counter tomorrow night. He said that he had an appointment and he would be late.

Also that I didn't have an appointment for the writing room...

Wednesday, 30 January 1957
This evening, I had fun working at the Equipment Counter. I wore my uniform with my nametag. I think a couple of GIs just came to flirt with me, as they never checked out any equipment. They asked me questions. Most wanted to know what company I was in and where was CQ. Some of them I recognized as my dance partners. One of them asked me for my phone number. I gave him my line that I was a student and I didn't have a telephone. When CQ reported to work he shooed them away from the counter. He was most appreciative of my help. I told him I enjoyed it and he could call on me anytime.

Before leaving the service club, I checked the music room for Montoya. It was empty...

Friday, 01 February 1957
A very upset Cordero phoned asking why I didn't let him know I replaced CQ at the club on Wednesday. He said he would have kept me company. Also, he tried to persuade me to let him come by for a few minutes because he had not seen

me all week. I told him it would be too late, and I gave him
a firm no and said good night...

Saturday afternoon she opened the laundry bag at the bottom of her bed
and dumped the soiled clothing on her footlocker, and she began separating
the whites from her colored blouses.

"Attention bay three." A voice blared over the loudspeaker. "Private
Terry has a visitor."

Mae looked up from where she was sitting cross-legged on the floor arranging
her shoes beneath her bunk.

"Isn't Cordero on company duty?"

"It must be Richard," she said as she started toward the bay door.

"Wait," called Mae. "You can't go down dressed like that. Here take my
WAC sweater."

She finished buttoning the knit garment that ended below her knees before
entering the lobby. It was empty and she walked over to look into the Day
Room. She turned to the CQ, "I'm Private Terry. You announced over the PA
that I had a visitor."

"He stepped out for a moment," said the private, motioning toward the
door.

She pushed open the glass doors and stuck her head outside. Richard
dressed in a red plaid shirt and gray slacks was crossing the walkway from the
direction of the parking lot.

"What are you doing here?" she asked.

He took her hand and pulled her through the door to the outside. "I thought
perhaps we could go to a movie or take a drive."

"I'm not supposed to be outside dressed like this," she said, indicating
Mae's long sweater that fit her like a dress.

"You look fine to me."

"If the Duty Officer comes by she might not think so."

"I want to talk to you. Let's sit in the car. If the DO comes, she can't see
what you are wearing." He walked ahead of her and opened the passenger
door. She got in; he closed the door, moved around to the driver's side and
slid behind the wheel.

"What did you want to talk about?" she asked adjusting the sweater over
her knees.

Resting his hands on the steering wheel, he stared straight ahead for
several long seconds, a forbidding hard line to his mouth instead of his usual
smiling face.

"I would like for you to explain what kind of relationship you have with Cordero. I have never seen him kiss you except on the hand or cheek."

"I explained that to you the other night. We are just good friends; I am not his *girlfriend*. As for him kissing me, I have never let any man kiss me."

"Is that so?" He sounded doubtful, and his eyebrows rose up a notch.

"It's true whether you believe me or not," she retorted.

"Tell me why is it you won't go out with me when you are considering dating Montoya? We've known each other much longer."

"I am very fond of you, Richard, but I think of you like a brother, the same as I do Cordero. I don't know why you keep bringing up Montoya's name. He has not asked me out and I doubt that he will. How about you answering some questions for a change?"

"Like what?"

"Like why did the two of you lie to me about Cordero's age?"

"How did you find out?"

"I saw his driver's license."

"I didn't lie to you, I just went along with him when he said he was the same age as myself."

"Actually, he seems older than you."

"He grew up in a tough neighborhood in New York where he ran with a street gang. Unfortunately, he got involved with marijuana and was arrested. Because of his youth he was given the choice of being locked up or volunteering for the Army."

"And what happened at Ft. Dix that he didn't want you to talk about?"

"I probably owe him my life. He took a knife meant for me, and he ended up in the hospital. As the result he has a large scar on his chest."

"Are you telling me that he saved your life, but here you are asking me to go out with you? Just what kind of a friend are you?"

"April, you as much as told me that you didn't consider yourself his girlfriend." He shrugged his shoulders. "I wanted you to go out with me. Are you going to tell him about our conversation?"

"No, I'm not, and I would appreciate if you didn't either. I care for him, and I don't want him hurt."

"I promise not to say anything to him."

"Just out of curiosity, what is the translation of his name in English?"

"Cordero means *lamb*, but don't ever call him that. It makes him fighting mad. He's been in more than one scrape over some guy teasing him about it."

"He was definitely misnamed."

"There is one other thing I should tell you. The night we were introduced I had bet him that he couldn't get you to play pool with us. But when he met you, he called the wager off, and he wouldn't take the money."

"Bet? You mean like betting on a race horse?"

"No, it wasn't like that. Please let me explain—"

"This is too much. I met him because of a wager? I better go before I lose my temper." She opened the door and got out of the car.

"Are we still friends?" he asked, as he walked with her to the door.

"Barely," she said. She started through the door he held for her, stopped and turned toward him. "By the way, I lost an earring the other night. It may be in your car."

"Sure. I'll look for it."

She walked slowly upstairs, her head filled with questions. Now she had two problems. But at least she knew why Richard never liked any of the girls she had introduced to him.

Friendship finds its own path, sets its own pace,
And travels in its own way.

Chapter 13

"Let's do something to celebrate getting our orders tomorrow," said Mae as she rinsed her toothbrush.

"Like what? The only places we can go are to the service club, movies or bowling. And neither of us bowl," she replied. April picked up her ditty bag from the shelf above the row of sinks and started toward the latrine door.

"We could go play pool. I haven't been out all week, I have barrack-itis," said Mae, following her out the door.

After April finished buttoning her black velvet weskit, she selected a pair of shoes, and she sat on her footlocker to slip on her black pumps. She stood and smoothed down her slim skirt.

"You look like you are in mourning instead of a celebration," observed Mae.

"Actually, I do feel sad. When we get our orders tomorrow, we may be assigned clear across the states from each other."

"We stayed together in basic training and this school. I still have hopes that we get assigned to the same post. We can always write to each other."

All the pool tables were in use when they arrived at the service club. Mae sat down to wait for a free table.

"I'm going to get a soft drink," she said and exited the room by the French doors. Instead of going to the soda fountain, April made a detour and went down the hall to the music room. It was empty. She returned to the bar, and bought a grape soda and sat down to listen to the jukebox. The Mills Brothers' "You Always Hurt the One You Love" was spinning on the turntable.

Suddenly Cordero slipped into the seat beside her. He held out his closed hand toward her.

"Chica, did you lose something?"

"You found my earring?" She asked, reaching out to take it.

"Rich found it in his car." He drew back his arm. "I've carried it with me all week. Would you mind if I kept it awhile longer?"

"Are you going to wear it?" She laughed. "Do you want the other one, too?" She opened her purse. Her dog tags fell out on the table as she fished around in her purse for the earring's mate.

"No," he said and he laughed. "I'm going to the field on Monday for two weeks and I want something of yours to keep with me while I'm gone."

"You are an *Indian giver*. Those are my favorite earrings."

"I promise not to lose it. I'll put it on my chain with my cross. I never take that off." He removed the heart from the ear clip and put it on the chain around his neck. He picked up her dog tags and put the matching earring on the beaded chain.

She took the last sip of her soda and scooted back her chair. "My friend Mae is here. We are going to play pool. Do you want to play with us?"

Later Cordero walked back with them to the Clerical School.

As they climbed the stairs to the third floor, she told Mae about the incident with her earring.

"I have the feeling that I'm never going to get it back. What a crazy thing for him to do."

"He's in love," said Mae.

"For Pete's sake, he's only eighteen."

"Age has nothing to do with love. Sooner or later he is going to tell you."

"I hope you are wrong," she said, slipping off her shoes and lining them up beneath her bunk.

Following morning chow, Specialist Faxon entered the bay and called attention.

"Students, I know you are all anxious to find out your post assignments." She held up a sheaf of papers. "As I call your name and assignment, please come forward and pick up a copy of your orders. Try to hold the noise down until I have given out all the copies. I'll try to answer any questions you may have about your new post. Pvt. Ames, assigned to Ft. Lee, Virginia, Pvt. Barnes, Ft. McPherson, Georgia, Pvt. Dela Cruz, Ft. Rucker…"

She hardly heard the squeals, sighs, and boos as the instructor went down the alphabet calling out the names of the privates and their new posts until she called, "Pvt. Honsberg, Arlington, Virginia."

Mae excitedly brought her orders to show her. "I can visit Washington DC from there."

"Pvt. Terry, Ft. McClellan, Alabama, Pvt. June Trell, Slocum, Georgia," continued Sp. Faxon.

She clasped the paper in her hand, not believing what she read. Special Orders Number 35 dated 04 February 1957. She scanned down to the circled number five in red, her name also underlined in red.

"Oh, no, Mae, we're going to be separated. I'm assigned to the Reception Company here as the Company Clerk."

"We'll write to each other and Virginia isn't that far away. You could visit and we'll go to DC."

"That would be nice. I've never been to the capitol," she said, absently.

"Neither have I."

"I just wish we were assigned to the same place," she said, sadly.

"Two out of three assignments aren't bad," said Mae. "You said that you liked this post and it is beautiful," she continued, "at least, you are familiar with Ft. McClellan. I don't know anything about the place where I am assigned. And you'll have some other classmates here with you. Pvt. Wells has been assigned as Mail Clerk to the same company with you, Newsome is going to Company A and Wilson and Girad to Headquarters Company. And what about the guys?"

"I was hoping to leave before they become problems."

"I think one of them already has," commented Mae.

Possibly both of them.

In the latrine the next evening, April finished combing her hair and picked up her makeup case.

"Do you want to walk to the service club with me? The Spanish Band is playing for the dance," said Mae, picking up her ditty bag from the shelf above the sink.

"I don't know if I'm going. Cordero never mentioned it last night." She capped her lip-gloss and dropped it into her cosmetic bag.

"After what you told me, I wouldn't want to be in your shoes," said Mae, shaking her head, negatively.

"What do you mean?"

"You have two guys crazy about you and you don't have any romantic notions toward either of them, that's what."

"I'll admit that in the beginning I was fascinated by Cordero's good looks and Spanish charm, but when I found out about his girlfriend and then his age..." She paused and took a deep breath. "I put on the brakes of my feelings so to speak. I was afraid to care about him that I would be hurt. And as for Richard, I made it clear to both of them that our relationship would only be that of friends. I'm sorry if they have made more out of our friendship than what it is."

"What you need is another diversion like that new piano player. I think he likes you. I noticed the other night, he played your favorite song the moment you walked into the club."

"That was just his way of an apology for being rude to me the first time I tried to talk to him."

"Is that so?" Mae arched her brows and closed her cosmetic case. "Are you coming with me to the service club?"

As soon as they walked into the ballroom, the next number the band played was "Cherry Pink."

Mae elbowed her and gave her a knowing smile, and she inclined her head toward the bandstand where Montoya was gazing down at her. He smiled and nodded his head.

It was impossible not to smile in return.

Before they found a table, a guy in uniform asked her to dance. Part way through the song she looked over the private's shoulder into the snapping black eyes of Cordero as he tapped the guy on the back.

"Hi," she said.

Instead of returning her greeting, he danced them right through the French doors to the patio.

"I went to pick you up and the CQ told me you were out," he said, angrily.

"It's nice to see you, too," she drawled in her best-honeyed southern accent. He looked so ridiculous scowling at her and her laughter bubbled up until she began to laugh.

Finally, he laughed, too.

"Fix my head with your magic fingers," he said, clasping both her hands, and placing them at his temples.

"Sit down so I don't have to reach," she said, dropping her hands to her side.

He sat at a table and she stood behind him and started a slow light massage. "I think the only reason you see me is to massage away your headaches. By the way, I got my orders this morning. I have to report to my new assignment on the 21st of February at—"

He got up so abruptly she had to jump back to avoid being hit by the chair as he shoved it back from the table.

"Chica, you can't leave. I'll be in the field."

"You never let me finish. I'm not leaving the post. My assignment is the Company Clerk at the Reception Center."

"A girl like you doesn't belong in the Army. You should go home."

"I am in the military for another year and a half. Besides, this is the only home I have."

"Why aren't you two inside dancing?" asked Richard, seating himself at their table.

"I was just telling Cordero about my orders. I have been assigned to this post. I thought he would be pleased but apparently he isn't."

"Well, I'm happy about it. Why don't you use my car to move to your new quarters? I was thinking about asking you to keep it while I'm in the field."

Standing behind Richard, Cordero shook his head negatively.

"Thanks for the offer but I don't want to be responsible for a new car."

Later when Richard drove Mae and her to their barracks, Cordero walked her to the door.

"I'll miss you," he said. "I want be able to see you for two whole weeks. Tomorrow, I have to get my gear ready for the field." Before getting out of the car, he took her hand, kissed her palm and closed her fingers over the warm spot.

> Saturday, 16 February 1957
> Dear Dreamcatcher,
> Tonight, it is raining and cold. I hope the guys are not getting wet. This storm reminds me of my basic training when it poured on us in the field…

> Sunday, 17 February 1957
> Today was our last Sunday for the *Three Months of Bay Three* to attend church together. Mae and June will be departing next Friday for their new assignments. It makes me want to cry to think about them leaving, especially, Mae. She is like the sister that I always wanted…

The Clerical School's graduation ceremony was held at the WAC Chapel. Afterwards, they marched to the parade ground for the conclusion of the activities. April's heart went into double-time and her arms broke out with goose bumps. Mere words could not described what she felt as her class came to attention and she lifted her hand proudly to salute the Stars and Stripes passing in review.

In the afternoon Mae and June each carried an arm full of clothes and draped them over the empty bus seats.

Some of the other girls pitched in to assisted Pvt. Wells with her baggage.

Mae and June remained on the bus and rode down to the WAC Training Battalion with her. When they reached the Reception Company, they helped carry her belongings inside.

While they aided Pvt. Wells, April went to report to the Orderly Room. She clutched a copy of her orders, walked down the corridor to the closed door, and rapped.

"Enter."

She opened the door, marched up to the desk, and sounded off, "Pvt. Terry reporting as directed." She placed a copy of her orders in front of the sergeant sitting at the desk.

"Oh, I remember you," said Sgt. Levy. "You took your basic training at Company B.

"I remember you, too," she replied. "It seems like only yesterday that I arrived and here I am back again."

"Your room is up on the second floor next to the kitchen. Where is your baggage?"

"In the Day Room."

"I'll get a couple of the recruits to help you with it." Sgt. Levy reached for the phone.

"That's not necessary, I have a couple of my friends with me, Mae Honsberg and June Trell."

"I remember them, too. I can't leave the Orderly Room so send them in to say hello before they go." She turned and took a key from the pegboard in back of her. "Here is the key to your room. For now you will have it all to yourself. At a later date you might have to share the room with someone. Did Pvt. Wells come down with you?"

"Yes, Mae and June are helping her with her luggage."

"Send her in. She'll have the room to the right of the kitchen on the third floor above you. Welcome to the Reception Company, Pvt. Terry," Levy said, dismissing her.

She met Pvt. Wells in the hallway. "Guess what? We have our own room. Mine is on the second floor and you're on the third."

"Cool," said Pvt. Wells. "I never expected a private room. Did you?"

"Huh-uh, but Sgt. Levy said we might have a roommate later on but not likely."

"I hope not. I like my privacy," said Wells.

"Sgt. Levy said for you to report to the Orderly Room."

She hurried down to the Day Room to share the good news with her friends.

On the second floor April unlocked the door and stepped back for Mae to enter with an armload of clothes, followed by June.

"Why are there two beds?" asked June.

"This room is for two people. Sgt. Levy said I might have to share the room in the future. But for now I am going to enjoy my own room. This is the first time in my life that I've had a room to myself." She clasped her arms across her chest and spun around gazing at the tall chest of drawers, the dressing table with a mirror, and the old familiar footlocker at the foot of each bed.

"Which bunk are you going to use?" asked Mae, looking at the cots separated by four metal wall lockers.

"The one next to the window, and I get to use all the lockers."

"You will have to go shopping to fill them," Mae said, putting the clothes across the bed nearest the window.

After they finished helping Pvt. Wells, April walked back down to the first floor with Mae and June. She said good-bye to them before they went to say hello to Sgt. Levy.

Hot dry sobs threatened to spoil her determination to remain smiling. She forced back her tears and raced upstairs to her room.

She slipped off her shoes and sat on her bunk wiping the moisture from her eyes. A sob erupted from her throat into the quiet of the room. She rolled over on her stomach, buried her face in her pillow as the tears began to flow unchecked.

Life is not what happens to you,
But how you react to it.

Chapter 14

Before going to eat the following morning, April walked up one flight of stairs to the third floor and knocked on Pvt. Wells' door.

The door cracked open exposing the girl's head.

"If you are going to chow you had better get a move on. We are expected in the Orderly Room at 0800 hours to report to the Commanding Officer."

"I never go to breakfast," said Pvt. Wells, running a hand through her unkempt hair.

"Okay. I'll see you later," she said, continuing on down the hallway toward the staircase.

After eating, she went directly to the Orderly Room. The door was locked.

"My, but aren't you the eager beaver to get started," said Sgt. Levy, arriving behind her. The sergeant unlocked the door and stepped back for her to enter. "That will be your desk in front of the window. It will be your job to make the lieutenant's coffee and take it to her each morning." She motioned to the coffee machine on a small stand in the corner of the room. "I hope you make good coffee."

"I don't drink coffee and I've never made a cup in my life," she confessed.

"Nothing to it. Just follow the instructions on the package and add a little extra. The lieutenant likes it strong and black. You'll find everything in the little cabinet behind the coffeepot. Use the filtered water from the cooler."

April dropped her hat and purse on her desk and went to the corner where an empty pot sat on the countertop above a small refrigerator. She opened the cabinet, picked up the package of *Maxwell House*, and began reading the instructions.

Pvt. Wells came in and greeted Sgt. Levy before dropping down on the vacant chair beside the sergeant's desk.

"Is it coffee yet?" A stout sergeant entered wearing fatigues.

"I'm sure you girls remember, Sgt. Waite, our supply sergeant."

"I sure do," she said.

Pvt. Wells nodded affirmatively.

"Would you taste this and tell me if it is okay?" She held out a steaming cup to Sgt. Waite.

At that moment another WAC walked through the open door.

"Let's give the first cup to Sp. Walters," she said, passing the cup to the dark haired specialist in dress uniform.

"Are you trying to use me for a guinea pig again, Sgt. Waite." The woman's eyes narrowed as she looked from the cup to the sergeant's grinning face. She lifted the cup and blew into the brew before taking a sip. "Now that's what I call a cup of coffee. I guess we'll keep you." She peered at the nametag on April's *Ike* jacket. "Pvt. Terry."

She let out the breath that she had been holding. "Anyone else who wants coffee, just help yourself."

"Attention," boomed Sgt. Levy. They all snapped to attention.

An officer entered followed by another lieutenant.

"As you were, ladies," said the tall officer. With a graceful stride she crossed the floor and entered the door at the end of the room.

Sgt. Levy made the introductions to Second Lieutenant Barron. The auburn haired officer bade them welcome and took her coffee and retired to the office opposite that of the Commanding Officer.

"Okay, Pvt. Terry, you better take the CO's coffee and report to her." Sgt. Levy motioned to the door with the name, Lt. Mary J. Theodoroff, Commanding Officer.

She poured coffee into a cup labeled CO and knocked at the door.

"Enter." The mature, feminine voice held an authoritative ring.

She walked to the desk and placed the cup down before snapping to attention and sounding off. "Pvt. Terry reporting for duty, Ma'am."

"At ease," the lieutenant said, returning her salute. She picked up the cup and sipped the black liquid. "Best coffee I've had in a week, now if you can type as well as you make coffee..." She smiled.

"I hope so, Ma'am. I've been typing for years. That's the first cup of coffee that I've ever made."

"Don't loose the recipe. Do you smoke? I can't tolerate cigarettes."

"No, Ma'am. I don't smoke."

"I think we'll get along just fine. Welcome to the company, Pvt. Terry." The commanding officer picked up a card from the desktop and handed it to her. "This is your Armed Forces Liberty Pass. Please send Pvt. Wells in," she said, by way of dismissal.

She snapped to attention with military precision—lifted her hand in a salute—about-faced and marched from the office.

"Pvt. Wells, the CO wants to see you." She stepped over to her desk, opened her purse, and slid the pass inside.

April sat down and typed up the Morning Report. It was a short report as there were only two names to add.

A tall sergeant entered with a box of pastries and set them on the countertop next to the coffee before pouring herself a cup.

"Did you meet Sgt. Owens when you passed through the center?" asked Sgt. Levy.

"No, I don't believe I did."

Sgt. Levy made the introductions.

"Bring your note pad, Pvt. Terry, and come to my office. I want to give you a list of the Company Clerk's duties. Did you make the coffee?" she asked as she closed her door.

In the late afternoon April covered the typewriter and straightened her desk. It had been an interesting day. She picked up the empty coffeepot and walked down the hall to the kitchen. When she returned with the clean pot, Sgt. Levy was on the telephone.

"Here she is now," she said. "You have a call on line one."

"Pvt. Terry speaking."

"Chica," said Cordero over the phone. "I just got back from the field."

"Cordero, how did you get this number?"

"I looked it up in the post phone book. I want to pick you up at 1900 hours. Can you be ready?"

"Sure. Did you know that this was my first day at my new job—"

"Tell me later, I've got to get cleaned up. I haven't had a decent shower in two weeks."

"Okay," she said and hung up the phone.

"Boyfriend?" said Sgt. Levy.

"No, just a good friend."

"He asked for Abril is that your middle name?"

"It's a nickname I picked up at Clerical School. Actually, it's April. He uses the Spanish pronunciation."

"Quitting time," said Sgt. Levy. "Let's close up shop."

In the car going up to the service club with Cordero and Richard, she told them about her private room and her job.

120

"I bet you were so busy that you never missed me at all," complained Cordero.

"I did miss you, and Richard, too." She caught Richard's gaze in the rearview mirror, and he winked at her.

Inside the ballroom, they had just found a table and sat down as the Spanish Band began their rendition of her favorite song.

She gazed up at Montoya on the bandstand; she was reassured by the brilliant smile that he winged her way, and she smiled back.

"You can dance with Richard—I'm too tired," said Cordero. He must have caught their exchanged gestures as he sent a smoldering glare in Montoya's direction.

Later while the band took a break, she went to the restroom. Carol Girad sat at the vanity powdering her nose.

"Hi," Carol said, catching April's reflection in the mirror. "How is your job?"

"So far, I love it, especially having my own room."

"How did you rate a private room? I share mine with two other girls at Headquarters Company."

"Actually mine is for two persons but I don't have a room mate. How do you like being the Company Clerk?"

"Okay except for the Morning Report. What a pain." Carol paused, wrinkling her nose. "Would you mind telling me which one of those two guys are you dating?"

"Neither. We just hang around together."

"I wish you'd send one of them my way."

"I'll see what I can do," she said, opening the stall door of the toilet.

She returned to the ballroom. Richard had brought drinks for them. She took a sip of her grape soda and grinned at him. "Thanks," she said, placing the bottle down on the table.

He smiled back at her, stood and pulled her up into his arms for the next dance number "At The Hop."

"Do you remember Carol Girad from the WAC Clerical School?"

"Is she one of those fat, ugly girls you keep trying to palm off on me?" He twirled her out and back into his arms.

"No, she's a cute blonde with dimples." She laughed.

Richard let out a burst of laughter.

"I like your face when you laugh," she said.

"I am glad you do. It's the only one I have." He flipped his sandy brows

121

up and down above twinkling blue eyes. "I thought I had died and gone to heaven the first time I heard a Kentucky girl speak to me."

"You really like to tease me, don't you?"

"If I do, it's because teasing is a way of showing affection for a person," he said without any teasing glint in his eyes.

"Too bad you don't make him laugh as easily as you do me." He jerked his head toward their table where Cordero sat.

"What's wrong with you two? He was in a good mood until we got here."

"I don't know. Maybe he misses being a member of the band."

"Or maybe it's a member of the band that makes him so sour."

"About Carol," she said, changing the subject. "She is here tonight. I think she likes you."

"She likes my car." He spun her around with dizzy, graceful precision.

"Why don't you ask her to dance?"

"Can't. I have to dance with you. Cordero told me not to let you dance with any other guy."

"Oh, now I have two big brothers instead of one watching over me?"

"I think you have the wrong idea about that."

The music ended and they returned to the table without her asking him what he meant by his unusual statement.

Cordero was absent-mindedly playing with the chain that encircled his neck that held her silver heart. She was on the verge of asking him to return it when he brought it to his lips before dropping it back inside the neck of his shirt.

Later, Cordero said good night, kissed the palm of her hand, and closed her fingers over the warm spot.

Cordero checked his watch for the second time as he stood outside the phone booth. It was 1625 hours. In another five minutes Abril would leave her office. What was taking this guy so long? The phone booth door opened.

"Okay, Rodrigues, it's all yours," said Cpl. Gomez, exiting the booth.

He entered and dropped a nickel in the slot and dialed her number.

"Good afternoon, Reception Company, Pvt. Terry speaking." Her sweet voice came over the wire.

"Chica, it's me," said Cordero.

"Hi," she said.

"There is something I want to show you. I'll pick you up at 1900 hours."

"What is it?"

"It's hard to describe. You have to see it."

"Aren't you going to at least give me a clue?"

"Nah, see you," he said. He hung up before Abril asked more questions.

Tonight he planned to be alone with her. Away from Richard and everyone at the service club. He had found the perfect spot while in the field this past week. Richard had prevented him taking her there last night by tagging along.

He wanted to hold her in his arms and immerse himself in her sweetness that had called out to him from the first time they met. He longed to taste her lips, to explore her luscious mouth with his tongue, open his heart, and declare his love.

Following the evening chow, April showered and dressed in a mulberry colored pinwale corduroy skirt with a matching short jacket over a long sleeved pink shirtwaist.

Instead of staying in her room, she went down to the Day Room to wait for the guys.

Cordero came swinging through the front entrance with spirit in his step and a smile on his handsome face.

"Aren't you in a good mood tonight," she said by way of a greeting.

"Hi," he said, and he kissed her cheek.

"Have a nice evening," said the friendly CQ as they went out the entrance.

"Thanks," she said over her shoulder.

"Where is Richard?" she asked as they approached the empty Chevy.

"He's already seen what I want to show you," he said, helping her into the front seat. "He stayed at the Beer Hall. We'll pick him up on our way to the dance." He closed the door and leaned in the window. He tried to kiss her on the mouth, but she turned her face and he kissed her ear.

"You've been drinking," she accused.

"Just a couple of beers," he said. He shrugged his shoulders and slid behind the wheel.

It was no secret he often frequented the Beer Hall with his buddies, but this was the first time he had picked her up smelling of alcohol.

He backed the Bel Air out of the lot, drove down Sixth Avenue, and turned left onto Tenth Street. They continued past the NCO Club, the 30th Chemical Company, and the Chemical School. She had never been beyond the school. Sky-high pine trees lined the sides of the pavement blocking out the moonlight. The car's headlights knifed through the blackness along a curving road winding up a steep hill.

At the top, he stopped in the middle of the road and turned to her.

"Close your eyes and don't open them until I tell you."

"It's so dark, I can't see anything with them open," she pointed out.

"Just do as I asked," he countered.

Even with her eyes closed she sensed when they left the pavement and drove onto a graveled road.

A few minutes later he brought the car to a halt and cut the engine.

He turned to her, but he remained silent. Was he just staring at her? What was wrong with him? Then he moved closer—a strong wave of alcohol and his cologne confirmed that. Her heart began to race. It was thrilling yet…very frightening.

"Chica, open your eyes."

The first thing she saw was a bright full moon shining through the pines standing sentinel a few feet back from the edge of the graveled lot. Cordero had parked the car in a clearing, elevated looking down on a lake. The breathtaking view was one of tranquility. The water shimmered and sparkled like cut glass beneath the moon's silvery light.

"It's beautiful. It's so beautiful," she repeated the words catching in her throat. "I've never seen moonlight on water before. It's like a giant mirror reflecting the heavens."

"Reilly Lake," said Cordero. "The other side is even prettier. It doesn't have all these trees blocking the view. Our company camped over there on bivouac last week. I would like to drive around and show it to you, but it's off-limits in the field training area."

He got out and came around to help her from the car. Cordero held her hand until they reached the edge of the water. He released it to bend down and scoop up a handful of rocks. First, he picked out a white flat stone, and then threw it at the lake. It skimmed across the surface of the water, and then sank. He pitched another stone into the water. It performed no better than the first. It too, fell short near the shore with a single loud plop.

"I use to be better at this," said Cordero, a half smile curving one corner of his mouth. Selecting another missile from his left hand, he hurled the rock into the lake. It too, fell short near the shore. "I must be out of practice," he said, shaking his head. He opened his hand, the remaining pebbles slipped from his fingers to the ground. He leaned down and hunted out a smooth, round stone. He flicked his wrist and sent it jumping and careening across the lake. Seemingly satisfied with the number of skips it achieved, he turned to her, a thoughtful expression on his face.

"That looks difficult," she commented.

"It is," he agreed tautly. Stooping down to pick up several more rocks, he hurled one sidearm across the lake. It skipped three times creating ripples in the dark blue water before disappearing below the surface. His strong arm shot out again, another stone clipped the water several times sending out more rippling waves. His rhythm of pitching never faltered until he had thrown all the pebbles. Cordero dropped to his heels and picked up another stone, turned it over, then discarded it, selecting a flatter one. This time he didn't try to skip the rock, but he shied it hard and high into the air. It soared heavenward, a few moments later it fell in the middle of the deep part of the lake sending waves all around until they reached the edge where she and Cordero stood. Small ripples played on the surface of the water then vanished.

"That was spectacular," she said, laughing and clapping her hands noisily. "You really are good."

"I'm glad you think so." A faint smile touched his mouth when he looked at her. "Would you like to try?" he asked, scooping up several stones and holding one out to her.

"No, thanks," she said, shaking her head.

Cordero let the pebbles fall from his hand and swiped his palm across his pant leg. Then he gave her a little half salute before moving away from the edge of the water.

She walked ahead of him, paused next to a tall pine, leaned against the trunk and looked out over the lake.

Cordero strode up in front of her. He braced one hand above her shoulder; the other hung loosely by his side.

Waves of curiosity emanated from her like ripples set off by a rock dropped into deep water. Confused, she lifted her eyes to stare into his face.

His pose was casual, but his nearness embraced her, surrounded her, until her breathing became forced. Her heart thrummed in a drum roll as she shifted uneasily against the tree. Her eyes scanned the lake over his shoulder. The water was smooth and tranquil; nothing like her accelerated heartbeat throbbing painfully at her temple.

Finally, her eyes settled on his. He clearly sensed her nervousness. He stepped closer letting his gaze rove over her features as he planted his other hand flat against the tree near her shoulder. His warm breath against her cheek smelled of alcohol and tobacco. Even without making physical contact, the position of his body crowded her against the rough tree.

He leaned closer until they were eye-to-eye then her surprise leapt to fear. She widened her eyes slightly, and she couldn't seem to stop her lower lip from quivering. She caught it between her teeth.

His mouth mashed against her lips, and she stiffened, her lips compressed, rejecting him. She trembled, her rigidly unyielding mouth shuttering beneath his. Stubbornly, she kept her lips sealed against Cordero's probing tongue. One of his hands came away from her head and grasped her just under her chin. His fingers squeezed until she opened her mouth to protest.

Silently, she screamed with fury as his tongue thrust its way in her mouth. Her brothers had warned her about letting a man French kiss her. It was the first step at getting her into his bed.

He kissed her wildly, passionately until she thought she would suffocate from lack of breath. When Cordero finally drew back, she swayed weakly against him, her breath came in short, openmouthed pants and her stomach knotted. He caught her arm steadying her. She took a deep breath and fought to calm the frantic cadence of her heart. Tears leaked from beneath her lashes as she jerked away and stared, stunned and disbelieving, into the licorice-black eyes of her best friend.

"How could you?" she gasped wiping her hand across her mouth, as though she could erase what had happened.

"I love you, Chica. I want to marry you and take you to New York with me."

"No," she said. "Don't say that. We're just friends. That's all."

What caused you to react will surely pass,
But how you continue can only be passed by you.

Chapter 15

"Forgive me. I'm sorry." Cordero moved within an arm's length away holding out his right hand, palm up. "Haven't you ever been kissed?" he asked, a rough edge in his voice. He caught her hand in his. In the wrist he held, her pulse jumped, but otherwise she stood unmoving and faced him with defiance and a proud tilt of her chin.

"No," she whispered, shaking her head, a deep flush crept from her neck to cover her cheeks.

"Chica, I'm sorry," he said in a rush. He let go of her hand and abruptly stepped back, his hands falling loosely at his sides. "I don't know what came over me." Two huge pools of topaz shimmered up at him beneath her golden lashes. Her gaze conveyed disbelief, hurt, and worst of all betrayal as she swiped at the tears streaking her cheeks.

"You should be sorry, friends don't act like that."

"All I did was kiss you."

"What happened just now was a mistake," she said, continuing to wipe at the wetness on her face.

"If there was any mistake, it was only that I figured you were more experienced."

She looked so beautiful standing there her face flushed with indignation. Her pulse beat in the high hollow of her throat, the stain of embarrassment coloring her cheeks as her hands fluttered in an empty gesture. Still she maintained her silence.

"Say something," he demanded, alarmed. "Damn it. Talk to me!"

"Don't you know what you have done?" She stared up at him with anger and pain mingled in her gaze. "We were supposed to be friends."

"We're still friends." He raised his voice a notch.

"Friends share a mutual understanding and they want what's best for each other. It isn't that way anymore. You want more than I'm willing to give."

"That's not so—I only want what's best for you. I always have."

"Richard was right. We can't be friends. You've proved me wrong. I can't trust you." Her voice escalated to a high pitch.

"I don't know what Richard has to do with us. Things change, just like people change. You're not the same girl I met a few months ago. I've always loved you. That hasn't changed."

"Oh, but *you* have changed. Your behavior has become rude. I can't talk to you anymore without you becoming angry for no reason at all." Her breathing was soft and rapid, betraying her uncertainty.

"You damn right." He clinched his teeth. "I can't be near you. And it's your fault."

"My fault? What's my fault?" she repeated.

"Someone should have explained to you about a man's body being sensitive."

"I don't know what you mean."

He crowded her against the tree and trapped her with one hand planted squarely on either side of her head in the depths of her hair. He pressed his weight against her soft, sweet curves, and she trembled along the length of his frame.

April's breast heaved against his chest. He held her against the abrasive bark with the rock like hardness of his aroused body. No man had ever drawn her against his body when he was aroused. Some of her earlier uneasiness returned.

"That's why I can't be near you without being angry at not being able to touch you." His voice carried a plea for understanding.

Her palms came up to press against his chest, as her mouth formed a shocked, "No!"

He dropped his arms and walked swiftly away. Leaning one hand against the nearest pine, he bowed his head. He pressed the tips of his fingers across his forehead before pushing away from the tree and stalking back to where she stood, stunned into total stillness.

"I think I'm losing my mind," he said, huskily. "Do you know what I'd like to do?"

Unable to speak, she shook her head, her pulse racing with the thrumming of her heart crowding into her throat.

"I want to strip off your clothes and taste and love every inch of you from the top of your head down to the tips of your toes and make you mine." His black eyes bored into hers. "I want to kiss you so deeply my passion will awake yours. To put my lips on your breast and lay you down and sink my body into yours—"

"Stop it," she hissed, covering her ears. "Stop it, Cordero—please! I don't want to hear anymore. You must be drunk or just plain crazy to say those things to me."

"I've only had a few beers. I'm not drunk, and if I'm crazy—you're the cause."

"That's not true. I've never given you any reason to speak to me in such a crude, vulgar manner."

"Is that what you call it? I call it love. Why do you think I let Richard dance so much with you lately? I can't even hold you without wanting to make love to you. When I'm near you, I can't think about anything but how delicious your mouth would taste or how much I want to bury myself in your sweet, soft body, so deep we won't know where I end and you begin." Cordero paused. "Are you willing to let me make love to you?" he asked, huskily.

"You've made a mistake if you think I'm that kind," she replied. The heat rose in her face. "I'm not like that," she said, shaking her head. "You have the wrong girl."

"You're the only girl I want. I promise I won't do anything you don't want me to. All you have to do is tell me to stop."

"No." She pushed hard against his chest, struggling frantically, the adrenaline pumping through her veins. She managed to slip under his arms and backed away from him. "Is this why you brought me here?" she accused.

"Nah," he denied. "I didn't ask you to come here with any thought in mind except to show you the lake by moonlight. You looked so sweet and irresistible I couldn't control my true feelings. I only meant to kiss you, but..." He shrugged his shoulders. "But once I kissed you, I couldn't help myself. I wanted you as a man wants the woman he loves. It's the most natural thing in the world to share the pleasures we can give each other with our bodies."

April held up her hand. "Don't say another word. Just take me back to my barracks," she said, a quaver in her voice. She hated that she sounded so weak, but she couldn't control her emotions as tears brimmed in her eyes.

"Don't cry, Chica. I never meant—" He cursed under his breath and muttered, "I swear I won't touch you."

She stumbled blindly back to the car and climbed inside, where she sat huddled against the passenger door.

Cordero flung himself behind the wheel breathing hard; his eyes roamed over her tear-wet face.

"You're right," he rasped. "I better take you back to your company before I do something we both will regret." Resting an arm over the steering wheel, he slanted a long look at her before speaking. "You're a virgin?" The dim interior of the car nearly hid the eyebrow he lifted in her direction but it couldn't disguise the cocky tone of his voice.

"I wasn't aware it was a crime to be a virgin," she said, with as much dignity as she could muster.

"I didn't mean it that way. I'm just surprised that a pretty girl your age could still be—"

"Where I come from," she cut him off, "being a virgin is a virtue, and not a disease the way you make it sound. It's considered a gift to be given to the man she marries and not to be shared with any other than her husband. Further-more, I don't think this is a proper subject, for two people of the opposite sex to discuss," she said, embarrassment flooding her cheeks with heat.

"You're right again—forget I mentioned it."

"Take me to my barracks or I'll walk."

Instead of starting the car, he cradled the steering wheel with both arms, clasping a wrist behind it. His nostrils flared, as he started straight over the dash into the dark. He lowered his forehead onto the wheel. Finally, he gazed over his shoulder at her.

She quickly looked away to avoid eye contact, suddenly more afraid than ever.

"Is it because I'm Spanish?"

"What?" she asked, turning to face him.

"I want to know if it's because I'm Spanish that you rejected my amorous affections."

"No," she said, without hesitation. "Your being Spanish has nothing to do with it. I told you—I'm not that kind of girl."

"In spite of what you think, my intentions are honorable. I asked you to marry me."

"And I gave you the reasons for my refusal. You've ruined something very precious. I'll never trust another man as long as I live." She paused. "Please, could we leave now?"

He started the engine without taking his eyes off her. Throwing the car in gear, he jammed his foot on the accelerator. The wheels squealed, spun in the dirt and gravel as the vehicle lurched forward.

Inside the car, the air fairly crackled as he drove at high speed, steering with one hand. The '57 Chevy careened down the curving, winding road, the pines blurred past the windows.

Several times she braced her hands on the dash breaking her forward pitch, not wanting to risk sailing through the windshield. She angled a glance, noted his white-knuckled grip on the steering wheel.

"Would you please slow down?" She reached over and touched his sleeve. "You're frightening me. I would very much like to reach my barracks in one piece."

"Sorry," he said, letting his foot up on the accelerator, bringing the car down to an acceptable speed. "I didn't mean to scare you. I never meant to harm you."

April felt the tears filling her eyes and the sting in her nose, and she turned to stare out the window. She blinked twice, gritting her teeth to stop the wobble in her chin. She swallowed hard, but the lump in her throat didn't get any smaller. With verbal combat forsaken, the remainder of the ride was short, no more than fifteen minutes that seemed uncomfortably long to her.

Cordero pulled into the Reception Company parking lot handling the car with a smooth expertise. He switched off the lights before cutting the engine and turned to face her.

"I'm sorry if my love offends you. Right or wrong, everything I said tonight was the truth."

She couldn't reply. April looked away from his smoldering, black eyes, knowing she would burst into tears if she tried to speak.

"Can I see you again?"

"I—I don't know," she stammered, placing her hand on the door handle.

"Stay put," he admonished, opening his door.

Ignoring him, she shoved the door open and jumped out. She stumbled forward, caught her balance and sprinted down the walkway. A car door slammed.

"Abril, wait! I want to talk to you."

Still she did not pause or look back, not even when she heard the thudding of footfalls over the pounding of the blood in her veins. Again she ignored him, increasing her pace running toward the building as fast as she could in her heels. Gasping for breath, she bolted through the entrance a few steps ahead of Cordero. She dashed past the startled private behind the CQ desk, rounded the corner into the corridor and ran up the steps. With trembling hands she fished the key out of her purse and unlocked the door. Tears were burning her nose and throat. She wanted to scream at her own stupidity for disregarding the little things that led up to her being in tonight's situation. In short, she wanted to erase the entire evening from her mind. She flung herself on her bunk and wept.

A few moments later, someone knocked on her door. She sat up and groped for the lamp switch.

"Yes?" she called. "Who is it?" She got up and went to the door but didn't open it.

"Pvt. Boyd. I'm the runner. PFC Rodrigues wants to see you."

"Please tell him that I've retired for the evening."

"Okay, Pvt. Terry, I'll tell him."

April removed her shoes and clothes and laid back down in her slip.

Minutes later, she was disturbed by another rap on the door. She dried her tears and cracked the door.

"I'm sorry to bother you again," said Pvt. Boyd. "PFC Rodrigues is still at the CQ desk, and he refuses to leave until he sees you."

"Have the CQ tell him if he doesn't vacate the building, she will call the MPs."

"Can she do that?" Pvt. Boyd's eyes widened.

"No, but she can call the Duty NCO, and she will call them if he doesn't leave."

Later, she put on her robe and went to the latrine to brush her teeth and wash her face. She returned to her room to find four messages under her door. Three were from Cordero, asking her to call him. The forth was from Richard. "Urgent that I speak to you. Please call me at 2016." She crumbled up the pink slips and threw them in her waste can. For the first time since joining the Army, she cried herself to sleep.

The following morning she skipped chow. Her stomach was too tied up in knots to eat. She showered and dressed in her blue suit and walked up to the chapel. Later as she walked back to her barracks, she tried to recall what the service was about. She brought several passages of scripture to mind but she was sure none of them was what the pastor used for reference in his sermon. She entered the building and started past the CQ counter to the corridor.

"Pvt. Terry." A private in a stripped exercise suit stepped out from the back entrance to the CQ quarters "I have several messages for you." The CQ gave her a bunch of pink slips.

Without looking at them she shuffled the papers in a neat stack, tore them in half and handed them back to the startled CQ.

"Please put these in your trash can. I am not accepting any calls from PFC Rodrigues." April inclined her head to read the private's nametag. "Thank you, Pvt. Lowell." She continued up to her room.

In her room, she exchanged her suit for a simple black skirt and long sleeved print blouse before going to lunch.

Four more messages awaited her at the CQ desk when she returned from chow. She gave them the same treatment as the previous slips before returning to her room. There she curled on her bunk trying to clear all the thoughts of Cordero and the night before from her mind.

Sunday, 24 February 1957
Dear Dreamcatcher,
I couldn't write last night. I would like to erase the evening from my memory like it never happened. It hurts me deeply that he had such a low opinion of me after all the time we spent together. I don't think I can ever trust another man...

Tuesday, 26 February 1957
I cried myself to sleep again last night. I know this sounds like a broken record or the words to a sad song, but I can't seem to help myself.
In the afternoon, I told Sgt. Levy about what happened at the lake. She thinks I should talk to Cordero. Just thinking about how he betrayed my friendship causes me to weep. He called twice while I was at chow tonight...

Wednesday, 27 February 1957.
I wish I could write that I went to sleep without crying last night. I even tried going to bed early. Nothing works. To make matters worse I forgot to tell the CQ that I wasn't taking any phone calls and Pvt. Mitchell, the runner came to inform me that I had a call. I sent her back with instructions to take a message that I wasn't accepting any phone calls.
Later, I went to the latrine and returned to find a stack of messages under my door that the runner brought up when she made bed check with the Duty NCO. You would think that after awhile Cordero would take the hint and leave me alone...

On Thursday morning as soon as April entered the Orderly Room, Sgt. Levy waved a pink slip at her.

"I spoke to PFC Rodrigues after you left the office yesterday. He gave me a message for you.

I promised him I would read it to you because I know you trash them without reading a single one."

"I know you mean well, Sgt. Levy, but I don't care to hear it."

"A promise is a promise and I keep my promises." She perched her reading glasses that were attached to a black cord around her neck on her nose. She read, "I wake up each morning thinking about you, and you are the last thing on my mind when I close my eyes at night to sleep. If you have any feeling for me at all, please call me and say you forgive me." Sgt. Levy looked at her over the top of her glasses and rolled her eyes. "Jeez, he's very romantic. I wish someone cared for me like that."

"Excuse me, I'm going to chow," she said. April hurried from the office before she cried in front of Sgt. Levy. Instead of going to the mess hall, she went up to her room. She slipped off her skirt, draped it over the chair, lay down on her bed, and wept. A half-hour passed before she went to the latrine and splashed her face with cold water. She returned to the Orderly Room and found it empty. A note on her desk informed her that Sgt. Levy had gone to escort a group of recruits to the supply depot.

Her Inbox held the pink message slip from Cordero. She picked it up, and after ceremoniously tearing it into several strips; she deposited it in the waste container.

She sat at her desk and typed the Reception Company Morning Report. She had to retype it twice before it was acceptable for the lieutenant's signature. She fared no better with the dental appointment slips but at least she could correct her mistakes where as with the Morning Report it was not permissible to make corrections.

Sgt. Levy returned at 1600 hours. Before taking her seat, she placed a stack of clothing allotment forms in April's Inbox.

"I see the message from your PFC Rodrigues is gone," she observed.

"He's not *my* PFC Rodrigues," she said adamantly. "I put it in *file thirteen*, with all his other messages."

"I apologize for interfering in your personal life. I felt sorry for the guy. If you really don't want to be bothered by him, you can type up a directive with a permanent standing order to the effect that you will not accept his phone calls or see him in person and attach it to the CQ message book."

She fed a blank sheet into her typewriter. "What do I write?"

"I'll type it for you," offered Sgt. Levy, as she inserted a page into the machine on her desk. Her fingers flew over the keys. A minute later she yanked the paper from the typewriter and cut off a portion. She handed it to April. "Be sure to sign it before you clip it to the call book at the CQ desk."

She read the less than three-inch strip of paper. Pvt. Terry as of this date, 28 February 1957, will not accept any visits or telephone calls from PFC Cordero Rodrigues. A line followed the text with her name typed beneath it.

"Thanks." She picked up her pen and signed the slip.

By 1620 hours, she had filed the copies of the clothing allotment forms in each individual recruit's file folder.

"That's the last of the form 151s," she said, closing the large metal file cabinet.

"You've been here all day by yourself." Sgt. Levy looked up from her desk, pulled off her reading glasses, letting them dangle by the cord around her neck. "Why don't you close up shop. I can man the phones until the CQ comes on duty."

"Sure you don't mind?" She looked up at the big wooden clock above the door, the minute hand crawling down on 1621 hours.

"Go ahead," said Sgt. Levy, glancing up at the clock. "I have to be here anyway. I'm the Duty NCO tonight."

"Thanks," she said, straightening her desktop before grabbing her garrison cap and signed slip. She scooted out the door, with "I'll see you in the morning," tossed over her shoulder.

In the vestibule, she stopped at the CQ counter, went around behind the desk and picked up the call book from underneath. She placed the strip of paper beneath the large black spring clip holding the CQ and Runner directives. Before replacing the book back under the counter she smoothed her hand across it, her fingertips touching the narrow strip of paper.

"That's that," she said softly.

That evening after chow, the runner knocked at her door and informed her of a phone call from Richard Sheets. Perhaps she should have added his name to the order, too.

Down in the Orderly Room, she switched the call to line two at her desk before answering the phone.

"Hi," said Richard's familiar voice. "I wasn't sure if you would take my call. You never returned any of my messages."

"I am not in the habit of calling guys on the phone unless it's for company business."

"I was at the service club tonight, and CQ asked about you. He wondered what happened that you never came to help some guy with a letter."

"I forgot—I've had a lot on my mind lately."

"The reason I called is Cordero. He's been spending all his money on booze and getting into brawls. I'm not lending him anymore and neither are the rest of the guys. I wish you'd make up with him before payday on Friday or he will continue drinking and getting into trouble."

"I'm sorry. That's none of my concern."

"Aren't you his friend? You really should talk to—"

"Not anymore," she interrupted, her voice thick and quivery.

"Is it because of the lie he told? I want you to know that I never believed him for one moment."

"What lie? What are you talking about?"

"Look, he was totally drunk when he said it and the next morning he swore he didn't remember saying it and that it never happen," he said, in a rush.

"What didn't happen? Richard, you're not making any sense."

"Cordero never mentioned your name. I swear it."

"Would you please tell me what my name has to do with a lie Cordero told?"

"I shouldn't have said anything. I thought you knew and that was why you refused to take any of his phone calls. I feel responsible because I loaned him my car to take you to the lake. When he came to pick me up at the Beer Hall, I expected to see you in the Chevy. I made the mistake of kidding him and asking if he had gotten his face slapped." He paused and her silence must have encouraged him to continue.

"One of the guys at the Beer Hall had a bottle of whiskey. Cordero and him got drunk in the parking lot. I was taking him to our barracks when he stumbled into some guy and started a fight with him and his friend. It was two against him. I tried to break up the fight, and I got punched in the mouth. After Cordero passed out in the car, I had to get Larsen to help me put him in his bunk. That's when he came to and started laughing and saying how *lucky* he was that he got *laid* at the lake."

"Oh, my God." she gasped.

"I tried to shut him up because I knew he had taken you there. He got pretty loud and boisterous. Several of the Spanish guys in the barracks were laughing and encouraging him. I didn't know what they were saying until a guy asked in English, *How was she*? He said something to the effect—that she was a virgin—she didn't even know how to kiss or anything but he had been a willing teacher."

She almost dropped the phone.

"If he hadn't been drunk, I would have beaten him to a pulp. He kept on rambling in Spanish to his audience until he passed out. The next morning when I asked him about what he told the guys, he swore that nothing happened. He said all he did was kiss you and when you cried that he took you back to your barracks. Is that true? Was that all that happened?"

"Yes, he kissed me, but I didn't cry because of that. It was because he had such a low opinion of me. He treated me like I was a girl with loose morals. He said crude, ugly things; telling me in graphic detail how he wanted to make love to me. No man had ever spoken that way to me. I'm so deeply hurt to think that he lied about me. All this time, I thought we were special friends—that I meant something to him."

"You do. He loves you."

"How could he and say what he did about me? Now I'll be afraid to leave my barracks for fear of seeing one of those guys that heard his awful lies about me."

"This whole thing has gotten to him. He really feels bad about the lies he told. Every night he's had me drive him to your company hoping you would talk to him. Tonight your CQ told him that she had a signed directive that says you won't see him or take any of his calls. Is that true? Did you do that?"

"Yes, I did. And now that he has shamed and humiliated me with his monstrous lies, I never want to speak to him again. You can tell him that for me." Her voice broke on a sob.

"Why don't I come by? We could just sit in the parking lot. I'll let you cry on my shoulder," he offered.

"No thanks. I wouldn't be good company. Besides, with the kind of reputation I have now, you don't want to be seen with me." She tried to laugh, to keep the banter light, but it sounded more like a sobbing. Embarrassment buzzed in her ears.

"April, I know that you are a sweet, decent girl."

"And what about the other guys in your barracks? What kind of opinion do they have of me?"

"I told you he didn't mention your name."

"Richard, he didn't have to. They've all seen Cordero and me together many times. Why didn't he just put it in the company bulletin, or better yet, hang a sign around my neck with *whore* printed on it? Do you know what all those guys will think every time they see me? There goes the whore that is sleeping with Cordero. No doubt they will wonder if they can sleep with me, too."

"April, don't say things like that about yourself. Are you sure I can't come by just to talk?"

"I'm going to take a shower and go to bed."

"At this time? It's too early."

"This week has been the loneliest time of my life. I've been so miserable, and I haven't slept well lately. I've cried myself to sleep every night since I went to the lake. I loved him and he has hurt me so…" She paused to wipe her tears. "Richard, do me a favor, when you see CQ tell him I won't be coming back to the service club to help the guys with their letters. I'm sure by now he must have heard what happened."

"If he did, CQ didn't mention it when he asked about you. I'll give him your message when I go to the club. It won't be the same there without you. I really would like to see you tonight."

"Not this evening, Richard. I was in the Orderly Room by myself the entire day. I'm really exhausted."

"Would you mind if I call you again?"

"Okay, as long as you don't mention your friend's name. And thanks for telling me about the lies he told."

"Don't thank me, April. I shouldn't have told you. I'll call you soon. Sleep well."

She sat staring at the phone long after she had said good night. It didn't matter what Cordero called it. He had tried to seduce her. When that didn't work he told her that he loved her and proposed. Cordero couldn't love her, could he?

Memories can be cruel.
We don't choose what we remember,
And what we forget.

Chapter 16

"How did everything go yesterday?" asked Sgt. Levy, peering over the tops of her reading glasses.

"Everything went smoothly," April, responded. She uncovered her typewriter and inserted a blank Morning Report into the carriage.

"I was referring to the problem with PFC Rodrigues."

"You wouldn't believe what happened." She exhaled and took a deep breath. "Last night, I got the shock of my life. His friend Richard called and told me that after Cordero brought me back here, PFC Rodrigues got drunk and bragged to practically his whole platoon that I slept with him. Not the exact words he used, but you know what I mean." She made a useless gesture with her hand. "I've never been so humiliated in my entire life. He's ruined my reputation."

"Jeez, I'm sorry to hear that, but if he was drunk, he can't be held responsible for what he said under the influence of the alcohol." Sgt. Levy pushed her chair back and stood.

"In a pig's eye. I don't believe that for a moment."

"Is he still calling you?"

"There were no messages under my door this morning. Thanks to you, the directive got results."

"I'm sorry I have to leave you again today." Sgt. Levy picked up her garrison cap and set it at an angle across her black curls. "I have to take the second platoon for inoculations."

"Better them than me." She shuddered.

April picked up the small desk calendar from her desktop and ripped off the page. She was glad to see the day end. It had been one tough week with

Sgt. Levy away from the office most every day. Except to go to the mess hall, she hadn't budged from the Reception Company.

She grabbed a copy of the *McClellan News* and stuck it under her arm before locking the office door. If she couldn't go anywhere on the post, she could read about it.

In her room, she kicked off her shoes, and she sat down at the vanity. Darn, she was going to miss Jerry and Dean's latest picture at the Flick. She could sure use a good laugh, too.

What was wrong with her? Why should she be hiding in her quarters like a thief when she had done nothing wrong? Just like when she was learning to ride a bike, she fell off a few times, but she got right back on until she mastered it. She would conquer her humiliation over Cordero's lies, too. From now on he no longer existed, and she would not let him deprive her of going where and when she wanted on the post.

She glanced at her watch. If she hurried, she had just enough time to shower and change before chow.

Refreshed, April chose a peach floral dress with a flared skirt and a matching peach jacket. After dinner, she considered going to the service club. She wouldn't go to the dance but she could go to the writing room, a letter for Mae was long overdue.

Determined to face her fears, she walked the short distance to the Hilltop Service Club. As she went up the steps to the entrance, she prayed that she would not encounter any of the guys that had been present when Cordero told his monstrous lies about her. She took a deep breath and pushed bravely through the club's glass door.

She strolled past the double doors of the ballroom, and the familiar notes of one of her favorite tunes, "Only You," floated through the wide opening. She continued down the long corridor to the writing room. It was empty with most everyone in the ballroom. She put her writing box on her favorite desk, checked the ink supply in her Waterman pen and began a letter to Mae. She briefly told her about her job and that she and Cordero were no longer friends.

Someone entered the room, and she glanced up from the desk. She recognized him as one of the many guys she had danced with in the past. He sported a new set of corporal stripes on the sleeves of his dress uniform.

"Abril." The GI paused in front of her desk and smiled at her. "Why aren't you in the ballroom dancing?" he asked.

"I am giving myself a rest. Congratulations on your promotion, Cpl. Conde. It's *Angel*, Isn't it?" She gave his name the Spanish pronunciation.

"You remembered my name," he said, seemingly amazed. "In a few days I am leaving for Germany, and I have no family or anyone to write me. I often see you here writing, and I wondered if you would write to me."

"Sure," she said. She addressed the envelope and placed a three-cent stamp on Mae's letter.

Cpl. Conde removed a scrap of paper from his wallet before sitting down at a vacant desk. Carefully, he copied the information on a sheet of stationery. The corporal folded it several times until it was the size of a playing card. He appeared to hesitate after he placed it on her desk as he stood smiling down at her.

April returned his smile, laid a clean sheet of paper on her desk, and began a letter to her mama.

"You have a beautiful *sonrisa*...smile. You are always smiling. Do you like being in the women's Army?"

"Most of the time." She stopped writing and looked up at him.

"You like to dance, don't you?"

"Yes, I do."

"Would you dance with me?"

"I planned to return to my quarters when I finish my last letter."

"Just one dance," he hedged. "I probably won't see you again before I leave to go overseas."

"I want to finish my letter." She indicated the half-finished page. "Then I'll come to the ballroom for just one dance." She held up her forefinger to affirm the number.

"I'll be waiting for you," he said, and strolled out of the room.

Ten minutes later she finished mama's letter, put on a stamp and addressed the envelope. She picked it up with Mae's letter and went down the hall to the equipment counter where she found CQ placing a pair of pool sticks on the wall rack behind the counter.

"Are you here alone?" he asked.

She whirled around making a pretense of looking behind her. "Yes. I guess I am."

He laughed; his black eyes glittered like glass.

She slipped her letters in the slot of the large mailbox at the end of the counter.

"I got your message from Richard. The guys are going to miss your helping them with their letters," said CQ.

"I'm sure you'll find someone else to *volunteer*," she replied, emphasizing the word.

"I wish you would reconsider. Who is going to correct my bad English?"

"I'll think about it."

"Beside writing letters what are you doing here tonight?"

"Proving a point. I'm not staying. I finished my letters and I'm returning to my barracks as soon as I have one dance. Here, keep this until I get back." She slid her stationery box across the counter.

"I'll be leaving soon," he warned her.

"Be right back," she called over her shoulder. She hurried in the direction of the ballroom.

The moment she entered the room a smiling PFC approached her and held out his hand. "Dance?"

A few minutes into the dance, Cpl. Conde cut in. She smelled alcohol on his breath. It didn't appear to affect his dancing. He began to sing along with the music in Spanish. She closed her eyes and for a moment, it was as if she was dancing with someone from the past until she felt the evidence of his aroused body against her hip. She plastered her palm against his shoulder and shoved in an attempt to gain space between them He spun her out and back, forcing his hips more firmly against her. His interest had grown to the point that there was no polite way for her to ignore it. Obviously, he wasn't in the least embarrassed by his body's reaction. She couldn't believe this was happening to her again. As soon as the music ended, she excused herself, and she fled from the room nearly colliding with CQ in the hall.

"Are you leaving?"

Still shaking from her encounter with Angel, she could only nod.

"I'm through for the night. Come on, I'll give you a lift to your barracks."

"That's okay. It's just a short walk."

"Come on," he insisted.

CQ picked up her box from behind the counter and led the way out to a blue Pontiac that had seen better days.

"This yours?"

"It don't look like much," he said, opening the passenger door and pulling the seat forward for her to climb into the back. "But it takes me where I want to go."

Out of the dark, Cpl. Conde appeared next to the car and spoke to CQ in Spanish. Angel folded the front seat and got in the back crowding her against the door as the car moved forward.

"Oh baby," he said. "I want you." Suddenly, he hiked up her skirt; his hand shot up between her thighs. His other hand groped her breast, as he leaned forward attempting to kiss her. Shame flooded her and as it did so, saving pride returned. Fury hummed through her veins, drowning shame and humiliation is a rising stab of anger so thick, and pure, she shook with it.

"Stop it!" Hauling back her hand, she slapped his face with all her strength.

CQ jammed the brakes hard and fast causing her to nearly pitch into the front seat.

The door on the driver's side was yanked open. Angel was unceremoniously jerked from the seat by his tie and shirt collar into the parking lot. His frightened cry was drowned by the low menacing growl of CQ as he backhanded Angel across the face. After muttering something in Spanish with Cordero's name, CQ dropped him on the pavement.

It happened so fast, she felt faint. CQ sat beside her wiping her face with his handkerchief. She had not been aware that she was crying.

Learn to follow your head,
Your heart is blind.

Chapter 17

"I promise he won't touch you again," CQ said. He guided her head to rest against his shoulder. She clung to him as though he was her only safety in the world. He held her lightly almost in fear of crushing her.

After her sobs became sniffles he gently settled her back against the cushioned seat.

"Are you okay?"

She nodded; he got out and closed the door, and rounded the vehicle to the driver's side.

"You sure you are alright?" he asked, his dark eyes catching hers in the rear view mirror before starting the car.

"I think so," she said, hesitantly and promptly burst into tears again.

This time he let her cry without interference as he drove past the club and down the hill. At the bottom he halted the car. "Which way to your barracks?"

"It's off Galloway Road next to the Fourteenth Army Band building."

By the time he pulled into the parking lot of the Reception Company, her sobs had dwindled to an occasional sniffle.

He folded the front seat forward and helped her out of the car.

"Thank you for what you did this evening. I'm sorry for weeping on you and getting your shirt wet," she said, her hand brushing at his damp shirt.

"It'll wash. It's okay to cry. You had a bad experience for which I feel responsible. Had I known he was drinking, I would never have allowed him in the back seat with you. He's been on leave and he will soon be going to Germany."

"I know. That's why I danced with him. What did you say to him when you used Cordero's name"

"If he knew what was good for him, he'd better leave you alone that you were Cordero's girlfriend."

"You know that's not true," she protested.

"Yeah. But Angel doesn't know it." He threw back his head and whooped with laughter.

April didn't laugh. She didn't even smile. She looked up at him in confusion.

"From all appearances, you were his girlfriend." His laughter stopped, and he became serious. "I've never seen him with any other woman on this post. You were *hands off,* to all the Spanish guys because they considered you to be his girl. I sure wouldn't want to be in Angel's shoes." He held her elbow as they walked to the front entrance.

She turned and thanked him again while he held the door for her to enter.

At the door to her room, April paused and reached for her purse beneath her arm. Clasped tightly in her hand, she still held CQ's damp handkerchief.

After stripping off her clothing, she put on her blue terry robe and picked up her ditty bag from the footlocker. At the door she turned, went back to the bed, snatched her pajamas from under her pillow, and the towel from the bunk rail.

She was in luck. The latrine was vacant. Sick with a feeling of contamination, she took off her robe and stepped into the shower. She adjusted the water temperature as hot as her skin would allow. Her tears mingled with the stinging spray as she turned letting it pelt every inch of her skin. Angel had barely touched her, but her body had a crawling sensation. She scrubbed at her skin until it was rosy red, tingly and burning in places. Stepping out, she grabbed the large towel from the bench beside the stall and briskly rubbed herself dry. Something she rarely did, she usually ran the washcloth over her body to remove the excess water. She pulled on her pajamas and belted her robe over them before leaving the latrine.

Back in her room, she climbed into bed. Too upset to write, she ran her hand lightly over the blue Dreamcatcher journal before putting it away and clicking off the light. What a disaster of an evening. Lately her life seemed to be filled with one tragic mishap after another.

Sunday morning in the chapel, she prayed a special prayer for CQ. Giving God thanks for protecting her from what could have resulted in a nasty situation that she shuttered to even think about.

Following lunch, she returned to her barracks and put away her hat and gloves. After rummaging through her locker, she exchanged her blue suit for a dusty rose jumper with a matching jacket. Last, she traded her black heels for a pair of low-heeled beige pumps.

Before leaving her room, she slipped the neatly folded white handkerchief from the dresser top in her purse. She went down to the CQ desk and signed out for the service club.

Inside the club, the ballroom was dark, she continued down the hall. CQ was coming from the direction of the restrooms and he ducked behind the check out counter where a private waited.

She opened her purse and removed his handkerchief before moving down the corridor. After the soldier left the counter with two pool sticks, she approached where CQ was filing an ID card in a metal box.

"Hi, Sir Galahad," she said, smiling and she held out the folded linen cloth. "I want to return this and thank you again for coming to my rescue."

"Who is Sir Galahad?" He returned her smile and slipped the handkerchief in his back pocket.

"You've never heard of him?"

"I don't think so," he said, rubbing his forehead. "There's a lot of guys on this post. Do you know which company he's with?"

She hid her smile as she explained that Sir Galahad was a *knight of old* that rescued damsels in distress.

"Sir Galahad. Hmmm." CQ threw back his head and laughed, his black eyes twinkled. "I like that." He picked up the small green file box and placed it beneath the counter. Then he brought out a dust cloth and swiped it across the shinny black laminated counter top at non-existent dust.

"Did you just get here?"

"Yes, I came to return your handkerchief."

"I guess you haven't heard about the fight at the Beer Hall last night." He continued to shine the counter top without looking at her.

"You're the only person I've spoken to since I arrived."

"Then, I'd better tell you before someone else does." He folded the orange cloth neatly in front of him and placed his hand palm down on top of it. "After I left you last night I drove to my barracks. Cordero came to my cubical and wanted to know if I had seen you at the club. I told him about Angel."

"Oh, CQ. You shouldn't have done that. It was none of his business."

"I saw no reason to lie to him. Besides, he got a little hot under the collar when I said I gave you a lift to your quarters. I had to tell him something. The truth seemed the best way to go. He asked me to drive him over to the Beer Hall. Angel was at the bar, and Cordero invited him out to the parking lot. They started throwing punches and Cordero had him on the ground. He was beating the hel—I mean the heck out of Angel. Then Cordero pulled a switchblade and threatened to cut him if he so much as looked at you again.

"Someone in the crowd called the MPs. It was all I could do to get Cordero back in my car before they showed up."

"Was he hurt?"

"Nah. He was so mad that Angel hardly touched him. Don't worry. He never mentioned your name."

"Just how could he warn Angel to stay away from me if he never *mentioned* my name?"

"Simple, they were speaking in Spanish. He told him to keep away from his *mujer.*"

"His *mujer*?"

"His woman."

"I know what it means. I just don't know how he has the nerve to tell another lie about me. It was none of his concern," she fumed. "Do you know what happened to Angel?"

"I heard he had a black eye and a busted mouth, probably some sore ribs."

"I meant what did the MPs do."

"They drove him to his barracks. After the way he treated you, you shouldn't care what happened to him. He got what he deserved."

"I'm just sorry it happened. I wish Cordero had stayed out of it. If I were a man, I'd teach him a thing or two." Her hands turned into fists at her sides.

"Abril, if you were a man there wouldn't be any problem." CQ smacked the counter with his palm, laughing.

"I'm glad you think it's funny. I certainly don't. Cordero's nothing but trouble. Now do you understand why I don't want anything more to do with him?" she asked, her hands on her hips. "Or any other guy for that matter," she added.

"Does that include, Montoya? He's playing chess in the game room. Why don't you go say hello?" He winked. It was more of a conspiratorial gesture than a flirtatious one.

"Don't try to change the subject on me. Was he at the fight?"

"Nah. He never goes to the Beer Hall. At least I've never seen him there," he clarified.

"Do you think he knows about it?"

"It's possible. Cordero got pretty loud when I took him to his quarters."

"Oh, that's just dandy." She pivoted sharply away from the counter, rapidly crossing the wide corridor.

Her face warmed with heat as she quietly opened the door and went in. Montoya was sitting in one corner of the room facing his opponent across a red and black-checkered tabletop. She didn't recognize the sandy haired guy wearing glasses opposite him. Montoya wore a white dress shirt; the cuffs rolled up to his forearms. Nearby three men concentrated on the game, none of whom she knew.

One of the guys next to her offered his seat.

"No, thanks," she whispered, "I'm not staying."

At first Montoya appeared unaware of her presence. Then he glanced up, tilted his head slightly and a smile lifted one corner of his mouth.

April returned his smile with one of hers.

While she watched the game his challenger took one of his five black pieces. In turn, he captured one from the other player leaving his contender with only two white pieces.

A few minutes later, she quietly left the room and strolled down the hall to the restroom. After checking her appearance in the mirror above the sink, she fluffed her bangs across her forehead, and washed her hands before exiting. She walked past the game room and wondered how the chess game turned out. She shrugged and continued down the hall toward the front entrance.

"Did you see him?" CQ called, as she neared his counter.

"Who?" She paused, turning to face him.

"Montoya?" asked CQ. He moved to the end of the counter where she stood. A wide grin spread across his face.

"Oh, him? Yes, he's still playing chess."

"Don't look now. He's coming this way."

Montoya came up beside her. He slid a box of chess pieces across the counter to CQ. He smiled at her showing his cute dimples.

"Who won?" she asked, returning his smile.

"I did," he said, his voice tingled with a husky Spanish accent. "Cpl. Blackledge was a worthy opponent. Do you play?" he asked, leaning an elbow on the counter top.

"No, I don't."

"I could teach you if you care to learn," he suggested.

"Thanks. That's very kind of you. I don't think I have the patience the game seems to require."

CQ handed a card to Montoya who fished his wallet from his back pocket. They spoke in Spanish while Montoya placed his ID in a plastic holder. He closed the black case and replaced it in his pocket before he turned back to her.

"Are you unattached?"

April frowned, not knowing how to answer him.

"Excuse me, I used the wrong phrase," he said, combing his fingers through his short, curly hair. "I meant to ask if you are here alone or meeting someone…" his voice trailed off.

"*Solo*," she said. The heat rose in her cheeks. The color flooding her face and her inability to keep her color constant annoyed her.

"You speak Spanish?" he asked, a look of surprise on his face.

"Just a few words and phrases that CQ taught me while I helped him with his English."

Montoya hesitated as if searching for the correct words before speaking slowly. "I am going to play the piano in the music room. Would you care to accompany me?"

She hesitated for a moment before replying, "Thanks. I'd love to."

"Good," he said linking her arm through his, and then covered her hand with his. They strolled down the corridor to the dark music room. He switched on the light above the piano and pulled out the bench.

"Sit here next to me," he said, before sitting down beside her. His fingers moved rapidly over the keys and began to play "Cherry Pink and Apple Blossom White."

"Thank you," she said, when the last note faded away. "That's my favorite song."

"I know," he replied, smiling. "I have played it many times just for you. Is there another piece you would like to hear?"

"La Paloma."

"I like that one, too," he said, and struck the first chords of the melody.

She stared in fascination at his hands, his fingers moving nimbly over the keys. All the while he played when she glanced at his face he was watching her and smiling.

"Here is another number I think you will enjoy."

"I've never heard it before," she said, when the music ended. "It's lovely. What's it called?"

"Celito Linda," he replied. "In English it means 'Beautiful Sky.'"

"Beautiful Sky," she repeated.

"Do you still like this one?" he asked, and began "Smoke Gets In Your Eyes."

The last note faded, he looked at her and she laughed as she recalled the disastrous time she had requested him to play the song. He laughed along with her.

Soon, Montoya had an audience. Guys and gals drifted into the room, and sat down calling out names of popular songs for him to play. "Play, 'Blueberry Hill,'" hollered one of the men.

As the hit tune ended, she recognized a familiar voice asking, "Where are the rest of the guys?"

Montoya's body blocked her view of those entering the door. She leaned back, turned her head to look around Montoya's broad shoulders.

Richard appeared surprised to find her sitting next to Montoya. He frowned and glared at her with a disapproving shake of his head and approached the piano.

"The band is not practicing this afternoon." Montoya had turned his head and spoke to Richard over his shoulder. "The WAC Band is playing for the next dance."

"Hi, April," Richard said, and she returned his greeting. He came within a few feet of the bench and stopped. His left hand rested casually on his hip, and he made a movement with his head toward the doorway.

Instead of looking where he indicated she glanced at the wall behind the piano where wall-to-wall mirrors lined three sides of the room. She caught the reflection of Cordero leaning against the doorjamb just inside the room. A purple bruise marked the left cheek of his dark brooding face. Briefly, his eyes held hers. Quickly, she broke eye contact glancing to where her hands rested in her lap, and her palms began to tingle. Her hands were feverish and moist with perspiration. Opening her purse, she pulled out a tissue.

"Are you coming to the dance?" asked Richard, looking down at her.

"I don't know," she said. She dropped the damp tissue in her purse and snapped it closed.

"If you do, save a dance for me."

"Sure," she agreed.

Richard executed his familiar British half salute and did an exaggerated about face and strolled back toward the exit.

She turned around and caught his reflection in the mirror. At the door he spoke to Cordero and they left together.

After Montoya finished playing "Stars Fell On Alabama," he glanced at his watch and closed the cover over the keyboard. He shifted sideways on the bench toward her.

"I'm not too good with words," he said slowly, "but could you keep one dance for me?"

"If I attend." She nodded. A movement in the mirror momentarily caught

150

her attention as most of the room's occupants filed out the door leaving only one couple in the back of the room.

"Tell me. How is it that you help CQ with his English?"

"I correct his speech and he teaches me words in Spanish. On Wednesday evenings I sit in the writing room and assist guys with answering their letters."

"Does the club pay you?"

"No," she said, and laughed. "It's a volunteer job like CQ's work at the equipment counter."

"I do not write to anyone in English. If I come on Wednesday would you help me by correcting me when I speak?"

"I don't think I am going to continue with it. I'll let you know what I decide."

The couple from the back of the room walked to the door and left, leaving it open.

April glanced at her watch, 1730 hours. It was time for her to leave if she wanted to make the chow line at the mess hall.

What if she asked Montoya to eat with her? Would he accept her invitation?

I don't know, but I've been told,
Army chow is served nine days old.

Chapter 18

Montoya grasped April's hand, and he assisted her from the bench. Her grip was firm and sure, surprisingly full of feeling. It was as if a short jolt of electricity passed between them at her touch. He held the small perfect hand immobile in his palm so delicate for a young girl in the position of a woman soldier. There was no doubt about it. He was thoroughly attracted to the little WAC. He admired the regal way she held her head. She had charmed him with her sunny smile and her lovely voice with its soothing lilt. Not to mention her fascinating eyes that changed to match the color of her clothes had captivated him beyond anything else. She now met his own gaze without shyness—no coy flirting—instead he detected nothing but innocence.

"Montoya, it's nearly time for chow at my mess hall. Would you be my guest and eat with me?"

This small young woman stood before him and boldly offered her friendship with a simple gesture. How flattering, but it was an invitation he had to refuse. His heart had started to pound like a giant sledgehammer. A fact he chose to ignore. It worried him no little bit, the way this girl had set things stirring inside him all of a sudden. And he tried to put it out of his mind for there was no point in pursuing her. Nothing could ever come of it.

"Thank you. No," he said.

"If you declined because you think you would be uncomfortable being the only man there, you need not be concerned."

April withdrew her hand. "On Sunday, many of the girls invite family members and male guests."

"That is not the reason I declined your invitation." His speech slow and calculated, he translated her foreign tongue to his own language. "I could not enjoy the food with all those women staring at me."

"I'm sorry you feel that way. I have never invited a guy to eat with me. It would have pleased me for you to be my guest," she said, in a matter-of-fact tone.

He couldn't think why he should care whether she was angry with him or not—after all he hadn't started the conversation between them.

Her eyes followed his movements as he meticulously unrolled his shirtsleeve and smoothed the white fabric down his muscular forearms. He did the same for the other sleeve before buttoning both cuffs. Then he yanked one cuff, positioned it at his wrist, and then the second one. Montoya angled a glance at her.

April tipped her head up slightly until their eyes met briefly. She wasn't smiling. A deep, pink blush stained her cheeks.

"Good night, Montoya," she said. She turned on her heel and hurried toward the exit.

With long swift strides, he reached her before she walked through the doorway and laid his hand on her arm.

She faced him and he gave her a slow smile as their eyes met. Then his gaze was drawn to her mouth, pursed in a little pout. He had the strangest desire to reach out and stroke a finger across her lips. The mere thought caused a rush of heat that stunned him. For a moment he could think of nothing to say.

"All right," he said lamely, for he was no hand with women. "I would be pleased to accept," he said, his voice sounding a bit husky. "Against my better judgment," he added.

"And why is that?"

"Like I said, I probably won't be able to eat with all those women watching me." He tipped his head to one side. Gazing down at her, he smiled in a gentle, teasing way.

"Let's go eat." He reached for her hand, they left the club, his fingers entwining with hers.

Whatever his reasons for changing his mind, she found herself keeping pace with Montoya as they cut across the parking lot to the walkway leading down to the WAC Battalion mess hall.

As they entered the building, April was aware of the stir of attention his presence caused around the room. There were several appreciative cat whistles.

"Where did you find the handsome *Latino*?" whispered Lt. Sousa, the mess officer.

She couldn't blame them. She had to admit that he possessed more than his share of exotic magnetism and good looks. He had a physical appearance that drew the eye. It had drawn hers, ever since she'd first seen him playing the piano in the ballroom. Her reaction then had been so out of character that she had pushed it out of her mind and ignored it, or at least, she had tried. It had surprised her because she had never before thought that way about any guy.

After they went through the mess line, she steered him to a table at the end of the room. She sat against the wall leaving him to take the seat facing her. With his back to the room full of girls, many of them gave him appreciative glances.

Without offering any conversation, his eyes focused on the tray, giving full attention to his food.

April examined him over the rim of her cup. The soft spicy scent of his after-shave invaded her nostrils. His features were strong and vying for attention in a face that would always be dominated by his deep-set eyes. Eyes the color of dark, rich chocolate. His blue-black hair was short and curly above a prominent widow's peak that interrupted his wide forehead.

He looked up suddenly, and his gaze locked with hers. The corner of his mouth curved up in a half smile, letting her know he was aware of her intensive inventory. Her cheeks warmed. She broke eye contact, glancing down at her tray.

In all her twenty years she had never been as affected by the sheer physical appearance of any man. *Get a hold of yourself*—she scolded. What was wrong with her? And why in God's green earth had she been so brazen to insist on him coming to eat with her? What had changed his mind when it was plain that he didn't want to dine with her?

After he finished all the food on his tray except for a slice of apple pie, she leaned forward.

"You won't be able to eat the pie," she whispered.

He paused briefly for a moment as if considering her words. Then he looked straight into her eyes and another inexplicable shiver coursed through her.

"Why would you say that?"

"Don't look now." She widened her eyes. "There are a dozen recruits and one lieutenant staring at you."

Montoya frowned and turned his attention back to his tray. He didn't know what to make of her statement. Then he glanced up and caught the teasing light in her topaz eyes. She was smiling. He answered her smile with one of his own. Her soft giggles mingled with his deeper, hearty chuckles.

Following their laughter, the tension between them eased, exchanging stories of their family and childhood over dessert.

Montoya finished eating, and he laid his knife and fork diagonally on the stainless steel tray. He could imagine what would have taken place had the situation been reversed and they ate at his mess hall. Although he found it mildly amusing, he continued to stare at her, his mouth quirking slightly at the corner. He could just sit all afternoon looking into her eyes, watching the expressions on her face, and talking to her, listening to her soft southern drawl. He hadn't enjoyed conversation with a woman in a long time, especially one that was so young and lovely.

"I've never seen anyone with eyes the color of yours. Did you know they have little green sparkles that glitter when you smile?" he said, smiling yet again. For a man who did not smile easily or often he felt a lighthearted grin tickling his lips in April's company.

"I hadn't thought about it."

"A penny for your thoughts."

"I'm not sure they are worth the investment." She shrugged and glanced meaningfully around the nearly empty dining hall. "I was thinking that we should leave so the KPs can clean up."

He picked up both trays and conveyed them to their proper place.

They crossed Galloway Road and walked past B Company to the end of her building. When they reached the three steps that led up to Company C, Montoya paused.

"Is it permissible to sit here?" he asked, indicating the cement steps.

"I guess so, although it won't be very comfortable."

"Do you mind?" he asked.

She shook her head.

They sat on the middle step and continued to converse until she noticed the lateness of the time. He glanced at his watch, where had the time gone? They had been talking almost two hours.

"I'd better be going inside." She stood. "It's getting late and 0500 hours comes mighty early."

He rose to his full height and took her small hand in his. A charge like summer lightning ripped up his arm.

"I…" He paused; not finding the right words that adequately described his feelings. This was unknown territory for him. He was not a man of few words, but one whose preference was limited. Expressions of almost any sort were difficult for him in this foreign language. "I want to thank you for inviting me

155

to dine in your mess hall, and I want to see you again," he finally said, once he found the correct phrase.

"I would like that, too."

"On the regular operator's day off, I run the projector over at the theater, and I have passes to all the movies. *The Conqueror*, staring John Wayne and Susan Hayward is the feature film for this coming week. I would be pleased if you would accompany me."

Montoya had used nearly the exact words she had to invite him to eat with her. He was a fast learner.

"I've been wanting to see that picture." April smiled and nodded. "The stars are two of my favorites."

At the front entrance of her barracks, he turned to face her. "Thank you again for the invitation to your mess hall."

"You are most welcome. And I want to return your thanks for inviting me to listen to you play the piano. I loved the music—you played beautifully."

"I thoroughly enjoyed the opportunity to spend time conversing with you," he said.

"I had a lovely time, too. Good night, Montoya."

"*Bueñas Noches*," he said, softly, gently squeezing and released her hand that he had held since assisting her down Company C's steps.

April stopped to sign in at the CQ Desk. Pvt. Cleary handed her three pink slips. One message from Richard and two from Cordero. She refused to let Cordero spoil the nicest evening she had spent in a long while.

"Please put these in your waste can." She handed the folded slips back to the private on duty.

"Excuse me, Pvt. Terry, did I do something wrong by accepting the messages from PFC Rodrigues. I noticed a directive on the clipboard that you won't accept any phone calls from him."

"No, Pvt. Cleary. You didn't do anything wrong, PFC Rodrigues did. Good night."

On Tuesday, April filed the last dental record in the metal cabinet and closed the drawer as the phone rang.

"I'll get it," said Sgt. Levy. She picked up the receiver, "Reception Company, Sgt. Levy speaking."

"It's for you, a PFC Montoya." She raised her black brows curiously.

"I hope I'm not disturbing your work," he apologized. "I called to ask you if you had changed your mind about continuing to work in the writing room on Wednesday evenings?"

"I would have to speak to CQ. He may have gotten a replacement."

"No, he hasn't. I took the liberty to ask and if it would be permissible for you to help me with my English if you returned. He said it was okay as long as it didn't interfere with the letters you assisted the other men in writing."

"All right," she replied, slowly. "I'll help you with your English."

"I shall see you there tomorrow night." He said good-bye, and she hung up the receiver.

"What was that all about, if I may ask?" said Sgt. Levy.

She briefly explained about the volunteer work she had been doing at the Hilltop Service Club.

"There may be a problem. I made up the Duty Roster this morning and you have duty the nineteenth. If you want I could switch with you? I'm on for Tuesday." She took the roster off her desk and showed it to her.

"You'd do that for me?"

"Sure, I don't have any plans for that evening. I'll just make the switch. You can type it up tomorrow." She placed the paper in April's Inbox after making the correction.

"Thanks a heap. I really appreciate it."

"It's gonna' cost you. I want to know all about PFC Montoya." Sgt. Levy waggled her eyebrows up and down.

"There's nothing to tell. He's just a guy who needs help with his English."

The phone rang again; Sgt. Levy answered and immediately hung up. "I guess you know who that was," she said.

April grabbed her cap and left the office slamming the door behind her.

After chow, she returned to the Orderly Room for her purse before going up to her room. The private from the CQ desk came down the hall toward her as she closed the door.

"Pvt. Terry, you have a call on line two."

"Do you know who it is?"

"PFC Larsen," said Pvt. Williams.

"Thanks, I'll take it here." She opened the door and went back into the office.

"Hello, April. How about taking in a movie with me?"

"I'm sorry, Larsen, I already have a date to see the film."

"Just my bad luck. I couldn't get in touch with you earlier. I phoned twice on Sunday, but I didn't leave a message as I was told that you don't return phone calls. What about the dance on Saturday night?"

"I already have plans." *I do have plans; the person just doesn't know it yet.*

"Then save me a dance," he said, and hung up.

I don't know, but I've been told,
At Fort Knox, there ain't no gold.

Chapter 19

Wednesday evening CQ left his equipment counter to meet her halfway down the corridor.

"Abril, you have someone waiting patiently for you in the writing room."

"I do?" she asked, innocently.

"You are free tonight. No one is coming for help with a letter. Montoya spoke to me about your willingness to help him with his English. I think it is good." He walked back down the hall with her and ducked behind his counter.

April continued to the open door of the writing room.

"Good evening." Montoya picked up a book and stood when she entered the room.

"Hi," she said. "Have you been waiting long?"

"Twenty-two minutes," he said, glancing at his watch. "I was early." The slightest hint of a smile touched one corner of his mouth.

She took her seat at her usual desk facing the door. He placed a textbook in front of her before taking his seat with his back to the door.

"This is my English book from the Jacksonville College where I am enrolled. There are some things that are not clear to me." He opened the book to a place held by a yellow slip of paper.

The door opened, and she knew without looking that it was Cordero. Her hands started perspiring and dampened the paper on which she wrote examples on from Montoya's English book. She took a calming deep breath before risking a quick glance at the doorway. He leaned casually against the doorjamb watching them.

Discarding the ruined page, she took fresh notepaper and quickly wrote out the explanation. She slid it across the desk to him. "See if this helps clarify your question."

After a moment, Montoya looked up from the paper. "I understand it now. It is so simple the way you show me. The book should have explained it like this."

A few minutes later, she heard the door close softly. She looked up; Cordero had left.

The hour passed swiftly. When it was time to leave Montoya insisted on walking with her to the Reception Company.

"The bus stop below your barracks at the corner of 6th Avenue is where I took the post bus Sunday evening. I learned that I can catch it in either direction and it goes to my barracks at the 30th Chemical Company."

She accompanied him to the bus stop talking with him until the bus arrived. He boarded and took a seat next to the window facing her on the sidewalk. She waved as the vehicle pulled away. Montoya smiled, and he lifted his hand to return her gesture.

On the following evening, they waited in the short line in front of the Post Theater ticket window. When it was his turn, Montoya stepped up to the booth and asked for one ticket.

"Forget your pass, Monty?" asked the guy behind the glass enclosure.

"The ticket is for my friend," he replied, indicating April and showing him a small blue card.

"It's on the house." The ticket agent waved them away.

Inside, they had their choice of seats in the nearly empty theater. Montoya stopped midway down the center aisle and turned to her.

"Is this okay?" He stepped back for her to take her seat and sat next to her. "I've seen just about all the movies since I arrived on the post. They have been a great help in my learning English. While running the projector, I saw them repeated four times."

"It must have gotten boring?"

"Not at all. Each time I watched the film I understood something that I had missed in the previous showing."

"Hmmmm. The private in the ticket booth called you, Monty. Would you object to me calling you that, too? I can't see you as Alberto, and Montoya sounds impersonal and unfriendly."

"By all means, please call me Monty. Did it disturb you when you were called Terry after you enlisted in the Army?"

"A little. I've never gotten use to it. After I was nicknamed April in Clerical School, no one called me Terry except for the officers and noncoms."

"How did you get your nickname?"

She related the story with the Hawaiians and Pao that nicknamed her. "Now when someone calls me Elaine, it sounds strange," she concluded.

"In Spanish the months are *Abril, Mayo* and *Junio*."

"I know. It's been a trial to get the Spanish-speaking people to pronounce my nickname correctly. You are one of the few that doesn't mispronounce it."

"That's because I am focused on trying to speak your language correctly. I confess I sometimes think of you as *Abril* as that is how I first heard your name." He stood. "The popcorn should be ready. What would you like to drink?"

"*Nehi* grape if they have it, or *Coke*."

"Be right back."

The screen lit up with a large red and white box of popcorn and an assortment of soft drinks with a printed announcement to purchase soda and popcorn before the start of the film.

She glanced behind her. The theater was now filled and sitting two rows in back of her was Cordero and Richard. She quickly faced forward. In her lap, her palms began to perspire. She opened her purse and dug out a tissue.

"April?" She looked up. Monty held two *Nehi* sodas by the bottlenecks in one large hand and a box of popcorn in the other. She took the bottles, and he slid into the seat beside her and placed the popcorn on the armrest between them before taking his drink from her hand.

The film rolled and they settled back to eat popcorn and watch the movie.

Twice during the picture, Monty slid his arm across her shoulders and each time she tactfully removed it.

Something touched her hair. She combed her fingers down the back of her head and removed a popped kernel of corn. Most likely one of her *shadows* had pitched it there.

The next time she felt it, she was certain of the guilty party as she plucked the popcorn from her hair.

The third time Monty's arm slipped around her, she glanced up at him. He started to move the arm; his eyes had a little boy look that seemed to say, *sorry, I forgot*.

"Leave it there," she whispered. After that no more popcorn landed in her hair.

The film ended and the house lights came on.

"Let's sit here for a few minutes until the crowd thins out," she suggested. She had rather not have to face her *shadows*.

"Good idea. I can finish my drink."

"I see you bought both sodas the same flavor. Do you like grape?"

"I like the taste much better than *Coke*."

"Me, too.

"We do have that in common. Did you like the movie?" he asked.

"Very much. Susan Hayward is a fantastic actress and I admire John Wayne."

"So do I."

"Just don't start speaking like him. 'Wall howdy, pilgrim,'" she said, doing a fair imitation of Wayne's voice.

"Say, that was pretty good," he said. He chuckled and she laughed along with him. They started moving up the aisle to the exit.

She breathed a sigh. There was no sign of Richard or Cordero. She briefly wondered if he had seen them when he went for their refreshments.

They both seemed to be in a reflective mood as they left the theater. She was conscious of his hand lightly resting at the back of her waist, but she didn't object to it. In fact, she was beginning to enjoy his protectiveness.

Outside along the curb, two buses waited in front of the theater.

"It's still early. Would you care to accompany me to the service club?" asked Monty.

"I don't think so. I try not to make a habit of staying out late on nights before a workday."

He held her elbow as they boarded the bus. They were fortunate to find two seats together. But as the bus filled some people were standing in the aisle. Monty got up and gave his seat to a WAC in uniform. He was pushed farther back in the bus and she couldn't see him until some of the passengers disembarked. Ten minutes later, they exited the bus at the stop below her barracks.

"Monty, you should have stayed on the bus."

"I wanted to talk to you. Could we go sit on the steps where we sat Sunday? I promise not to stay long." Montoya took her hand and slipped it through the crook of his arm. They walked past the front entrance to the three steps at the end of the building that led up to the next level. He seated her on the middle step before seating himself on the top step above her.

"April, I wanted to tell you that I am on Guard Duty Saturday night. The 30th Chemical Company leaves for the field Saturday morning, and I'll be joining them after I am relieved from duty."

"Oh," she said, "that's too bad. You'll miss the dance."

"In this Army your time is never your own," Monty observed. "Could we go to the club tomorrow evening?" he asked. "That is if you are not busy," he added.

"I don't have any plans. I could meet you there."

"I prefer to call for you."

"Really, I don't mind meeting you at the club."

"I do. You are an unusual girl."

April looked at him as though confused; a frown marred her forehead. He wondered if he had used the right word to describe her. Did she think he meant she had a flaw of some sort or think her strange?

"I give you a compliment when I tell you I think you are unusual."

She looked up at him, her eyes shining, cheeks flushed, and in that instant he knew that he had never seen a more innocent, vibrant girl. And never had he felt more vital in the company of a female.

For a moment, she simply stared up at him as a bright blush covered her cheeks. She suddenly stood and smoothed her slim skirt before descending the steps.

"Do you have to go in now?" He got to his feet.

"It's time. Thank you for a pleasant evening. I enjoyed the movie." She thrust out her hand.

"So did I." He gave her hand a gentle squeeze. The thought crossed his mind…was she waiting for him to kiss her?

They walked in silence to the front entrance and he held the plate glass door for her to enter.

"Good night, April," he said, hesitated and knew he didn't want to rush it. So he walked away.

The following evening, in the music room of the service club, April sat on the bench next to Monty. After ending the last request he closed the piano cover and stood.

"Let's go someplace where it's not so noisy and we can talk." He cupped her elbow and guided her out to the corridor and down the hall to the writing room. The room was empty and he motioned her to a table in the far corner. He held a chair while she sat down, and then he took the seat opposite her.

"There is something I need to ask you," he said slowly. He folded his arms one on top of the other across the table. "If I'm out of line, just say so."

"You can ask me anything." She nodded.

"It's about Rodrigues—"

"Oh," she said, interrupting him.

"I've noticed," he continued, "that each time I've been with you, he shows up. For example, tonight he drove behind the bus when I came to pick you up. And he followed us here. Last night, he trailed us to the Post Theater. Are you aware of that?"

"Yes," she admitted. "I don't know why he's doing it." She bit her lower lip. "We were friends until a couple of weeks ago. He said things…things that hurt me."

"He is not your friend. I should have told you that I was in the barracks the night he came in drunk, bragging about what happened at Reilly Lake—"

"Yes, I know. Richard called me," April said. Her face burned with embarrassment. "I had already made up my mind to stop seeing him before Richard told me about his lies."

"Did Richard tell you everything?" He raised one black eye brow.

"He told me enough," she said. Her attempt at laughter was bitter.

"The things he said, no gentleman would say about a woman he cared about."

"Now I understand," she said, rising from her chair, "the reason you hesitated to eat with me. Please excuse me." She took a step away from the table.

"Where are you going?" He quickly got to his feet clasping her forearm.

"To my barracks." She brushed off his hand. "Good-bye, Montoya." She got halfway to the door before he caught up with her.

"Wait—I never said that I believed him."

"It doesn't matter. The damage to my reputation has…" her voice trailed off.

"Please," he said, "sit back down." He pulled out a nearby chair and guided her to be seated. "What happened? Can you tell me? That is if you don't mind." He sat opposite her, still holding her hand across the desk. His eyes caught hers, full of compassion.

"I'd rather not," she said honestly. "It hurts me to even think about it."

"Discussing it might make the pain less," he replied.

"Everything he said was a lie. We were never lovers." She sighed and took a deep breath before continuing. "We had never been alone together until that night. He suggested and said things that frightened me, and then he kissed me. I had never been kissed before."

Montoya raised both eyebrows in reaction.

"It's true," she confessed. "I had never let any guy kiss me. I didn't exactly give him permission—I felt invaded—he made me cry."

Montoya muttered a word in Spanish that she didn't understand. He squeezed her hand and released it.

"Did he try to force you?"

"It's according to how you mean that. He never touched my body with his hands, but he tried to seduce me with words. He described in detail how he wanted to make love to me. I told him that I wasn't that kind of girl and demanded that he take me back to my barracks."

Stillness came over Monty's face of tightly controlled anger.

"Cordero said he was in love with me, that he wanted to marry me. I imagine he said that to try and persuade me to let him have his way with me. I told him as much."

"What did he have to say?"

"Oh, he denied it. Swore that he loved me, and he wanted to marry me. After I learned about the lies he told I sent a message to him that I never wanted to see him again. Since then I have refused all his telephone calls, and I won't see him when he comes in person to my barracks. But I cry myself to sleep every night." April held out her damp hands. "Touch my hands. They are usual cool but just at the mention of his name they perspire like this."

Two big tears slipped down her face as he took her hands in one of his. Monty pulled a tissue from the box on the desk; he blotted her tears and dried her hands.

"Are you still in love with him?"

"You don't understand about our relationship." She took a deep breath. "I was never his girlfriend. The love I had for him was not the kind of which you speak. I loved him as a friend—like a brother, I trusted him, and he betrayed that trust. He humiliated me with his lies and he hurt me—deeply."

"Rodrigues is not worth your tears. Forget about him. We won't mention his name again."

"Are you sure you don't mind being seen with me? A girl with a damaged reputation like mine?"

"I don't claim to be a saint. I know how it feels to be hurt by someone you trusted. I was engaged to a girl in my country. Her name was Esther, and because she was divorced, my father objected to my marrying her. He persuaded me to go to New York to attend college. With my little knowledge of English it was impossible to enroll. Instead I got a job and I planned to send for her, but she stopped writing. Later, I learned she was seeing someone else."

"I'm sorry," she whispered and reached impulsively for his hand, laying a comforting hand on his.

"I got over it," he shrugged, looking down where her hand covered his. "I need to ask you for a favor."

She removed her hand and gazed at him silently.

"You know Reynaldo Riviera that the guys call *Little Fish*."

She nodded.

"He was engaged," he continued, "and the girl broke the engagement and gave back his ring." He took a diamond ring from his shirt pocket. "Reynaldo pawned it to me. I am going to the field and my footlocker has been broken into a number of times because I use to keep money in it. I am afraid of losing the ring if I take it with me." He picked up her left hand and dropped it into her palm. "I want you to keep it for me while I'm gone." He paused, "You have small hands, I bet it will fit you."

April slipped it on her ring finger. It fit like it was made for her. She held her hand at arm's length admiring the sparkling stone.

"It looks so pretty. Why don't you wear it?" he suggested.

"I haven't agreed to hold it for you." She pulled off the ring and held it with the thumb and forefinger of her right hand. She rotated it in her fingers. "No initials," she said.

"I would think not. This is the second girl he has been engaged to since I've known him."

"And they both had the same size finger. How convenient and coincidental."

"Not necessarily. He's not a very big guy. It follows that his girl friend would be small."

"Reynaldo has good taste in jewelry." She slid the ring back on her finger. "Sad that it didn't extend to the girls he chose. I think I *will* wear it—that way I won't lose it."

"Thank you for doing me this favor. I wouldn't want anything to happen to the ring. Someday, Reynaldo might get lucky and find the right girl."

Later as she was walking down the corridor with Monty, she found herself constantly glancing at the glittering ring on her finger.

He grasped her left hand as they went out the entrance. "The ring looks like it belongs on your finger," he commented.

When they reached C Company's steps, they automatically sat down.

"I'll be in the field for a week. Will you miss me?"

"Maybe a little bit," she teased.

"You'll go to the dance Saturday and forget about me."

"I'm not going," she said.

"Why not?"

"I changed my mind, and for another—I don't have an escort."

He put his arm around her like he had in the theater and hugged her to his chest. The rapid ticking of his heart was so reassuring.

"What was that for?" she asked.

"Because, I am going to miss you."

"I'll miss you, too."

"I better go. It's almost time for my bus." At the door, he squeezed the hand he held. "I'll call you when I return from the field. Good night—sleep well." He turned and strolled down the walkway toward the bus stop whistling a popular tune.

Saturday, 09 March 1957

Dear Dreamcatcher,

My *ring* got a lot of attention this morning until I told everyone that it was on *loan*. I had to explain how I came to be wearing it. Everyone had a good laugh. Lt. Sousa remarked that perhaps it would become permanent. "Not a chance," I told her.

After lunch I took the bus to Anniston to shop for fabric. I purchased three dress lengths and a pattern. I borrowed the company sewing machine from the supply department. Sgt. Waite said I could keep it in my room, as she never uses it. The sergeant remarked that it weighed more than me, and she carried it up to my room.

I almost forgot to mention that last night was the first time I went to sleep without crying since the incident at the lake. Perhaps it was the ring...

Yes is a wish.
No is a dream.

Chapter 20

Wednesday after evening chow, April dressed in her burgundy skirt and matching weskit over a pink long sleeved blouse. She picked up her stationery box and walked to the service club. Inside she paused at the equipment counter to speak to CQ.

"Do I have anyone to help with a letter tonight?"

"No. A lot of the guys are in the field this week," replied CQ.

"So is Montoya," she remarked.

"Are the two of you going out together?" He smiled and looked inordinately pleased with himself.

"We are just good friends."

"He's a real swell guy. You've helped him a lot with his English and me, too."

"I'm glad to help—"

"Wow! When did you get that?" he asked, staring at the ring on her left hand.

"Before you get any wrong ideas, the ring doesn't belong to me. Reynaldo pawned it to Montoya, and I am holding it for him."

"Let me see if I understand this." CQ scratched his head. "Reynaldo put the ring up for a loan from Montoya but you are holding the ring. Doesn't he trust Montoya?"

"Montoya's footlocker had gotten broken into and since he was going to the field, he asked me to hold the ring for safe keeping. Simple." She smiled.

"That doesn't explain why it's on your finger."

"Well, I didn't want to lose it, and it fits my ring finger. I'm going to write some letters." She turned to walk away, "See you later," she said, over her shoulder as she continued down the hall.

Like the rest of the club, the writing room was empty. She arranged her stationery folder on her usual desk and took out two letters. One from her mama and the other her brother, Jackson. After finishing her first letter, she folded it and picked up an envelope. Funny how she always seemed to know the moment Cordero was near.

Dressed in fatigues and wearing combat boots, he leaned against the wall inside the open door. His arms were folded across his chest, looking for the entire world like his namesake—a sleeping lamb with slitted eyes.

She lifted her chin and met his dark smoldering gaze. His eyes kindled with a glow above a blade straight nose, and then they took on an odd glitter as they focused on the ring on her left hand.

"What are you doing here? Aren't you supposed to be in the field?"

"I went on sick call." His black eyes searched her face with an intensity that both terrified and mesmerized her. Shivers iced down her spine as he pushed away from the wall and took a step toward her. In a few long strides, he was across the room; with the swiftness of a striking snake he seized her left hand. His powerful grip was too much for her slender bones, drawing a gasp of pain from her. Before she could stop him, he stripped the ring from her finger, and he tossed it carelessly into the breast pocket of his fatigues.

"Give it back," she demanded, holding her hand palm up.

His arm shot out and grabbed the hand she extended. He jerked her out of the chair into his arms.

"You'll not marry Montoya. You know nothing about Spanish men. I don't want to see you get hurt."

She detected liquor on his person and raised her hand to strike him. His strong hand grasped her arm, held it tight. Twisting and pushing at his hard chest, she struggled against his punishing grip.

"Easy, baby," he whispered.

Cordero's grasp tightened. He pulled her close until her exertions created an intimate friction between them. Abruptly she froze, feeling the effect her movements were having on him.

"Please, Cordero, let me go," she begged, breathlessly, straining against his hold. "Haven't you done enough? Don't you know the lies you told led to my being molested?" she accused.

"I'm sorry—I never meant for you to be hurt." His words slurred, and his chin dropped to rest on the top of her head.

"You've been drinking."

"Not enough," he said.

"You're making a big mistake. That ring you took doesn't belong to me."

He placed her hand over his racing heart. "Your nearness causes this." And then he snatched her other hand and pulled it down to the front of his fatigues, fitting her fingers over the hot ridge that bunched against the rough fabric. "This is what happens every time I'm near you. You're making me crazy with wanting you."

"You...you...how dare you." She couldn't think of one single adjective that was adequate to describe him.

"How dare I do what? How dare I love you? I would say this is a fair indication that I want you."

"I don't care to discuss your private parts," she hissed, trying to jerk her hand free, but he wouldn't allow it. "I will *never*, forgive you for this." Her voice was almost a whisper.

April had not been angrier in her entire life as she was at that moment. With all her strength she wrenched her hands free. She pummeled him with her fist and at the same time she kicked his shins.

In one hand he grasped both hers together and pulled them painfully behind her back. There was no gentleness in him as he held her helplessly pinned against the length of his body.

Without warning he kissed her. The kiss was rough—brutal—bruising. She struggled to free herself, but he held her easily forcing her to submit... His tongue stole inside, a heated intrusion, so intimate an action her breath left her in a rush that made her light headed, with a pounding pulse in her ears. It was like an invasion, an assault on her senses that was overpowering. A scream rose in her throat and lodged there in frozen silence.

He dropped her hands, and he tried to embrace her. She shoved hard against his chest, but she managed only to break the contact between their lips. Feeling helpless, her hands fell to her sides.

"You—you coward. Take your hands off me before I scream this building down around your ears..."

Immediately, he released her and stared down at her for a moment before he spoke. "Stay away from Montoya." He turned with military precision and marched out the open door.

Her knees became liquid and she melted into a chair beside the door. She gently massaged her stinging wrists. They were of no importance. But the bruising on her heart would stay with her far longer than any marks on her flesh.

She circled her arms on the desk and dropped her head, burying her face against them. Her shoulders shook as she sobbed. Slow painful tears trickled down her cheeks onto her hands. She had no idea how long she sat weeping with her head cradled on the desk. It seemed like hours, but it must have been only minutes for her heart was still thundering in her ears like a run away tank. And her lips still tingled from the encounter with Cordero.

Someone called her name and a gentle hand touched her shoulder as a handkerchief appeared next to her face.

"Did he hurt you?"

She accepted the cloth and swiped at the wetness on her cheeks before rising to a sitting position.

CQ stood in front of the desk with a concerned look in his glittering eyes.

"I'm sorry. What did you say?"

"I asked if you were hurt. I met Cordero in the hall. He seemed pretty torn up about something."

She held up her ring less left hand and quickly dropped it in her lap when she saw the ugly bruise forming on her wrist. "No," she lied. "He took Reynaldo's ring. I tried to stop him. I told him it didn't belong to me. He had been drinking, and he wouldn't listen."

"Don't worry about the ring. I'm sure when he cools off he'll return it to Montoya. The guys in our barracks are ribbing him pretty hard saying Montoya stole his girl."

"That's not true," she raised her voice in protest. "I was never his girl. You know that."

"Do you have a handkerchief in there?" CQ pointed to her black purse on the desk across the room. "This one's wet."

"What? Oh, no. I have some *Kleenex*."

CQ crossed the room and retrieved the small bag. With hands that trembled, she removed a packet of tissues. He took the package from her, opened it, fished out a tissue, and blotted her tears.

"You always seem to be rescuing me," she sniffed. "You have become my hero on more than one occasion."

"Have I?"

"I think you must be quite the *knight errant*." She nodded.

"I don't believe I've ever been anyone's hero before." A chuckle sounded in his voice.

"Do you make it a habit of saving damsels in distress?" she asked, assuming what she hoped was a lighthearted tone.

"No. It's only you I seem to be rescuing." His smile widened, flashing gleaming white teeth against his dark skin.

In her lap her hand touched her bruised wrist. The pain brought tears to her eyes. She hated lying to CQ about not being hurt, but she didn't want his pity. Carefully, she smoothed her sleeves down to cover the red marks.

"I'm sorry," she stammered as the tears overflowed. "I can't seem to control the waterworks. It's been like this ever since..." Her voice broke miserably.

"Cordero *es stupido*—savage fool," he said, mixing his Spanish and English. "Do you feel okay now?" He handed her another tissue, and she dried the last of her tears.

"I'm fine, really," she managed to say without her voice quivering. But inside she was shaking.

"You look kind of pale. Get your things. I'm taking you to your quarters."

"That's not necessary. I—"

"I insist. I was about to leave anyway."

"Okay, Sir Galahad," she agreed. "I promise not to make a career out of being rescued."

CQ took her by the elbow and left the building with her. Gallantly he shortened his steps to compensate for her much shorter stride as they walked through the club parking lot to his car.

A few minutes later, CQ tucked her hand into the crook of his arm and walked her to the door of her barracks. At the entrance, she turned to him. "Thank you again...for everything."

"It was my pleasure, Abril. Damsels in distress are my specialty." He winked at her and left.

We are Delta Company,
And we like to party.
Party hardy all night long,
Keep the party goin' strong.

Chapter 21

April pasted a false smile on her face and strode jauntily into the Reception Company's Orderly Room.

"Morning, Sgt. Levy.

"Good morning, Pvt. Terry. The lieutenant wants to see you."

"Oh, brother. What did I do now?" She glanced up at the clock. "I'm not supposed to be at my desk for another quarter of an hour. She is never here this early. Has she had her coffee?" She dropped her cap on her desk and continued to the stand that held the empty coffeepot and began measuring the grinds. "I guess not," she answered her own question.

"I don't think it's anything you did," said Sgt. Levy, peering over the rim of her reading glasses. "It just might be something nice."

"Have you been crystal ball gazing again, Sergeant?"

"You know I don't own one. But after what you told me last night, I checked out your daily horoscope. It said you were due for a change and good things were in store for you." The sergeant fluttered her eyelashes.

"That's a relief. Things sure couldn't get any worse." She wiped her hands on a paper towel, walked over, and picked up a small desk calendar from the sergeant's desk. She studied it for a moment before putting it back. "It's too early for my promotion to PFC."

"For the love of Petunia—report to the lieutenant and get it over with," said Sgt. Levy. She snatched up the calendar and repositioned it on her desk.

"I'm going—I'm going," she said, grabbing a steno book and ballpoint pen before stepping to the coffee stand and pouring a cup of coffee.

She marched across the room to the closed door with the gold lettering on the obscure glass panel. She checked the buttons on her *Ike* jacket, and tightened her arm over her steno pad. Then she transferred the coffee cup to her left hand with the pen. She rapped sharply twice.

"Enter."

Inside the door, she paused, gazing at the sharply, dressed woman behind the desk. Standing tall, she stepped lively to the desk and deposited the coffee before coming to attention and sounding off. "Pvt. Elaine Terry reporting as requested, Ma'am." She snapped a short salute that the officer returned before giving her *at ease*.

"Have a seat, Pvt. Terry." The lieutenant indicated the chair beside her desk where April usually sat to take dictation.

"Do you prefer to be addressed as Elaine or April?"

"April is my nickname. I answer to either name, Ma'am."

"I see that your desk sign has *April* on it."

"Sgt. Levy made that, Ma'am. She prefers April."

"I understand that you attend all the dances at the Hilltop Service Club."

"Yes, Ma'am. I do enjoy dancing."

"The Third Army Special Services Staff is putting together a show. The production is to be performed in Atlanta, Georgia. It will be taped and segments of it shown on TV. How would you like to be a part of the dance troop?"

"Wow! I mean that sounds wonderful, Ma'am."

"You don't have to give me your answer today—take a few days to think about it. A total of nine girls from this post will be chosen to participate. The 45-day TDY would begin the first week in August. This is an information sheet that should answer any questions you might have." The officer handed her a light green printed-paper. "Look it over and give me your answer by this Friday.

"Now for the big news." Lt. Theodoroff leaned forward and folded her hands on the desktop. "As of April the first, the Reception Company is converting to a training company as part of the WAC Battalion Basic Military Training Program. Our new name is Delta or Company D. Additional officers and cadre will be assigned including a first sergeant, which will lighten some of your duties. With the increase of cadre, you won't pull Duty NCO as often nor your Morning Reports be as lengthy."

"That is good news, Ma'am."

"I thought that would please you," said the lieutenant. She smiled. "Do you have any questions?"

"The information about the company conversion, is it confidential or can it be discussed with other company personnel, Ma'am?"

"I'm glad you asked. It was kept confidential for a while until it was recently made official." She took another light green page from her desk. "This is your new Job Description for Company Clerk. I borrowed it from B Company. We will be adapting it for our company policy. Pay close attention to article number eight. It's an additional duty for you. You will be understudy for the First Sergeant. That's about it—unless you have more questions."

"No, Ma'am," she said. She stood at attention, saluted and waited for the lieutenant to return her gesture.

"Dismissed."

This time she entered the Orderly Room with a genuine smile on her face.

"Well?" said Sgt. Levy. A big smile spread across her mouth, her black eyes squinted into tiny slits.

"You knew all the time," she accused. "Did you have anything to do with me getting offered the TDY?"

"A little," admitted Sgt. Levy. "I thought a change of scenery would do you good. Make some new friends—especially male friends. You are going, aren't you?"

"We shall see…" She sat down and began reading the Job Description for Company Clerk.

A thumping noise disturbed her. She looked over at Sgt. Levy, drumming her fingers on her desk.

"Well, how long do you intend to keep me in suspense?" asked the sergeant.

"The lieutenant said I should give it some thought. As soon as I know— I'll tell you." She returned to reading the directive. She scanned down the first two articles. They were the same duties she had now. Number three, answer the telephone and take accurate messages in the absence of the First Sergeant. Next, she read number eight. Understudies the First Sergeant, particularly in duties involving the duty rosters, reports, formations, etc., in order to replace the First Sergeant efficiently during any short absences.

On Friday, she gave her acceptance for TDY to the commanding officer.

After the evening chow as soon as she stepped into the building, the CQ hailed her from behind the counter.

"You've got a call from PFC Montoya."

"Thanks, Private. I'll take it in the Orderly Room." April continued down the hall to the office. She unlocked the door, laid her garrison cap on the desk, and picked up the phone.

"Hi, Monty." She spoke lively into the handset.

"Hello, April," he returned, coolly. His greeting was not as friendly as in the past. "How are you?"

"Fine, but you don't sound so cheerful."

"I just got back from the field. It was a rough week. I haven't even had a chance to shower. I'm waiting for my section's turn in the latrine."

"I know how that is. I had a shower schedule in basic training."

He was silent. There was no use putting it off. She had to tell him about the ring. "I want to explain about Reynaldo's ring," she blurted. "I hope Cordero returned it to you. He acted like a crazy person—"

"The ring was returned to me. It was entirely my fault. I'm sorry it happened. Just forget it."

"How could it be your fault? Look—he took it from me. I didn't give it to him."

"I said to forget it. What happened is not important. I have the ring. Let's not speak of this again," he said.

"Okay, if that's the way you want it," she agreed. "I won't mention it again."

"I called to tell you the Spanish Band is playing for the dance at the service club tomorrow night. I have to be there at 1900 hours to rehearse if you'd like to come and listen."

"I can't. I didn't plan to go to the dance, and Sgt. Levy invited me to the movies."

"You know I can't dance and play the piano, but I want you there. Won't you at least come to the dance at 2100 hours?"

"All right, I'll have to disappoint Sgt. Levy. I have a new dress that I made. It's yellow, my favorite color."

"I bet it's pretty. Yellow is very cheerful, green is my special color. What time can I call for you?"

"There's no need for you to come to my barracks. I can walk to the club."

"I don't like the idea of you going alone."

"Okay. I'll go with Pvt. Wells or one of the girls from B Company."

"Don't be late," he warned. "See you."

"Good night, Monty." She placed the phone on the rest. For a moment, she sat thinking about what he said about Cordero returning the ring. How she would have liked to know what Cordero said when he gave it back to Montoya. And better yet, what Monty said to him. From the timber of his voice, he had not sounded happy about the incident. Maybe it was a good thing that she didn't explain how Cordero took the ring and the way he treated her. She should take Monty's advice and forget it.

But dismissing unpleasant things didn't make them go away. It was just not the way life worked.

After getting dressed in her yellow, sleeveless frock, she walked up to the third floor and knocked at Sgt. Levy's door.

"Golly jeez—you're as pretty as a buttercup. How many crinolines do you have on?"

"Two, do you think my skirt is too full?" She twirled around in the center of the room.

"It's perfect." The sergeant moved to her vanity and unclipped an artificial nosegay of three daisies from beside the mirror. "Here, pin this in your hair." Sgt. Levy handed the flowers to her. "Not like that. Let me do it." The sergeant carefully unpinned the holder, smoothed April's hair behind her left ear and secured the flowers. "There," she said, adjusting the daisy cluster and fluffed April's bangs out above her right brow. "How's that?"

"I like it," she said as she turned her head to one side and viewed herself in the mirror above Sgt. Levy's vanity. "I think I'll start wearing my hair like this in the evenings." She glanced at her watch. "I'd better get going before I get scolded for being late."

Music wafted from the ballroom as she entered the service club. According to the large clock at the entrance, she was a quarter hour early. Through the open doors of the ballroom, she viewed the couples dancing. Cautiously, she picked her way around the twirling dancers until she reached the bandstand.

The music ended and CQ stepped up to the microphone. "The band will have a short break. Take this time to visit the *Coke* Bar. We'll return at 2100 hours to begin tonight's dance."

"Ahs," echoed around the room. Many of the couples took his advice and headed toward the French doors.

Montoya got up from the piano bench. His eyes held hers as he strode to the edge of the platform and hopped down to her level. He wore a white dress shirt with a string tie and a red cummerbund above dark trousers. Silently, he took her hand and turned her around. Her skirt swirled out, circling her legs.

"You made this dress?" he asked, his voice sounded doubtful.

"I cut and sewed it myself," she confirmed, proudly.

"It's lovely and you're wearing your hair different. I like the flowers."

"They're not real." She touched the daisies with her fingertips.

"I was about to ask if I could smell them," he teased.

"You wouldn't like the fragrance. Daisies have a musty odor."

"How about something to drink?"

"No, thanks. There must be a mob at the soda counter."

"We have our own refreshments. Come on. I'll show you." He grasped her hand and walked with her up the steps leading to the stage. Behind a dark green curtain at one end of the platform, a card table held an ice chest, a package of paper napkins and cups.

Monty raised the cover on the blue container and took out a bottle of *Nehi* grape. He used the bottle opener attached to the end of the cooler. He poured a cup and handed it to her before pouring one for himself.

"You remembered that I liked grape soda."

"It's what I like, too, and after seeing you in that dress, I may change my favorite color to yellow." He grinned down at her. "I have a special seat for you over by the piano." He indicated an overstuffed, brown chair near the piano bench.

"Where did that come from?"

"CQ borrowed it from the TV Room. He said you should have a comfortable chair."

"That's my Sir Galahad."

"You'll have to explain that to me sometime, but right now it's time I got back to work—uh playing." He took their empty cups and tossed them in the trash container beside the card table before escorting her to the chair.

"Am I being punished?" she asked.

"No—I just want to keep an eye on you and make sure you stay out of trouble." He gave her a wink, grinning as he took his seat at the baby grand.

The band was playing their third selection when the truth hit her. None of the guys would come up on the stage to ask her to dance.

From on the platform, she spotted Reynaldo standing on the floor. She caught his eye and gave him an Indian point with her head. He looked to his right, to his left before touching a finger to his chest and mouthing *me?* She nodded vigorously.

"Are you allowed to dance?" he whispered. He gazed from her to Montoya and back.

"Sure," she said. "I've never been to a dance and not danced."

Following the waltz, a Latin rhythm swept over the crowd, and she was gathered into familiar arms. She gazed up into Richard's sparkling blue eyes.

"You still remember the *merengue*," he commented.

"I had a good teacher."

"You are looking particularly pretty tonight. I like the new hairstyle. It's very becoming. Your eyes are topaz with green specks—looks like I'll have to change the color of my Chevy."

They both laughed.

"Have you seen Cordero?"

"No. I haven't been looking for him."

"You walked right past him when you came in. He's been standing in the same spot all evening. He hasn't taken his eyes off you since you entered the ballroom."

Cordero's presence was strong—her hands began to perspire.

Richard changed directions and she faced the entrance. She lifted her head and looked across the room, bravely meeting Cordero's smoldering glare.

"Do you see him?" asked Richard.

"Yes," she said softly. "Please move me away from this area and stop speaking of him or you will have to find another dance partner."

"Sure," replied Richard, and he switched direction. "How is it you're dancing with different guys? Doesn't Montoya object?"

"I dance with whomever I choose."

The number ended and the band began their rendition of "Til I Waltz Again With You."

"Rich, this is my dance." Larsen tapped Richard on the shoulder. "You've had your turn."

"Hi, Tex. How's your horse?" She moved easily into Larsen's arms as he swept her around the floor. He waltzed holding her the proper distance from him.

Larsen's hand tightened on her waist as he moved her in graceful patterns, dipping and whirling in large circles in perfect rhythm to the music. "I understand you recently lost an engagement ring."

She missed a step and gave an inaudible gasp as she recovered. "You most likely know more about it than I do."

"Cord was the maddest guy I have ever seen."

"Be a Texas gentleman and don't use his name in my presence."

"Whatever you say, pretty lady. When are we going out together?" he asked, as he swung her into a turn.

"I don't think it would be a good idea. My personal life is private. I want to keep it that way."

179

"I don't get it?"

"It should be obvious."

"Because I'm friends with…I can make new friends."

"Right now he needs all the friends he has."

"After all the lies he told. You still care for him." It was a statement, not a question.

"Feelings aren't something you turn on and off like a light switch," she said, then added, "unfortunately."

The music faded and CQ announced that the band would take a short break.

"I'll call you in case you change your mind," Larsen said, releasing her in front of the platform.

She went to the refreshment table, waiting for Montoya to leave the piano.

"I saw you dancing the *merengue*," CQ spoke from behind her.

"You guys sounded great," she said, turning to face him.

"*Gracias, Señorita*."

"*De nada*," she said. "How many damsels have you rescued lately?"

"A couple," he said, his black eyes glittered.

"And what do you hope to gain from those you rescue?" she asked.

"One day one of them might rescue me." He winked boldly.

"That seems only fair," she agreed.

She selected a grape drink from the ice chest, attempting to open it.

"Here, let me do that." Montoya came up behind her and took the bottle out of her hands. "It's a little tricky."

"I was just telling CQ how great the band sounded."

"I'm going out to smoke," said CQ. He turned and walked away.

"This may be the last night I play with the band."

"Why?"

"I'm thinking of resigning."

"You can't mean it. You enjoy playing with the band. Why would you quit?"

"It's simple. I cannot play and watch you at the same time."

"Monty, you can't be serious. You would miss playing the piano." April leaned toward him and retied his string tie making the loops even beneath his collar. "There. That's better," she said, pressing the ends against his shirtfront.

"I can play the piano in the Music Room on Sunday afternoons." He glanced at his watch. "Our break is almost over. For our next number we are going to play 'Cherry Pink.' I hope you will sit," he indicated the chair beside the piano, giving her a meaningful look. "And listen."

She didn't dance; she sat quietly in the seat. But for the remainder of the evening she danced every number. She caught Monty looking at her several times, from a distance, the heat still simmered in his eyes.

So he wasn't as immune to her as he pretended to be. She felt a little vindication at that thought, but he had never kissed her when he bid her good night.

It was after 2300 hours when he walked her to her door and said good night, just like that. Not so much as a handshake.

The following day after lunch, she washed her hair and put it in rollers. She wrapped a scarf around her head and went to the laundry room to wash her shirtwaists and press her uniform for the next day.

A private knocked on the open door and entered. "Excuse me, Pvt. Terry, you have a phone call from PFC Montoya."

"I'll be right down," she said, turning off the iron and sitting it upright on the board.

She hurried to the first floor and answered the phone at the CQ counter. "Pvt. Terry, speaking," she said, formally.

"April, I called to apologize for last night and ask you to pardon me."

"There is no need for an apology, I enjoyed the music. I told you when you left me at my door that I had a pleasant evening."

"You know what I mean. I would like to come by and take you to the club and make it up to you."

"I'm sorry, but I can't go. I just shampooed my hair and I'm busy doing my laundry."

"You aren't just saying that because you don't want to see me any more, are you."

"I have no reason to lie to you. It disturbs me that you think I would."

"I didn't mean it that way. You know I don't always use the right words."

"Perhaps you should explain just why you called to apologize to me."

"For my behavior last night. I didn't like sharing you with all the guys that were dancing with you."

"Apology accepted."

"Thank you. How about going with me to the movies on Thursday?"

"I'm sorry, I can't." There was a moment of silence. "I'm on Duty NCO that night. I am free Friday, Saturday, and Sunday. Pick one of those days."

"I choose all of them," he said, and laughed.

"Okay, it's a deal as long as I don't get a better offer," she said, laughing along with him.

On Monday, the Reception Company added three new cadre members to the Morning Report. Master Sergeant Craig, a very petite older woman with extremely short hair. She wore blue tinted glasses and spoke in a raspy voice. The two platoon sergeants, Wilcox and Gwynn, were in their late thirties with dark hair and skin like old shoe leather.

Early in the evening on Thursday, the runner knocked at April's door.

"A Major Vega is on the phone for you."

"Did he ask for me by name?" she said, closing the door behind her.

"No, he asked to speak with the Duty NCO."

She followed the private down to the first floor.

"I'll take the call in the Orderly Room," she said. She picked up the receiver and used her best professional voice. "Pvt. Terry Speaking."

"This is Major Vega from Post Headquarters."

"Don't you know you can get in a lot of trouble impersonating an officer?"

"How did you know it was me," asked Monty.

"I recognized your cute accent."

"Are you going to report me?"

"I just might the next time you say good night to me like you did Saturday night."

"I promise it will never happen again." He chuckled.

"I'm going to hold you to that promise."

"I called about the movie tomorrow night. *Anastasia* is playing. It's highly rated and stars Ingrid Bergman and Yul Brynner. Would you like to accompany me?"

"Yes, I would like very much to see the film. I've already agreed to spend the next three evenings with you."

"I know, but I wanted to make it official. I'll call for you at 1800 hours."

Following the movie on Friday night, they went to the service club. Montoya entered a Ping-Pong game and April sat and watched since it was not her game. She much preferred a game of pool. She noticed Monty using both hands but he seemed to favor his left hand. He was the winner of all four games.

Later, they left the club and strolled down to sit on their favorite steps. They talked for a while until she mentioned it was time for her to go inside. She got to her feet.

Would he just say good night? Or would he try to kiss her. She turned her head gazing at him standing behind her, so close his thighs brushed against her full skirt.

I don't know, but I've been told,
Eskimo pie is mighty cold.

Chapter 22

"April, I'd like to kiss you good night, if it would be permissible?" Monty asked, softly. He raised his thick brows up a notch. "Do you mind?" He picked up her hand slowly giving her a chance to withdraw it. He laced his fingers through hers feeling her pulse against his fingers, and it echoed his own heart's cadence. Nothing in his life had ever felt so right.

She didn't move her hand. Instead she looked down at their entwined fingers, gazed back at him, and smiled. She was close, close enough for him to smell the fragrance of her perfume. It was sweet, light, and utterly captivating.

"I...um...no. No, I don't mind," she stammered.

"Do you have a tissue in your purse?"

She opened her small bag and handed him a *Kleenex.*

He folded it carefully and swiped it across her mouth.

She jerked back. "What are you doing?"

"Cleaning your lips. I very much dislike the feel of lip rouge and besides, the men at the barracks have a grand time ribbing any man returning with it smeared on his face."

"Well, things sure have changed. I can recall my brothers getting lipstick on their faces and saying they weren't going to wash for a week."

Monty threw back his head and laughed and she joined him.

She took the tissue and removed the rest of her lip-gloss. "Are you satisfied," she asked, moistening her colorless lips with the tip of her pink tongue. Her eyes were wide and soft as she stared up at him.

Without replying, he reached for her, both hands framing her face.

"Monty," she whispered, as his mouth descended on hers.

He tasted the sweetness of his name on her lips as he brushed his lips across her mouth and watched her slowly close her eyes. Through sheer force of will he managed to keep the kiss gentle, and he lightly kissed her lips again.

Her awkward response was tentative, hesitant and unsure as if she didn't know what to do. But she didn't push him away. Gradually, she returned his kiss, tilted her face toward his to meet his lips. His mouth smiled beneath hers. She stiffened. Her eyes fluttered open.

"You are laughing at me because I don't know how to kiss," she accused, her eyes wide.

"No. I was smiling because it was the sweetest kiss I have ever had."

"You're only saying that because—"

He silenced her with a kiss that was deep and thorough, once more tasting the sweet, luscious flavor of her unpainted mouth. He absorbed the quick flash of heat that caused his blood to sing. It left them both trembling in its aftermath.

He drew back breathing heavily. "Any complaints?" he asked.

"Complaints?" she echoed, softly, blinking up at him.

"I refer to the way I am bidding you good night." He caught her gaze, his hands holding her at arm's length.

"None," she whispered, so low he barely heard her.

Entering her room, April leaned against the door. With her eyes shut tight, she relived Monty's kiss, experiencing it again down to the very soles of her feet.

Sighing, she kicked off her shoes before sitting down on the bench in front of the vanity. She didn't look any different. Delicious warmth like sweet honey had spread slowly over her entire body when he kissed her. For a moment, she'd nearly lost the ability to think. She touched her lips softly with her fingers. They tingled again, reminding her of the heat of Monty's mouth against hers and her cheeks grew warm. A kiss of discovery perhaps, or recognition. Tender and so sweet and wonderful. An unexpected tremor of excitement shimmied throughout her body.

The following Saturday night, April dressed in her new pink and white-stripped dress. She combed her hair back behind one ear the way Sgt. Levy had done the previous week and pinned an artificial, pink and white carnation in place. She fluffed her short bangs above her right brow and swiped pink lip-gloss across her mouth. After slipping her stocking feet into a pair of white pumps, she picked up the matching handbag from her dresser.

On the third floor, she knocked at Sgt. Levy's door. The sergeant opened it and gave a long, low whistle. "Montoya better put a chain on you tonight."

April waited for Monty in front of her barracks. Appreciation showed in his eyes at her appearance. He whistled like Sgt. Levy, only louder.

"I'll be the envy of all the men at the dance."

"If that's meant as a compliment, I thank you."

"It is. You must know how lovely you look."

"Sgt. Levy did mention something about you needing a chain for me." Laughter bubbled up in her throat.

"That might not be a bad idea," he murmured, taking her arm and walking toward the parking lot.

"Aren't we going to the dance at the club?"

"I got a lift from Cpl. Blackledge. That black Mercury in your parking lot belongs to him. He's waiting to give us a ride."

Minutes later, they stopped and paused in the entrance to the crowded ballroom of the Hilltop Service Club.

"One of the graduating companies must have gotten their liberty passes," observed April. "Looks like all the tables are taken."

"I see a few vacant ones over by the French doors," said Montoya, stretching up, looking over the heads of the dancing couples. "Instead of trying to get through this mob, let's go get some sodas and enter from the patio."

"An excellent idea," she agreed.

Moments later, he placed two grape drinks on the table before pulling out a chair and seating her.

"I'll be right back," he said. "Don't move from this table."

She angled her head to peer around the couples as he skirted the edge of the floor. At the end of the room, he headed toward the stage, and she lost sight of him as the dancers obstructed her view.

"May I have this dance?" A deep drawl came from behind her. She swerved to gaze up at a guy with a crew cut.

"I'm sorry, I'm with someone."

The soldier shrugged and strode away.

"I can't leave you alone for a moment, can I?" said Montoya, slipping into his seat.

"He only wanted to dance. I told him I was sorry to turn down his kind offer, but I was tied to this table," she said, doing her best to suppress her laughter.

"Maybe I should have taken your sergeant's advice." Monty chuckled. "I won't leave you unattended again."

The WAC Band's trumpet player sounded the first notes of "Cherry Pink." Montoya stood and extended his hand.

"I believe this is our dance." Montoya said, grinning from ear to ear. As they left the table, he put his hand on April's waist, guiding her to the edge of the swirling dancers.

"You arranged for the band to play my favorite song," she said.

He nodded and smoothly drew her into his arms.

"You realize that we have never danced. I've watched you dance many times with other men to this music. I wanted this number for our first dance together." He pulled her snug against him, pressed her cheek to his shoulder and kind of wrapped himself around her.

The enchanting melody seemed to penetrate every part of her, as they moved in harmony with the music. She closed her eyes and relaxed letting him guide her through the movements. After a few jostles and bumps by the other couples, she opened her eyes to find Monty with his closed. Dancing with his eyes shut might explain why he was not the expert dance partner like Richard, but he moved with a natural easy grace. He hummed along with the melody and surprised her by singing the chorus in English. April had never heard Monty sing, and she was pleased to discover he had an exceptional baritone voice. She was disappointed when the tune ended, and they returned to their table.

"You have a marvelous voice," she complimented him. "Why did you never sing with the band?"

"I play by ear—when I sing I lose my concentration. I must have a one-track mind. Just like when I tried to play and watch you at the same time, I made a lot of mistakes." He chuckled as the band began another number.

"This is my song." He stood and held out his hand.

He swept her into the midst of the couples to the music she recognized as "Beautiful Sky."

Before the next number began, a PFC asked her for the dance.

"Sorry, this is our dance," said Montoya. And then he looked at her with innocence. "You didn't want to dance with him? Did you?"

The next selection was a fast rock tune "Let The Good Times Roll."

"I don't dance this music," he apologized, returning with her to their table.

"Then I'm sure you won't object to Schafranec partnering me."

"Mind if I borrow your girl for this number?" asked Jerry Schafranec, entering through the French doors.

"The choice is hers," said Montoya, shaking his head.

"What a *crush*, huh?" said Jerry, as he skillfully spun her out and back to the beat of the music. "They announced the dance is in honor of Company A's graduation."

Jerry certainly knew how to rock and roll. For someone so tall, he moved with surprising speed, with none of the awkwardness usually associated with a guy of his height. His movements were fluid and graceful, and she relaxed in the security of his partnership. He twirled her around, and she laughed with sheer exuberance. The volume of the music rose as Jerry met her, released her, and then caught her again.

"It's called *Cinderella Night* because the girls have to be back in their quarters by midnight. All those graduating from Basic Training are given their first Liberty Passes since entering the military. I still remember mine," she said, breathlessly.

"I remember it, too. We danced to this same tune. I think the WAC Band plays the same songs at all the dances."

"We did? I don't remember you. But I danced with so many guys that night. There were fewer women than men attending the dance. They are more equally matched tonight."

"I see you in the company of Montoya a lot lately. He's one of the nicer guys," Jerry commented.

"Yes. I think so, too," she agreed. She was well aware that Jerry was comparing him with Cordero. When the music ended, Jerry kept hold of her hand and escorted her back to where Montoya stood beside their table.

"Thanks, that was fun," Jerry said, pulling out a chair and seating her. "Thanks for the loan of your girl," he said, turning toward Montoya.

Monty nodded his head and sat down opposite her as Jerry turned and walked out through the open French doors.

For the rest of the evening she danced only with Monty. His intense glare and impressive broad shoulders deterred her would-be partners.

On their favorite step, he spread his handkerchief for her to sit. He went through the same routine with the tissue wiping off her lipstick before he tipped her chin up. This kiss was different from the first time; his lips were firm and possessive. For an intense moment she forgot everything and what she was doing. His lips slid from hers to beneath her chin, kissing the fluttering pulse at the base of her throat. She felt her senses reel and her insides melted. How could he make her feel so much? Her hand drifted over his chest, the hard thumping of his heartbeat against her palm. His kissing her seemed so right. She felt no fear even though she knew so little about him in the short time since they met. It was as if she had known him forever.

The following morning, after lunch Monty called inviting her to keep him company at the Post Theater while he ran the projector in place of the regular operator. She declined with the excuse that she had seen the film and needed to wash and dry her hair after she finished her laundry.

Sgt. Levy came into the laundry room while she was ironing and asked about the dance.

April mentioned Monty's unusual habit of wiping off her lipstick before he kissed her.

"Why don't you go to the PX and purchase a tube of that new *Coty* Everlasting lipstick," suggested Sgt. Levy. "I would like to see him try wiping it off. I bet that would make him crazy."

They both cracked up laughing.

Later, in the afternoon, Richard phoned, not the best time since her hair was still wet. She wrapped a towel around her head turban fashioned and went down to the Orderly Room.

"Hi," he said. "I saw you dancing last night but I couldn't get near you."

"Yes, it was very crowded," she agreed.

"It wasn't the crowd that kept me away. It was Montoya. Didn't you tell me that you danced with anyone you pleased?"

"I did, but it pleased me to dance with him. We had never danced together because he was always playing the piano."

"Cordero watched you the entire time until you left. Do you have any idea what it's doing to him to see you in the arms of another man? He is continually drinking and getting into brawls."

"He made his choice when he lied about me. Whatever he is doing is not my fault. So don't try to make me feel guilty."

"What about the fight with Angel? You heard about that didn't you?"

"Yes, I did. Cordero shouldn't have interfered."

"Cordero is really hurting. Why don't you at least talk to him and give him a chance to apologize?

"I can't. He is not the only one that's hurt," she said.

"I know, but you could stop it just by seeing him."

"I don't care to continue this conversation. Good-bye, Richard."

She placed the receiver back on the rest. Despondent at the tears seeping from her eyes. It had been four weeks since she stopped seeing Cordero, but it seemed more like four months. How long would it take for her to stop weeping?

I don't know, but I've been told,
The WACs in Company D are mighty bold.

Chapter 23

Thursday, 28 March 1957
Dear Dreamcatcher,
This morning after I typed the Morning Report I straightened the office of the commanding officer to ready it for the new CO. Lt. Helena Babyk is expected to arrive the first of April.

I went with Monty to the Post Theater to see *All Heaven Allows* with Rock Hudson and Jane Wyman. A real heart breaker. I had to explain some of the scenes to Monty.

Following the movie we came to sit on our favorite steps. Monty was a riot trying to wipe off my lipstick. He said that I had outsmarted him, but I should be warned that he was not a man to get angry, that he got even. After the way he kissed me tonight, I plan to stop seeing so much of him. I don't want either of us to get hurt. I have a good start as he is on Guard Duty tomorrow night and I have Duty NCO on Saturday. Sgt. Levy offered to swap duty with me if I wanted to go out. She treats me so nice, almost like I'm her daughter…

Monday, 01 April 1957
I had a five page Morning Report because of the twenty-four trainees that came in over the weekend. We weren't supposed to get any recruits until today. Lt. Babyk arrived with two assistant platoon leaders, Sgt. Dunn and Sp. Faulkner. The lieutenant is an attractive tall blue-eyed blonde with a bubbly personality and a contagious smile. Formerly a recruiting officer from Texas; she has a delightful western drawl. Dunn is medium height with large

black eyes and dark complexion. Faulkner is petite with brown eyes and short dirty blonde hair. She has a tendency to giggle after each statement…

Wednesday, 13, 1957
Monty called but I was too busy to talk but a few minutes. He said he was tired because he had cut the guys hair in the barracks as he does every Wednesday afternoon. He is saving his money to buy a car.

He said if I didn't see him Saturday he would come stay at the CQ desk until I did. He is getting too possessive but I don't know how to put a halt to it without hurting him. It seems to be a natural Spanish trait or something…

Saturday, 06 April 1957
I saw Monty tonight and what a reception I received from him. We went to the dance at the club, but we didn't stay long. We had a slight disagreement about him letting me dance with Chico. His argument was that if I danced with him then all the other guys would expect to dance with me, too. Monty was still in a temper when we reached my barracks so I just said good night and went inside…

Sunday, 07 April 1957
This morning Monty called just as I was leaving for church and said he was sorry about Saturday night. He would try to control his temper in the future.

Monty told me that Monday was his birthday and asked me to call him…

Monday, 08 April 1957
Tonight, I called Monty for his birthday. It was the first time I broke my rule and called a guy. I told him but I don't think he believed me. Monty said he was twenty-six and asked what day was my birthday, as he knew I was born in April. I replied it was the nineteenth, and then he asked if I minded telling him my age. He said he knew it wasn't polite to ask a lady her age. I told him it was okay, and I would be

twenty-one on my birthday. He suggested we celebrate our birthdays on Saturday. I had to tell him that I was sorry that I couldn't because I was on duty and again tomorrow night…

Friday, 19 April 1957
Happy Birthday to me.

This morning, Sgt. Levy surprised the lieutenant and myself with a cake as we both have a birthday this week. Lt. Babyk's is tomorrow.

When Monty came to take me to the service club, he gave me a gift. Before I unwrapped it, he told me it wasn't much as he was saving to buy a car, but it was something I needed. A blow dryer for my hair. Monty said that I would not have any more excuses for not seeing him because I had washed my hair and it was wet. I think he is trying to outsmart me.

Monty did quit the band. They have a new piano player, Eduardo. CQ announced the next song was dedicated to a young lady celebrating her birthday. "Feliz cumpleaños, Abril." The guys played "Cherry Pink" for me.

It was late when we returned and I thanked Monty again for the hair dryer and he kissed me good night. Oh, so sweetly.

When I entered my barracks tonight, the CQ handed me a pink message slip. I didn't read it until I reached my room. In the space for the caller's name was written, "Person didn't give name." The message read, "Happy Birthday, Chica." I noticed the time of the message was 1930 hours. Cordero had called few minutes after I left to go to the service club. I was determined not to let myself cry over him and spoil my birthday.

But I did…

Friday, 26 April 1957
All this week, I have felt depressed. Sgt. Levy says I have the *over 21 blues*. I've never heard of it, but I hope I get cured soon.

We have a full company and I spent the entire day typing their medical and dental charts for next week.

> Monty called and told me the swimming pool was opening tomorrow and asked me to accompany him. I said that I had not learned to swim and he offered to teach me...

On Saturday afternoon, April arrived at the pool before Monty. She went to the ladies changing room, unzipped the back of her peach, flowered sundress and pulled it over her head. Beneath it she wore her new black swimsuit. She hung her dress in the metal locker, picked up her red beach bag and towel, and walked out to the fenced Olympic sized pool. At the deep end near the diving board were two guys and a girl in the water. She recognized the female as Ruth Bryza, one of the nurses from Noble Army Hospital. She waved to her.

"Come on in," Ruth called. "The water is marvelous!"

"I can't swim," she said, shaking her head negatively.

Ruth swam up to the edge of the pool. "How did you get by without learning? I thought it was mandatory for all military personnel to swim."

"It is, but I enlisted in the fall and the pool was closed. I don't think I could learn."

"I bet I could teach you. It's easy," said Ruth. She grasped the metal ladder and climbed out of the water. She wore a light blue swimsuit with a matching cap.

"Thanks for the offer, but I panic every time I get in water over my head."

"So what are you doing here if you don't swim?" asked Ruth.

"I'm meeting someone."

"The Spanish guy that plays the piano?"

"Alberto Montoya. Do you know him?"

She shook her head. "I've often seen the two of you together. Are you going steady?"

"Just good friends."

"Have you told him about your TDY assignment in August?"

"How did you know about that?"

"I saw your name on the list. I'm going, too."

"That's great news."

"My boyfriend, Don, threw a fit when I told him." Ruth unsnapped her bathing cap and shook out her auburn curls.

"I guess I'm a coward, Montoya doesn't know about my assignment. I'm going to the other end, this deep water makes me nervous," she said. "Want to join me?"

"I'm meeting Don. I just saw his car pull into the lot. See you later," Ruth said, over her shoulder turning in the direction of the gate.

April glanced at the water and shivered. Goose bumps raised on her arms. She walked rapidly towards the low end of the pool. Before she sat down, she spread her towel on the concrete deck. The large towel had a black and white skunk with four-inch high red letters spelling out KEEP OFF.

She glanced up and waved to Montoya as he walked through the gate. When he reached where she sat, he jerked the tails of his red-checkered shirt loose from his slacks.

"Hi," he said with a smile that made her feel warm inside. He paused beside her. "I hope that sign doesn't mean me," he said, indicating her towel.

She shook her head and laughed.

"That's a relief," he said and pulled his shirt over his head without unbuttoning it.

It confirmed what she had guessed about a muscular frame beneath his clothes. He bent to place his shirt on the towel, his muscles rippled in his back. She watched in fascination as he revealed the width of his shoulders and the strength of his broad chest. The sun sparkling off the water danced across his dark skin dusted with black hair. Her breathing became shallow as her eyes followed his hands to the closure on his black pants. With deft flicks of his fingers, he unbuttoned the top button and pushed down the zipper of the front placket. The trousers slid along on his hips, a narrow line of black hair disappeared beneath the white fabric of his swim trunks. He stepped out of the slacks and picked them up.

"What did you do with your clothes?" he asked, neatly folding the leg creases of his pants.

"There are lockers in the restroom where you can hang them."

Monty fished his wallet from his trousers and handed it to her. "Hold this for me."

Without his shirt hanging over his backside, his narrow, firm buttocks were revealed. She watched mesmerized as he strode to the men's room at the other end of the pool.

She gasped at her own un-maidenly boldness at gaping at a man's pleasingly shaped derriere and furthermore, her enjoyments of such a pleasant sight. She continued to chastise herself for being too aware of his broad and naked chest save for the curling dark hair matting the center.

Montoya came out of the men's room and glanced to the far end of the pool where April was seated. She was more beautiful than he imagined, evenly proportioned with shapely legs. His swim trunks became snug and he shifted uncomfortably, surprised that his body reacted to the sight as well as the sound and even the thought of her.

He strode to the edge of the water and dived in. He swam the length of the pool and back and over near enough to speak with April without raising his voice.

"Come on in. The water's fine," he said. "You aren't going to learn to swim sitting on your towel," he teased.

She smiled and put on her white bathing cap, walked down the steps and waded out to where he waited in water above his waist. He took her hand and moved them into deeper water.

"The first thing I'm going to teach you is how to float," he said. He placed his hands under her back and lifted her until she was horizontal on top of the water. Each time she started to sink, he lifted her up again until finally after several attempts she was floating on her own. Next, he showed her how to kick her feet and use the basic arm strokes to propel herself around in the pool on her back. But each time she put her head under the water, she panicked and grabbed him around the neck.

"I'm sorry," she said, loosening her grip. "The water frightens me. When I was small, I saw my best friend's brother drown. It left a lasting impression on me."

"I understand," he said, "but you must put your trust in me. I won't let anything happen to you."

"I do trust you. It's just that every time the water covers my face, I panic."

"Here, put your arm around my shoulder, and kick your feet the way I showed you. With your left arm reach forward and make paddle strokes away from your body. We are going to swim together around the pool. Anytime you feel afraid, all you have to do is stand."

They made several circles around the shallow end of the pool.

"Oh, this is fun," she said. "I feel like I'm really swimming."

"You are," he said. "If I let you go, you would swim on your own."

"No," she said, and clasped him tightly about the neck.

"Don't worry," he said, chuckling. "I wouldn't do that to you. We are going to swim to the deep end and back."

"I-I don't know…"

"Trust me. Nothing will happen."

April held him tighter around the shoulders when they reached the six feet marker. She continued to tighten her arm until they were at the twelve-foot depth.

"I believe someone is trying to get your attention." He jerked his head toward the diving board.

Larsen waved from the diving board just before he jumped up to plunge into the water.

"Nice dive," he said. "Before long you'll be doing that."

"Don't bet on it," April said. They laughed, turned and headed for the shallow end. Once they reached the steps, he assisted her out of the pool, and he remained in the water.

"I'm going to take a couple of laps around the pool before I get out," said Monty. He turned and swam toward the deep water.

Grace in motion, April observed, impressed by the play of muscles on his back as he swam, strong strokes across the length of the pool and back to the metal ladder. He climbed from the pool; droplets of water running down his body glistening in the sun like crystal tears, caressing every line of muscle and sinew.

The sight of him stole her breath away. She'd never seen a more perfect male body.

She handed him a towel, and continued to smooth lotion on her legs while he dried himself. "Perhaps, I should put some of this on your back and shoulders."

"I never burn," he said, sitting down beside her. "This is my natural color." He shrugged his shoulders. "It smells nice, why not? Go ahead." He turned his back to her.

She poured a glob of lotion in her hands and began to smooth it across his back. She was covering his left shoulder when her hand encountered a single, coarse, black hair. It was all of four inches long, without thinking she plucked it out.

"Ouch!" he yelled, jumping up from his sitting position as if a bee had stung him. "What did you do?"

"I didn't mean to hurt you," she said. She stood holding the thick strand between her thumb and forefinger.

"Do you know how long that hair had been growing?" he asked. His eyes riveted on the single hair. It was apparent he was upset, his brow wrinkled and he fixed her with a level stare.

She shook her head in bewilderment.

"That was my *lucky hair*, it's been there ever since high school."

"I'm sorry," she said, her voice contrite. "If I had known it was so important, I would never have..." Her words ended in confusion and her cheeks burned in embarrassment. Her eyes gazed at the wiry hair between her fingers. She opened them and dropped it like a guilty child caught with something forbidden. It fluttered to the pavement.

She snapped the top on the lotion bottle and dropped it in her red tote bag. After she bent and grasped the large towel, she shook it and folded it meticulously in half then in fourths.

Montoya sighed. He took a step toward her, curled his hand around her wrist, its touch at once strong yet gentle.

"What are you doing?" he asked, his voice husky.

"I'm going to my barracks," she answered, refusing to look at him.

Holding onto her arm, he reached out with his free hand and touched her cheek, turning her face until she was forced to meet his gaze.

"Why?" he asked, plucking the beach towel out of her hands.

"It doesn't matter," she waved her hand, dismissing the incident.

"Really? I don't wish for you to leave."

"I beg your pardon." Her tone was polite but she let him hear the anger underlying it.

"I said that I don't want you to go."

"I think it's best that I leave."

"Look, I'm really sorry. I over-reacted. It was just a silly old hair." Montoya whipped the towel open and spread it back on the cement. "I wouldn't want you to burn. Let me put some of that lotion on your back."

"I guess I do need some lotion," she agreed, peering over her shoulder at her pinked skin.

"It will be my pleasure," he answered, assisting her to sit on the towel.

She handed him the bottle and he knelt behind her and began applying the creamy lotion over her back and shoulders.

> Saturday, 04 May 1957
> Dear Dreamcatcher,
> I went to the pool today. I'm not sure if I learned to swim, but I learned to float. I also discovered that Montoya has a hot temper. While putting lotion on his back and shoulders, I pulled out a long ugly hair from his shoulder. He pitched a

fit over it, saying it was his *lucky hair*. At first, I thought he was teasing but when I realized he was serious I almost left the pool to return to my barracks. I allowed him to put lotion on my back and I think he forgot about his hair. I know I did. Of all the guys at the pool, his physique was one a sculptor would appreciate with one exception. He has a lot of dark curly hair on his chest, which I don't like. Maybe I could pluck them out, too…

Friday, 10 May 1957
Tonight, I went to the movies with Monty. He operated the projector so we stayed in the projection room. It is very interesting how the changes over of the reels are made. A little circle of light shows on the corner of the screen when it's time to switch to the next reel…

Saturday afternoon, April rode the bus to the pool to meet Monty. She arrived early and met Ruth Bryza at the entrance. They stood near the deep end of the pool talking.

Without warning someone scooped her up and tossed her into the pool.

"She can't swim," yelled Ruth.

"Help." she screamed, sailing over the water, splashing upside down on her backside. Water filled her mouth and nose, terror and panic flooding her mind. She sank to the bottom of the pool. Suddenly, there was someone next to her grasping her under her arms and yanking her to the surface.

Holding her face out of the water, Larsen swam halfway across the pool until the water was at his shoulders. He lifted her into his arms and carried her toward the shallow end.

"You can put me down, the water here is not deep." The fear on his face was replaced by a smile.

"No, I'm rescuing you from downing." He continued to carry her to the end of the pool, mounted the few steps, strode over to a concrete pillar, and lowered her to sit on it.

"Braza said you couldn't swim. Is it true?"

"Not a stroke."

He looked at her in disbelief. "But I've seen you swimming with Montoya in the deep water."

"I was holding to his shoulder, he was swimming, not me."

198

"I'm sorry. I didn't know. I was not trying to drown you. Please accept my sincere apology for such a dumb, stupid prank."

"April, are you okay?" asked Ruth, rushing up out of breath. "It was too late to stop him, when I saw his intentions."

"I'm fine, just a little shook up," she replied.

It was lucky she had on her bathing cap and even luckier that Montoya wasn't there. Larsen might have gotten punched in the nose.

The following Saturday she returned to the pool with Monty. April was floating on her back when she suddenly sank. In a swift movement, Monty grasped her shoulders jerking her from beneath the water. His hands moved down and held her around the thighs and hoisted her high above his head, her limbs clasped securely yet painlessly by arms hard as steel.

"Put me down." Her hands clutched his upper arms and the hard biceps flexed as he held her a little closer.

Slowly, he allowed her legs and lower body to slide down his taut muscled form. His heart pounded beneath her cheek and the straining ridge of his manhood pressed against her abdomen. Her arms fell away from his shoulders as if she had been burned.

The pleasure of love lasts but a moment,
The pain of love lasts a lifetime.

Chapter 24

April's feet touched the bottom, and she stepped back, her hip brushing against the part of Montoya that ached to possess her body. A tremor shook him and an automatic blush spread quickly up her neck and cheeks. Plainly enough, she'd felt his untimely reaction to her.

The friction of April's body moving over his could scarcely have been more inciting. A hot shaft of desire pulsed through Monty pushing the front of his swim trunks into a new shape. Embarrassed, he was unable to stop the slow flush that climbed his throat. His body had responded like some randy teenager to the feel of her flesh against his; rather than the rational twenty-six year old man he thought himself to be. He edged his hips quickly away from her. Determined not to show April more than he had already, he turned his back and waded into the deep water. Just why her opinion of him mattered so much? It just did. He swam a few laps around the pool before returning to where she was drying off.

> Saturday, 25 May 1957
> Dear Dreamcatcher,
> I have given up on learning to swim. After what happened in the pool last week with Monty, I didn't even get my feet wet today. I sunbathed while he swam. I took my camera to the pool and we took pictures. I think I got some nice ones of him and the two of us together.
> Since tomorrow is Mother's Day I told Monty I was going to call my mama. He asked if he might be allowed to meet her over the telephone. I agreed…

All the pay phone booths were occupied at the service club. April and Monty each stood in a line waiting for a phone. Monty got the first free booth.

They squeezed into the small compartment. Monty closed the door and leaned his back against it. She sat on the small seat, dialed the number, and deposited the correct amount for the first three minutes.

"Elaine, I was hoping you would call. How are you?" her mama asked.

"I'm just fine. I hope you are having a nice Mothers' Day," she said.

"As well as can be expected with three of my children absent. Gene called earlier."

"That's swell. I have my friend, Alberto Montoya, here with me. Remember I wrote you about him. He would like to speak to you," she said.

"Sure, put him on the phone."

"Here, Monty," she said, handing him the receiver. "She likes to be called Inez."

"Hello, Inez," he said. There was a pause.

"That's my father. If I'm going to call you Inez, you must call me Monty." He spoke into the receiver. "I am very pleased to be speaking with you, too." Monty gazed down at her, smiled and winked.

He was quiet for a few minutes; he seemed to be listening intently.

"Is that so?" he said, still smiling from ear to ear. "I hope it was all good." There was a long silence before he spoke again. "Yes, I will."

Another break in his conversation.

"I promise. You have my word on it," said Monty, followed by a very long pause.

"It was nice talking with you, too." He handed her the phone. "Your mother wants to speak to you."

"His voice reminds me of Desi Arnez on TV. Don't you think so?" said Mama.

"A little, they both have Spanish accents, and he has a marvelous singing voice like him, but that is as far as the resemblance goes. Monty is quite tall. We took pictures by the pool yesterday, as soon as I get them developed I will send you some."

"He sounds very nice, if he looks as well as he sounds."

"I think so. I better hang up; there is a long line outside this booth waiting to use the phone. I love you, Mama. Take care," she said.

"I love you, too, Elaine. Bye-bye."

"Let's go to the soda counter and get a cold drink, and you can tell me what my mama said. You didn't say much, she seemed to be doing most of the talking."

Monty set the two grape drinks on the table and pulled out a chair for her.

201

"So," she placed an elbow on the table and rested her chin on one fist. "What did she say to you?"

"Oh, the usual, if I thought her daughter was intelligent and beautiful—"

"I want to know what my mama really said." She punched him lightly on the arm.

"She cautioned me to take special care of you. I promised her that I would. I guess that makes me responsible for you." He grinned at her.

"She said that?"

"Yes, she did, and I gave her my word," he replied with all seriousness.

Thursday, 06 June 1957
Dear Dreamcatcher,

This has been one hectic week. We graduate our first group of trainees tomorrow.

As if I don't already have enough to do, I was informed of a new duty. I'm to have Post Staff Driver every thirty working days and a separate roster for weekends. I had to report to the Motor Pool for a military license. A smart aleck corporal there told me that the only available vehicle for my exam was a deuce and a half truck, five-speed, stick shift. I saw three jeeps on the lot and asked why couldn't I use one of those for my test-drive. He told me they were all assigned to the mail clerks. He was surprised when I drove the ton and half truck without any problem, except for getting into the cab. Lucky for me I wore my fatigues, as he had to boost me into the cab.

Monty called me later and I told him about my new duty. He wanted to know if any of the officers I chauffeured would be male.

I was hoping for a nice quiet night but I didn't get my wish. I was called to the First Platoon's Bay because of a disturbance. Two of the girls were in a fight over my friend, CQ Del Valle. One of the girls, a black Hispanic, Maria, had told Shirley, a southern girl from Georgia, that he was black. I told her that I knew him and we were friends and yes, he was black. I thought Shirley was going to pass out. It seems she had kissed him. Perhaps I should have told her not to worry; the color doesn't rub off. After I left the bay, I had a good belly laugh over it. Just wait until I see CQ. Am I ever going to tease him…

Friday, 07 June 1957

Today was my first experience as a Post Driver. I had to report to the Motor Pool after breakfast to pick up my vehicle. A new '57 Ford station wagon fully loaded with automatic shift. Not only did I drive the WAC Duty Officer but also a male major. He said I was the first female driver he had ridden with, and he complimented my driving. How about that?

In the afternoon, accompanied by Sp. Walters, I drove a group of our girls to the Birmingham airport. Later I picked up new trainees from the bus and train depots twice in Anniston. It made the day go fast, and I rather enjoyed my driving duty…

On Saturday night April and Monty walked to the service club. While the band took a break,

Monty bought soft drinks at the soda fountain, and he carried them out to the patio.

A gentle rain begun to fall, making a peppery noise on the overhead canopy. Not like one of those old-field soakers that rained so hard that if she looked up with a smile, she'd drown. Occasional raindrops could be heard splattering on the edge of the floor tile near the outside door.

"Let's walk to my barracks," she said. April sat the empty bottle on the marble table and stood.

"In case you have not noticed, it's raining."

"I don't mind a little rain. It's a warm evening, and I doubt we'll melt," she said, going toward the exit. "Haven't you ever walked in a summer rain?"

"You must be joking. Why would anyone want to walk in the rain?"

"Obviously, you have missed some of the finer free treats of life."

"I'd hardly call getting soaked a treat."

"Come on. You'll like this, I promise," she said, going out the door.

"And if I don't," he asked, following her.

"Trust me. Take off your shoes." Before he could protest further she hunched down and slipped off his shoes then yanked off his socks. She tied the laces together, slung them over his shoulder, and did the same with hers.

April stepped out from under the awning into the warm gentle rain with her face turned up and her mouth opened to catch the drops.

"Taste it, Monty. There are few things sweeter than summer rain."

"You are something else," he said, slowly, shaking his head. He stepped out from beneath the canopy to join her in the softly falling rain. "I can never figure you out."

"Why would you want to?" She smiled, amused.

"I don't know," he said, turned and walked backwards, smiling at her through the glistening drops. "I just do."

By the time they reached the bottom of the hill the rain had ceased.

"The rain can cause problems." Monty indicated the wet cement steps where they usually sat.

She gazed toward the steps and back up at him, her lashes dipped shadowing her topaz eyes with glistening wet lashes. For a few moments, he simply looked at her taking in the soft flushed curve of her cheeks, her mouth the color of a ripe peach. She caught her lower lip with her teeth; a shiver of pleasure touched his heart.

"I guess nothing is perfect," she said, and shrugged her shoulders.

Instead of words, he bent down and lightly kissed her. Just the faintest touch of lips to lips; like a gentle raindrop falling on a flower petal. Angling his head to one side, he traced the curve of her mouth. Her lips beneath his were moist and velvet soft as he brushed another chaste kiss across her mouth.

He drew back breathing heavily. She had the most bemused expression on her face. Arrogantly pleased, he smiled. April obviously had been just as affected by their kisses as he'd been. And for some unexplained reason, he felt wildly ecstatic. He wanted to shout—to swing her around and around until they were both dizzy. And more than anything, to kiss her again.

He did just that, loving the way her eyes warmed and her lips softened under his. If he could he would continue kissing her the entire night, holding her and wanting her. Wanting her with an ache that had no cure.

Her lips tasted of fresh rain and her mouth a warm, sweet contrast to the damp cool air. After all, there was something to be said about walking in the rain. Sweet rain tasting kisses.

Sunday, 09 June 1957
Dear Dreamcatcher,
After lunch, Monty came to see me. He had been trying to phone me, but all the pay phones in his barracks were occupied. He told me he was going to the field tomorrow for two weeks.

We strolled up to the club and sat on the patio talking. He told me how much he had disliked the service and the post until he met me and now everything had changed. And how much he enjoys my company and he looks forward to the weekends and spending time with me. I have the feeling he is getting serious. I like his company, too, but I am not going to get my heart broken again. Once was enough...

Friday, 21 June 1957
Hooray! Today, I got my PFC stripes, and a pay increase of $15.00 per month. Now I have the task of sewing them on my uniforms...

On Saturday after the evening chow, April added a matching jacket over the blue flowered sundress and picked up her beige handbag before leaving her room. Downstairs, she signed out at the CQ desk.

A short while later, she entered the Hilltop Service Club and walked down the hallway to the Equipment Counter where CQ was studying some papers. He looked up when she approached.

"April, what are you doing here by yourself?"

"Montoya is in the field, and I got so bored in my barracks, I had to get out for awhile."

"Try to stay out of trouble."

"I'm not worried. I always have you to rescue me," she said, smiling up at him.

"Not for long. I just made corporal and I'll be going to Germany in a few months."

"Congratulation. I'm going to miss you. Guess what? I got my PFC stripes yesterday."

"How about that? We should celebrate. Come on. I'll buy you a soda." He stuck a closed sign on the counter, and joined her in the corridor.

She linked her arm with his and accompanied him to the soda fountain.

They sat at the refreshment counter talking and making a few mock toasts.

"To you keeping out of trouble while I'm gone," said CQ, lifting his glass.

"While we are on the subject of trouble, it seems we have that in common," she responded, clicking her grape drink against his glass.

"How so?"

"You," she pointed an accusing finger at him, "were recently the cause of a fight between two girls in one of the platoons of my company."

"You heard about that, did you?" He threw back his dark head and laughed. When his mirth subsided, he said, "Did that surprise you?"

"Yes, it did. I was on duty, and I had to break up the fight. Lucky for you, Shirley was assigned to another post after she graduated from basic training. She was so furious that she wanted to scratch your eyes out."

That prompted him to laugh again. "I was innocent. She kissed me at the dance."

"Not for one moment do I believe that you were innocent. Your eyes are too mischievous. It would have been a shame if she followed through with her threat. It's your eyes, the girls just can't resist them," she said.

"I'd better get back to work." CQ finished his drink and slipped off the barstool. "You try to stay out of trouble."

"You, too."

They left the counter laughing.

She went to watch TV until a guy sat beside her and tried to start a conversation. She remembered what CQ had told her, got up and returned to her quarters.

> Friday, 24 June 1957
> Dear Dreamcatcher,
> I am glad to see this week come to an end. We graduated another platoon, and I had tons of extra paperwork. I have been in the Orderly Room by myself most all week as Sgt. Levy and MSGT Craig have been occupied with escorting the trainees to class and showing training films.
> Monty called late tonight. He just got back from the field, and he has to return on Monday.
> He purchased a roll of color film, and he said I should wear something colorful tomorrow...

On Saturday afternoon, she had just stepped into a pair of strappy sandals when someone knocked on her door. She finished buckling her shoes before opening the door.

"PFC Terry, You have a visitor in the Day Room," said the freckled faced private. "A PFC Montoya."

"Thank you," she said, glancing at the girl's nametag. "Pvt. Welby, tell him I'll be down in a few minutes," she said, and closed the door.

From the footlocker at the end of her bunk, she took out a white clutch purse and dropped her dog tags and keys inside. She turned the thumb lock on her doorknob and closed it on her way out.

Monty stood when she entered the Day Room. He wore a crisply, starched white shirt and freshly, creased black trousers. A leather camera case was slung over his left shoulder.

"You must have read my mind," said Monty. "I was hoping you'd wear that dress." A wide grin spread across his face.

"You said to wear something colorful," she said, smoothing down her skirt over the crinoline at the hem of her favorite yellow outfit.

"If we hurry we can catch the bus to Post Headquarters. There are some pretty flowering shrubs there that I want to use as a background."

Aboard the bus, Monty removed the camera from its leather case, opened the back, dropped in a roll of film, and snapped it closed.

"With this roll I can take thirty-six pictures for slides."

"I've never seen a camera that makes slides before."

"I made my own slide projector from a mirror and lens that projects the pictures on a screen or a white wall."

"It must have been difficult?"

"Not at all. I found the directions in an issue of *Popular Mechanics*. I just followed the instructions."

"My older brother had a subscription to that magazine. I always thought it referred strictly to automobiles."

"No, it's anything mechanical. It offers a number of good articles."

"I would be interested in seeing your projector."

"As soon as I get the film developed, I'll make a show for you." He returned the camera to the case.

"This is our stop," he said, and stood, held out his hand steadying her as the bus came to a halt.

They exited the bus in front of a large two-story white stucco building topped by a red barrel roof. Ornamental shrubs and colorful plants landscaped the surrounding grounds. At the base of the walk leading up to the structure were tall bright pink and red blooming bushes.

"Oh, they're beautiful," she said, walking toward the plants.

"Don't get too close," warned Monty. "They have large, sharp thorns. Don't move. I want a picture of you in front of the flowers." He snapped a couple of pictures, then motioned to the iron railing that formed a balcony at the end of the building. "Let's get a couple of shots up there."

"Are we allowed on the balcony?"

"Sure. I haven't told you, but I'll be working here this summer." He took her hand and they went up the steep walk and climbed the steps to the porch that ran the length of the building.

"Does that mean you'll be changing barracks?"

"No, it's just for a few months, but it's possible I could get permanently reassigned to Headquarters Company." He let go of her hand, placed both his hands on her waist, and hoisted her up to sit on the wide top railing.

She glanced over his shoulder at the turquoise and white Chevy parking across the street.

"Don't fall off," he cautioned. He stepped back, opened the lens cap of the camera and snapped the photo. "That's going to be a beautiful picture," he said. He took another one before lifting her down.

She gazed back at the street as Cordero stepped out of the car and leaned against the hood staring in their direction. Richard sat behind the wheel.

Monty's eyes followed hers. "Oh, you noticed them, too?" he remarked.

She didn't comment; she just nodded.

Monty clasped her hand and walked with her to the steps. "Stand here, I want to get a shot from down there." He ascended the steep stairs and focused the camera on her.

"What will you be doing here at Headquarters?"

"Typing, cutting stencils, running the Post Bulletin, reports, stuff like that."

"You know how to do all that?"

"More or less. I worked in an office before I was drafted. And would you believe I'll be working for a WAC captain?"

"I don't know if I approve of that," she teased him.

"I think she's older than me," he said, defensively.

"Age is not a factor when a good looking man is involved."

"So, you think I'm good looking." The tops of his ears turned beet red and he studied his shoes before looking up and catching the amused look on her face.

"I told my mama that you were handsome."

"Did you?" He replaced the lens cap on the camera. "Noncoms aren't allowed to fraternize with officers."

"Is that supposed to make me feel better about your assignment?" she asked. "I'll envy you working in these beautiful surroundings."

"Yes, well, I wanted to take some shots of you on that picturesque bridge across the street, but I don't care for our audience. We might as well leave."

"Would you like to return to my barracks with me and eat in my mess hall?"

"No, I'm all sweaty. I want to go to my quarters and take a shower. That guy burns me up the way he follows you around like a sick calf mooning for its lost mother. I sometimes feel you encourage him."

"The word is *mooing* not mooning. I most certainly do not encourage him. I have not spoken to him since he took Reynaldo's ring. I would be curious to know what he said when he returned it to you."

"I don't want to discuss him period. You think this is amusing."

"No, I do not."

"Then why are you smiling so much?"

"If you must know, I don't want them to know we are having an argument."

"It would appear every time we've had a disagreement, Cordero is at the bottom of it. He's always watching you. I don't like him looking at you one bit."

"It's a free country. I can't help it if he follows me."

"So, you admit he follows you." He fisted his hands at his hips and turned to stare across the street.

"I believe you brought it up first with the *sick calf*. I've changed my mind about going out with you this evening. I think you better go take your shower and cool off."

"Let's go before I say something I'll regret. The bus just passed, it will make the circle and come back in a few minutes."

The ten-minute ride to her bus stop was made in silence.

"I'll call you later." Monty touched her arm as she stood to exit the bus.

She didn't reply, just nodded. What would he say if he knew of all the *crank* phone calls?

Montoya called her at 2200 hours; she went down to answer his call in the Orderly Room.

"Why didn't you tell me you made PFC?" asked Monty.

209

"How did you find out?"

"CQ told me. He got his corporal stripes the next day."

"I didn't want to mention them since you hadn't gotten your promotion."

"You know that doesn't matter to me."

"It does to me. It's an extra $15.00 a month pay increase."

"Look, I'm sorry about this afternoon. I don't know why I let that guy get to me. Yes, I do…it's because of the lies he told about you."

"I know. It bothers me, too."

"When I see the way he looks at you—I get so angry—I lose control of my temper. Please forgive me. I shouldn't have said those things to you. I know it's not your fault. I really can't blame him for looking at you. If I were in his place, I'd be doing the same."

"Cordero is trying to cause trouble between us. I wish I had never met him."

"So do I," Monty agreed. "I'd like to finish the roll of film. Could I come by tomorrow afternoon? I promise not to give you a hard time."

Sunday, following chapel, April went to the mess hall still dressed in the white, sheath dress of China brocade that she had worn to church and carried her white lace hat.

Monty was waiting in the CQ area with his camera when she returned to her barracks.

"Hi. You're early," she greeted him. "Have a seat in the Day Room and I'll go change."

"Don't. I like what you're wearing."

"Then I'll go freshen up. I'll only be a minute."

"Bring the hat," he said.

In front of the service club, they sat on the steps of the walkway leading up to the entrance. By setting the timer, Monty held the camera in his hand and snapped a close up picture of them together. And then he leaned under her broad, brimmed hat and kissed her.

"Now you know why I wanted you to wear the hat," said Monty. "It makes a good cover." And he kissed her again.

He took several more pictures before they went inside the service club.

On Monday April returned from evening chow and paused at the CQ desk.

"Pvt. Lucas, I'll be in the Orderly Room if you need me." She continued down the hall to the office and unlocked the door.

Before starting her work, she carefully removed her starched cap and placed it on Sgt. Levy's empty desk. From the stack of files on her desk, she picked up a handful, went to the metal cabinet, and began placing them in alphabetical order in the corresponding folders.

A knock on the door interrupted her before she finished filing the last of the medical records. Pvt. Eagan from the fourth platoon stood in the hall with Pvt. Lucas.

"Pvt. Eagan said she heard screams coming from Pvt. Wells' room," said Pvt. Lucas

"Are you sure it's not her radio?"

"One of the girls knocked on the door. She doesn't answer. I put my ear to the door and it sounds like someone moaning," said Pvt. Eagan.

"I'll check it out. Thank you, Pvt. Eagan. Return to your bay." She selected a key from the pegboard behind Sgt. Levy's desk.

"Come with me, Pvt. Lucas."

She hurried up to the third floor and stopped at the room next to the kitchen. No sound came from the room that she could hear through the door. She knocked hard on the door.

"Pvt. Wells? This is PFC Terry." There was no response, but she heard a faint moan.

"Pvt. Wells, are you okay?" The noise increased.

She used the key to unlock the door and pushed it open. The overhead light revealed Pvt. Wells lying in her bunk on top of bloody sheets. Across her stomach, her arm covered a baby streaked with blood.

"Oh, my God." April quickly closed the door and stepped back out into the hall. "Go back to the CQ desk and call the post ambulance. The number is beside the phone. Give them my name as the Duty NCO and say that I authorized the call. Tell the operator it's an emergency that a girl just gave birth. Then go up to Sgt. Levy's room and tell her that I need her in Pvt. Wells' room. And don't discuss this with anyone else. Do you understand?"

"Yes, PFC Terry," replied the wide-eyed girl.

She opened the door, entered, and locked it behind her. Carefully, she stepped around the large wet puddle on the tiles and approached the bed.

Pvt. Wells' eyes were closed. The baby across her stomach rapidly moved its hands up and down, mewing like a kitten.

"Peggy, are you awake?"

"I haven't passed the afterbirth. Is my baby okay?" Pvt. Wells opened her blue eyes and looked up at her.

"I think so. The baby is moving."

"Get a towel from my footlocker and clean her nose and mouth."

"For Pete's sake, girl why didn't you tell someone you were pregnant?" She removed several towels from the footlocker. With one towel, she carefully wiped the baby's nose and mouth and cleaned some of the blood off her face. Using another towel, she covered the baby that was still attached by the unbiblical cord to the exposed lower body of Pvt. Wells.

"I didn't want to get kicked out of the service."

"I still can't believe this." April shook her head. "I just thought you were gaining weight."

Someone knocked at the door.

"PFC Terry?" Sgt. Levy's familiar voice sounded from the other side.

She unlocked the door and Sgt. Levy stepped inside dressed in a pink chenille robe and wearing pink fuzzy bedroom slippers.

"Golly-jeez," said the sergeant, her black eyes big as saucers.

"Watch the puddle," she said, closing and locking the door.

"Did you know she was pregnant?" asked Sgt. Levy.

"I had no idea," she said, shaking her head. "Will you stay with her while I go down and call the Duty Officer and wait for the ambulance?"

"Sure, who is the DO tonight?"

"Fortunately, one of our officers, Lt. Barron."

"That's good.' Sgt. Levy approached the bed. "Hi, Peggy. How do you feel?"

"Not so hot right now."

"Boy or girl?" asked Sgt. Levy, lifting one corner of the towel.

"A girl," supplied Peggy.

"Looks like she'll have red hair, and she has your blue eyes," observed the sergeant.

April unlocked the portal, turned the button on the knob and closed the door. She double-timed down to the Orderly Room. She grabbed the handset and dialed.

After two rings a familiar voice answered. "Lt. Barron speaking."

"Ma'am, PFC Terry speaking. You're not going to believe it, but Pvt. Wells just gave birth to a baby girl."

"Th-that's impossible," sputtered the lieutenant. "She didn't look pregnant."

"I didn't think so either, Ma'am."

"Have you called the hospital?"

"An ambulance is on its way, Ma'am."

"I'll be right over," the officer said, and hung up.

She closed the office and went out through the CQ area to the front walk.

At the end of the block, an ambulance pulled into the parking lot with the emergency lights flashing and a blaring horn. Midway, she met the two EMTs rolling a stretcher on wheels.

"Sp. Cooper and PFC Wakefield," they sounded off with their names.

"Hi, guys, I'm PFC. Terry. Follow me."

"I understand you have a new company member?" said Sp. Cooper, leaving the tall EMT to push the gurney and walk beside her.

"I guess you could say that," she agreed.

"This is a first for me," said the brawny specialist.

"You've never delivered a baby?" She stopped abruptly on the walkway. "Pvt. Wells hasn't passed the afterbirth nor has the unbiblical cord been severed."

"Don't worry, old Coop has delivered a handful of kids," said the leggy EMT coming to a halt behind her. "What Coop meant was this is the first time a WAC has had a baby in one of the training companies."

"No one knew she was pregnant," she said, walking hurriedly toward the building.

At the entrance, Pvt. Lucas held the double doors open.

"Pvt. Lucas, Lt. Barron will be here soon, so be on your toes. I'll be up in Pvt. Wells' room if I haven't returned before she gets here."

"Yes, PFC Terry."

"She's on the third floor."

"Just my luck," groaned PFC Wakefield.

They came up the stairs behind her bumping the wheels of the gurney against the steps.

She ran on ahead and unlocked the door. A large bath towel had been placed over the puddle on the floor.

"How's she doing?"

"The afterbirth is out. I'm going to get dressed and go to the hospital with her," said Sgt. Levy. She exited the room just as the men arrived wheeling the stretcher.

April stood back and observed the efficient EMTs taking care of Peggy's baby.

"Coop, would you look at them blue eyes. She's wide-awake," said PFC Wakefield.

"Use the pink blanket," said Sp. Cooper.

"PFC Terry, would you hold her while we clean her mom up?" asked PFC Wakefield. He held out a pink bundle to her.

"This is a first for me," she said, taking the wrapped infant in her arms.

"What's that?" asked the EMT.

"My first time to hold a newborn."

Sgt. Levy came hustling in. She now wore a pink blouse and petal pushers.

"Oh, let me hold her," The sergeant extended both arms. "She's so tiny. I bet she don't weigh more than a sack of sugar."

The EMTs carefully transferred Pvt. Wells to the gurney and covered her with a blanket.

"Let's go," said Sp. Cooper. "One of you can carry the baby."

"I will," said Sgt. Levy, following behind the stretcher.

Lt. Barron met them in the CQ area.

April saluted and reported to her.

"You've had a busy night," said the lieutenant.

"Very unexpected, Ma'am," she replied.

The officer handed her a form. "Fill this and type up a detailed report. You can give them to me in the morning."

"Ma'am, it's the 4th of July. Are you working?"

"In all the excitement, I forgot. Please leave the paperwork on my desk."

"Yes, Ma'am."

Outside the building, she caught up with the gurney as it was being loaded into the ambulance.

"Thanks a bunch, guys. You were great."

"Don't mention it—all in a night's work," said Sp. Cooper.

"Peggy, I'll see you at the hospital tomorrow," she said, giving her hand a reassuring squeeze.

Sgt. Levy got into Lt. Barron's car. The lieutenant backed the beige Plymouth out of the lot, trailing behind the emergency vehicle.

She returned to the Orderly Room and began typing up the paperwork.

At 2200 hours, Sgt. Levy entered the office shaking her head. "I can't get over her delivering her own baby and none of us knowing that she was pregnant. She and the baby are okay."

"Neither can I. She must have been terrified. We went through basic training and Clerical School together, and I never suspected she was pregnant."

"Those big coveralls camouflaged her condition," said the sergeant, standing and stretching. "I'm turning in. Do me a favor. If anyone else gives birth tonight, call Sgt. Waite."

They left the office laughing.

"Wait up. I'll walk up with you. I have to take bed check," called April.

"Sorry, but you will be appointed the company mail clerk until we get a replacement."

"It's okay by me. I always wanted to drive that cute, little jeep."

Wednesday, 03 July 1957
Dear Dreamcatcher,
You won't believe what happened tonight while I was on Duty NCO…

Your left, your military left.
Don't get out of step.
Your left—your right—your left.

Chapter 25

Thursday, 04 July 1957
Dear Dreamcatcher,
Last night was quite a shock for St. Levy, and me. I am the official mail clerk until we get a replacement for Pvt. Wells. Sgt. Levy will take over my desk while I pick up and deliver the mail.

I went with Sgt. Levy to the Post Exchange to get a gift for Peggy's baby. It was my first time there. The sergeant said she did not frequent the place because she had a tendency to buy things she didn't need, as the prices are so low. Sgt. Levy was right about that. Everything was on sale. I purchased two outfits for Peggy's baby, one pink and the other yellow. Sgt. Levy bought a new arrival gift that included everything for the baby's bath.

In the evening we went to see Peggy at the hospital. The baby is real cute, red hair and blue eyes. Peggy named her Barbara Ann. She wouldn't say who was the father. Sgt. Levy calculated that she was expecting when she joined the service but may have not known it. I don't understand how she passed the physical, but Sgt. Levy assured me it was possible...

April released the roller, pulled the Morning Report from her typewriter, and placed it in the lieutenant's Inbox.

"Sgt. Levy, I'm going to pick up the mail." She plucked the jeep keys off the board behind the sergeant's desk.

"PFC. Terry, come into my office," the lieutenant's voice sounded over the intercom.

She pocketed the keys, picked up her steno book, and knocked on the CO's door.

Lt. Babyk looked up from the papers on her desk and indicated for April to be seated.

"You had a busy night on the third. I've read your report and that of Lt. Barron. You are to be commended on the efficient way you handled a delicate, unpleasant situation. A copy of my letter of commendation will be placed in your 201 File."

"Thank you, Ma'am. Sgt. Levy was very helpful, too."

"Your orders have been cut for TDY." She handed her Special Order Number 161 along with a letter. "You'll be leaving on August 8th with eight other girls from the post. I am sure you are going to enjoy this assignment."

"I hope so, Ma'am."

Lt. Babyk nodded. "You'll be receiving a directive on what to take with you on TDY. That's all, PFC Terry."

She closed the door and turned to face a grinning Sgt. Levy.

"The lieutenant gave me a letter of commendation," she waved the papers in the air.

"I know," said Sgt. Levy. "I typed it."

"And a copy of my TDY orders. I leave in thirty days.

"Have you told PFC Montoya?"

"Not yet."

"Don't wait too long," warned Sgt. Levy.

"I'll tell him soon."

"Are you happy to be going?"

"I'm not sure. I dislike leaving the company short a cadre member."

"You're not to worry. I'll take over your duties, and a mail clerk replacement will be here before you leave."

"I hope so. I'm off to pick up our mail."

A quarter of an hour later, she pulled into the long line in front of the Mail Facility in back of the Post Office. The huge building was constructed of cinder blocks painted a pale yellow. An enormous open bay was sectioned and divided into what resembled a miniature of the mail slots in the mailroom for sorting letters. A steep concrete ramp ran the length of the bay beneath the long high counter. There were spaces for six vehicles at a time. Each driver backed into the appropriate opening and showed his or her mail card then signed off on a clipboard beside the company's name. The sack of out going mail was given to the worker and the mail for the company was put in the back of the jeep.

"You're new," said the tall, good-looking sergeant coming from behind the counter.

"PFC Terry from Company D," she said, removing her helmet and placing it on the seat. "I'm the temporary mail clerk until our company gets a replacement."

"Sgt. Banner," said the smiling soldier. "I'm in charge of the Post Mail Facilities. If you have any problems, let me know. What happened to Pvt. Wells—she get reassigned?"

"Medical discharge," she replied, without offering any further information.

He was not in green fatigues like the other workers, but wore a tailored Khaki uniform and his short light hair was the same shade as his clothes.

She replaced her helmet, drove down the ramp, out to the main road, and back to Company D.

Later in the afternoon Monty called and she agreed to go to the service club with him. They watched TV and played a game of pool before returning to sit on Company C's steps. He had told her that he wanted to talk and the club was too noisy. She was sure their brief stay was mainly because Cordero and Richard were also at the club and they appeared to be following them.

She had sensed he was nervous and tense when he forfeited their last game of pool by ramming the cue ball into a pocket.

"I was thinking of you the whole time I was in the field. I couldn't wait to get back to see you. Did you miss me, too?"

"It's only natural that you missed me. We've been spending a lot of time together," she said, trying to evade his question.

"Were you thinking of me, too?" he pressed.

"I enjoy your company but some days I was so busy I couldn't think of anything but my job," she said, honestly. Try as she might she could not deny the powerful attraction that existed between them, or prevent it.

"I don't know what's wrong with me. I think I must be falling in love with you," Monty said.

She remained silent for a moment for she had no idea how to handle her feelings for him. And that scared her because he threatened her emotions in ways no guy ever had before.

"You can't be," she said finally.

"Why not?"

"Because—"

"Give me a reason," Monty interrupted.

"We've only known each other a few short months. You're just lonely, that's all."

"I'm not lonely when I'm with you."

"Don't mistake that for love," she warned.

"I have tried to avoid you," he admitted, "to deny these feelings I have for you. When you get to know me better, you'll learn I don't act on impulse, especially about something as important as this." He took a shaky breath, and then said, "I do love you."

"I think perhaps that I'd better go in." She stood.

He rose to his full height, cupped her face between his large hands and kissed her. His lips were open and moist, but unlike the other times, his tongue touched hers. Just enough to make her breath catch in her throat and her heart beat erratically.

Shyly, she touched his tongue in return, and she was rewarded with the sharp sound of his indrawn breath. It was good to know that she wasn't the only one affected by their kiss. Heat exploded in her cheeks and she pulled away from him, hurried down the steps and through the front door of the building.

With his fingers linked together behind his head, Monty lay in his lumpy bunk and stared at the dark ceiling. He couldn't sleep. His thoughts strayed to April. Her image reached into his heart like a soft, sweet song. He wished he were better with English so he could express to her how he felt. He needed the words to tell her how much a part of him she had become.

He liked everything about her, her sweetness, her amazing personality, and he admired her spirit. She sparkled when she smiled; it was as if the sun came out from behind a cloud, so brilliant.

April had said what he felt was loneliness. That was all his attraction to her was—just loneliness. But he knew better. It was like an awakening inside him, as though he had never loved until now. She was the part of him that had been missing his entire adult life. His natural yearning for a compañero de alma—soul mate. A man's one and only love.

How could a woman he'd known for such a short time have become such a vital part of him? It seemed one day she was a girlfriend of someone else and the next she was the most important thing in his life.

God and His angels must be laughing now, but surely they had known what they were doing when they'd had him inducted into the military and sent to this post in Alabama.

That had only been the beginning. Since then he met and fell in love with a tiny WAC no taller than his shoulder, who neither understood his language, customs nor him, no more than he did hers.

Saturday, 06 July 1957
Dear Dreamcatcher,
    I decided not to see Monty tonight because I think it best if we stop seeing so much of each other. I think he was hurt because I couldn't return his sentiments about the way he had missed me. Also Monty mentioned that he was falling in love. That made me wary and uncomfortable. I am not ready for any kind of commitment. I tried to blame it on loneliness and the fact that we spent so much time together.
    Sgt. Levy and I went to the hospital to visit Peggy and baby Barbara. She was happy to see us. I don't think she is looking forward to going home and facing her parents...

Sunday, 07 July 1957
    After returning from chapel this morning, I asked the CQ to take messages, because I didn't want to talk to Monty. I guess it's cowardly of me trying to avoid telling him about my TDY.
    In the afternoon I went over the suggested list of clothing to take with me. Shorts and tops will be worn for rehearsals because it is extremely hot there. A few dresses if we plan to go out and for attending church. Also a swimsuit and appropriate clothes for horseback riding for those who are interested...

Thursday, 11 July 1957.
    Picking up the mail twice a day and making distribution plus my duties as Company Clerk have kept me going like a house on fire. I have been so busy that I have neglected writing in my journal.
    Since the first time I went to pick up the mail, and I met Sgt. Banner, he has come over to say hello while I waited for

my mail sack. Today, he personally brought out my mailbag and put it in my jeep. Then he asked me if I would have dinner with him this Saturday night at the NCO Club. It came as a total surprise. I declined, and said I was busy.

Monty called after chow in the evening. He asked if I was avoiding him. I reminded him that since Pvt. Wells left, I had two jobs. I said I was tired and I wanted to stay in my room and rest. Then he asked me to go to the Post Theater with him tomorrow night. I told him that I couldn't go because we had a platoon on KP and I had to take their mail to the mess hall. He was so sweet, saying that he wished he could come and help me. Before we finished talking, I relented and agreed to go to the movies on the condition that I would come straight back to my barracks. He said he didn't like having to wait until Saturday to see me, but there was nothing he could do about it…

April sensed there was something bothering Monty all through the movie. He barely laughed at the funny scenes, and he was quiet on the bus ride back to her barracks. He tucked her hand in the crook of his elbow as they walked from the bus stop toward her building.

"You didn't much like the film, did you?" she asked.

"It was all right." He shrugged. "I had something on my mind that I wanted to ask you."

They paused midway down the walk. Monty gazed down at her with sad brown eyes then threw back his head expelled a deep breath looking up at the dark sky.

"Do you want to stop seeing me?" he asked.

"Is there a reason that I should? Is that what you want?"

"No, but it seems like you don't care to go out with me anymore," he said.

"I'm not dating anyone else if that's what you mean."

They continued walking.

"I didn't think you were. It has been a whole week since I saw you."

"Now I have Duty NCO every eight days and one day on a weekend per month plus my new duty of Post Staff Driver once every thirty days. With my new responsibility of Company Mail Clerk and my regular duties, I don't have much free time."

"I didn't know—I thought the problem was me. If I could only take some of your work load."

"How sweet of you. Once we get the replacement for the mail clerk, it won't be so bad." She stopped as they had reached the short walkway that led to the front entrance and turned to face him. "I have to go in. Thanks for the movie and thank you for understanding."

"I don't want you to go in." He brought a finger under her chin, raising her face to his. He lowered his head, brushing her lips softly. His hand moved along her arm up to the nape of her neck and his fingers splayed in her hair. Then they were running lightly up and down her bare arms until the little bumps of pleasure trembled on her skin.

April leaned back effectively breaking his embrace, his broad chest heaving as she stepped away from him. For a moment she stood staring up at him. She met glowing dark eyes filled with emotions she had never seen in them before. A heat spread through her body that made her cheeks flush, and left her feeling as if she had run a race in hundred degree temperature, all breathless and weak-kneed.

"Good night, Monty." She turned, hurrying into the building and didn't stop until she reached her door.

Monday morning April picked up the jeep keys and left the Orderly Room. She met MSGT Craig in the corridor.

"PFC Terry, I'm glad I caught you before you left. I wanted to tell you about the two cadets that came in last night. They were put in the empty cadre room on the third floor, and they will be housed with us for the next eight weeks training for OCS. When our new mail clerk arrives, she will be sharing your quarters temporarily until they leave. Sorry about the inconvenience."

"Oh, that will be a problem where to put the rest of my civvies. I'm using three of the four lockers in my room."

"I'll have Sgt. Waite put an additional one in the room. You'll find a copy of the cadets' orders in your Inbox for the Morning Report."

"Thanks."

Ten minutes later, she expertly backed the jeep into an empty stall. She jumped out of the vehicle to face Sgt. Banner standing on the loading ramp, hands on his hips.

"How was your weekend?" asked the hazel-eyed sergeant.

"Good."

"There's a new show at the NCO Club on Thursday. How about going to dinner with me?"

"I have Duty NCO that night."

"Friday?"

"Huh-uh, I've got a date."

"I suppose you've got a date for Saturday, too?"

"Nope," she shook her head. "I'm the Post Staff Driver."

"What does a guy have to do—to get a date with you? What about Sunday?"

"Sorry, that's my day of rest. I'm pulling double duty until we get another mail clerk."

"When will that be?"

"In a couple of weeks."

"I had better work fast if I'm going to persuade you to go out with me," he quipped, smiling.

She left the mail facilities smiling, too.

> Saturday, 20 July 1957
> Dear Dreamcatcher,
> I had a pleasant day driving. In the afternoon I picked up one trainee from the Anniston Bus Depot. In the evening after chow, I had to drive a male major around the post. We made stops at the NCO Club, bowling alley, Post Theater and the Hilltop Service Club. It seems strange opening the car door for a man. But that goes with the job…

> Friday, 26 July 1957
> Monty was upset because he couldn't see me all week. His company is on night maneuvers and he is not free until tomorrow. This meant I get an extended reprieve on telling him about my TDY.
> Sgt. Banner hasn't given up asking me for a date. I had come to the conclusion that there must be something wrong with him. Such a good-looking guy and he doesn't have a girlfriend. I finally asked him and he told me that he had been seeing a WAC and she was transferred to Ft. Lee, Virginia. I guess he is normal after all…

Saturday evening at the Hilltop Club while the band took a break, as usual, she and Monty took their sodas out to the patio. For once her *shadows* were not in attendance.

She took a sip of the grape drink and set the bottle on the small table. She placed her hand over his.

"Monty, there is something I have to tell you. Like a coward, I've been putting it off. I would have told you earlier this week but you weren't available. It's not something I could tell you over the phone."

"If it's something bad," his hand stiffened beneath her palm and he shut his eyes for a moment. "I don't think I want to know."

"You might think so. I won't be able to see you for a while. Forty-five days to be exact."

"Don't tell me that." Anger flashed in his eyes.

"It's true. I'm going to Ft. McPherson on TDY for forty-five days. I leave in two weeks."

The violence with which Monty arose startled her. He leaped up, knocking over his soda. She grabbed for the bottle and righted it but not before it splashed the contents across the tabletop.

"You can't." He stood with his hands fisted on his hips watching her sop up the liquid with paper napkins.

"I'm on Special Orders. I don't have a choice."

"If you wanted to stop seeing me, all you had to do was tell me. You needn't have gone to such lengths."

"I don't follow what you are saying. And if it's what I'm thinking. It's best that I don't."

"How long have you known about this TDY?"

"Awhile."

"Just how long is *awhile*? One week—three weeks—a month—or two months?"

"I don't like your attitude. This is not something I have any control over."

"I'll make it easy for you. After tonight, I won't bother you anymore."

"If that's the way you feel. That's just fine with me," she answered in a voice to match his.

Without another word, he turned with military precision and stalked from the table. After his broad shoulders disappeared through the swinging doors of the soda bar, she sat back down and finished her drink. She had never expected him to react like that to her news.

Before leaving the patio, she returned the two empty bottles to the refreshment stand and went to the ladies room. She walked slowly back to her barracks her thoughts on Monty's reaction to her up coming TDY.

She marched up to the CQ desk and read the trainee's nametag.

"Pvt. Adams, I'm PFC Terry, if anyone other than a member of my family calls, take a message. I'm not taking any calls for the rest of the evening."

After her shower she opened her door, lying on the tile were three messages from Monty.

"I'm not calling him back," she said. "Let him cool his heels for awhile."

> Wednesday, 31 July 1957
> Dear Dreamcatcher,
> Monty hasn't phoned since leaving the messages on Saturday night. I guess he meant what he said about not *bothering* me again. Perhaps it is for the best. He didn't belong in my life anymore than I did in his.
> Sgt. Banner asked me for a date. I was almost tempted to accept, but I don't need another problem...

April finished typing the Duty Roster, and then underlined her name next to August 2nd. She covered her typewriter before getting up to post the notice on the bulletin board.

"Are you going out tonight?" asked Sgt. Levy.

"No. I'm cleaning my room before the new mail clerk arrives tomorrow."

The phone rang.

"Company D, Sgt. Levy speaking." There was a pause. "Please hold." She pressed a button on the base of the phone. "PFC Montoya for you." She raised her eyebrows.

"Sure."

"See you in the morning." Sgt. Levy retrieved her cap and left the room.

She sat down before picking up the handset and punched the hold button to release the call.

"PFC Terry speaking."

"I thought you weren't taking any calls except from your family," said Monty's familiar voice.

"That was only for Saturday evening."

"You never returned any of my calls. I called three times."

"I know."

"I regret the way I acted. I'm sorry, please forgive me. I want to see you tonight and apologize properly."

"I can't go out this evening. I'm getting my room ready for the new mail clerk."

"When can I see you?"

"How about Friday?"

"I have CQ Duty tomorrow. Can I see you on Saturday?" he asked

"Sorry, I'm on Duty NCO."

"What about Sunday?"

"Okay, you could meet me here after church and go to lunch with me in my mess hall."

"How about if I come over after lunch?"

"Are you afraid of a few hundred girls?"

"What time do you return from church?"

"At noon, just in time for chow."

"I'll be there at twelve sharp," Monty said, and hung up the phone.

The following morning, April entered the Orderly Room and placed a tray of Danish on Sgt. Levy's desk.

An attractive black girl in dress uniform sat next to MSGT Craig's desk, her feet crossed at the ankles.

"Here she is now," said the first sergeant. MSGT Craig got up and walked around her desk.

The private rose, uncoiling herself with an elegant movement. She stood a head above MSGT Craig. Tall and willowy she smiled showing even white teeth.

"PFC Terry, this is our new mail clerk, Pvt. Saymone Black, recently graduated from Clerical School."

"Welcome to Company D," April said, extending her hand.

"Thanks," said Pvt. Black. Her hand was cold.

"You go ahead and pick up the mail and I'll get her squared away as soon as Sgt. Waite returns from mess. After you finish with the mail shoot Pvt. Black over to the Motor Pool and get her a military license."

She picked the jeep keys off the board and put on her cap. "I'll be back soon."

April met Sgt. Levy in the hallway outside the door. "Morning, Sgt. Levy. I left some pastries on your desk. The new mail clerk is here."

"Is she nice?"

"Just like her name."

"What?" Her dark eyebrows came together in a frown.

"I'm late—see you later."

She dashed down the steps to the mailroom, unlocked the door, grabbed the outgoing mail sack, and slung it over her shoulder.

226

As she drove to the mail facility, she recalled the First Sergeant's expression when she introduced her to Pvt. Black. She hadn't sounded too pleased with her. Was she prejudiced because of the girl's color? If that were the case then how would she handle it?

GI brush and GI comb,
Gee I wish I was home.

Chapter 26

April backed the jeep into the Company D lot, hopped out and grabbed the light mail pouch. She slung it over her shoulder and hurried into the building, going directly down to the mailroom.

Pvt. Black was standing at the supply counter talking with Sgt. Waite. The mail clerk wore a set of new fatigues and carried a helmet.

"You better have a letter for me in that sack," called Sgt. Waite.

"I wouldn't count on it. There's not much in the bag." She demonstrated, holding up the almost flat pouch.

After she unlocked the door to the mailroom, she stepped back and let Pvt. Black enter.

"This is your domain, not very big is it?"

"It sure is small," agreed the private, turning around in a little circle.

"Look at it this way. It'll be less to clean." She took a key from a peg on the wall. "The key for the mail bag is kept here. Always put it back after unlocking the sack." She dumped the mail in a shallow carton on the desk. "Not much mail this morning, it will be twice this amount in the afternoon. Here is the way I sort the mail. Pick up a handful of letters and shove then in the proper pigeonholes in alphabetical order. X, Y and Z share the same space. Over there on the bulletin board is a list of all the girls in the company with their service numbers. Once in awhile you'll come across a name you can't read. You have to check the serial number to find out to whom the letter is addressed. Familiarize yourself with the list of names. You'll also find some mail for girls that have transferred. Those are in the green file box on the desk. As the trainees leave the company after graduation, you have to make up a little card for each one and file it in the box. Oh, here's one that's at Clerical School." She picked up a half-red and half-blue pencil. "With this colored pencil line through the address using the red part like this," she demonstrated. "Then print the new address below with the blue end of the pencil."

"What if the name is not on the list or in the file box?"

"Good question. You line through company D in red and print in blue *not at this company* and put it back in the mail pouch with the outgoing letters."

"Now that we've alphabetized all the mail. I start with A and group all the letters for each name. If there is two or more for the same person I put one of these rubber bands around them." She handed a few bands to Pvt. Black.

"If anyone mails a package, you have to weigh it on the scale on the work table. The postage rates are posted above it on the bulletin board. So far they only receive packages. I haven't had to send out any." She moved to the small barred window and pulled open a small drawer beneath the shelf. "This is where the stamps and money is kept. You order stamps each Monday. I'll show you how to do that later. Bring the letter for Sgt. Waite and your helmet. We are going to the Motor Pool for your military license. You do drive, don't you?"

"For about five years."

"You won't have any problem. All they do is give you a driving test around the area to familiarize you with the post regulations and speed limit."

April drove forward onto 6th Avenue. "It's just a few blocks from here." She hung a right on 10th Street and drove one long block before making a left on 7th Avenue. "Here we are," she said, parking the jeep and hopping out. "That's Sgt. Kerbeck coming toward us. He's in charge of the Motor Pool."

"I see you finally got your replacement," said the ruddy-faced sergeant coming to a halt beside the vehicle.

"Sgt. Kerbeck—Pvt. Black." They exchanged greetings without shaking hands.

"Pvt. Black needs a military license."

"You come to the right place. Cpl. Owens is out giving a test now. Come on to my office and I'll start the paperwork."

Forty-five minutes later April handed the jeep keys to Pvt. Black. "Bessie's all yours."

"Bessie?"

"That's what I call the jeep…it's a habit. I name all the vehicles I drive."

"Bessie. I can live with that. Say what time is mail call?"

April glanced at her watch. "In fifteen minutes. We gotta hustle."

"How do we manage with a speed limit of twenty-five miles per hour?"

"I'll race you to the jeep," said April.

Out of breath with five minutes to spare, April stopped at the CQ desk, flipped on the switches of the PA system.

"Your attention, please. Mail call," she said, loudly as Pvt. Black came through the front door huffing and panting.

"Girl, you sure can run."

"I got a head start, I hopped out before you backed the jeep in. Go down and bring up the mail tray."

"I hope I can pronounce all the names," responded Pvt. Black.

"You'll do okay. After you give out the mail come down to the mail room in case some of them want to purchase stamps."

Thirty minutes later she closed the mail window and turned to Pvt. Black. "Well, how was it? Any questions?"

"It's a lot to remember. What happens if it rains?"

"If it's raining mail call is held in the Day Room. In a few days, it'll be like second nature to you. Let's go eat."

"I have to go up to my room—our room and get my hat. I don't want to wear this helmet to chow," said Pvt. Black, removing her steel shell.

"My garrison cap is on my desk. I'll wait for you in the office, and we can walk together."

Over lunch, she told Pvt. Black about her upcoming TDY assignment.

"I heard about it. I'd give my eyeteeth to go. I'm a jazz and impressionistic dancer."

"Yeah, you would have fit right in. I'm not a professional, I just love to dance."

"Tomorrow night, I'm performing a number in the Third Army Variety show at the service club. After chow I'm going up to the club to rehearse. Wanta come watch?"

"Sorry, I can't. I'm the Duty NCO tonight. I wasn't going to the show because the guy I'm dating is on CQ Duty. But since you're in the program, I'll be sure and see it."

"Oh, you have a boyfriend on post?"

"Nothing serious, just good friends." She placed the utensils on the empty tray and scooted back her chair from the table at the same time as Pvt. Black.

"Tell me about our first sergeant. Is she as tough as she looks? It appears her face would crack if she smiled," asked Pvt. Black as they crossed Galloway Road.

"I wouldn't say she is all that cut and dried. You've seen the stuffed animal collection on my bed. Recently I forgot to remove them for a Saturday inspection. That's one of the rules, nothing on the bed except what belongs there when we have inspection. She told me the lieutenant thought they were cute. I apologized and said it wouldn't happen again. I braced myself for a *chewing out*. All she said was to be more careful in the future. After that, she asked me to feed her puppy, Nicky while she was away one weekend."

"Are we allowed to have a pet in our room?"

"No," she said, laughing. "Don't I wish? There is a kennel over by the band building. MSGT Craig brought Nicky to the office a couple of times when she first got the black cocker spaniel."

She opened the glass door and held it for Pvt. Black. "I see my CQ and Runner are here for instructions," she said, nodding toward the two recruits in PT dresses behind the CQ counter.

"Do you mind if I observe since this is something I will be doing?"

"In eight days to be exact."

"Oh, brother." Pvt. Black rolled her eyes.

The private stood by and listened intensely as April went over the information with the two trainees. After she finished speaking to the girls, they left the CQ area and walked down the hall to the staircase.

"Any questions?" she asked.

"Not about the duty. Is it true the mail clerk that I am replacing gave birth to a baby in her room?"

"I have been encouraged by *the powers that be* not to discuss it." She made a motion with her fingers that resembled quotation marks. "It's true. I was on duty that night. That's all I'm allowed to say."

"I understand. What do I do now?"

"Until 1400 hours, it's your own time. That's the time we go pick up mail. I'll be going with you and show you the procedure at the mail facility."

The following evening, April adjusted her crinoline and smoothed down the yellow skirt of her dress.

"That's a pretty outfit. I see you have a sewing machine. Did you make your dress?" asked Pvt. Black

"Yes, I did. The machine belongs to the company. If you want to use it—help yourself."

"Thanks. I make my own costumes. What little there is of them," said Saymone, laughing. She opened her locker, pulled out a skimpy white garment, and held it up. It was made of jersey, straight lined without a waist, the short skirt flared at the hem. A pair of black leotards was clipped to the hanger. "I call it my Greek creation," she said, showing her how it fastened on one shoulder with a single gold leaf. "This is what I'm wearing tonight for my dance number. Wanta walk up with me?"

"Sure, I'm ready when you are."

"I just have to get my shoe bag." Pvt. Black removed a black, leather tote bag from her footlocker and picked up her outfit on the hanger.

April held the door and turned the thumb bolt in the doorknob so it snapped closed locking the door behind them.

They entered the club and went straight to the ballroom. It was dark.

"We are early," said Saymone. "I have to go practice before the show." She turned to walk up the stairs to the stage.

"Oh, dang it," she said, pausing and turning around. "I forgot my key."

"That's okay. I'll wait for you at the soda counter after the show is over. We can walk back together unless you were going someplace later."

"No—that's good," Saymone said, continuing up the steps. "Be sure to get a good seat," she called over her shoulder.

She left the ballroom and strolled down the hall to the equipment counter.

"What are you doing here? Isn't Montoya on duty?" asked CQ.

"Yes, he is. I came to see the show. Our new mail clerk is going to dance. Anyone from your company in the show?"

"Nah."

She glanced at her watch. "I'd better go if I want to get a good table."

"I just might close up and see the show, too."

"You should," she said, and walked away.

She found a vacant table near the side of the stage and sat down. In a matter of minutes the room filled. The curtain opened and the WAC Band began the show with the "Star Spangled Banner."

Just as she sat back down, CQ walked up to the table. "Mind if I sit with you?"

"Not at all," she said, indicating a vacant seat.

He moved the chair over next to hers facing the stage and sat down.

As the overhead lights started dimming, she glanced over at the doorway. Cordero filled the entrance. He leaned against the doorframe, frowning intently, staring in her direction. Her eyes roamed the room for Richard, but she didn't spot him. The lights went out and the show started.

A guy dressed in a red and blue clown outfit juggled balls, hoops and some shapes like bowling pens while riding a unicycle. After the juggler a black trio called the "Dewdrops," two guys and a gal, crooned their rendition of "Too Young." The next contestant was a Spanish guy that sat on a stool and played his guitar while he sang "*Malagueña.*"

When the applause ceased, she whispered, "Do you know him?"

232

"Nah, I think he's from the MP School."

"Maybe you could recruit him to sing with the Spanish Band."

CQ shrugged without replying.

"Saymone Black with her interpretation of 'Who Cares,'" announced the MC.

The piece was best described as mood-music more romantic than jazzy. The dance ended with Saymone doing a slow motion split with her torso bowed over one outstretched leg.

"What did you think?" she asked above the applause.

"Interesting," replied CQ, "but I prefer to watch a couple dancing."

Several more entertainers presented their talent until the last one had been seen. At the conclusion of the program, the overhead lights came on.

"I'm leaving." CQ stood and placed his chair under the table. "Can I give you a lift to your barracks?"

"Thanks, but I promised to wait for Pvt. Black at the soda fountain and walk back with her."

"I could drive you both."

"It's a nice night for walking."

"I'll accompany you to the refreshment counter."

CQ must have seen Cordero watching them sitting together at the table, and he was playing Sir Galahad again. At the entrance to the soda bar he bade her good night.

She waited in line for a soda and took a seat near the door where she could watch for Saymone.

Cordero entered, went to the counter and ordered a drink. He carried it across the room where he sat at a table with a direct view of her. April got up, walked over to the jukebox, and then returned to sit in the opposite chair putting her back to Cordero and the door. She wondered where Richard was as those two were like a pair of bookends.

Saymone appeared in front of her carrying her costume over her arm with a leather bag slung over one shoulder.

"How did you like the show?"

"Great. You are very talented. Would you like something to drink before we leave?"

"No thanks. I just want to get home—to the barracks and a hot shower."

"Let's go," she said, picking up her handbag from the table. She avoided looking in Cordero's direction as they filed out of the room.

They reached the end of the long covered porch to the entrance and she glanced back at the double doors of the club. Behind them, Cordero pushed through the set of glass doors.

"Do you know that guy?" asked Saymone, looking over her shoulder. "I'm sure he followed us from the soda fountain."

"I know him," she said. "Let's cut through the parking lot to the sidewalk below. It's shorter."

Cordero trailed them at a distance down the hill. After they reached the last set of steps, she stopped, turned and glanced back. He had paused to light a cigarette. Cordero held a match to the tip and stared straight at her over the flame as it illuminated the blackness. A moment later the aroma of tobacco stung the night air. He stood in the dark shadows, like a ghost, with only the red flare of the cigarette revealing his location before he turned and climbed the steps leading back to the service club.

She walked ahead of Pvt. Black through the front entrance, stopped at the CQ desk, signed in and continued up to the second floor to unlock their door.

"What was that all about?" asked Saymone, closing the door.

"It's a long story that I don't talk about." She undressed leaving on her bra and panties and slipped on her robe. Before leaving the room, she hung her dress and crinolines in her civvies locker.

Pvt. Black entered the latrine while April was brushing her teeth and stepped into the stall next to the door. At the end of the room, she chose a shower and turned on the water full force, effectively covering the sound of her weeping. She lingered until she was sure Saymone had returned to their room before leaving the latrine.

The light was out in their room and the illumination from the hall disclosed the other girl in her bunk.

April closed the door and made her way to bed in the dark.

Why did she still allow Cordero to affect her that way?

> Sunday, 04 August 1957
> Dear Dreamcatcher,
> Today was the last day I could see Monty before I leave on TDY because he has classes on Monday and I am Duty NCO on Wednesday. I promised to spend the day with him. After lunch we rode the bus to Post to Headquarters to take some more pictures.
> Monty consented to eat lunch and dinner with me in my mess hall without any persuasion on my part. He is getting

234

accustomed to the girls whistling at him. But the tops of his ears still turn red as a beet when they show their appreciation.

After chow, we walked to the service club and Monty played the piano for me along with a lot of other request for the guys and gals sitting in the music room.

At 2200 hours we strolled down to sit on our favorite steps. He confessed that he loved me, and I couldn't answer when he asked me if I loved him, too. He said he would write me every day while I was away.

He said good night with the sweetest kisses that he has ever given me...

Monday, 05 August 1957
Everything went smoothly with the mail. Pvt. Black is doing a swell job. She told me Mark Banner had asked about me when she went to pick up the mail.

Monty called tonight before he went to his classes. Again, he told me that he loved me. He asked me if I didn't love him, too. I still couldn't answer him...

Tuesday, 06 August 1957
Monty called and we talked for a long time. He told me how much I meant to him and how he was going to hate this post without me...

After chow on Wednesday evening, Pvt. Black entered the building in front of April. She stopped at the CQ desk.

"Any messages?" Saymone asked Pvt. Travis.

"Sorry," the trainee said, shaking her head.

"PFC Terry, a PFC Montoya has called three times. He didn't leave any message."

"I may as well stay down here," she said. "He'll call back,"

"Why don't you call him?" inquired Pvt. Black.

"That would be against my principles."

Saymone pursed her thick lips and raised her penciled eyebrows.

The phone rang.

"Company D, Pvt. Travis speaking. It's for you," the CQ said, handing April the receiver.

"Hi. Let me put you on hold. I want to take your call in my office." She punched the hold button before returning the receiver to the cradle.

Pvt. Black left the CQ area with her.

"Aren't you going out?" she asked, pausing in the corridor.

"Nope. I wanta get a plenty of rest. I'm on Duty NCO for the first time tomorrow night. See you later," said Saymone, turning in the direction of the staircase.

April hurried into the office and picked up the phone on her desk before switching on the lights.

"Monty, I'm sorry that I took so long."

"I was wondering if you had forgot about me."

"I was talking to our mail clerk, Pvt. Black. Tomorrow, she's pulling her first Duty NCO."

"Is she nice?"

"She's okay. She wishes she was going to Ft. McPherson on TDY."

"So do I, but I wish she was going in your place."

"I'll be back before you know it."

"I don't know how I'm going to stand being on this post without you."

"You can go to the movies, play the piano at the service club—"

"It won't be the same without you."

"What about the letters you said you would write me? You can write them at the service club."

"Will you write me everyday?"

"I promise to write as often as I can."

"You know I love you. Do you love me?"

She remained silent, unable to answer him.

"Monty, I have to hang up. It's almost time for the Duty Officer to make her rounds."

"April, please stay true to me. Don't break my heart." Monty's voice sounded husky.

"Forty-five days is not so long. I'll be back before you miss me."

"That wouldn't be possible," he said quietly. "I miss you already."

She closed her eyes against the sudden hot sting of tears and swallowed with difficulty caused by the dryness in her throat.

"Good-bye, Monty. I'll miss you." She answered in a strangled voice.

She drew the phone from her ear, holding it to her chest for a moment. Her eyes squeezed closed, and she struggled to make sense of her feelings and the tears running down her cheeks.

She did care for him. It may not be the way he loved her. She was afraid of being hurt again, and neither did she want to hurt Monty.

April pulled a handful of tissues from the box on her desk. It wouldn't do for the Duty Officer to see her crying. She waited in the Orderly Room until the officer came and departed before going to her room.

"Is everything okay?" asked Pvt. Black, as she closed the door.

"I just told the guy that I've been dating good-bye on the phone. It was more difficult than I had anticipated."

"Was that the same guy that followed us to our barracks the night of the show?"

"No. That's someone else."

"Why was he following you?"

"I don't know. He's been following me ever since I stopped seeing him. He even follows me when I'm with, Monty, the guy I've been dating."

"What does Monty think about it?"

"Mostly he ignores him. They are in the same company, and they previously played together in the Spanish Band." She briefly relayed the incident concerning Reynaldo's ring.

"You're not afraid of him after what he did?" asked Pvt. Black.

"No. But I am concerned that he and Monty may get into a fight. The guy carries a switchblade."

"He sounds dangerous to me. I think it's a good thing you are leaving the post for awhile."

"I'm inclined to agree with you."

I don't know but I've been told,
While goin' through the chow line,
Don't take more than your belly can hold.

Chapter 27

Thursday, 08 August 1957
Dear Dreamcatcher,
I was the last passenger picked up by the bus before it left the post at 1530 hours. Our driver, Ken, kept us laughing and singing enroot to Ft. McPherson. We made one restroom stop along the route, arriving just in time for chow. The post is small compared to Ft. McClellan. The women's barracks are made of wood and ancient but with a fresh coat of paint.

We are not in a bay, but a large room that accommodates twelve. The bunks are wood and stacked three high attached to the wall. My bed is on the top. I have to climb a ladder to my bed. I'm thankful it's equipped with a guardrail.

I was told to report to the motor pool in the morning to pick up a vehicle for transporting the girls and myself to and from Chastain Park...

Friday, 09 August 1957
I was assigned a '57, nine passenger Ford station wagon. I get to drive as long as I'm here.

It was a forty-five minute drive to Chastain Amphitheater. The enormous theater seats two thousand people. I had some difficulty finding my way because Peachtree Street branches out in three directions.

In the afternoon we were measured for our costumes and shoes. After evening chow everyone got together at the NCO Club to meet the cast and the Production Staff of approximately one hundred and fifty persons. Each of us was given a rehearsal schedule.

Because of the heat, most of the time we will be using the air-conditioned NCO Club.

Our first rehearsal is on Saturday at 1300 hours. We were informed that we might stay as late as 2300 hours and we would be eating at the club on the nights we practiced there...

The following morning, April quietly left her bunk. Since all the other occupants were sleeping, she carried her clothing to dress in the latrine. After returning from the mess hall, she went to the Day Room and finished a letter to Monty that she had began several days ago. It had been four days and he would surely be upset at not hearing from her. After dropping the letter in the mail slot, she set out on foot to explore the post.

The small post chapel sandwiched Troop Row, where she was quartered in the WAC Detachment, between it and the HQ building. She strolled toward the distinctive horseshoe shaped structure of the Third Army Headquarters. In the center of the U shaped walk stood a tall flagpole. Beyond the pole was the main guard gate. Off Wetzel Drive, she came to a pool and sat in one of the patio chairs beneath a large, yellow umbrella.

"Put on a suit and come on in, the water's great," said a deep masculine voice from behind her. In the pool was one of the guys that she met at the NCO Club the night before. He swam over to the area where she sat, put a hand on the pool rim and vaulted onto the cement.

"I don't swim," she replied; gazing up at the tall, wet blond-haired man.

"Bob Nathan from Oklahoma." He stuck out a dripping hand, grinned apologetically and quickly let it fall at his side.

"April Terry, Kentucky," she said, suppressing a giggle.

"Kentucky," Bob repeated. "Then you must like horses."

"Yes, very much."

"Have you seen the stables next to the amphitheater?"

"No, but I heard about them. We were told to bring riding gear if we were interested."

"I often ride there when I'm not playing my trumpet with the band." He paused running his hand through his wet hair. "How about going horseback riding with me before our rehearsal this afternoon?"

"I can't. A station wagon was assigned to me as the driver for the girls in the chorus line."

"What about going tomorrow? Everyone will be in the park for the cook out."

"I do plan to ride tomorrow, but I can't go with you. I'm dating a guy back at Ft. McClellan."

"I understand. I didn't mean to come on so strong. While riding, I like company. Any objections if we meet at the stable and ride together?" He grinned down at her.

"I guess that would be okay."

"See you later," he said, before entering the pool. April watched him swim to the deep end and make a couple of spectacular dives from the diving board.

That afternoon, the rehearsals began with the Carnival scene. April danced with the chorus line in the *Girly Sideshow*. At 1800 hours, a break was called for the dinner served by the NCO Club kitchen staff. After chow, the rehearsals resumed. She returned to her quarters at 2300 hours.

Early the following morning, she climbed down from her bunk and slipped her feet into her sneakers. The room was dark with very little light coming in around the lowered shades. She stumbled over several shoes before reaching the entrance and engaging the automatic door holder. With the dim light from the hall, she managed to locate her locker, and she fumbled around for her shoes. Beige pumps were exchanged for her sneakers. She selected one of the three outfits she brought for church, a peach floral print with a solid peach jacket. From the top shelf, she pulled down her ditty bag and quietly went out, closing the door behind her.

After breakfast, she returned to her quarters to find the rest of the girls just getting up. She took her stationery box and went to the Day Room. She finished a letter to Monty and dropped it down the mail chute before going to church. At the conclusion of the sermon, she rushed back to her quarters and changed into her riding clothes. She threw a pair of black shorts, a sleeveless leopard print blouse and her sneakers into her beach bag.

The rest of the group dressed in shorts and sneakers milled about the room.

"Hey, Terry," called Trask, "aren't you going to wear shorts?"

"Got them right here," she said, holding up her red bag. "I'm going horseback riding."

"What time are we leaving?" asked Bryza.

"At 1300 hours, we are to be at the Wetzel parking lot ready to go. We better get a move on. It's a quarter of now."

An hour later, April pulled into the park behind the military bus carrying the members of the Third Army Band.

"If any of you guys hitch a ride back to the post with anyone let me know before time to leave, okay? This vehicle departs at 1900 hours."

They agreed with various acknowledgements.

Nathan was waiting at the stables talking with a balding, white haired man with more fuzz on his face than his head. He introduced her to Stanley, the stable hand, who had to be at least seventy-five years old.

"Come on," said Nathan, "let's go pick out a mount for you. I'm familiar with all the horses. Most of them are sweet natured, not a mean one in the bunch."

As they walked down the aisle between the stalls, the horses hanging their heads over the Dutch doors welcomed them with whinnies and nickers. She stopped in front of a sorrel with a white streak down the face.

"What about this one?" she asked.

"Blaze is a real sweetheart. You'll like him," replied Nathan. "Mickey is my mount in the next stall. I ride him regularly." He walked up and scratched the big bay behind the ears.

Fifteen minutes later, they rode out of the paddock together. The bridle path was lined on each side with shady oak trees, providing them with a pleasant, cool thoroughfare.

With a light tap, she sent Blaze into a trot. Nathan matched her pace, and she encouraged Blaze to canter.

She laughed as Nathan passed her. She'd seen his quick grin of challenge and answered it by urging Blaze into a full gallop. Her mount was no match for Mickey. On a rise Nathan pulled up, and he turned to wait for her.

They exchanged stories as they walked their horses back toward the stable. Nathan told her about his youth on a ranch in Oklahoma. April shared her life on a farm with narratives about the broncos that her brothers had tamed and broke in their teens.

As soon as she left the livery, she went to change her clothing in the restroom beneath the amphitheater. After tying her hair back with a white scarf, she washed off the dust along with her makeup. She shrugged at her reflection in the mirror. She had forgotten to bring her lipstick. Oh, well, at least her face was clean.

She climbed the ramp to the stage with a few muscles objecting to her horseback ride.

At one end of the mammoth stage, the mess staff had set up grills and tables with food. Across from the barbecue facilities, a dark skinned guy painted on a large piece of scenery. She ambled over to get a better look at the painting. It appeared to be a lot of trees with cherry blossoms. The tall, black haired artist dressed in khaki shorts and paint splattered T-shirt dabbed pink petals on the trees.

"Hi," she said. "Those are pretty cherry blossoms."

"Thanks," he said. He glanced over his shoulder briefly at her and went back to painting.

"Whose kid are you?" He spoke with a heavy Spanish accent.

"I beg your pardon?"

He turned and faced her. His eyes were black and mischievous like CQ's. "Aren't you one of the kids in cast of the German Townspeople and Paris scenes?"

"Nooo." She drew out the word slowly. "I'm one of the dancers in the chorus line."

"Don't tell me you're a WAC. You're too young." He looked her up and down before his eyes locked with hers. "How old are you?"

"I don't usually discuss my age with strangers, but since you asked—twenty-one this past April."

"Coulda fooled me, Niña," he said, sticking the long handled brush behind his ear. "I woulda said you were about thirteen—fifteen at the most." He grinned, showing even white teeth.

"I was horseback riding—I washed off my makeup with the dirt," she said, making a useless gesture with her hand.

"Alexander Ayaso. My friends call me Alex," he said, extending his paint-splotched hand. "Please excuse the paint."

"April Terry," she replied, accepting his pinked hand. "I don't mind the paint. I want to study art after I my ETS."

"Have you ever painted with acrylics?"

"Only with oils," she answered, shaking her head.

"This is much faster. You don't have a long wait for the paint to dry. The best part is that it cleans up with soap and water."

"It doesn't smell either," she said, taking a deep breath through her nose.

"Here, show me what you can do." He gave her the brush from behind his ear and handed her his palette containing a large glob of pink paint and a smaller one of white.

She painted on several pink blossoms before Alex handed her another brush.

"This one's for the highlights," he said

She lightly touched the tip of the brush to the edges of the petals and then she stood back to admire her work.

"They look better than mine," Alex declared.

"That's because my favorite song is 'Cherry Pink and Apple Blossom White,'" she quipped, and was rewarded by his deep chuckle. She laughed along with him.

"How would you like to help me paint the scenery?"

"I would love it, but I have rehearsals."

"I meant on your free time in the mornings."

"I don't think I could. I'm the driver for eight of the girls in the chorus."

"What if I cleared it with Hickey? Would you help me paint?"

"Who is Hickey?"

"The Post Commander, Lieutenant General Thomas Hickey."

"Oh," she said. "That *Hickey.*"

"What do you say?"

"Sure. Why not?"

A loud clanging drew her attention across the stage to a short guy in white wearing a gob hat whacking on a large triangle.

"Come and get it," he shouted.

"Time for chow, Niña. Let's get washed up," said Alex, striding toward the restrooms.

After Alex filled his plate he sat at her table.

"I had an assistant assigned to do this job with me but he got into a car accident. By the time paperwork goes through the chain of command for a new one, the show will be over."

"Ayaso, that's Spanish?" She surprised herself by saying her thoughts out loud.

"Mexican," Alex clarified. "I was born in El Paso, Texas. My parents were *wetbacks.* I hope that doesn't make a difference in your working with me?"

"Of course not. At my post, I date a fellow from South America. I had a friend named Cordero from Puerto Rico."

"You said *had*—did the lamb turn out to be a wolf in sheep's clothing?"

"You might say that. Let's just put it down as a bad experience and leave it at that."

"Sure. Tell me about the fellow from South America?"

"His name is Alberto Montoya. I was helping him with his English and one thing led to another." She shrugged. "He says that he's in love with me."

"How do you feel about him?"

"I'm not sure as I've never been in love. I don't think I know the meaning of the word."

"Love is wanting to be with that one special person all the time. And when you are away from each other it tears you apart. You desire to spend every waking moment with her."

"Terry," said Judith, pausing at their table. "I won't be riding back to the post with you tonight."

"Okay. Have you met Alex? He's the artist designing the scenery." She introduced them and they exchanged greetings.

"See you at the barracks," said Judith, walking away.

"I still have an hour and a half before I leave to go back to the post. We could do some more painting," she suggested.

"You haven't eaten anything." Alex indicated her full plate.

"I'm not hungry. I don't eat much."

"Then you must be in love." Alex grinned and winked at her.

"I'd rather paint than eat," she said.

Alex stood, picked up her full plate, sat it in his empty one, and placed them in the garbage.

The next day after breakfast, April drove to Chastain Park. Alex was at work on another backdrop, a large cathedral for the Paris street scene.

She finished painting the cherry blossoms in silence. She found her thoughts straying to Monty. Maybe she was in love with him?

"You are too quiet," said Alex.

"That's because I can't paint and talk at the same time."

"How long can you stay?"

"I have to leave by 1100 hours. We are rehearsing the Carnival scene starting at 1330 hours at the NCO Club until who knows when?"

It was well past midnight when she returned to her quarters.

> Monday, 12 August 1957
> Dear Dreamcatcher,
>
> What a blue Monday. I still have not received a letter from Monty.
>
> I helped Alex finish the painting of the cathedral this morning. He insists on calling me Niña because he first thought I was one of the children in the cast.
>
> In the afternoon I collected the girls and we went to the NCO club to rehearse...

Tuesday, 13 August 1957

After breakfast I went to the park to paint with Alex. We worked on the backdrop for a Paris café, until I had to return to the post. I drove the girls to the NCO Club for the costume fittings of the German Octoberfest.

We didn't have rehearsals until 1700 hours and we all went to the pool. I put on lotion and sunbathed beside the pool. We finished rehearsing the Carnival Scene where Glen, the strong man, picks me up above his head and spins me in the air. The first time, I was so startled that I shrieked. The director didn't like it and he had Glen pick me up several times.

Glen's wife was there and she told me not to worry that he had never dropped anyone.

I have been writing in the Day Room. There are four phone booths and only one is in use. If I had change I would call Monty. I just want to hear his voice. If I don't get a letter tomorrow, I'll call him in the evening. While I was painting I was thinking of him, and he has been on my mind the entire day. And again tonight during rehearsals, I was wondering what he was doing and if he thinks of me...

In the evening she returned from the park to find a welcoming letter on her bunk. She quickly opened it and began to read.

Fort McClellan, Alabama
August 13, 1957
Darling,

You don't know how happy I was today with your letter that I've been awaiting since the day you left.

There is one thing I didn't like, and that is the time that you took to drop the letter into the mailbox from the time it was written.

Since the day you left 'til now, I have had a terrible time. Like yesterday when I was hoping to get your letter.

Well, your dearest letter finally arrived today and it tells me how hard you are working in the show.

Around here things goes the same but I miss you, and I can't help feeling blue and wanting to see you.

245

Darling, please be careful in climbing up to your bunk. You are so tiny to be going up so high, and I don't want you to get hurt.

Tell me, April; do you miss me when you go to the pool? I hope you won't let somebody else take my place neither at the NCO Club nor at the movies. If you do, you are hurting someone that loves you like no one else could ever love you in this world.

Since you've gone, I've not been swimming because I couldn't stand to be there without you.

Please, come back soon. Meanwhile, take care of yourself.

Loving you always,
Monty.

She read the letter twice before putting it away inside her journal.

Wednesday, 14 August 1957
Dear Dreamcatcher,
We finally finished rehearsing the German Scene. If I never dance another Polka, it will be fine with me. The scene opens with a village square that has a bandstand in the center. PFC Lehman is the Burgermeister who gets the towns people together for a beer festival.

My costume is a full, dark green skirt trimmed with lots of red ruffles worn with a yellow, embroidered, off the shoulder blouse. The girls wear white Dutch hats and the guys have green, small brimmed, mountain hats with a white feather in the hatband.

Bryza is here with me in the Day Room writing to Don. We have the place to ourselves...

Immediately following breakfast, April drove out to the park. The mess staff was busily setting up their cooking facilities at the opposite end of the stage where Alex painted the scenery.

"Ili," she said. "What are we painting today?"

"A Japanese garden for scene four."

"Looks more like sand for a beach."

"It's a rock garden." He held up paint stained hands. "Would you mind getting me a cup of coffee before you start?"

She crossed the stage to the coffee stand and picked up a cup.

"Can I help you with that?" asked a masculine voice from behind her.

"Yes," she turned around. "I'd like a cup of coffee."

"I don't think we've met," said the short male dressed in white. "I'm Sgt. Yates, everyone calls me, Cookie."

"PFC Terry."

"Do you want cream and sugar?"

"I don't know. The coffee is for Alex."

"He drinks it black. Are you his new girl?" he asked, scratching his left ear using a hand with a tattoo of a dragon on his upper arm.

"No." She was quick to reply. "We're just friends. I'm helping him paint the scenery."

"I shoulda known. You're too young for him. A piece of advice. Watch out for him. He was a sergeant like me until he got into a brawl over a girl. Lost her and his stripes."

"Thanks," she said, picking up the steaming cup and walking back across the stage to Alex.

"Was that little midget flirting with you," Alex asked, taking the cup of coffee.

"He wanted to know if I was your girl."

Alex threw his head back and laughed, almost spilling the hot coffee. "And what did you tell him?"

"The truth, of course."

"He probably didn't believe you."

"Why wouldn't he believe me?" she asked, allowing a frown to crease her brow.

"I have a bit of a reputation for being," he paused. "Somewhat of um…a lover." His eyebrows raised and lowered rapidly.

"And a fighter?" she added.

"I guess you heard about my stripes."

"Yes, I did. I outrank you. So you best behave around me unless you want to find another painter."

"Have I done anything wrong so far?" he asked.

"Let's keep it that way," she said. She selected a large brush and dipped it into a can of sand colored paint.

Age is a matter of the mind.
If you don't mind, it doesn't matter.

Chapter 28

That afternoon in the Wetzel Drive parking lot, an MP patrol car rolled up next to April's vehicle and stopped. The driver got out and approached the van full of girls. April rolled down her window as the corporal stepped up to the door.

"PFC Terry?"

She nodded.

"Cpl. O'Reilly. Lt. Col. Reeder has assigned me as your escort to the park. If you need me to stop for any reason beep your horn twice."

The sharply, dressed MP returned to his vehicle and gave the hand signal to move out.

"Oh, he's cute," said three of the girls in unison.

A short time later, April pulled into the lot behind the patrol car. "I think I broke my record. That's the fastest we've ever gotten here."

The rehearsals that afternoon began with the *Apache* dance number in front of the outdoor Paris café.

In the right wing, April sat in a blue Renault watching the dancers. As soon as they finished their number, they took seats at the vacant tables. After she put the small car in gear, she drove it to the center of the stage and parked in front of the café. She got out, and gave the keys to an attendant who drove the vehicle across to the left wing. While she sipped coffee at one of the tables, a derelict slyly approached and stole her purse. Pvt. Voir, a soldier sitting near by saw what happened and rescued her handbag. She thanked the private and invited him to her table to share a cup of coffee.

A short distance away, a group of young students accompanied by a nun were singing "Ava Maria" in front of the cathedral.

She and Pvt. Voir left their table and ambled over to listen to the choir.

After the rehearsal, the director excused the actors, but he asked that the dancers and choir stay for another run through.

She moseyed over to the scenery department and picked up a brush. She dipped it into the brown paint for the bottom of the palm trees. On a tall ladder above her, Alex painted the tops of the palms green.

"Niña, are you coming to the NCO dance tonight?"

"I don't think so," she replied, shielding her eyes to glance up.

"I feel guilty about your painting when you should be enjoying your free time."

"I told you. I love to paint and dance, too. And I've been to the pool and gone horseback riding."

"With the Oklahoma cowboy," Alex added.

"I didn't go with Nathan. He was already at the stables, and he helped me chose a horse."

"Lucky him. So why not come to the club tonight? I would like to see you in something other than shorts. I've never seen you wearing make up—not even lipstick."

"My boyfriend doesn't like me to wear lipstick." Her face warmed. *Why had she told him that?*

"I promise not to tell him." Alex raised his brows and made a sign of the cross above his heart. "You need to relax a little. Why not come to the club?"

"Maybe I will just for a little while."

Back at the post, she showered, put on her robe and arranged her hair in the style Sgt. Levy had showed her. Instead of a flower, she used a large rhinestone clip. Carefully, she applied eye shadow and cherry pink lipstick before returning to the room. From her wall locker, she pulled a dark blue sheath dress of China brocade. She hunted in the bottom until she located the matching pumps. The zipper stuck on her dress, she walked over to where Shirley was sitting on her bunk, filing her nails.

"Can you give me a hand with this?"

"Wow," Shirley said. "Do you look different?"

"It's the make up. I haven't been wearing any."

"You should use it more often," the woman said, adjusting the zipper. "I like your hairstyle, too."

"Thanks."

"I think someone is going to be in for a surprise tonight," said Shirley, clicking her tongue.

Music blared from a five piece combo as April entered the NCO Club. Her eyes were drawn to a table where Alex sat gazing at a drink in front of him.

"Alex?"

He looked up at her and rose from the table. Alex made no pretense of his surprise. His mouth hung open at a ridiculous angle while he looked her up and down with wide unbelieving eyes.

"Is this the same paint dabbled girl who was wearing a pony tail an hour ago? What have you done with my Niña?"

"I just rearranged the paint. Its called makeup."

"You know," he said, a slow grin transforming his handsome face, "I certainly would never make the mistake of thinking you were a kid tonight." He pulled out a chair and she sat down.

She had never seen Alex dressed in anything but shorts and a T-shirt. He wore a pale, blue, silk shirt beneath a navy blazer stretched over wide shoulders. A pair of soft gray loafers replaced his sneakers below light, gray slacks.

"What would you like to drink?" he asked, dropping into the chair beside her.

"Whatever you're having."

"Ginger ale? I'm on the wagon."

"That's fine."

Alex signaled a waitress. "Another ginger," he said. He reached out and spread his fingers through hers. "Want to dance?"

She nodded in agreement.

"I can't get over how fine you look." He pulled her into his arms. "Amazing what a little paint can do."

She relaxed and let the joy of the music take over as Alex guided her through the movements. For the next few minutes neither spoke, only moved with the rhythm, adjusting their steps to each other. He was a marvelous partner, smooth and graceful as he swept her around the floor.

The music ended and they crossed the parquet floor back toward the table.

Alex had been surprisingly quiet during their dance for someone who was usually very talkative, as if he were considering some matter of grave importance that had nothing to do with her.

"Cpl. O'Reilly is sitting at your table," she informed him.

"Do you know him?"

"I just met him today. He's been assigned as our escort to and from the post."

"Better watch out for that Irish MP. He's a love 'em and leave 'em guy," warned Alex.

"He doesn't interest me. I've only dated Spanish guys."

"What about Nathan? He follows you around like a lost puppy."

"I told you, I never went out with him. We were merely at the same place at the same time."

Cpl. O'Reilly stood as they neared the table. He inclined his head. "Alex."

"O'Reilly," Alex acknowledged his greeting.

"April, may I have the next dance?" asked the corporal, grinning down at her.

"You'll have to ask Alex." She shot a glance at the surprised artist.

"How about it?" he asked, his hands resting on his hips.

"Sure," said Alex, slipping into his chair. "Just dance where I can see you."

She suppressed a giggle as she went into the open arms of the frowning MP. She missed a step. "Sorry," she apologized.

"How about us getting together Saturday night?" asked O'Reilly.

"I have rehearsals."

"I meant afterwards."

She shook her head. "We sometimes rehearse 'til midnight."

Out of curiosity she glanced back at the table. Alex was talking with someone dressed in a light blue sport coat over dark trousers. The guy turned and walked toward the bar and she recognized Lt. Salgado. It appeared everyone dressed up tonight. She had never seen him in anything but his uniform. Even when the guys of the 101st wore T-shirts and khaki shorts for practice, he was always in full dress uniform.

Cpl. O'Reilly thanked her for the dance and left her at the table with Alex who was still grinning.

"Well, You've done it now. O'Reilly will think we're going steady." His grin turned into a hearty chuckle.

"I don't think so. He asked me for a date."

"What did you tell him?"

"That I had to work."

"You just might have given him a different message," said Alex, shaking his head.

"What does that mean?"

"What do you think?" There was a husky seductive quality in his countering question that sent the heat rising in her face. "He may have labeled you as my property," said Alex, laughing.

"What's so funny about that?"

"I was laughing about the lieutenant."

251

"You mean Salgado? I saw you talking to him while I was dancing with O'Reilly."

"Yeah. He was asking me about you. The lieutenant didn't recognize you—thought you were a civilian."

"Is that so?" She took a small sip of her drink.

"I set him straight. I let him know you were a noncom and off-limits to him, and besides, you didn't date Puerto Ricans since you had a bad experience with one."

"You didn't tell him that?"

"Nah. But I should have." Alex chuckled. "I did say that you were a WAC and spoken for."

"I'll have you know I am quite capable of speaking for myself."

"Don't look now, but here comes your *puppy*."

"Shhh," she said. "He'll hear you."

"April, I wasn't sure it was you. You look spectacular," said Nathan, stopping beside the table.

On the platform, the musicians struck a chord of a familiar song.

Nathan held out his hand to her. "April, may I have this next—"

He never got the chance to finish. "Sorry, Nathan," Alex cut in smoothly, "but she has already promised this dance to me."

She had no choice but to follow when Alex practically dragged her into the middle of the dance floor. Still rather stunned, she gaped up at him. "Why did you do that? Maybe I wanted to dance with him."

"Trust me"—his tone was clipped—"you didn't. Why get his hopes up and bust his bubble?"

"He's really very nice. Besides I told him the reason I wouldn't go out with him because I am dating a guy back at McClellan. Speaking of which, I have to leave after this dance. I want to write a letter to Monty."

"That guy must be someone special."

"I think he is."

They danced in silence until the tune ended.

Alex led her toward the exit, but he retained possession of her hand.

"Do you need a ride back to the WAC Detachment?"

"No thanks. I drove the staff car."

"Too bad that you are leaving. I'd rather dance with you than paint."

"Maybe we could change places."

"I could never fit into your costumes," Alex said, smiling. "Come on, I'll walk you out to the lot."

Later in her quarters before going to bed, she wrote a letter to Monty, although she had not gotten one from him to answer.

The following morning she went to the park to paint with Alex—minus any makeup.

"I see I have my Niña back. I had a great time last night. I haven't laughed so much in a long while. Since the cast is rehearsing the Hawaiian Scene here this afternoon, there won't be any rehearsals at the club tonight. Instead, there's a special show at the NCO Club followed by a dance. Why don't you go with me?"

"I can't," she said.

"We could go as friends," he suggested, wiping his hands on a paint rag.

"I've been around that block before—never again," she said, grabbing up her paint can and brush.

Following lunch in the park, she joined the other eight girls to practice the hula with the guys of the 101st Airborne.

Friday, 16 August 1957
Dear Dreamcatcher,

In the afternoon we rehearsed the Hawaiian Scene. The eighteen members of the drill team with their rifles makes two lines while myself and the other eight girls dance down between them as Lt. Salgado puts them through some fancy drills. I can see this scene will take a lot of practice. Each time the men mess up, they have to fall down and do ten push-ups, and the next time it is twenty and so on.

In the show the men will wear their helmets, gloves, belts, boots all dipped in florescent paint with their Khaki uniforms. Also their rifles will be painted.

We girls will wear florescent-sprayed leis around our necks, hair, ankles, and wrists. Also our hands and the tasseled belt around our waist will be coated. Black lights will be used to make the paint glow. I can just imagine the spectacular scene.

A letter from Monty was waiting on my bunk when I returned from the park. He tells me he may be moving to Headquarters to work permanently with Capt. Putman. It's not definite yet, but he is hoping for the approval. He would have a nice easy job working in her office.

He scolded me for not writing more often. He had told me when I left he wanted a letter from me every day. In my letter to him I reminded him that those were his words not mine...

Sunday, 18 August 1957

This was our first day off. After church, I treated myself to a movie, *Jumping Jacks* with Dean and Jerry. It was hilarious. I wrote Monty, told him to be sure, and see the film when it comes to the post...

Monday, 19 August 1957

It was great to get a good night's sleep. The first one that I've had since I have been here.

We are still rehearsing the Hawaiian number. The drill team is perfect when they practice by themselves but when we girls start doing the hula they start messing up and have to do pushups.

This evening I found the sweetest letter from Monty waiting for me on my pillow. He had gone to see Sgt. Craig's little dog at the kennel and he said that Nicky misses me, too. Later, in the evening, he went to the service club and met a girl from my company that knew both of us. I have to check this out when I get back to the post...

Tuesday, 20 August 1957

In the morning, I painted with Alex.

This afternoon, we rehearsed the Hawaiian scene until I thought my hands would fall off.

Tonight I found another adorable letter on my bunk from Monty. So loving and tender, it made my eyes misty just to read it. It's good that his classes have started back at Jacksonville College. They will keep him occupied...

April arrived at the park to find Alex sitting at a makeshift table with a stack of plum colored folders spread over the top. He looked up when she approached. He was minus his usual T-shirt and shorts. Instead he wore a dress uniform. He handed her a colorful foldout program.

"These are good," she said, examining the six scenes of the show he had illustrated with cartoon type line drawings. The front was on colored paper with three black arrows running around a white globe printed with YOUR ARMY AROUND THE WORLD in the center. The inside fold listed all the scenes and the names of the cast members.

"Thanks. I have to approve them and deliver them back to the printer. Could you work by yourself tomorrow if someone helps you with the ladder and backdrop boards?"

"Sure. I'll ask Nathan to help. He is always standing around watching us paint. Might as well put him to work."

"I already have someone coming to help you. Anyway, Nathan might get the wrong idea that you will go out with him."

"I hadn't thought of that."

"Since you will be up on the ladder, do you have some long pants to wear?"

"All I have are the jeans that I use for horseback riding."

"Wear them. I don't want you to attract an audience because I won't be here to handle anyone who gets out of line."

"What the *Sam Hill* are you talking about?" she asked, one hand resting on her hip.

"When you paint, Nathan and the guys stand around watching you wiggle your back side."

"I have you know I've never done any such thing," she denied adamantly, and instantly felt a burst of heat on her face.

"Yes, you do. You just aren't aware of it. It's when you bend down or stoop over to paint the bottom of the boards."

"Why have you never told me that they were ogling me?" she demanded angrily.

"I didn't want to spoil their fun," he said, chuckling.

"Well, maybe I shouldn't help you paint anymore." She glared at him, both hands fisted on her hips.

"Niña, I'm sorry for teasing you. I'm depending on you to help me finish the painting in time for the show. Please accept my humble apology." He dropped down on one knee, his hands clasped together in a prayerful manner.

"Since you put it that way." She didn't mean to laugh, but she couldn't help it. Alex looked so funny kneeling in front of her. "Get up. I'll come paint in the morning."

"Thanks," he said, raising to his full height and brushing at his trouser leg. "Vic Castillio will be here to help you."

"He's Spanish?"

"Of course." He smiled. "Don't worry, you'll be safe with him around." After lunch, the 101st Drill team finally got the Hawaiian rehearsal right.

Thursday, 22 August 1957
Dear Dreamcatcher,
When I got to the park, Cpl. Castillio was waiting for me. He is from the Dominican Republic and he's tall and black. Now I know why Alex was smiling.

The corporal handed me a short sleeve fatigue shirt and said that Alex wanted me to wear it to keep the paint off my clothes. Alex knows that I never get paint on me. The shirt hung down below my knees. A tape of Alex's name was sewn above the breast pocket and the impression where his sergeant's stripes had been could be seen on the sleeves.

Nathan and a couple of the guys from the band did come over to ask what I was doing on the ladder. They didn't stay for very long. Nothing for them to see?

I ate lunch with Vic who is mannerly and quiet. I learned that he is one of the stagehands in charge of the scene changes for the show.

In the afternoon, we rehearsed the Japanese Scene. So far, it is my favorite. We will wear black wigs and beautiful silk kimonos. There are four girls in the scene including myself. Don Gibson sings while we dance with our fans in the garden. Even though we were not in costume, everyone applauded after we finished. It gave me goose bumps.

After I returned to my quarters tonight, I found a short, but very sweet letter from Monty…

The following morning, April carried Alex's freshly washed and ironed shirt on a hanger with her to the park. Alex was waiting for her with a wide grin on his face as she approached him.

"Niña, you did a great job. I didn't expect you to get so much done."

"Maybe it was because I didn't have an audience," she quipped as she handed him the hanger.

"No. You keep it to wear when you paint."

Monday, 26 August 1957
Dear Dreamcatcher,
This started out to be a blue Monday. It is raining. I went to the mailroom; the clerk was nice enough to go through the mail, and I had not one letter but two from Monty. Now it isn't a blue day after all.

Monty says the men at his barracks are *ribbing* him because he writes to me so often. And telling him that I am driving him crazy. He got the slides back that he took at HQ just before I left and he made a show for the guys in their Day Room. He said even his First Sergeant heard about the slide show and asked him to show them again for him.

He was upset because they are planning a company party on the fourteenth of September and I would not be there. He doesn't know it but I will be back at the post by then. I am not going to tell him yet but wait and surprise him.

I called Monty from the NCO Club tonight. He was so happy to hear my voice. I could have talked to him all night but I had to go back to my rehearsals. As we were saying good-bye, he said, "I love you." And I told him that I loved him, too. It seemed so natural. I don't know where the knowledge had been all this time, but it suddenly struck me that I loved Monty. My feelings changed into love without my knowing how it happened. I wish he were here to hold me in his arms where I am cherished and safe...

Wednesday, 28 August 1957
I painted all morning and then went to rehearsals at the club at 1300 hours.

Tonight when I returned to my quarters I had two letters from Monty on my bunk. He was thanking me for calling him and saying how happy that I had made him when I said that loved him. He told me that everyone at the service club asks about me. He thinks he will print a directive with all the information about the show and me and hand them out...

Thursday, 29 August 1957
Tonight, on my bunk, I found a very upsetting letter from Monty. Richard and Cordero have returned from area eight

and they are together with Monty in the same barracks. He told me not to worry, that they are now friends. Friends? How can he even think that?

Apparently, he has forgotten what Cordero did to me with his lies. He still doesn't know what transpired between us over Reynaldo's ring. I haven't forgotten, and I will never forgive Cordero's behavior. I am so furious; I most likely won't be able to sleep a wink tonight...

What you want and what you get,
Are often two different things.

Chapter 29

Following a sleepless night, April drove to Chastain Park.

Swift to see that she was disturbed, Alex had said, "What happened to your cheerful smile, Niña?"

"I didn't sleep well last night."

They painted in silence until Alex climbed down from his ladder.

"Your eyes are red, have you been crying?" he asked, gazing at her intensely.

"No. I'm too angry to cry." She jabbed her brush at the canvas backdrop for the café.

"Do you want to tell me about it?" He shoved his paintbrush into a can of soapy water.

She briefly related the details about Cordero, the knife he carried, and the fight over the ring. How he and Monty were back in the same barracks and her concern for his safety.

"Maybe, your boyfriend is telling you they are friends because he knows that you are worried." His eyes caught hers for a moment before he went back to cleaning his brush.

"I don't understand how he can say that he is a friend with someone who hurt and humiliated me the way Cordero did."

"Were you in love with this Cordero?" asked Alex, the brush he was cleaning held idly in one hand.

"I loved him like he was my brother. Monty thought I was in love with Cordero when he met me."

"If you had loved him, you would have forgiven him," said Alex.

"There were times I wanted to forgive him because I cried myself to sleep countless nights. But my pride wouldn't let me."

"Have you ever considered that you may have transferred the feelings for Cordero to your boyfriend? And what you think is love is only gratitude?"

"I only recently told Monty that I loved him when I spoke with him on the phone from the NCO Club." She put the finishing touches on the café windows and dropped her brush in the can of soapy water.

"When you return to your post, if Monty asks you to marry him, how will you answer?"

"I hadn't considered it." She was already shaking her head. She took a deep breath and exhaled. "I don't know."

"You better start thinking about it. Weddings are a natural consequence of two people falling in love."

She stood staring at Alex for a long time as she quietly accepted the logic of his arguments. Hot tears flooded her eyes as the emotional turmoil inside her became too much to control. She turned away sharply trying to force the tears back. Too late, they overflowed and ran down her cheeks.

"I'm sorry, honey," said Alex. He put aside his brush and wrapped his arms around her, leaning her head into his chest, one hand stroking her shoulder. "I didn't mean to make you cry. I wouldn't hurt you for the world. Go fix your face. Let's knock off for today and go eat at the club."

In the NCO Club Alex went to the bar and brought back a drink topped with whipped cream and placed it in front of her.

"What's this?" she asked.

"Brandy Alexander. It'll make you feel better."

"I've never drunk anything other than wine made by my grandpa."

"You've not had any hard liquor?"

"Never." She shook her head.

"One of these can't hurt you."

April slowly sipped the concoction. "It's delicious." She had to admit, after eating she felt much better but still confused.

The cast rehearsed the grand finale and the director informed them that they would have a dress rehearsal on Labor Day. A chorus of moans and groans followed his announcement.

After the rehearsal, Alex stopped her on her way out of the club. "Are you okay?" he asked.

"I'm fine. What are you doing here? I thought you left after dinner."

"I wanted to be sure that you were okay. You better not let Monty see Glenn throw you up in the air like he did in that last scene tonight," he teased.

"Glenn scared the life out of me the first time. Maybe I should have had a couple more of those brandy drinks."

They laughed together.

"I have to go to the printers in the morning. If you could meet me at 0900 hours at the park, we can put the finishing touches on the backdrops. I promise not to upset you again."

April had difficulty sleeping and missed breakfast. She dressed and went directly to the park. Alex was already painting. They continued painting until lunch without talking. Alex bought them lunch from one of the park vendors, and they sat at one of the picnic tables.

At the end of the paint session, she helped Alex put the materials away before leaving for the club.

Later in the NCO Club, Alex sat at the same table with her as they ate dinner. While waiting for the rehearsal of the grand finale, they drifted into the bar and Alex fed some coins into the jukebox.

"This song is for you," he said. He took her hand and led her onto the small floor, drawing her into the circle of his arms. He sang along with, "You'd Be So Easy To Love."

"I didn't know you liked country western music."

"Sure. I'm from Texas, ma'am," he drawled.

The next selection was "Heartaches." And before it ended, the tears started slipping down her face and they wouldn't stop.

"Do you know what I do to young ladies that cry and wet my shirt?" he asked, looking down at the damp spots on his T-shirt.

She sniffled and shook her head.

He kissed her on both cheeks.

"Stop." She removed her arm from his shoulder, put it against his chest, and pushed. "Don't ruin our friendship."

"Maybe I want more than a friendship," he said, calmly.

"I have to get some fresh air." She slipped out of his arms, and headed for the door.

Outside it was beginning to get dark.

"I'm glad I found you." She recognized Glenn Vandal coming up the walk. "I want to practice the lift and spin with you before our rehearsal tonight."

With the grand finale over, she exited the club with Bryza and drove to the WAC Detachment.

Monday, 02 September 1957
Dear Dreamcatcher,
Not enough of the cast showed up for work today and they cancelled the pre-dress rehearsals. Except for Bryza

261

and myself, I think they all had too much to drink last night.

After dinner I wrote Monty a letter. I couldn't seem to say what I really wanted to tell him. Lately, I have become confused and unsure about my feelings.

For the rest of my stay here on the post, I plan to avoid being alone with Alex...

Tuesday, 03 September 1957

I am sorry I mailed the letter to Monty yesterday. It was so cold and uncaring.

Today was "pay back" for yesterday. We worked long hours into the night. Alex took two rolls of film with my camera of the entire rehearsal...

Wednesday, 04 September 1957

Tonight our rehearsal went smoothly; I don't see how we can get any better.

I had a newsy letter from Monty. Reynaldo has announced his engagement for the third time. My little friend, Chico had a fight at the Beer Hall with Wayne, the new piano player in the Spanish Band. I was sad to learn that CQ left for Germany. I knew he was being transferred but I didn't expect him to leave until I returned. I had promised to write to him when he went overseas and continue to correct his English. When I go back to the post I plan to look up his orders and get his address. I always like to keep my promises...

Thursday, 05 September 1957

Tonight we had a full dress rehearsal starting at 2000 hours, as they wanted to check the lighting. A lot of people showed up to see our run through so we had quite an audience. We finished our rehearsal at 2200 hours and I returned to my quarters, hoping for a letter from Monty, but no luck...

Friday, 06 September 1957

We were instructed to rest this morning. In the afternoon, I wrote a friendly letter to Monty. I don't know how to write to him anymore. I know that I've hurt him with the cold uncaring letters that I've written recently. My feelings toward him are totally confused. I don't know if they are real or out of gratitude as Alex suggested.

Tonight the show went smoothly despite the extra lights and cameras used to film the production. The director was pleased with our performance. He announced that a party would be held at the NCO Club after the final show tomorrow night...

A hissing sound woke her. April sat up in her bunk, gazing around the darkened room.

Someone had propped the door open and a patch of light was visible from the hall.

"Pssst. PFC Terry. I have a letter for you," said a familiar voice.

She looked over the railing at the dim outline of a person waving an envelope at her.

"I'm sorry I forgot to leave it on your bunk yesterday," whispered the mail clerk.

"Thanks. What time is it?" she asked in a low voice, reaching down to take the letter.

"A few minutes past 1100 hours."

"I'm getting up. Please leave the door open," she said, climbing down the ladder. At the bottom she slipped into her sneakers and picked her way over the discarded shoes on the floor to the opening.

In the latrine she opened the envelope with a trembling hand and began to read.

6-Sept.-57
Hi Elaine,
I am sitting here in my barracks tying to write to you and sew at the same time, a new chemical shoulder patch. The old one was damaged.

I couldn't write to you yesterday 'cause I came back late from school and I didn't feel like writing to you, though I was trying to call you from the college. I wanted to talk with you about the letter I got from you yesterday. It sure made me confused about you caring for me anymore. Also you sounded like you were writing just to keep a promise. I don't want you to become enslaved to your word. That is why I didn't write yesterday and because you don't like me to write to you this way when I am not in a happy mood. How could I laugh with a letter like yesterdays? I hate writing to you this way.

Forgive me.

I think you shouldn't write to me anymore and this will be my last letter to you.

Our phone in our barracks is out of order. Sometime if you feel like calling me you could use the one at the CQ desk. (5160)

I wish the best of luck for you in your show.

Alberto Montoya

April re-read Monty's letter. He had addressed her as Elaine. Something he had never done. *Should she call him?* She read that part of the letter again. Now her feelings were so confused it might be the wrong thing to do. *Perhaps this is the way it is supposed to end?*

As the tears streamed down her cheeks, she pressed her hand over her lips to hold back a sob. She laid the letter on the shelf above the sink and washed her face in the cool water. The paper towel dispenser was empty. She opened a stall and ripped off a handful of toilet tissue, drying her face and hands before picking up Monty's letter.

Following lunch, April went to the pool to sunbathe. But it only reminded her of the happy times she spent with Monty. After a few minutes, she returned to her quarters. It was empty and she undressed and climbed up to her bunk. She couldn't sleep for thinking of Monty. She wept hot tears into her pillow. It was the wrong time to be crying, her eyes would get all red and puffy. An hour passed, and she forced herself to get up and go take a hot shower.

She had six hours before she had to go to the amphitheater. Time enough to go to the movies. The schedule posted inside the Day Room listed the picture as a comedy. *The Ambassador's Daughter,* starring Olivia de Haviland, just what she needed to cheer her up. It turned out to be a film about a French ambassador's daughter who sets out to prove all enlisted men are not womanizing predators. She found herself watching for the circle of light for the change over of the reels. It started her thinking of Monty and that made her weepy. She walked out of the theater before the movie ended.

Later, she waited until the last minute before leaving for the parking lot where she knew Cpl. O'Reilly waited to escort them to the park.

At the theater, she immediately went to wardrobe and picked up her costume for the opening scene.

Alex and Vic were backstage making some last minute adjustments of the scenery.

"Hi," said Alex. "I tried to call you this afternoon."

"I went to the movies," she answered.

"Is anything wrong?"

"Nothing," she said, quickly.

"Are you sure? You look kind of sad. Are you sorry this is the last show?"

"Actually, I'm glad it will finally be over."

"Your eyes aren't smiling. Looks like you've been crying. Do you want to tell me about it?"

"There's no time. I have to go to the make up department," she replied.

"We'll talk at the party after the show."

A few minutes later with her make up applied and dressed in her German costume, April pasted a false smile on her face, waiting for the curtain to open on the first scene. Her heart wasn't in what she was doing. But like the saying, *the show must go on.*

Once the production began it was a practiced routine. In a daze, she changed from one costume to another for the appropriate scenes.

Following the last curtain call the director compliment the cast on a show well done. Had she not been expected to drive the girls to the party she would have skipped it.

Back at her quarters, she took down her hair from the bun she wore in the last scene. She brushed it back behind one ear, fastened it with a pink flower, and slipped into her pink and white-stripped dress.

The party began with a speech by Col. Reeder, the Special Services Officer, complimenting the different departments, actors, dancers and musicians. That was followed by congratulations form Major Hoskins, Production Supervisor, and Director PFC Robert Fass. Then the Production Coordinator, MSGT Tatel thanked all the departments, lighting, makeup, wardrobe, sound and set designs. The shortest and best speech came from Lt. Williams, the Entertainment Officer. She told everyone to enjoy the food and the party, that they had earned it.

There was a ton of food, but she didn't feel like eating. Alex grabbed her arm and escorted her to the chow line. She took some sliced turkey, coleslaw and a spoon of potato salad. They sat at a table with Vic. O'Reilly tried to make it a foursome, Alex told him the empty seat was taken.

She picked at the food on her plate while Alex and Vic polished off all their food. Vic went back for seconds.

"Let's get some air," Alex suggested. "The loud noise and the heavy cigarette smoke are starting to get to me." He took her arm, walked her out to the parking lot, and stopped beside a red and white Ford convertible. He opened the door and she sat down. She ran her hand over the black and white leather.

"Is this yours?"

"Yeah."

"What happens when it rains?"

"I get wet."

"I can't believe it doesn't have a top." She looked over her shoulder, searching the space above the back seats.

Alex pressed a button on the dash; a grinding noise startled her as the back of the car raised almost perpendicular to the ground. Suddenly, a red top came out of the trunk and the retractable hardtop slid in slow motion to cover the car.

"Wow! That was impressive. I've never seen anything like it."

"If it had been raining, we would have gotten drenched," remarked Alex. "I'm trading this Skyliner as soon as the new Fords are out."

"I see what you mean. It takes too long for the top to get in place. But it sure is pretty with all the chrome trim and detailing."

"Now do you want to tell me what's wrong?"

"No, I don't want to discuss it."

"Bet I can guess. Your boyfriend got jealous."

"I haven't done anything to make him that way. I haven't gone out with any of the guys here that have asked me."

"Then what's the problem?"

"It's me. I'm afraid of committing myself. Monty said I shouldn't write to him anymore and he wasn't going to write me."

"I've got eighteen more months left if I don't re-enlist. I will have a total of fifteen years of service. I'll be thirty-four in October and I'm not getting any younger. I want to get married and have a family. If I came to see you—"

"Why are you telling me all this?"

"Because I want to come courting when you return to your post."

"You—what?"

"I want come visit after you go back to Ft. McClellan."

"No. You can't do that. My life is already complicated enough."

"Is that what I represent to you—a complication?"

She pressed her lips together without commenting.

"I know you think there's a big age difference between us." He continued in the wake of her silence. "Let me tell you something about love. It's not like becoming of a legal age when you can vote or drink alcohol. Love is ageless. Your age or mine doesn't matter. Love happens with the right person."

"Then I guess I have never found the right person."

"Maybe you have. I think you are afraid of loving in return."

"I don't care to continue this conversation. It's becoming much too personal," she said, opening the door of the Skyliner. "Excuse me, Alex. I'm going back inside to say good-bye to the gang."

She had no sooner entered the club than Nathan approached her and asked her to dance.

"I guess this is good-bye, Nathan," she said, slipping into his arms. "I'm leaving for Kentucky as soon as I can clear post."

"April, I would have liked to have gotten to know you better."

The music ended and he returned her to the table where Alex now sat with Vic. Nathan kissed her cheek before she sat down and he walked away.

"What's with the Oklahoma cowboy?" asked Alex.

"I was just telling him good-bye. I'm leaving as soon as I can clear post. I still have seven days left before I report back to Ft. McClellan."

"I thought you would be staying for a few days. The bus isn't returning to your post until Monday afternoon."

"I know, but I want to visit my family in Kentucky."

Bryza approached the table. "Are you leaving soon? The rest of the girls are staying for awhile."

"I'm ready to go. I'll be right out."

"It's been great fun working with you, Alex. I learned a lot about painting and life, too." She held out her hand.

"This is not good-bye." He took both of her hands and squeezed them before letting them go. "We still have to talk. I'll see you before you leave."

She and Bryza drove in silence the short distance to their quarters.

Saturday, 07 September 1957
Dear Dreamcatcher,
Tonight's show was a huge success with all two thousand seats filled and people sitting on the aisles. I don't remember

much about the production, as my heart wasn't in it.

With the letter I received from Monty this morning I am totally confused about my feelings. I know I've hurt him with the letters that I have recently been writing to him. And now he doesn't want me to write to him anymore and said he would no longer write to me. I don't know what to do. Also, Alex has become a problem…

The following day, she skipped breakfast, washed, and dried all her soiled clothing. In the afternoon she drove off post, ate lunch, and returned to pack her suitcase. For fear of running into Alex, she avoided the mess hall at dinner.

On Monday she learned that she would have to report back to Ft. McClellan before she could go to Kentucky. Since she had the car, she ate off post, ending up out at the park, and went to see the horses. Stanley gave her carrots to feed to Blaze and Mickey. Before leaving the park, she took a drive past the empty Amphitheater. It looked so lonely and deserted.

Monday, 09 September 1957
Dear Dreamcatcher,

After I turned in my linens, I signed out and the CQ asked if I was PFC Niña Terry as I had signed Elaine Terry. I told her it was a nickname, and she handed me several messages. They were all from Alex.

Following lunch I returned the Ford to the motor pool, and we boarded the military bus at 1400 hours. Everyone was pensive on the return to the post. None of the singing and joviality like our initial trip.

As soon as I arrived at Company D, I went to the Orderly Room to get permission to go to Kentucky. Lt. Sousa signed my pass because the CO was in a meeting.

In the evening, Sgt. Levy came to my room, asking about the show, as we hadn't talked earlier when I was in the Orderly Room. I remarked about having my room to myself again, as all Pvt. Black's things were gone. I asked Sgt. Levy how Saymone was doing and said she was in a room of her own.

After I finished packing, I told Sgt. Levy about what had happened with Monty and she persuaded me to call him to let him know I had returned. He was not in his quarters. I forgot that he goes to school on Mondays. Just as well. He might not have wanted to talk to me...

Tuesday, 10 September 1957

I arrived at Mama's early this morning while it was dark. I wish I had stayed at the post. But at least, she was glad to see me. I finally told her what had happened and showed her Monty's letter. She said that from their phone conversation she thought he sincerely cared for me.

She asked me about Cordero and why I stopped seeing him. I told her the whole unpleasant story. After I finished telling her, she said a strange thing that she thought he behaved normally for a man in love. Mama told me a person couldn't be held accountable for the love others give them unasked for. Also that I could not prevent or stop his pain. She thinks I cried because I have always been tenderhearted and I regretted the hurt I've caused him. Perhaps she is right.

At Mama's suggestion, I wrote a note to Monty letting him know when I would return to the post and included my phone number. (As if he didn't already know it by heart.) After mailing the letter, I felt better, and I finally stopped crying...

Friday, 13 September 1957

When the taxi drove through the Galloway guard gate, my heartbeat accelerated. It was as if I was really coming home. I arrived at 1645 hours after the cadre left the office.

After chow I went down to the Orderly Room hoping the phone would ring. I knew it wouldn't but I sat a long time in the dark before returning to my room after midnight.

Tomorrow is the party at the 30th Chemical Company. I am tempted to go. But I don't want to run into Cordero, although he could still be on leave...

Sometimes in trying to spare others pain,
We can cause more pain.

Chapter 30

Cordero watched Abril standing outside the Day Room gazing at the couples swaying to the music. The sight of her brought back old memories. She was a burning fever in his blood, a yearning in his soul and an ache in his heart.

Her petite curved body was silhouetted in the light streaming threw the open door. Did she have any idea how appealing she was in a dress that made him think of pink cotton candy? It emphasized her narrow waist. A cluster of white flowers that sparkled like they were dusted with tiny diamonds held her hair at one side of her face.

Their eyes caught as if a physical line connected them. She drew him toward her through the dancing couples across the room like a magnet. His pulse raced and his mouth grew dry.

Never breaking eye contact with her, he cut across the floor heading in her direction. For a moment it was as if no one else was in the room except the two of them.

He wove his way across the floor toward her, side stepping the entwined couples until he was standing in front of her. Her heartbeat fluttered at the base of her throat where he longed to place his lips. What did it mean? That she was as excited to see him, as he was to see her? The soft scent of lilacs floated to his nostrils striking an unexpected chord of familiarity.

His eyes raked her from the top of her honey blond hair to the tips of her strappy white sandals. They flickered over her again slowly studying every detail, and when he finally found his voice, it was with a cool, indifferent tone.

"What are you doing here?"

"I might ask you the same question. Aren't you supposed to be on leave?"

"I returned this morning. You shouldn't be here." The words sounded too gruff, even to his ears, but he couldn't staunch the deep emotion that turned them so harsh.

"I was invited," she said.

"Montoya's in his cubicle. He's not coming to the party. Have the two of you broken up? He looks as if he lost his best friend."

"I don't recall asking you about him."

"You're right. You didn't. I was just trying to be friendly. We were friends once. Remember?"

"We aren't friends. Not any more," she said, simply.

"It's curious that while you were away, Montoya and I were on good terms. He even cut my hair for me before I went on leave." He fingered his short curls. "This morning, I asked if you had returned from TDY and he practically took my head off. He told me to mind my own business. I was just trying to be friendly." Without touching her he braced his hands on either side of the wall behind her head.

"What do you think you are doing?" she asked. A frown marred her normally smooth forehead.

"I know what I'm doing. The question is, do you?"

"Like I said—I have an invitation—"

"I wasn't referring to the party. I meant your relationship with Montoya."

"That's none of your business," she retorted. With the palms of her hands she shoved at his chest.

The touch of Abril's hands on him sent pleasure streaking through his body like fragmented bolts of lightning.

"Come dance with me." He motioned toward the floor where couples swayed to the music.

"You're not afraid of embarrassing yourself?" Her eyes drifted down to below his belt buckle and back up to hold his gaze.

He cocked up one black eyebrow and lifted the corner of his mouth in a half smile.

"I got over that."

He looked into the green-flecked topaz eyes that had fascinated him since that first night in the service club. She was uncommonly nervous, he could see it in her eyes.

She turned and started walking out of the doorway, and he moved to block her way as she tried to step around him and her frown deepened.

He didn't allow it. His long arm reached out and stopped her cold. For several moments he did nothing but hold her. She was stiff but unresisting in his arms.

Swiftly, both his hands cradled the back of her head, gently gripping it as he brought his mouth down on hers. Ignoring her cry of alarm, he kissed her

271

as he had never kissed her before. This kiss was long, deep, and satisfying. Her hands came up to grasp his wrists. It wasn't a gentle kiss. His mouth plundered hers, expressing months of frustration, broken dreams and shattered hopes.

He gathered her against his body, letting her feel the evidence of his passion. He wanted her in every way it was possible for a man to want a woman. And to his sorrow, he knew she didn't want him in the same manner.

As he looked into her eyes, they began to mist, she pushed frantically at the solid wall of his chest, drawing great gulps of air as their lips parted.

"Cordero. No. Please." She blinked, apparently struggling against a display of emotions.

"Tell me if Montoya has ever made you feel this way." His breathing was uneven as he dragged his mouth from hers. "Has he ever made you feel a tenth of what I do?"

She looked away, her lower lip slightly swollen from his kisses, quivering despite her obvious efforts to still it. As she shouldered past him, his hand shot out, slowing her movements, and captured her arm at the elbow. He swung her around to face him.

"I've tried to stop loving you and I can't. I love you, Abril," he stated solemnly. "I loved you from the beginning, and I probably always will."

"I don't understand—how can you hurt me so easily…" Her voice trembled. "…if you love me so much?"

He loosened his grip and let his arms fall to his sides.

"I hope you don't find out too late that you had what you wanted and threw it away." He stepped away from her. "Because you were too damn proud to admit it."

Their gazes held for a long moment. She glared one final dark look before lifting her head in a proud, haughty manner, turned and hurried down the cement steps.

Through clouded eyes, he watched her walk away, his heart aching for what might have been. He stood staring after her. He committed to memory the graceful way her hips swayed, her natural easy stride carrying her away from him until her lovely shape was swallowed up in the dark of the night.

Damn it. Would he never lose his obsession of her? For several months, he had been under the impression that he had gotten over loving her. The very sight of her stirred emotions he had believed dead.

Cordero hadn't realized that a person never stopped feeling the ache of loss; he had just grown use to living with it. He pressed his fingers between his brows. There was a pressure in his chest and behind his lids. He shut his eyes tightly waiting for the sudden rush of pain to subside once again, but the relief never came.

True love is an acceptance of all that is,
Has been, will be, and will not be.

Chapter 31

Saturday, 14 September 1957
Dear Dreamcatcher,
  It was a mistake to go the Chemical Company party tonight. I had a run in with Cordero. I don't even want to write about it. Except to say I think my mama was right. I feel guilty because I unintentionally hurt him. I saw the pain in his eyes tonight and I felt it in my heart. It leaves me feeling helpless that I can neither do anything to erase nor prevent it…

Sunday morning, April showered but didn't get dressed for church. She put on a T-shirt and pair of white shorts. Not feeling up to eating, she skipped breakfast. Instead, she returned to her bunk, her arms curled around her body thinking of Monty.

Much later, a loud knocking on her door made her jump off the bed and she jerked the door open.

"You have a call from PFC Montoya," said the breathless trainee.

April rushed out barefoot and had to return for her sneakers. She stepped into her shoes and flew down the stairs.

"Yes?" she spoke into the receiver, breathlessly.

"Meet me at 1500 hours in the music room of the service club." There was no emotion in Monty's voice. He didn't even identify himself.

"Okay," she replied. "I'll be there." The line went dead. April replaced the phone in its cradle and glanced at her watch. 1400 hours. She had missed lunch.

She jogged back up to her room and took her ditty bag to the latrine. Carefully, she applied a small amount of make up and lip-gloss. Next she combed and brushed her hair, letting it curl around her shoulders. Back in her room she discarded her shorts for a yellow crinoline before taking out the yellow dress that Monty favored.

She arrived at the club a quarter of an hour ahead of the appointed time. As she walked down the corridor, familiar notes of the piano wafted from the music room. She picked up her pace, hurrying until she reached the door. It was closed. Her hand trembled as her fingers wrapped around the knob.

Monty sat in the darkened room at the piano playing "Cherry Pink." He stood, came around the bench and stopped. She searched his eyes for traces of anger, but there was nothing there but a raw, painful anguish that tore at her heart. For a long moment they stood staring at one another in silence.

April wasn't aware that she was holding her breath until she tried to find the air to greet him and it wasn't there.

"Come here," he said softly, as if afraid he would startle her. He held out his arms to her. A wry smile twisted his mouth.

"Oh, Monty," she cried, launching herself into his waiting arms, nearly choking on a suppressed sob as she hugged him. "I'm sorry. I'm so very sorry."

For a while they stayed wrapped in each other's arms. After a time he pulled back slightly. She opened her eyes.

"Did you mean it when you said that you loved me? Because these last weeks without you have been hell," he said, huskily, staring down at her.

April's arms slid around his neck and pulled his head closer to hers. Her mouth met his in a gentle kiss. The need for words ended as Monty took over, changing the kiss into a hungry embrace that left no doubt as to the depth of his feelings. Her response was equally revealing.

How could she have ever doubted her love for this gentle, passionate man? She closed her eyes and pressed close to him heedless of the public room and that at any moment someone could walk in and see them. It felt good to be in his arms again. So right to be cradled against his heart. A sense of relief washed away the heartbreak that had haunted her these past unhappy days.

Neither of them spoke. They just stood holding each other until she stopped crying.

"Let's go." He picked up her hand and entwined her fingers with his.

She didn't know where they were going but she went with him. They walked out of the club and down the hill to sit on the steps at the end of her barracks. It had been a long time since they had sat there. She rested her head against his chest in silence.

"Are you hungry?" she asked.

"No. Are you?"

"I haven't eaten all day. Would you mind waiting in the Day Room, while I go wash my face and powder my nose?"

Half an hour later they sat in her mess hall eating. He kept smiling ever time she looked at him. She gazed up at him again and saw that he was trying hard not to laugh.

"What's so funny?" She finally asked.

"You are," he said. "Did you really think I would let you go so easily? I'll never let you go, no matter what happens."

Monty took a white packet from inside his jacket and slid it across the table. "Del Valle left this for you."

April's name was written across the front with Sir Galahad in the upper left-hand corner. She picked up the legal-size envelope and tore it open. A snowy white man's handkerchief fell out on the table. She smiled, refolded it and placed it in her purse. She glanced up at Monty.

"You aren't curious?" she asked, closing her purse, dropping it back in her lap.

"Del Valle sealed the envelope in front of me. He said you would know what it was for."

"I'm glad I don't have to explain it to you. It's a little complicated, and you might not understand the reason behind it."

"He thought highly of you and cautioned me not to lose you." Monty took a forkful of food and chewed vigorously.

After they finished eating, they walked down Galloway Road and around by the band building.

"Let's stop and say hello to Nicky," she suggested.

"He's not here anymore. I visited him once while you were away and the next time I came, Nicky was gone. A different dog was in his kennel."

"I hope nothing happened to him. Tomorrow, I'll inquire about Nicky."

They walked back to the steps at the end of her barracks. She sat on the top step and he stood in front of her. He took some letters from his jacket pocket that she recognized as her last two correspondences that she had written him from Ft. McPherson.

"I am giving these back to you. Your previous letters were very precious. I kept them to read over and over except for these two. I found no love in them for me." He picked up her hand and pressed them in her palm.

She clutched the letters and got up, her back to him.

"April." His hands on her shoulders turned her around. Monty lifted her chin with his finger and looked deeply into her eyes. "Tell me, April. Have you stopped loving me?" His voice was gentle. He could have been speaking to a bedeviled and perplexed child for all the tenderness in his tone.

She gazed at the letters and back to his face. There she saw the hurt she had caused by her foolishness. Her eyes misted.

"Monty, I tried to stop caring because I felt my emotions were getting out of control. All the attention I was getting while I was gone confused me. Stupidly, I listened to bad advice that persuaded me it was wrong to love you. I wanted you to stop loving me so neither of us would get hurt. Until I thought I had lost you, I didn't realize how deeply I cared for you. At this moment I care more for you than when I went away. Do you forgive me?"

"If I didn't, I would be hurting myself, too. You came to the 30th Chemical party last night." It was not a question.

"I did, but I didn't stay. Before I got all mixed up, I had planned to surprise you…" She made a feeble gesture with her hand. "After I returned from TDY I tried to phone you. But you were at school, so I went to visit my mama. She encouraged me to write the letter to you from Kentucky. When I returned to my barracks I hoped you would telephone me. Friday night, I sat in the Orderly Room waiting until past midnight for your call that never came."

"After the last letter I wrote you, I vowed not to bother you anymore. I reasoned that since I was the one injured, it would be up to you if you wanted to continue our relationship. I imagined that was why you came to the party. And that is why I phoned you this afternoon. You'll never know how difficult it was for me not to call you on Friday as your letter suggested."

"I understand," she said.

"Walk with me to the bus stop." He thrust out his hand to her. She placed hers across his broad palm. His long fingers closed around hers. His thumb traced little circles over the backs of her wrist, sending tiny shocks of awareness up her arm. He was not touching her with anything but his hand on hers, but she was aware of the heat of his body, the smell of the familiar scent of Old Spice and cinnamon that always clung to him.

They no sooner reached the corner than the bus appeared. Before boarding he leaned down and kissed her on the cheek.

"Cordero did me a favor by telling me that you came to the party." His deep voice vibrated close to her ear.

She walked slowly back to her barracks thinking about what Monty had told her. Apparently, Cordero had not told him everything that transpired between them.

She pushed through the entrance doors and signed the CQ book. The trainee behind the counter turned the book around to read her signature.

"Oh, PFC Terry, you have several messages." The private handed her three pink slips.

"Thank you," she said. She glanced at the first paper. It had Alex's name and phone number with a request for her to call him. The second and third messages were the same. She crumbled them in her hand as she walked away from the counter. Once she reached her room, she pitched them in the wastebasket. This was the first time she had recalled Alex since leaving Ft. McPherson. She did like him as a friend. He was fun and easy to talk with and they had gotten along well together, but she could never be what he wanted. And she had learned the hard way that some friendships between men and women were not meant to be.

Early the following morning she walked into the Orderly Room. The sign on her desk stopped her dead in her tracks. *Acting First Sergeant Terry.*

"Good morning Sgt. Terry," said Sgt. Levy, behind her.

"Is this some kind of a joke?" She whirled around to face the grinning sergeant.

"No. That's one of your duties to replace the first sergeant in her absence."

"Oh, well. How long will she be gone?"

"Permanently."

"Permanently?" she echoed.

The world is full of people,
Who make excuses for their failures.

Chapter 32

"You better sit down and let me catch you up on all that happened in your absence," said Sgt. Levy.

"I can't imagine—" April plopped down on the chair next to the sergeant's desk.

"When you got back from TDY you had asked me about Pvt. Black having her own room. It all started with her. She is under house arrest in Pvt. Well's old room."

"What on earth for?" April's eyes widened.

"There is a board case pending against her. It appears that she is a lesbian."

"I don't believe it. We shared a room together." She stood her hands on her hips.

"Believe it. It's true. All I can tell you is she and Craig got into it. They pointed fingers at each other. Craig was another board case. A week ago she was given a Dishonorable Discharge. I knew there was something strange about Craig from the moment I met her. And that's not all. The WAC Battalion Mess Hall officer, Lt. Tolbert was also implicated. If you recall those two were thick as thieves."

"Wow. And I thought my TDY was exciting. What a shock." She sank back down on the chair.

"Not only have you got an extra duty as Acting First Sergeant but Friday you are on Guard Duty. However, there is a plus—for the time being you have been relieved of Post Staff Driver Duty."

"What do you mean by Guard Duty?"

"An EW under house arrest has to be guarded against her escaping. You are responsible for seeing that she gets fed and escorting her to and from the latrine. The rest of the time you sit outside the door until bed check and lock her in the room at night."

"When did all this happen?" she asked.

"About three weeks after you left," Levy replied.

"From day one, I could tell that the first sergeant didn't like Pvt. Black. But I thought it was because of her color. Now I understand what was the problem." She nodded her head.

"It was because Craig was prejudiced against her that started the whole mess. It just snowballed and got nasty. We are not to discuss the case with anyone outside the company. It's not something the *big brass* up on the hill wants spread around."

"You mean I can't even tell Monty." She widened her eyes.

"I'm repeating what I was told. You'll find a directive on your desk about how to handle it. I always say what people don't know can't hurt them. Since Pvt. Black was your roommate for a short time, you will be asked to fill out a questionnaire. And the lieutenant may want to ask you some questions, too."

"Oh, my God. I hope they don't think I'm like Pvt. Black and MSGT Craig."

"Don't refer to her as Master Sergeant. Her stripes were taken away before she got her DD. Don't worry, I'm sure that no one will think you are in anyway like them."

"I surely hope not. Was she under house arrest too?"

"I'll say—she cussed a blue streak the entire time. Not only that—Craig threw a tantrum and smashed things in her room. Sgt. Waite had to take everything out but the bed and mattress to prevent her from throwing something through the window."

"Imagine that." April shook her head. "How sad to end her career like that. What about our trainees, were they told about Master—I mean Craig?"

"Fortunately we had just graduated our last platoon when this happened. The trainees in the company now have never even heard of Craig and they don't know about Black, as there aren't any platoons on the third floor. You're right. It is a pity Craig threw away a twenty-three year career like she did. She could have retired in two more years and been sitting pretty. Now she has nothing."

"Oh, what about the mail?"

"We have a new mail clerk, Pvt. Axel. She should be down any minute. You'll like her."

"What room is she in?"

"Sgt. Waite moved down to Craig's old room and Pvt. Axel took hers."

"Good. I don't want any more roommates."

"I can't blame you. For the time being I'll take over doing the Morning Report and some of your other clerical duties. Until the company gets a replacement, you are going to be extremely busy as Acting First Sergeant. I've written out a list of your duties besides taking Reveille and Retreat and marching in the parades." Levy shuffled through the papers on her desktop. "Here," she said, picking up a typed page and handing it to April.

"Why weren't you made the Acting First Sergeant?" she asked after glancing at the list and back at Levy.

"Chain of Command. As the Company Clerk, you are next in line. For another reason, my bum knee won't allow me to march in the parades. I have been medically excused from marching for the remainder of my service."

"I'm sorry. I didn't know that."

"I do miss the parades, but I got use to it."

"So that's why you never went to any of our parades. From now on Pvt. Axel will drive you in her jeep to the parade field for any parades that you want to attend."

Later that evening, April unlocked the Orderly Room to take Monty's phone call. She walked to her desk, picked up the receiver, and punched the button beneath the red light.

"Hi, Monty, how was school?"

"It was okay, but I had rather been spending the time with you. What about your day? Was it difficult getting back to work?"

She sighed. "You are not going to believe what happened while I was gone. And you must promise not to repeat a word of what I am going to tell you." Briefly she relayed the information about Craig and Black and that she was now the Acting First Sergeant.

"Are you for real? You're joking, right?"

"I'm afraid not. It's the truth. And not only that, Black is still in the company under house arrest. On Friday I am pulling Guard Duty."

Monty's hearty laughter came over the wire.

"It's no laughing matter."

"I was just picturing you pacing up and down the hall with a M-1 on your shoulder."

"I don't have a rifle. I sit outside her door, escort her to and from the latrine, mess hall, and then lock her in after bed check."

"Wait 'til the guys hear about this. They won't believe me."

"No. You promised not to tell anyone. I'm not allowed to discuss this outside the company. I only told you because I don't want any secrets between us."

"That's what I like to hear. And I won't talk about it with anyone but you. You have my word on that. Now tell me that you love me."

"You know that I do."

"I want to hear you say it," said Monty.

"PFC Alberto Montoya, I love you with all my heart. Satisfied?"

"I love you, too," he responded.

> Wednesday, 18 September 1957
> Dear Dreamcatcher,
> It seemed strange not to go the service club tonight. It just wouldn't be the same without CQ.
> Monty called and we talked for a long time. Before he hung up, he asked if I had been issued a rifle.
> Very funny...

Friday morning, April set the tray on the floor, fished the key from her pocket and unlocked the door. She knocked and picked up the tray before entering.

"When did you get back?" Saymone sat on her cot dressed in wrinkled PT clothing.

"A week ago," she said. She crossed the room and placed the tray on the vanity. "I would have come to say hello but I was told the *prisoner* wasn't allowed visitors."

"Were you surprised to find out about me?" Pvt. Black moved to sit on the bench in front of the dresser and unwrapped her eating utensils.

"Shocked is more the word for it." From against the wall, April picked up a folding chair, opened it and sat down.

"What did you think when you heard about me?" Saymone nibbled on a strip of bacon.

"How do you feel about me?" she answered with a question of her own.

"You're definitely not my type," said Saymone, laughing. "You still dating the same guy?"

"Yes, but we've had our share of problems."

"Do you want to tell me about them?" the woman asked, vigorously stirring her coffee.

"You have enough problems of your own."

"You got that right." She laid the spoon on the tray and sipped from the cup.

"I want you to know that I don't judge you because of your so called *lifestyle*. I liked you and I think we could have been friends."

"Thanks. That's the nicest thing anyone has said to me in a while."

"I could tell you about my TDY. That is, if you want to hear about it?"

"Do I ever. I'm dying to know all about it."

"I'll go get my pictures while you finish eating." She stood, picked up the folding chair and carried it with her. In the corridor, she leaned the chair against the wall and locked the door.

A few minutes later she unlocked the door and passed the packet of pictures and the three-page program of the show to Saymone who had moved her chair over by doorway.

"The photos are in order of the six scenes of the show. In the second scene near the Cathedral of Notre Dame, notice the scenery in the background. I helped the artist paint it and the rest of the backdrops. The last night of the show was taped. In December, excerpts will be shown on Ed Sullivan's Christmas program."

"No kiddin'?"

"That's what we were told."

"Are you one of these girls?" Saymone held up one of the pictures of the hula dancers in the Hawaiian scene.

"I'm the third girl from the left."

"Oh, yeah, now I make out your face under all that long hair. Is this you?" Pvt. Black showed her a picture of the Japanese dancers.

"Yes, that's me beneath the black wig."

"Pretty outfit and fans."

"That was my favorite scene of the whole show. I loved the costume and the fan dance."

"What about this?" Saymone pointed to the picture of her in a leopard skin leotard high above Glenn's head. "What did your boyfriend say when he saw this snapshot?"

"I haven't shown the pictures to him yet."

"Are you going to show this one to him?"

"What do you think?"

They looked at each other and laughed.

"Great photographs. Who took these?" asked Saymone, putting the photos back into the envelope.

"The artist that designed the sets. He also did the artwork for the program."

"A very talented guy," remarked the private as she handed the pack of pictures and program back to her.

"Yes, he is," she agreed.

"Could I take a shower before lunch?"

"Sure. Get your things together."

After her visit to the latrine, Pvt. Black exchanged her PT outfit for a plain white blouse and dark skirt.

Much later, April stopped at her room, dropped off the program and photographs on their way to the mess hall.

"It feels good to get out of that room. Except for you and Sgt. Levy, all the other cadre have brought the meals to my room." In front of the building, Saymone extended her arms, twirling around in the middle of the walkway.

"What are your plans once you are discharged? Do you have folks in…ah, I believe you said you were from Louisiana?"

"Yeah, but I'm not going back. I think I'll try New York City—ever been there?"

"No, I haven't, but that is where my boyfriend lived before he was drafted." She pushed through the door and held it for Pvt. Black to enter the mess hall.

They each picked up a metal tray and moved slowly down the food line. She selected an empty table in the section reserved for cadre. April folded the two extra chairs and leaned them against the sides of the table before taking her seat.

"I really don't care for hot dogs," she said, eyeing the chilidog on her tray. "But I like chili."

"Neither do I," said Saymone. "I had rather have a juicy hamburger."

She looked up, smiled and nodded as Pvt. Axel took a seat a few tables away.

"Have you met the mail clerk?"

"Not really. Sgt. Levy pointed her out to me. She hasn't been allowed to guard me. I guess they are afraid I might corrupt her." Pvt. Black shrugged and rolled her eyes toward the ceiling.

That was probably true, as she hadn't been allowed to type any of the woman's testimony. She would have liked to read Craig's case. Sgt. Levy knew all about it since she had typed the papers. But she wasn't talking. That was for sure.

In the evening, April escorted Pvt. Black to the mess hall for dinner. Then at 2200 hours, after a visit to the latrine she locked her in the room.

The following Sunday evening, April sat at the piano with Monty. He finished the last notes of "Cherry Pink," and he lifted his hands from the keys.

"I have some good news to tell you. I've made arrangements to buy Cpl. Pete Pinellas's car. He is leaving for Germany next Friday. The car will be mine Tuesday after I give him the balance of what is owed. Wait 'til you see the light green '53 Plymouth. There's not a dent or a scratch on it anywhere."

"Oh, Monty, that's wonderful."

"There is just one problem. I know how to drive, but I don't have a license. Blackledge is going to go with me to take my test on Friday. He got a book for me when he was in Anniston. Could you help me study so I will pass the written test?" He got up and pulled a small book from his back pocket.

"Let's go to the writing room and start studying." She stood and took his hand.

> Friday, 27 September 1957
> Dear Dreamcatcher,
> Monty called tonight letting me know that he passed his written driving test. We talked for a long time until I had to make bed check.
>
> I stopped and knocked at Saymone's door. I spoke to her through the closed door, telling her good-bye, and wishing her luck. She goes before the board on Monday and I won't have the chance to speak with her again. She thanked me for not turning up my nose at her like the rest of the cadre…

> Saturday, 28 September 1957
> Today's date reminds me that this is my anniversary of one year in the service. It has been an exciting year. A real learning experience for me.
>
> Monty and I went to the movies and saw, *Payton Place* with Lana Turner. The picture was kind of sad. At the end when the screen went blank and the theater was dark, Monty leaned over and gave me a big, sweet kiss. "This is why I brought you to the theater," he whispered in my ear…

Monday, 30 September 1957
Dear Dreamcatcher,

While our cadre and officers were at Saymone's trial, I was alone in the Orderly Room most of the day. Only they call it a *Board Case*. Sgt. Levy returned around 1500 hours and told me Pvt. Black had been discharged. That was all the information I was given.

Monty called me tonight before he went to school. He is very happy and excited about getting his car tomorrow, and I am happy for him, too...

Tuesday, 01 October 1957

Tonight Monty came over to show me his car. It is all he said, a clean vehicle with low mileage. He took me for a drive around the post. Monty is not a skilled driver or perhaps he was nervous as he stalled the engine several times because he let the clutch out too soon. We didn't sit on our steps and I teased him and said I missed sitting there but the car was more comfortable. And private for his sweet kisses...

Thursday, 03 October 1957

After chow I accompanied Monty to the Jacksonville College. While he was in classes, I browsed the library. On our way back we stopped at Lees' Drive-in Restaurant. I introduced him to grilled cheese with hot chocolate. I can't believe that he had never eaten the sandwich. He loved it.

Chocolate kisses are the sweetest...

Two days later, on Sunday, April signed out and walked to the parking lot to wait for Monty. He arrived and greeted her with a kiss on the cheek. Then he walked around the Plymouth and held the door to the driver's side open.

"You drive," he said.

"Okay." She slid behind the wheel and adjusted the seat and mirror before starting the vehicle.

"Just listen to that motor purr," he said. "Pete had the engine tuned and the oil changed before he sold me the car."

"It has a nice sound," she agreed, pressing the clutch and brake to come to a stop at the corner sign. She made a right and continued up Galloway Road then around WAC Circle to WAC Headquarters and back down by the row of Battalion Training Companies and pulled into Company D's lot.

"She drives like a dream."

"She?" he repeated.

"All vehicles are referred to as feminine. Don't ask me why. I've never figured it out."

"I could think of a few reasons," he said, laughing. "However in my country the *motor car* is considered masculine. But since we are in yours, I give you the honor of selecting *her* name."

"I already know the name. It's Lizzie."

"Then Lizzie it is."

> Thursday, 11 October 1957
>
> Dear Dreamcatcher,
>
> These past days have gone by speedily. My duties as acting first sergeant and Monty's classes have kept us from seeing each other since Sunday. He called me before he went to school tonight. Monty wanted me to come to class with him but I have a backlog of work in the Orderly Room. We have a platoon graduating this weekend. I have to arrange for transportation for those that are not going to Blueberry Hill. I promised to take a break and go to the movies with him tomorrow night...

> Friday, 12 October 1957
>
> This morning I marched in my first parade as the Acting First Sergeant for our Fourth Platoon's graduation. I was the last body in the back of the company.
>
> In the evening Monty and I went to see a comedy picture about Japan, Joe Butterfly, staring Audie Murphy.
>
> It was great having our own transportation and not being dependent on the bus...

On Saturday, the phone rang in the Orderly Room at 1130 hours.

"Let the CQ on duty pick it up," said April.

"It might be important," replied Sgt. Levy, reaching for the telephone. "Company D, Sgt. Levy speaking. It's for you," she said, pushing the hold button and putting down the receiver. "PFC Montoya."

"What are you doing this afternoon?" Monty asked.

"My laundry—nothing too exciting."

"How would you like to accompany me this afternoon? I washed Lizzie and I'm going to find a nice shady spot to put on the wax."

"Sure."

"I'll pick you up right after lunch."

"Okay," she said, and replaced the handset.

"Well, that was short and sweet," remarked Sgt. Levy.

"Monty wants me to go with him to wax his car.

After chow, she opened her civvies locker and moved the hangers around until she found the black jeans she wore for horseback riding. Hurriedly, she dressed and went down to the CQ area.

Monty came through the door just as she signed out.

"What are you wearing?" he asked. "You can't go out dressed like that." He took a stance with his fists on his hips surveying her.

"This is what I wear when I go horseback riding. I can't very well go climbing around over your car in a dress. Now, can I?"

"I didn't say you had to help me."

"Just what is it you object to? I wore fatigues in the field and when I was the mail clerk."

He took her by the elbow and urged her into the Day Room. "I never saw you in pants. I don't like the way they show off your...you know what I mean."

"I'm afraid I don't," she said, suppressing her laughter, and putting on a solemn face.

"Those pants show all your curves. It's okay for me to see you but I don't want any other guys looking at you," he said, lowering his voice to a whisper.

"I'll be right back," she said, hurrying from the room.

In a few minutes she reentered the Day Room wearing her long WAC sweater over her pants.

"How is this," she asked, turning her back letting him see where the length of the sweater ended.

"I guess it will do," said Monty, still not sounding any too happy about the pants she wore. "Just be sure you wear it when you leave the car."

Inside the vehicle, she edged away from him so that she wouldn't be touching him.

"I want you next to me," he said, hauling her against his hip.

Monty drove out Tenth Avenue onto a winding road cut through a hill. The trees on the hillside had such pretty colors of red, gold, and orange. On the other side they stopped beneath a tall spreading shade tree. Monty put on the wax and she helped with the buffing of the vehicle.

After they finished he arranged a blanket at the base of the thick trunk, and assisted her to sit. Monty lowered himself until he was sitting on the ground beside her. He angled his body, laid his head on her lap, and gazed above them.

"Do you know the name of this tree?" he asked.

"It's called a sycamore. Do you have them in your country?"

"I don't think so. I've never noticed one like it there. The bark is very unusual the way it scales in places leaving white patches."

"If you break off a small branch, you can peel it with your fingers and the underneath bark is green not white."

Monty rose with easy athletic grace and took out his pocketknife. His body blocked her vision as he stood in front of the tree.

When he finished, he stepped back for her to see the letters A and M within a large heart on the trunk.

With her fingertips she outlined the heart that enclosed their roughly carved initials.

"This is our tree," he said.

He pulled her into his arms and kissed her. One of his many kisses that turned her legs to spaghetti. Her heart did a tiny flip.

Saturday, 26 October 1957
Dear Dreamcatcher,

I've seen very little of Monty these past two weeks because of his school and our combined company duties. He has called me every evening, and we talk for hours.

Tonight we went to a dance at the Hilltop Service Club. We didn't stay long as Monty became annoyed at the guys for cutting in. We left the ballroom and went to the patio, where he told me that he didn't want anyone else to touch me. He is becoming so possessive, and I don't know what to do about it. I'm sure part of his behavior was because Cordero was at the dance and he seemed to be everywhere I looked staring back at me. Monty couldn't have avoided seeing him, but he didn't mention his presence.

I had hoped Cordero would get over his obsession or whatever it is with me while I was on TDY.

Apparently he hasn't...

"It's for you," said Sgt. Levy, pressing the hold button before replacing the handset.

April glanced up at the clock with the hands on the twelve and the four.

"Don't get nervous. It's PFC Montoya."

She punched the red button. "Hi, Monty."

"Are you working tonight?"

"I hadn't planned to, why?"

"I want to see you. I haven't seen you all week."

"Don't you have school tonight?"

"My classes were cancelled because it's Halloween. Can I pick you up after chow tonight?"

"Lucky you. Yes, I would like that. See you later."

After chow she dressed in her yellow dress, took a white shawl, and went down to wait for Monty in the parking lot.

When she was safely inside the car, he walked around, opened his door, and slid behind the wheel. He put the key in the ignition but he didn't start the car. He leaned over and kissed her cheek.

"I'm glad you wore that dress. You look beautiful."

"Are we going to the party at the club?"

"What party?"

"There's a Halloween party at the service club. I've not attended one since high school. You don't celebrate the holiday in your country, do you?"

"No. But I've heard about it from my nephews in New York. Do you want to go to the party?"

"Sure, it might be fun."

Monty settled behind the wheel and twisted the key in the ignition. He flicked on the radio before backing out of the lot. Classical music flooded the interior as he drove the short distance to the service club.

He slowly cruised the parking lot until he pulled into a vacant spot and turned off the ignition.

Her eyes riveted on the turquoise and white reflection in the rearview mirror, that of a '57 Chevy parked in the row of cars behind them. Monty's eyes followed the direction of hers.

Resting his hands on the steering wheel, he stared straight ahead for several long seconds, a forbidding hard line to his mouth.

"Do you want to go in?" he asked, turning to her.

"I don't think so," she said, glancing out the window at the white Pontiac pulling along beside them. "The club isn't the same without CQ. Besides, we're not dressed for a costume ball."

"Not everyone is wearing a costume." He called her attention to the couple getting out of the car next to his Plymouth.

"Come on—let's go inside."

At the entrance a witch wearing a pointed hat gave them two half masks.

"Do I have to wear this?" The black mask dangled from his hand by an elastic band.

"Yes. You do," she said, carefully slipping her white mask over her hair." You can be the Lone Ranger and I'll be Tonto."

Monty frowned as she helped him with his mask.

Although the evening was early, the room was crowded. Each time the club supplied free food and drinks, it resulted in a heavy attendance. Only about a third of the couples wore costumes. The rest had on a half mask similar to the ones she and Monty wore.

In attendance were several black clad witches like the one that had greeted them at the front entrance. A red suited devil partnered a white uniformed nurse. Next to them, a female vampire and a Dracula danced together. Numerous pirates, gypsies, and a hillbilly in coveralls, barefoot with a blackened front tooth and tousled hair added to the originality.

"Look at him," said Monty, drawing her attention to a guy in a grass skirt. Two coconut halves were strung together across his chest. Around his head he wore a colorful lei and another encircled his neck. He partnered a fairy godmother carrying a wand with a star.

A black caped magician came up, produced a large red paper carnation from a silk, and handed it to her.

"Thank you," she said, taking the posy and pretending to whiff the fragrance. He smiled, bowed and walked away.

They continued around the edge of the floor and she encountered several costumed couples that she was unable to figure out whom they represented.

A fellow walked past them carrying a large baby bottle with a blue bonnet tied under his chin.

"Would you look at that?" remarked Monty. Other than the head covering, the guy wore only a diaper. "He has to be the bravest soldier here."

"He certainly is the coolest." She stifled a giggle.

"Monty. Over here." Jerry dressed, in fatigues, waved from a near by table. It held a large platter of small shaped sandwiches, assorted cheese, a bowl of chips, and a pitcher of red punch next to a stack of clear plastic cups.

"In case you are wondering, I'm a mail clerk. Why aren't you guys in costume?"

"We are," she said, "me Tonto, him Lone Ranger."

"April, you should have braided your hair," Jerry said, laughing.

The WAC Band struck up "Rock Around the Clock."

"Monty, do you mind if I borrow your girl?" Jerry looked at her and waggled his eyebrows above his glasses.

"As long as you remember to return her." He grinned and stood as she and Jerry moved to the dance floor.

Cordero lounged against the far wall with one knee raised, bracing himself with one foot behind him. With his arms crossed in front of him, he watched the couples dancing.

He noticed Abril the moment she entered the room. He would have recognized her with a bag covering her head. Now his eyes gazed at her honey gold hair gleaming beneath the lights as Jerry swung her out and back into his arms. He watched her just to enjoy her movements; the yellow skirt whirling around her legs and trim ankles. And the way the roundness of her hips emphasized her tiny waist. He studied her slender hands, remembering the feel of them on his head and neck.

She was laughing up at the 30th Chemical Company's mailman. He couldn't hear her over the noise of the crowd but her laughter filled his mind as she returned to the table where Montoya waited.

The band played another selection and she changed partners, gliding around the room in the arms of Montoya. A stab of pure dislike for the guy holding her sliced into his chest. Seething with fierce anger, he pushed away from the wall turning his back on them. He had no right to feel betrayed but that didn't change how he felt. He'd never been jealous over a girl in his life but there was no mistaking the nearly blinding rage he felt each time another guy slipped his arm around Abril's small waist.

To his embarrassment, he felt a sting in his throat and in the back of his eyes. He had to get out of the room before his unshed tears became reality. A good stiff drink would help—several drinks. Cordero turned and gazed at her once more, before exiting the ballroom, walking quickly outside into the night. He welcomed the cool air that dried the moisture he was ashamed for anyone to discover.

April and Monty were making their way back to the table when the bugler sounded the first notes of "Cherry Pink." Strong arms tucked her close, his

292

cheek resting lightly against her hair, as he slipped an arm around her waist, moving her easily to the rhythm of the music. He turned her, his thigh brushing briefly against hers, and a shiver of heat slid over her skin.

Earlier when he had put him arms around her to dance, a tremor had raced through her body when he brought her within the circle of his arms. She was entranced by the slight smile on his lips and in his eyes. A smile that seemed created for her. Closing her eyes, she had leaned into him, resting her forehead against his starched shirt where it escaped his jacket. Warm solid muscle shifted beneath her palms, fingertips and forehead.

She now found herself confronted by an overwhelming female reaction to a male. Her face felt flushed, her heartbeat accelerated twice its normal rate. So when Monty's arm tightened a fraction, gently urging her closer, she allowed it. She'd never thought herself a sensual person, but he stirred a heightened awareness of her own body that led to an irresistible curiosity to feel his nearness. Her skin became acutely sensitive to the touch of Monty's legs as they brushed hers, to the hardness of his shoulder beneath her cheek.

April no longer felt the floor beneath her feet, only the pressure of his hand on her waist and the warmth of Monty's arms.

"I could dance like this all night," she said, lightly trying to ignore the heavy thud of her heart and the press of his hard chest against her breasts. The thick muscles of his thighs flexed smoothly against hers as they swayed to the rhythm of the music.

"So could I," he agreed. Someone bumped them and he opened his eyes. He smiled sheepishly at her. "Sorry."

No sooner had they returned to their table than a loud drum roll sounded followed by an announcement for all the contestants to line up for the costume judging.

The participants were directed to form a circle in the center of the dance floor. They marched around to Sousa's, "Stars and Stripes Forever," until all of them had been eliminated, except for a lady vampire, the hula dancer and baby. After, the vampire was eliminated the band struck up a few bars of "Cry Baby" and faded into a fast beat hula. The guy in the grass skirt gave it his best shot and had everyone laughing and applauding his antics.

Finally, it was announced a tie, the baby for originality and the hula dancer as the most comical.

The bandleader informed the baby that several of the ladies had volunteered to burp him and change his diaper. Uproarious laughter and loud stamping of feet followed the announcement.

293

Jerry removed his eyeglasses and swiped at his eyes with his handkerchief then cleaned the lenses before putting them back on.

A guy in a blue suit approached the table and held out his hand.

"April, may I have this dance?" he asked, his blue eyes through the slits of the half mask matched his suit.

She glanced up at Monty. He nodded, though much slower this time.

She placed her hand in his and moved with him to the dance floor, her skirts swaying. She placed a hand on Richard's shoulder, fingering the rough texture of his jacket as he bent his sandy head above hers. He settled a hand at her waist and swept her into a graceful turn. His long strides moved them in graceful patterns, holding her carefully away from his body in a very correct waltz position.

"He acts as if he owns you."

"What do you mean?"

"Montoya. You had to get his permission before you could dance with me."

"It's merely a courtesy since he's my date. Why do you dislike him so much?"

"Because of Cordero."

"I was under the impression that the three of you had become friends while I was at Ft. McPherson."

"It's true, Montoya did a favor for Cordero, but we are far from being friends. He acts like he is better than everyone."

"I, too, got that impression when I first met him. But I learned he's not that way. Actually, he is shy and reserved, afraid of offending someone with his lack of understanding of American customs and our language."

"If you say so. Did you see Cordero?"

"No. I wasn't looking for him."

"He was here for awhile watching you dance. He left when you danced with Montoya. It tears him up to see the two of you together."

"I'm sorry for him, but he was the one who destroyed our friendship."

"Cordero doesn't see it that way. Montoya separated you and him."

"That just isn't true. You of all people should know there was nothing between Cordero and me—except what was in his mind. His monstrous lies are what cost him my friendship."

The waltz ended and Richard held her elbow while he escorted her back to the table.

"Thanks for the dance," he said. He took his leave without speaking to Monty or Jerry.

"I'm claiming the next dance," said Monty, "even if it's a rock and roll tune."

He pulled her snug against him, pressed his cheek to the top of her head as they danced to a slow number.

"Did you know that last guy I danced with was Richard?" she asked.

"Uh-huh—did you?"

"Yes. I knew who it was. Thanks for letting me dance—"

"Shhh—don't talk." He tightened his arm around her waist bringing their bodies closer together.

Toward the end of the song, the music grew increasingly romantic and slow. Monty held her with both his arms wrapped around her. And she had told Richard he was shy. He had never held her like this, so near she felt each of his fingers through the fabric of her dress. The easy movement of his muscular legs now almost supporting her since her knees had turned to liquid. She inhaled the fresh spicy fragrance of his cologne as her hand came to rest against his chest over his heart.

Several dances later, Monty glanced at his watch, "My watch and my stomach tells me its time to go to Lee's for a grill cheese sandwich. Do you mind if we leave?"

After saying good night to Jerry, they left the building and walked down the grassy slope to the car. She pulled her stole around her and gazed up in awe. It was a perfect Halloween night, with perfumed breezes, a full moon, and a sky awash with millions of brilliant stars. Their glittering points of light spread across a black velvet sky—so many more and so much brighter than in Kentucky. She could almost reach up and pluck them down. There must be a lot of truth in the words of the song "Stars Fell on Alabama." She hummed a few bars of the popular tune.

"Did you ever see so many beautiful stars? There must be thousands of them, so close I could reach up and touch them. Are they like this in your country?"

Monty smiled a slow, lazy grin that bracketed his mouth with deep dimples, emphasizing his full sensuous mouth. His smile left glittering highlights in his eyes like the stars above them.

"I don't believe so," he said, opening her door and helping her inside the car.

Much later, after Monty finished his sandwich, they left the restaurant, entered the post by Galloway Gate, and parked in the lot at Company D.

"Now that I've had my grill cheese, I feel like I've been to school."

Monty moved over next to her and picked up her hand. He stroked the insides of her fingers, brushing his thumb around the base of hers in a soft caressing movement. His subtle exploration made her warm and breathless. Her entire senses focused on his hand that caressed hers.

He shifted away from her, settled back behind the wheel still holding her hand.

"Will you continue to go to school when you leave the Army?"

"I expect I will."

"Monty, what are your plans after your tour of service ends?"

"I know that I'm not good enough for you," he began. "That is...you wouldn't want to marry me, would you."

She widened her eyes and met his gaze evenly.

"Why don't you ask me?"

True love is a decision,
An action, and a commitment.

Chapter 33

Words in English did not come easily to Monty when he felt most deeply. Somehow he always found himself saying things that meant nothing, leaving unsaid all the important ones he wanted to express.

He wanted to speak his heart now but found himself wordless when he looked into her eyes. There was much he wanted to convey to her.

"April." This time he spoke calmly. "Will you marry me and share my life? Without you I am nothing. I want to marry you and make you happy. Will you be my wife and let me do that?"

Not until he said the words did he realize how right it was to propose marriage. He had known he was in love for a long time. But his mind had not let his heart know he desired to marry her.

"Yes," she answered him, softly. "I would very much like to share your life."

That was all the encouragement he needed. His arms closed around her fiercely possessive as he pulled her against him. Embracing her, cradling her face, he kissed her eyelids, the corners of her mouth before his lips covered hers. When he tasted her tears, he lifted his head to gaze down at her.

"What is this? My proposal has made you weep?"

"These are happy tears," she said, "like when I cry at a happy ending in the movies."

"I feel like crying, too—you've made me the happiest man on this post." He used his thumb to catch her tears and his lips brushed her wet eyelids and her damp cheeks.

"When did you first know that you loved me?" she asked.

"I can't say for sure. It wasn't something that happened all of a sudden. It was a gradual thing. Now I cannot remember not loving you. You are the love of my life."

"What a sweet thing to say." She laughed. The sound was like sunshine in his soul. "Oh, Monty. Am I really your love?" She reached up and touched his cheek.

"I think of you that way. I am not good with English, especially when I am with you. I get all mixed up—afraid I will say all the wrong words."

He wound his arms around her until she was cocooned up close to him. He was not willing for any space to part them. Monty liked the way her body melted into his arms each time he kissed her. Every soft curve of her seemed to fit perfectly against him. But he had to cool the fire that blazed so brightly between them before he lost total control.

Something in Monty's gaze was making her blood shimmer wildly through her body, leaving confusion in its wake. His mouth descended on hers, rough in his hungry demanding need. Everything disappeared—the car where they sat locked in each other's arms—everything but *him*. She clung to Monty and sighed.

Never had she expected him to ask her to share a lifetime. How happy he made her. All the years of wondering if she would ever find anyone to love...who would return her love.

"I feel as if you were made for me," he said, echoing her thoughts. He kissed her once again.

The familiar heat raised up that set her heart racing and turned her bones to liquid. Moments later he ended the kiss and straightened.

"On Saturday afternoon, I'll pick you up and take you to Anniston to buy your ring."

"No," she said quickly. "I don't want an engagement ring."

"Why not?"

"Let's save the money for our house. I only want a wedding band."

"We haven't discussed where we will live yet. I have a job waiting for me in New York. I would like to get married during the Christmas holidays. That is—if it's okay with you."

"I was thinking about October when my ETS is up."

"April, I meant this Christmas. I don't want to wait that long."

"How is that possible? Where would we live?"

"We could live off post."

"It would be too complicated, and housing is expensive. Wouldn't it be better to put the money toward our own home? Besides, I need more time."

"Of course, you are right. It would make more sense to put the money into our own place. I just don't like waiting."

"It's only eleven months. Just think, we'll have all that time to plan our future and get to know each other better, too."

"I already know all I need to about you."

"You don't even know if I can cook."

"You can—can't you?" he asked, frowning slightly. "I know you sew beautifully."

"Yes, I can cook, too. But I might not know how to make your favorite foods. That's one of the many things I want to learn about you."

"Do you know how to make a grilled cheese sandwich?"

"As a matter of fact, I do and apple pie, too."

Monty grinned. "I'll make a list of the foods I like to eat."

"I'll want to know your dislikes, too."

"I promise to eat everything your pretty little hands prepare for me. I might not like it, but I'll eat it."

"Can I have that in writing?"

They laughed together.

As soon as he kissed her good night and left, she hurried up to the third floor. The ribbon of light under the door meant Sgt. Levy was still awake. She knocked softly.

"Come in, Sgt. Terry."

"How did you know it was me?" she asked, opening the door, and sticking her head inside.

"Who else comes knocking on my door at this late hour? Prince Charming?" Sgt. Levy sat in bed holding a book. She closed it and laid it on the bedside table. "What has you grinning like the cat that got the cream?"

"Tonight, Monty asked me to marry him."

"And?" Sgt. Levy removed her glasses and put them next to the book.

"I said *yes.* "

"I'll be-jeezed. Did he give you a ring?"

"No. He asked me to go with him to town on Saturday and pick one out. I said no. After that fiasco with Reynaldo's ring, I don't want that scene repeated."

"Do you really think Cordero would do anything?"

"I don't know. And I don't want to chance it. I convinced Monty that we should save the money for our house."

"That does make sense. But it's too bad you won't have an engagement ring." Sgt. Levy puckered her mouth and shook her head.

"I don't mind. I've never cared much for jewelry."

"So, when's the wedding?" Sgt. Levy waggled her eyebrows.

"Not until after my ETS, sometime in early October of next year." She clasped her hands together.

"Why wait that long?"

"I'm not ready to get married. We need time to get to know one another. To tell you the truth, it scares me to think about it." She twisted her fingers together several times before dropping her hands at her sides.

"Maybe you shouldn't have accepted his proposal," suggested the sergeant. "How long have you two known each other?"

"We met on the 5th of January. Nine months and twenty-six days."

"Well, it must be love. I'm happy for you."

"Thanks."

"Have you thought about how your mother will react to the news?"

"Not really. She spoke with him on the phone when I called her on Mother's Day. She seems to like him although she doesn't think we have much in common. I read somewhere that sometimes it's the things you don't share that are the most important."

"You mean opposites attract."

"Something like that. He's so different from anyone I have ever known."

"What about Cordero? They're both Spanish."

"Monty is nothing like him except for being Spanish. He's shy, sweet, considerate, and a gentleman."

"You forgot to mention, he's also handsome and has the body of an athlete."

"Sgt. Levy. You surprise me."

"I still look—there's nothing wrong with my eyesight. My glasses are just for reading."

"I'll say good night and let you get to sleep. I think I'm too excited to go to bed."

"I guess you'll have a lot to write in your diary tonight?"

"I sure do. Good night and thanks for listening to me."

"Good night, Chica—oops—sorry I forgot." Sgt. Levy grimaced, wrinkling up her nose and shutting her eyes.

She closed the door and leaned against it. Sgt. Levy had slipped and called her by Cordero's pet name for her. It shouldn't bother her. But it did.

Saturday, 02 November 1957

Dear Dreamcatcher,

I marched in the parade this morning. I felt so exhilarated afterwards. In basic training many of the girls complained that marching making them tired. For me, it makes me peppy and alive like I could lick my weight in bobcats.

Monty picked me up after chow. Again he brought up the subject of a ring. I insisted that the money be saved for our house and that I only wanted a wedding band when we married. I hope I put to rest any notions he has about giving me an engagement ring.

We drove out Rocky Hollow Road south east of Summerall Gate. I had never been on the road. It's like a different place, makes you think you are in the country and not a military post at all. We saw several whitetail deer. Monty parked beneath a shady tree and polished his *baby*. I think I have a rival in that green Plymouth...

Saturday, 09 November 1957

Monty and I attended the dance at the service club, mostly because I wanted to go. We didn't stay long. Soon as guys started trying to cut in he wanted to leave.

When I told him it was time to take me back to my barracks, he told me that a year from now I'd be his wife and he wouldn't have to kiss me good night and leave me. He said the time is not going fast enough for him, and he would like to drive somewhere other than this post. Actually, I am very content being here at Ft. McClellan. I am happy listening to Monty talk about our future. It seems a long way off to me, and if it wasn't I think I would be frightened...

April straightened the peplum on the jacket of her blue suit. This was the first time she'd worn it since the day that she enlisted. The jacket fit much better now that she had filled out in the top. She smiled, at her reflection in the mirror on the back of the door. Before leaving, she picked up her navy hat and gloves and locked the door behind her.

The auburn haired girl behind the CQ counter looked down at the sign out sheet as she paused to sign out.

"Oh, Sgt. Terry. I didn't recognize you out of uniform. I just sent the runner up to call you to the phone," the trainee indicated the receiver on the counter top.

"Thanks, Private. I'll take the call in my office." She fished the keys out of her purse as she walked down the hall.

As soon as she identified herself an angry male voice came over the wire. "Is it true?"

"Who is this?" she asked.

"It's me, Richard. I want to know if you are marrying Montoya. Someone told Cordero that you two were getting married and for a week he has been trying to drink himself unconscious. I saw you at the dance Saturday night, but I didn't notice a ring. I called to find out if the rumor is true."

"Not that it's any of your business, Montoya proposed and I accepted. I'm not wearing a ring because it's my choice. As far as Cordero's behavior, that's his choice."

"Don't you know that he is so crazy in love with you that he can't see straight? How can you do that to him?"

"I didn't ask him to love me. I can't control another's feeling no more than anyone can mine. Now if you'll excuse me, I have to go. I was on my way to church and I don't want to be late." She quickly replaced the handset before Richard could reply.

Richard's call totally distressed her. Had Monty not planned to pick her up after church in front of the chapel, she would have remained in her barracks.

She excused herself from going to the service club and asked him to take her to Company D. Back in her barracks; she took a hot shower and dressed in her nightclothes before returning to her room. She lay down on her bunk, rolled onto her side and drew her legs up close against her body in a fetal position. Then she covered her face with her hands, muffling her sobs.

I don't know but I believe,
I'll be home for Christmas Eve.

Chapter 34

Saturday, 16 November 1957
Dear Dreamcatcher,
Tonight my thoughts are like leaves scattered by the wind. They are flying every which away. I have been extremely depressed the entire week since speaking with Richard on the phone...

Friday, 22 November 1957
Monty has gone to the field for the next two weeks. It is getting cold—I hope he is keeping warm...

Saturday, 30 November 1957
This has been an extremely busy week for me overseeing the cleaning of the building and getting the trainees ready for this morning's Command Inspection. We had an excellent inspection and the parade went smoothly.

In the Orderly Room I spoke with Major Sullivan who conducted the inspection. She complimented me on the fine job I was doing as the First Sergeant. I took the opportunity to ask if she had an idea when our company would get one. She said there weren't any on the post at the moment that qualified.

I was feeling lonely so I wrote Monty another letter. While I was looking in my stationery box for an envelope I picked up the packet of letters that he wrote me when I was on TDY. I re-read all forty of them. They made me laugh and even cry. I can see how he got so deep in my heart and why I fell in love with him. I felt a lot less lonely after reading his letters...

Saturday, 07 December 1957

Our trainees were in the field. I spent the days going back and forth for the different exercises. It is rather cool and we have been wearing our winter fatigues. I like this uniform. It is so comfortable that I even wore it in the office all week. I'm sure Monty would not have approved.

Monty returned from the field and he called me at 2200 hours. He was waiting for a shower before going to bed. He thanked me for my memos and apologized for not writing but neither he nor any of the guys thought to bring any writing materials…

After eating lunch in the mess hall on Sunday, April entered Company D letting the screen swing closed behind her.

"Sgt. Terry," called the CQ. "You have a message." She handed her a pink slip.

She read the paper: "I'm on my way over, Monty." She glanced at the time. It was a quarter of an hour ago. He must already be in the parking lot.

"Thanks, Private," she said over her shoulder as she pushed her way back through the screen door.

April shaded her eyes and gazed toward the parking lot. It was vacant, but at the corner of Galloway Road, a green car was turning onto 6th Avenue.

She dashed down the sidewalk and launched herself at Monty as he emerged from his Plymouth. His arms tightened around her and he hugged her so close, the beating of his heart radiated through their clothing. She returned Monty's fierce embrace until it seemed they must crush each other.

"I think you missed me," he said, a teasing glint in his chocolate brown eyes.

With his arms around her she was caught against him. Her body relaxed and leaned into him. Her eyes fluttered shut, and she felt secure. April liked that. She also liked the strength of his arms holding her. The solid comfort of his body beneath her hand, resting against his chest, gave her such comfort. It was as if her senses had suddenly come to life. She was actually aware of the scent of his flesh, the nearness of him, the steady thudding of his heart, even the texture of the concrete beneath her feet, the fragrance of cool air that floated over her, the rhythm of her own beating heart.

He lowered his head and kissed her with warm firm lips. She moaned and he took the kiss deeper. Monty ended the kiss and she opened her eyes to find him with an odd smile playing around his mouth.

"April," he said, in a deep husky tone of voice. "What am I going to do with you?"

Before she could even begin to sort out his meaning, he kissed her again. Like none they'd ever shared. A kiss that took away her breath and muddled her mind.

"I think I should go to the field more often." He smiled and walked her around to the passenger side of the car and opened the door for her to get in before seating himself behind the wheel.

She smiled back and started to settle on the seat beside the door, when he laid his arm over the back of the seat and stared at her.

"Come over here," he said, in a voice that made her toes curl. He patted the space next to him. She moved closer without a single protest and felt the reassuring warmth and strength of his body touching her thigh.

He reached over and placed his hand on her hip scooting her tight up against him.

"That's more like it," he murmured, starting the car, easing it into gear.

He drove down Baltzell Gate Road and around by the Post Headquarters. The huge building resembled a stately house with intricately paneled front double doors. Gleaming white walls provided a sparkling contrast to the red barrel tile roof and the graceful wrought-iron railings that bordered the balconies on the upper floor where he had taken her picture in the summer.

"I put in for my Christmas vacation. I am leaving on the fifteenth, and I return one day before you do from New York," she said.

"That's good. I couldn't stand to be on the post again without you." He reached down and grasped her hand and squeezed it gently

"Where are we going?" she asked, when he drove past the Chemical Corps' barracks.

"To Reilly Lake. I know you've seen it before and I imagine you still hold unpleasant thoughts about the lake. That's why I have avoided going there. I want to replace those memories with some happy ones."

Her palms began to perspire and she clasped them together in her lap. She gazed out the side window at the array of red and gold trees sliding by, none of which she had seen that night so long ago. They rounded a curve and there before her was the lake, tranquil and peaceful.

Monty pulled the car onto the gravel parking lot and cut the engine.

They stared at each other for a long moment before he spoke.

"I have something for you, an early Christmas gift. He slipped his hand into his jacket and took a flat white box from the inside pocket. He held it out to her, but she didn't take it. Instead she eyed it uncertainly for several seconds.

"Monty, I haven't a gift—" she began.

"That's not important," he cut in.

With a shy smile, she took the box and opened it. For several moments she stared at the gold ID bracelet with a heart formed out of diamond chips next to her engraved name.

"Oh, Monty," she whispered. "It's precious. Thank you."

"Here, let me," he said and lifted the trinket from the velvet box and turned it over to reveal the engraving on the back *With love, Monty.* Then he snapped open the cover, inside was a small photo of him. "I didn't have a recent picture that would fit inside. This one was taken in New York before I entered the service. Put one of you next to it so we can be together," he suggested.

She raised her right arm and he pushed back the sleeve of her jacket, and then clasped the bracelet around her wrist.

"It's lovely, Monty. Thank you very much," she said, holding her arm out and turning her hand to admire his gift.

"You're welcome very much." He turned her palm up and pressed a warm kiss against the inside of her wrist. The faint scent of Old Spice filled her senses, her pulse fluttered beneath his tender caress.

"Our company was camped across the lake while we were here. Several times I walked around to this side at about this time of day."

Several hours passed as they remained talking and bringing each other up to date on the past two weeks they had been separated.

The sun had nearly dropped completely from the sky, and in the pink and amber twilight of another gorgeous Alabama sunset, the lake was awash with red and gold reflections.

"It is beautiful. I'm glad we came. Thank you for bringing me and thank you for this." She held up her hand with his gift encircling her wrist.

"My pleasure. Now, if we hurry we can make the last seating at your mess hall," he said, starting the car.

"When do I get to eat in yours?"

"Never. I'm not sharing you with a couple hundred other guys." He turned and looked over his shoulder as he backed out of the gravel lot.

Saturday, 14 December 1957
Dear Dreamcatcher,

With all my duties as Acting First Sergeant and Monty's classes, I have not seen him since we went to the lake on Sunday. We have talked on the phone each night. He is upset because he is pulling CQ Duty tonight and we couldn't be together. Tomorrow night, he is driving me to the bus station in Anniston.

We graduated two platoons on Friday. After the inspection and parade this morning I was exhausted. I still have to supervise the girls that are leaving the post tomorrow. I have made arrangements for their transportation to the train and bus stations and for the ones flying out of the airport in Birmingham. Eleven of the girls will be going up to Blueberry Hill in the morning. I guess the Cinderella dance went without incident, as I didn't get any complaints. I was not in attendance since Monty was on duty...

Late Sunday night, after checking her suitcase inside the station, they returned to the car to wait for the arrival of her bus. He scooted her over next to him until their bodies were touching. His hand captured hers and his thumb soothed the center of her palm sensuously. Whether he was doing this unconsciously or on purpose didn't matter. The effect was the same. Tingling warmth spread up her arm, her senses fluttering in awareness of how vulnerable were her emotions. His warmth and passion moved over her like a wave of heat on a hot Alabama afternoon.

He tucked a loose lock of hair behind her ear, and trailed gentle fingers across her cheek, letting them slide down the edge of her jaw to tilt her chin. April gazed at him in mesmerized silence observing the way his eyes darkened and became almost black.

Monty brought his arms up to pull her closer, until she was pressed so tightly against him that she could feel the frantic beat of her own heart against his unyielding chest.

His head lowered to hers, and his breath was warm on her mouth. There was no haste in his kiss. He took his time, slow—sensuous; every move of his lips increased the deeply buried heat in her body. She kissed him back, hungrily, her hand tunneling through the crisp hair at the back of his neck. Moisture formed behind her lids and slipped down her cheeks.

"These are not happy tears." He raised his head and looked at her searchingly.

"How can you tell?" she asked, wiping at her eyes.

"They taste salty." He winked at her. "Happy tears are sweet."

"The passengers are boarding the bus. I better get in line."

Monty walked her over to the group waiting beside the bus. He leaned down and kissed her cheek.

"I love you," he whispered in her ear. "Don't forget to call me in the morning."

She waved to him from the window as the bus pulled out of the station. To pass the time she opened her overnight case in the empty seat beside her and took out her writing materials. The last thing she remembered was the letter she started to Monty.

A jolt and screaming brought her awake. There was complete chaos and confusing on the bus, people moaning, lying crumpled in the aisle. The driver made his way between the seats helping them up, checking each passenger.

"Are you hurt?" he asked her.

"I'm okay," she replied. "Just a little shook up."

A short time later an ambulance arrived and took one elderly lady off the bus. Some of the other passengers complained of bruises but none were hurt seriously. They were given forms to fill out about the accident. She was told the bus hit a puddle and skidded off the road almost turning over.

Because of the delay she arrived at her mama's house at 0430 hours on Monday. She went right to bed and to sleep.

She awoke with a start. What was the time? The shades were closed and the room was dark. She turned on the bedside lamp and glanced at her watch, 1100 hours. Monty expected her to call before noon. She jumped out of bed and threw on the same clothes she had draped over the chair that morning.

The living room was empty. Mama must be in the kitchen starting lunch. She picked up the phone and dialed. She glanced out the window. It was raining. It reminded her of the times she and Monty walked in the warm summer rain, and his rain sweet kisses.

"Thirtieth Chemical Company, PFC Montoya speaking."

"Monty, what are you doing answering the phone?"

"I've been camped out here all morning waiting for your call. You had me worried. I thought something had happened to you."

"It did. The bus skidded off the road, and we had a two hour delay."

"Were you hurt? Are you okay?" he asked in an anxious tone.

"I'm fine. I was sleeping when it happened. Some of the other passengers were bruised and banged up, and one elderly lady was taken away in an ambulance."

"Thank God, you're all right. You had me worried when you didn't call."

"Guess what? It's raining. I was just thinking of the times we walked together in the rain."

"Funny you should say that. It's raining on the post, too. I was remembering the same thing. But we couldn't walk in this rain. It's too cold."

"Here, too. If it gets any colder, it will turn to snow. I hope so. I haven't seen snow in over two years."

"You should come with me to New York. I heard on the news this morning that it is snowing there."

"You didn't invite me or I would have," she teased.

"It's not too late."

"I wish I could."

"I know," he said, softly.

"I better hang up—I don't want to run up Mama's phone bill. Have a safe trip. I love you."

"Me, too."

She held the receiver for a moment before placing it back on the cradle. Quickly, she snapped open her ID bracelet to gaze at Monty's photo. She sighed.

"Elaine." Her mama stood in the doorway. "How long have you been up?" She crossed the room to hug her.

"Just a few minutes." She closed the cover on her bracelet. "I had to call Monty. The bus was delayed and I got in at four thirty this morning."

"Come out to the kitchen and tell me all about it while I fix you a nice breakfast."

Sunday, 22 December 1957
Dear Dreamcatcher,
   Yesterday I had my first letter from Monty in New York. He too, had some transportation problems. A pipe broke on the train and he said it was like a river running down through the train car in which he was traveling. He told me how happy my letters made him when he arrived and found them waiting for him. I have written to him each day since I arrived in Kentucky.

Mama has been trying to get me to go out as she sees how lonely I am. I had rather stay here and write to Monty. Then I am not so lonely...

Tuesday, 24 December 1957

I got so bored that I volunteered to baby-sit. Mama had promised to watch a neighbor's two children, Terrill age five and his sister Valerie nine, while their mother picked up their toys on lay-a-way at one of the department stores.

My granny came down from the hills to spend the holidays with us so I now have a roommate. She looks so fragile I am afraid to hug her.

Everyone has gone to bed. I am writing in the living room. Earlier, I had tried to write a letter to Monty but I kept getting the pages damp with my tears. Extremely salty ones...

Sunday, 29 December 1957

This afternoon, I had a sweet letter from Monty saying he spent a quiet Christmas playing with his nephews and their toys.

I had a call after dinner tonight from my recruiting sergeant. Mama must have called and told him I was here. Sgt. Matar invited me to appear as a guest on a local radio program tomorrow evening...

A casually dressed, Sgt. Matar in a dark sport coat worn over a light blue shirt opened at the neck met her in the impressive lobby of the WKTG Radio Station. She was glad she had not worn her uniform but opted for a long sleeved rusty-colored tweed dress.

"Hello, Sp. Terry. I saw you enter the parking lot in the Pontiac Chieftain. I thought by now you would have persuaded your brother to let you have the convertible on your post." He steered her down the corridor and around the corner through an open door.

"No. That's his baby." She gazed around the room that held an enormous mahogany desk with matching chairs, several cabinets and water fountain in one corner.

"Take a seat." He indicated a chair near the desk. Instead of sitting behind the desk, he perched on one corner. "I must say you have changed. The military must agree with you. Your mother told me that you recently became engaged."

She briefly related how she met Monty and the incident at the mess hall with the apple pie. The sergeant laughed with her over the pie story.

"You are a guest on a program called *You Asked For It.* Persons call and request for a record to be played and get a chance to ask you a question about your career." He glanced at his watch. "It's almost time for the show to begin. Let's go over to Studio A."

Down the hall she and Sgt. Matar entered a room with a glass panel separating them from where a handsome man in his mid thirties sat between turntables in front of a mike. He glanced up and waved before he came out to greet them. His intense blue eyes matched his silk shirt cuffed at the sleeves. Tall and wiry, he wore his golden-brown hair slightly longer than was the fashion. Probably in keeping with his *show biz* image.

"Elaine, this is Steve Wolfe, the host of the program. Steve meet Sp. Terry, a member of the Women's Army Corps.

"Elaine was one of the WACs featured in the recent Third Army production of *Your Army Around the World.* The one I was telling you about that a clip was featured on the Ed Sullivan Show a couple of nights ago."

She shook hands and exchanged greetings with Steve before they entered the glass enclosure.

"How did you feel about seeing yourself on TV?" asked Steve.

"Unfortunately, I was on duty the night it aired, and I never got to see it," she said.

"Too bad. From what Sgt. Matar told me it was a spectacular show. They should do more programs like that to promote public relations and good will between the military and civilians."

"I understand the Third Army Special Services Staff produces a similar show every five years," she informed him as he motioned for her and Sgt. Matar to take a seat behind the long counter.

She sat where Steve indicated in front of one of the mikes. He placed a set of headphones on her head and plugged the cord into the unit in front of her.

"Four—three—two—one," counted Steve. He pointed to a fixture on the glass. It turned to a bright red. "Good evening WKTG radio fans. This is Steve Wolfe welcoming you to *You Asked For It.* This evening, I have in the studio with me a young woman who is a member of the Women's Army Corps, Sp. Elaine Terry. She will be taking your request and answering your questions about her position in the service." He paused. "Hello. You are on the air with Sp. Terry."

"Hello, this is Sue Kyle. I would like to hear 'Young Love.' My question is what made you enlist in the Women's Army Corps."

"Sue, that isn't easy to answer. It was a combination of things. If you've heard the commercial on the radio, it has a lot to offer a young woman—travel, job opportunities, education, advancement, and a month's paid vacation is a wonderful plus."

After the music ended, she took the next call.

"Danny Murray here. I would like to know what you do in your job in the service."

"At the present I am the Acting First Sergeant of Delta Company in the WAC Training Battalion at Ft. McClellan, Alabama. I oversee the training of new recruits for the first eight weeks of their enlistment."

"Do you carry a gun?"

"No, I don't, Danny. But I used an M-1 Rifle in basic training. What song would you like to hear?"

"How about "If I Didn't Care," by the Ink Spots."

"Sure thing, that's a favorite of mine, too."

The disk ended and she answered the next call.

"Phil Brennan. Tell me about the post where you are stationed. I am thinking of enlisting and would you recommend your post?"

"Phil, that's more than one question but I'll try to give you the answers as briefly as possible. I'm stationed at Ft. McClellan, Alabama, said to be the showplace of the Third Army Military Posts. It's the home of the Women's Army Corps, The Military Police Academy, and the Chemical Corps. It's a beautiful post and I highly recommend it if you're thinking of enlisting. It might interest you to know that the ratio of women to men on the post are six to one."

"Did I hear you correctly, there are six girls for every guy?"

"That's right. Now what can I play for you?"

"'Ramblin' Man' by Hank Williams."

After that call a stream of guys and gals called wanting to know more about the post and what it had to offer. She replied to one girl's inquiry that it was the place to find the man of her dreams. That got a large response from the females.

When the show was over she stayed a few minutes talking with Steve and Sgt. Matar.

"We are having a New Years Eve party here at the studio tomorrow night," said Steve. "I would like you to come as my guest. Sgt. Matar is going to be here, too."

312

"Thanks, but I have already made plans. And thank you for having me on your show. It was fun. I thoroughly enjoyed myself."

"Nabil, try and persuade her to come to the party," said Steve.

"Nabil?" she questioned.

"That's the sergeant's first name."

"Oh, Nabil, yes, of course," she said, recovering and trying to swallow a giggle.

"I'll walk you out to your car, Sp. Terry, and you can tell me about your plans now that you are engaged," said the sergeant, holding the door for her.

Late in the afternoon on the following day, she placed a call to Monty in New York. She let it ring ten times before she finally hung up the receiver. She went to her room and got out her paper and pen careful not to wake Granny napping on the bed.

Mama had cooked all her favorite foods for dinner. After she dried the last plate, she put the stack of dinner dishes in the cabinet with the others they had used. She closed the door as the telephone rang. Sure it was Monty, she dashed out to the living room to grab the phone.

"Hello," she answered cheerfully, on the second ring before her stepfather could get out of his recliner. He mumbled something rude under his breath, glared at her and settled back in his chair.

"Hi, darling," said Monty, brightly.

"I tried calling you this afternoon. Since no one was home I wrote you a letter." She picked up the base of the phone, stretched the wire out into the hall, and closed the door.

"It's so good to hear your sweet voice. I went to ice skate in Central Park with my sister and nephews. You better not mail my letter. I'll be leaving before it gets here," said Monty.

"I'll send it to Ft. McClellan. That way it will be there when you arrive.

"Good idea. I wouldn't want to miss out on reading one of your dear letters. I still have the ones you wrote me from Georgia. I brought them with me to read when I get lonely."

"I did that with yours while you were in the field. I wish I had brought them with me to Kentucky. Several times a day I look at your picture in my pretty ID bracelet."

"I bet you can't guess what I'm doing. I'm babysitting for my sister. She and Jorge went to a New Year's Eve party. Are you and your parents going out to celebrate?"

"That's sweet of you to do that for them. We aren't going out, we have a big dinner on the first of January."

"I better say good night. I just wanted to call and wish you a Happy New Year. Just think this time next year we will be going out to celebrate together. Darling, won't that be wonderful?"

"Yes—Happy New Year, Monty." She hung up the receiver and clutched the telephone against her chest. Her throat had closed and a chill had run down her spine when Monty mentioned them being together this time next year.

Quietly, she returned the telephone to the small table inside the living room and went to her room.

She could not shake the anxiety that something would happen to prevent them from marrying. Moisture filled her eyes with the strangeness of the feeling deep inside her.

Always believe in yourself.
Don't give up your dreams.

Chapter 35

Friday, 03 January 1958
Dear Dreamcatcher,
A pleasant surprise awaited me on my return from leave. My portrait was hanging in the Day Room. I have the honor of representing Company D as WAC of the Month.

Everyone was glad to have me return especially Sgt. Waite who filled in as First Sergeant in my absence. By the end of this month, Sgt. Levy informed me that our company would be getting a replacement. I really don't mind. Its kind of fun running the company...

Early Sunday morning, April followed the Runner down to the first floor.

"Pvt. Currans, after I pick up the phone in the Orderly Room, please hang up the receiver at the counter."

"Yes, Sgt. Terry."

She hurriedly unlocked the door and grabbed the phone on her desk.

"Hi, darling, did I call too early?" asked Monty.

"Not at all. I just got back from breakfast. How was your trip?"

"Nothing unusual happened on my return train ride. It's so good to hear your voice."

"I'm glad. If I'd had your car I would have met you at the station."

"I got in much too late. That's why I didn't call last night. Can I come over now?"

"I'll meet you in the parking lot."

Twenty minutes later, as soon as the car came to a halt, Monty whipped open the door. He bodily picked her up and hugged her so tightly she lost her breath.

"Get in," he said, holding the door for her.

"Where are we going?"

"Somewhere I can kiss you properly without an audience." He indicated the girls returning from the mess hall going into the barracks.

A few blocks away, he abruptly stopped the car in the middle of the road. He leaned over and kissed her.

"Monty. Be careful. Never do that on a main road."

"I won't," he said, as a big grin spread across his face. "I'll pull over to the curb first."

"You used to be so shy. It took you the longest time before you kissed me that first time."

"I was just making sure that you wanted me to kiss you. I didn't want my face slapped."

"And all that time, I thought it was because you didn't like me well enough."

"That's the problem. I liked you too much. I was afraid you weren't ready for another relationship. But tell me about your leave. Did you have a good time visiting with your mother?"

"I would rather have been with you."

"Me, too."

He pulled over and parked under a shade tree. He reached across her, opened the glove box, and took out his camera.

"I want to take some pictures of you to send to my father when I write him."

"Why didn't you tell me when you called? I would have worn something nice?"

"You look adorable as always." He kissed her on the tip of her nose.

"I hope your father will think so."

"He will." He reached out and took her hand in his, raising it to his lips, feathering kisses across each knuckle. And then he placed a warm kiss at her wrist before he released her hand again to open his door.

Since their engagement, Monty had showed her every courtesy when they were alone. He had accepted the limits she placed on their lovemaking. Yet all the time she was aware of his restraint. It was evident in the way his eyes darkened and in the controlled tension in his body when they kissed, but he respected her desire not to preempt their wedding night.

Monday, 20 January 1958
Dear Dreamcatcher,
This afternoon I had an interview with Major Sullivan in connection with the WAC of the Month. She commented on the splendid job that I was doing as Delta Company's Acting First Sergeant. The major emphasized that at the end of my ETS—I should consider going to OCS. Since I was not wearing a ring I did not mention that I was engaged. Sgt. Levy had cautioned that it could have some bearing on my not getting selected the Post WAC of the Month...

Thursday, 27 January 1958
These busy days have given me the taste of what a First Sergeant's job entails. Arranging for the recruits' inoculations, clothing warehouse charts, and escorting them to the PX.
I have only seen Monty one night this week and only for a few hours because of his classes and my extra work. And tomorrow evening he is on CQ Duty...

April peeled off her gloves and tossed them beside her hat on the desktop.

"It's cold out there this morning," she said, taking off her jacket and draping it on the back of her chair.

The phone rang.

"Good morning, Company D, Sgt. Levy speaking."

There was a short pause.

"Yes, Ma'am. She's right here."

"Major Sullivan for you on line two." Levy held up her hands with the fingers crossed.

"Good morning, Ma'am," she said.

"Congratulations, Sp. Terry. You have been selected for the Post WAC of the Month. You will be attending a two-day field orientation arranged by the Defense Advisory Committee on Women in the Services. Some dignitaries from your home state have been invited along with Mrs. Harriet Reeves, a Professor and writer of Political Science from Frankfort, and Capt. Regina Hornak, recruiting officer from Ashland, Kentucky."

"I am honored. Thank you, Ma'am."

"The paperwork with the information will be sent to your CO. An appointment has been scheduled with Post Public Information Center for pictures. At this time it is my pleasure to inform you of an additional honor. You will become a member of the WAC Color Guard as the right guard next to the American Flag. What say you to that?"

"Somebody pinch me...um...I mean that is an *honor.* Thank you, Ma'am." She hung up the phone and slowly sank down on her chair.

"I know you made the Post WAC of the Month." Sgt. Levy jumped out of her seat and crossed the room. "But what else did she say?"

"Sgt. Levy, you're not going to believe it."

> Wednesday, 04 February 1958
> Dear Dreamcatcher,
> Monty was proud of me being honored as Post WAC of the Month and becoming a member of the Color Guard. But I don't think he is too happy with the time the duties will take away from my free time to be with him. I told him that at least my duties and obligations as WAC of the Month would end on the last day of this month.
> I had my first color guard practice Tuesday evening so I couldn't go to school with Monty. My first official parade will be in Anniston for the Washington's Birthday Parade. I wear white gloves with my dress uniform and a white silk neck scarf with the Third Army patch.
> Sgt. Williams of B Company is the American Flag bearer and Sgt. Greene from Company C carries the WAC Flag. Sp. Nancy Phelps of Company A is the other color guard. I tried on the harness that holds the flags. It looks easy but it is very difficult, especially if it's a windy day...

Two weeks later, she met with the color guard in back of Company B where they boarded a military bus for Anniston.

The weather had cooperated and given them a glorious, sunny day for the parade. It was cool but she was comfortable with the long sleeved T-shirt she had been instructed to wear beneath her shirtwaist.

By 1000 hours everyone was in place at the starting point of the parade. She removed the cover from the American Flag and it unfurled with a snap in the breeze. She and the other members of the color guard took their position behind the WAC Band.

Emotions ran riot through her as always, stirred by the pageantry and flourish of "The Stars and Stripes Forever." Notes from the tuba sending chills up her spine and it was not from the cool weather. This elation and thrill of patriotism moved her to a soul stirring experience, leaving her exuberant as she proudly stepped out next to the splendor of the American Flag, a symbol of duty, honor, and country.

Following the parade, Monty drove over after dinner and they sat in his car talking in the parking lot.

"I hope you don't want to go to the dance tonight," he said. "I don't think I could stand up to dance after marching in my heavy combat boots. And my head still feels like I'm wearing my helmet." He smoothed a hand through his hair, letting his arm drop around her shoulder.

"That's okay. I'm too excited to be tired. I don't understand why your company didn't wear dress uniforms for the parade."

"It's not what the Decon Unit wears when we are working."

"I looked for you but I couldn't spot your face beneath all those helmets."

"You looked real sharp marching with the Color Guard. You don't know how proud I was to tell the guys that my girl was marching next to the American Flag." He pulled her close against his chest.

"I felt proud, too," she whispered.

He bent his head to kiss her. He intended it to be a tender caress, sweet and lingering, but when her lips clung and opened beneath his, he found he wanted more. Before he could consider the wisdom of what he was doing, his hand was navigating the curve of her neck and the valley between her breasts. Her skin was like warm silk beneath his questing fingers.

April gasped at the intimate contact. She stared from his hand and back to hold his gaze.

"What are you doing?"

"My hand is cold, I found a *packet* for it to warm in," Monty said, looking innocently at her.

"The word is *pocket*, and you will have to put your hand in your own pocket," she scolded.

"But I like yours much better," he insisted, a smile creasing his face. "It's soft and so nice and warm."

Although she shouldn't allow him such a liberty, she couldn't bring herself to push his hand away. She had never been touched that way before, yet with Monty there was no thought of shame or embarrassment.

"Someone could walk by. What would they think?" she asked.

"They'd think we were necking. And they'd be right." He chuckled.

Heat warmed her upper body and she tingled in the center of her most private part. She had never known sensual pleasure. His lips continued to explore her temple, her ear lobes and the hollow in her throat. She could only lift her face to him to experience all the wonderful new feelings trembling through her.

"My pocket is getting warmer," he said, switching hands before his mouth settled over hers again.

His lips left her mouth, finding the hollow beneath her chin, the pressure point under her ear and moved to the curve of her throat again where her pulse beat in double-time.

He sucked lightly at her neck, whispering words of love against her skin that made her shiver. Taken by surprise, she drew in a sharp breath unable to move, shocked by the desire that began low in her belly.

He molded her to him, his fingers caressing her through her blouse then falling into the dark shadow between her breasts and lingered there.

"Monty?"

"It's all right," he said, soothingly.

His sweetness did it. It was that yearning tenderness that assured her. The way he pulled her tight against him, not suggestively but cradled her body as if it were fragile and precious. The way he trembled faintly. The way he kissed her.

It felt so right she silently fell into agreement with him and relaxed. She closed her eyes and responded fully to the explorations of his hand, enjoying the rapturous feel of his fingers as they caressed the sides of breasts. Her nipples instantly beaded under his soft manipulations.

How could something be so new and yet so familiar? A glorious feeling bubbled up inside her making her want to laugh and cry at the same time. She was acutely aware of the scent of his after-shave lotion, the warmth of him, even the cadence of her own beating heart.

In an odd way it was as if her life had been on hold while she waited for Monty to find her. Each morning she awoke happy and excited, knowing she would see or talk with him that evening. At night she laid her head on her pillow, her mind full of dreams she'd never dared to believe possible, never believed were meant for her.

The following morning she exited the shower in the latrine. She stepped in front of the sink, took off her shower cap and removed the curlers from her hair. A small bruise on her neck below her ear startled her. A hickey. She had

320

heard of them—seen them on other girls, but never had one herself. She leaned into the mirror and touched the injury. The spot stung where Monty had nipped her, but there was a feel of pleasure overlaying the twinge of pain. The brand left her with a sensation of being claimed and wanted. Had he been aware of what he did? Did he intend to mark her neck?

She returned to her room and dropped down on her bunk. With eyes closed, she relived the sensual memory of Monty's hand on her breast and his mouth moving over her neck. How his lips had nibbled and sucked at her flesh, her sound of pleasure and the way she had shivered against him when he kissed her throat.

With a sigh, she got up and went to one of her civilian lockers. She pulled out several blouses before selecting a pink one that buttoned up the front with a ruffle at the top. After dressing she checked her appearance in her vanity mirror. The high ruffle covered the small spot on her neck.

After church she walked to the parking lot where Monty waited in the car. He seated her beside him and eyed her blouse. A grin creased his face.

"Did you wear that blouse to deter my wandering fingers?" he asked, one corner of his mouth lifted in a half smile.

"No," she said, and she pulled down the ruffle to expose the purpling bruise. "It's to cover this brand."

Monty stared in disbelief. "Don't tell me—I did that last night."

She nodded her head and smoothed the cloth up over the injury. "I'm afraid so."

"I'm sorry…I never meant to hurt you. I don't know how could I do such a thing to you?" A look of regret marred his face. "Please forgive me. I promise I'll never do that again." He draped his arms around the steering wheel and rested his head on them. "I feel so rotten."

"Monty," she said softly, laying her hand on his shoulder. "It's not as bad as it looks. There's no pain unless I touch it."

He straightened away from the wheel. His dark face drawn, his eyes searched her gaze.

"You are not just saying that to make me feel better?"

"Honest. It doesn't hurt. My skin bruises easily."

Monty leaned toward her and gingerly moved the ruffle away from the purple mark.

"Who ever sees this will think I'm a monster," he said, allowing the fabric to stand around her neck.

"No one is going to see it. This week I'm wearing my wool fatigues with my neck scarf. One of our platoons is in the field and I'm going out to check on them and later this week I will be keeping score at the rifle range."

The following morning, April adjusted the yellow scarf around her neck before entering the orderly room. After greeting Sgt. Levy, she moved toward the coffee stand.

"No need to make coffee this morning. The lieutenant called and said she would be in the field most of the day. I left the Morning Report on your desk to take out with you."

"Okay," she said. She picked up the medical records from her Inbox and walked over to the metal file cabinet.

She touched the scarf protecting the spot on her neck as she had several times already, putting her finger on the place where Monty left his mark Saturday night.

Warmth flooded her insides as she recalled the liberties she had allowed him with his *packet.*

"Sgt. Terry," said Sgt. Levy. "Are you hiding a love bite under that scarf around your neck?"

"What makes you think I'm hiding anything?" She whirled around, her hand going automatically to the bruise.

"I've noticed you gently touching the left side of your neck a couple of times. Am I right?"

"I can't keep a secret from you, can I?"

"I have just the thing for it." The sergeant leaned down rummaging in her bottom desk drawer. "Here," she said, handing her a tiny amber colored bottle.

"*Tincture of Arnica,*" she read the label. "I've never heard of it."

"Dab some on—it'll clear up your bruise in no time, and it won't soil your scarf or discolor your skin. Be careful and not get it into your eyes," Sgt. Levy cautioned.

After going to the latrine and applying the liquid, she returned the bottle to Sgt. Levy.

"Anytime you need it. Help yourself. On second thought, maybe you should keep it," said the grinning sergeant.

"Thanks, but I don't anticipate getting any more of these," she said, and touched the scarf covering her neck. "If you could have seen Monty's remorseful face when he saw it the next day you'd know what I mean. I felt sorry for him."

As the days passed, her position as Acting First Sergeant settled into a repetition of military duties and exercises. All her off duty time, she reserved for Monty.

> Saturday, 15 March 1958
> Dear Dreamcatcher,
> Our First Sergeant arrived today. Sgt. Alma Vinson. A tall woman in her early forty's with light brown hair and sparkling, blue eyes. She is extremely nice and friendly, too. I got quite a start when I returned from breakfast and saw her car in the back of the building. It's a '57 Bel Air like Richards' and the same color, too.
> I spent most of the day bringing her up to date on what phase of training each platoons is in at the present.
> Just in time to drive many of our girls to the different transportation facilities, I resumed my duty as Post Staff Driver
> I marched with the color guard in the parade this morning. For me, marching is still as thrilling and exciting as the first time I stepped out to the beat of the drum…

In the Orderly Room—seven weeks and ten parades later, April sat in her chair with her foot propped on a stool. Sgt. Levy and Vinson stood in front of her.

"It's only a little sprain. I'm sure it will be okay by Saturday's parade," she said.

"Take your shoe off and let me have a look," said Sgt. Levy.

"Look, it's swollen," said Sgt. Vinson. "I think I'd better run you over to the hospital and let the doctor take a look at your ankle," she said, putting on her hat.

"I'm sure it'll be okay with some ice and an ace bandage," April insisted.

Thirty minutes later, after an X-ray she sat in a wheel chair in Captain Miller's office at Nobel Hospital.

"How did this happen?" asked the captain.

"I twisted my ankle stepping off the curb coming from the mess hall."

"I was referring to the small lump on the inside of your ankle."

"Oh, that. That's been there since I was a child. My leg got caught between a wooden wagon and a concrete coal house when a car backed into the wagon I was sitting in."

The captain pressed firmly on the inside of her leg.

"Ouch. That smarts, sir."

"Has it bothered you over the years?"

"No, sir. Not that I recall."

"Since you are here, I'm going to schedule you for exploratory surgery tomorrow."

"Sir, you can't. I have a parade to march in on Saturday."

"I'm afraid you aren't going to be doing any marching for awhile." He pulled her medical record over in front of him and began to write. He stopped writing, closed the file and picked up the phone on his desk. "Have Sgt. Vinson step into my office."

Later in the evening, Sgt. Levy returned with Sgt. Vinson and brought the personal items April requested along with her journal and box of stationery.

After the sergeants left, she wrote Monty in the field, explaining what had happened. She told him it was nothing serious and not to worry.

Early the following morning her friend, Bryza, prepared her for surgery.

"I don't know why I'm shaving your leg. It's as smooth as a baby's bottom. You're lucky not to have any hair on your legs," said Bryza, blotting her leg with a towel. "Now lie down on the gurney. I'm going to give you an injection—there—that didn't hurt. Did it?"

"Like a bee sting."

"Terry, you don't have a thing to worry about. Capt. Miller is the best surgeon in the hospital. Now I want you to start counting backwards from one hundred."

"100—99—98—97—96—95—94—93—92—91—90—89—80…"

"I think she is under," said Bryza.

No, I can hear you. She tried to speak but there was an odd numbness all over her body.

"Does she know?" asked Braza.

"No. I thought it best not to alarm her," said a male voice, she recognized as Capt. Miller.

First, the strength drained out of her body. Then the room spun for a moment, tilted and swirled around her. The light dimmed and the sounds faded away…

Time is like a medicine.
But there is excruciating pain,
That goes with the healing process.

Chapter 36

"Sp. Terry." A voice from far away repeated her name insistently, over and over again.

The face above her faded then reappeared in a blurry shape. Slowly, the features came together and gained clarity.

"Bryza?"

"Terry. You're finally awake. You've been sleeping like a baby, and you missed your visitor."

"What visitor?" She glanced at the empty chair beside her cot, then at the chrome rails around her bed and down at her left foot. Only her toes peeked out from the cast-like wrapping with a clear tube extending out from the side.

"He didn't give his name. It was a Latin dressed in fatigues. He asked about you and I told him you were still in the Recovery Room. He waited for over an hour until you were brought to the ward. I was keeping a close eye on you. Each time I passed down the aisle he was just sitting here holding your hand. Before he left he did the strangest thing. He kissed the palm of your hand, closed your fingers over it, and then placed your hand back under the blanket."

"Monty must have come in from the field."

"It wasn't him. This guy was thinner," said the nurse.

"I think I'm going to be sick."

Bryza lowered the rail, assisted her in sitting up and held a plastic tray under her chin. She gagged several times.

"It's the anesthesia making you nauseous. I'll get you some cracked ice. You can't drink or eat anything for awhile because it will just come back up." Bryza walked down the aisle to the front of the large bay-like room and exited through the tall double doors.

April's bed was in the middle of a room of approximately twenty-four beds. All the beds to her left were vacant, and no one occupied the bed on her right. The first three beds held male patients, as did the six across the aisle from her. They all seemed to have foot or leg problems. Two guys had their legs up in the air with wires attached to a pulley.

Bryza returned with a small bowl of ice.

"Dinner will be served soon, but I'm afraid that you can't have anything to eat as yet. Later tonight I'll bring you something."

"That's okay. My stomach is too upset to eat. When can I see the doctor?"

"He was here to see you after your visitor left, but you didn't want to wake up. Capt. Miller will see you in the morning when he makes his rounds. Let me know when your pain becomes too much."

"I don't have any pain. In fact, I haven't any feeling in my foot."

"You will. The doctor left something for it."

"What's that tube sticking out of the wrapping?"

"That's a drain tube. The doctor will explain it to you tomorrow."

Tuesday, 06 May 1958
Dear Dreamcatcher,

I had surgery on my leg this morning. I still don't understand why it was necessary, as I haven't talked to the doctor.

While I was still unconscious, a mystery visitor came to see me. There are a lot of unanswered questions going through my head right now.

In the evening Capt. Fraser and Sgt. Levy visited with me. After they left a male nurse brought me a bowl of Jell-O. That was my dinner...

Wednesday, 07 May 1958
Capt. Miller spoke to me this morning. He said the lump he removed was benign. It could have been malignant, and that is why he immediately scheduled the surgery.

Because I still can't keep anything down, I get injections for the pain. They must be very strong as they put me out.

Bryza told me that my mystery visitor was here again in the afternoon while I sleeping off the pain medication. She said he wore fatigues and sat beside my bed holding my hand, and she didn't notice when he left.

In the evening Sgt. Vinson and Sgt. Gwynn came to visit me. The first sergeant said Sgt. Levy spends the day talking to herself. That's nothing new…

The following afternoon, Bryza approached the bed carrying a small tray with her medication.

"Terry, don't look now but your mystery visitor is here. For the past ten minutes he has been standing outside the doors watching you through the glass. I don't know what to make of him unless he is waiting for me to give you this shot so he can come sit with you while you sleep."

She sat up and peered around the nurse in time to see someone wearing a helmet move away from the glass.

"Was he wearing a helmet?"

"Yes. Do you recognize him?" Bryza put the tray on the table and pulled the curtains around her bed.

"No. I only caught a glimpse of a helmet."

"Do you want me to find out his name if he comes in the ward this afternoon?" she asked, preparing the injection.

"Would you, please," she said, laying back on her pillow, and closing her eyes.

The last thing she remembered was the sound of Bryza raising the rails on her bed and opening the drapes.

Friday, 09 May 1958
Dear Dreamcatcher,
This afternoon, Sgt. Vinson and Sgt. Levy came to visit and brought me an unusual potted plant. It has big fuzzy leaves like an African violet with large flowers in shades of lavender and white.
They also brought my mail. A letter from my mama, who doesn't know about my surgery, and a cute card that Monty made for me. He will visit me on Sunday when he returns from the field…

April tried to raise her eyelids. Her limbs felt heavy yet at the same time light and limp. Unable to move, she lay there conscious of the bandage on her foot and of someone holding her hand.

She opened her eyes. A man's face swam before her as if she were gazing through a cloud of gray smoke. Rapidly blinking her eyes, she tried to bring the image into focus.

"Monty," she whispered. Her eyes drifted shut and she floated on a cloud. A sense of euphoria blocked out all thought as she felt herself slipping down into a vacuum.

Much later, a hand touched her cheek, drawing her back from unconsciousness. She came awake slowly, disoriented and confused.

Monty was standing beside her bed holding a bouquet of yellow roses and daisies. She took a few shuddering breaths, aware that he was staring anxiously at her with a frown on his face.

"Darling, you gave me a scare." He leaned down and brushed her lips with his. "You were so still." He handed her the flowers and sat down. "I got these at the commissary. I know you like yellow."

"They are lovely. Thank you," she said, sniffing the fragrant roses before placing them beside her on the bed. "Were you at the hospital earlier?"

"No. This was the earliest that I could get here." He reached out and clasped her hand, his thumb making small circles on the back of her hand near the base of her thumb sending out electric charges like lightning in a summer storm.

"It's just as well. I have been sleeping most of the afternoon because the pain medication they are giving me puts me to sleep."

"Tell me about your ankle. How much longer do you have to stay here?"

"The doctor took out the drain tube this morning. I start physical therapy on Monday."

"What kind of physical therapy?"

"For my ankle. The doctor said I wouldn't be able to walk without it. Some muscles and tendons were cut to remove the growth, and now my foot won't flex to take steps."

"If this is a joke, I'm not laughing."

"I couldn't believe it either when the doctor explained it to me. I cried after he left the ward."

Monty scooted his chair over next to the bed, putting his arms around her, and resting her head against his shoulder.

"Don't worry. I know you're going to be okay."

"I wish we were sitting in your car."

"Why?"

"So you could kiss me properly."

Monty laughed and she joined him.

Sunday, 11 May 1958
Dear Dreamcatcher,
Monty came to see me this afternoon. While I ate my dinner, he went out to grab a quick bite to eat. When the nurse came to give me my pain medication, he kissed me and left the hospital at 2200 hours.

Bryza informed me that the mystery visitor had been watching me through the glass door entrance and he had left just minutes before Monty arrived. She speculated that they had passed each other in the hall.

I told her his name was PFC Rodrigues and if she saw him again to tell him that I wanted to see him when I was awake...

Monday, 12 May 1958
My therapy began this morning with Sp. Gavin Rankin. The therapist is short, middle aged, and muscular with unruly black hair.

The therapy room is large, filled with equipment and padded tables. In the center mounted on waist high holders are two metal bars spaced thirty inches apart and ten foot long. I sat in a chair beside a deep tub and submerged my left foot in a warm water filled vessel. Sp. Rankin turned on a switch and I had the sensation of hundreds of tiny needles penetrating my foot and leg. It's called a whirlpool bath and my treatment lasted for thirty minutes. Afterwards, he lifted me onto a table and massaged my foot. He kept apologizing for hurting me, and he said it was okay for me to yell. I didn't cry out but it hurt enough to bring tears to my eyes. Lastly, he had me try and walk between the metal bars. I could barely touch my toes to the floor. How agonizing and discouraging...

Tuesday, 27 May 1958
After fifteen therapy treatments I am learning to walk with crutches. I never expected being this long in the

hospital. I am not allowed to return to my barracks because I cannot maneuver the stairs. I don't have anymore whirlpool treatments, but I practice lifting small weights with my foot and I still get the painful massages...

April kept her eyes focused on the area between the bars, willing her foot to work. She took a small short step with her right leg, and then a shorter step with her left leg. The sharp pain brought instant tears to her eyes. With each step the punishment was less. Beads of perspiration trickled down between her breasts. She kept at it, pushing herself to limp the length of the rails until she reached the end.

"You did it," said Gavin. He helped her into the wheelchair. "I knew you could do it."

He wheeled her down the corridor to the ward, and then stopped beside her bed. "Do you want to stay in the chair or get back in your bunk?"

"I'm exhausted. I would like to lay down for a bit."

He scooped her up in his burly arms and deposited her gently in the middle of the bed. The specialist leaned over and pulled up the chrome rail.

"Do you have to raise both rails? I feel like I'm in a baby's crib," she complained.

"This bed is pretty high off the floor," he said, shaking his head as he raised the other rail. "You could fall off. I'll see you tomorrow."

April punched her pillow and looked around at the sterile ward. She settled back to listen to the muffled sounds coming from the corridor, personnel and visitors passing up and down the hallway. She sighed, closing her eyes, inhaling the antiseptic smell that always made her queasy.

Monday, 02 June 1958
Dear Dreamcatcher,
This morning, I was released from the hospital. I am walking with a cane. Correction— better make that limping. For the next two weeks I am on light duty. I have to return twice a week to the hospital for therapy during the next six weeks. Also I am not allowed to drive for another additional month.

During my hospital stay, I gained five pounds. I guess that says something for Nobel's hospital food...

Saturday, 07 June 1958
This afternoon Monty took me to the WAC pool. He said
I needed some sun after my long stay in the hospital. I didn't
go into the water as I am still wearing an ace bandage.
Monty commented that the weight I had gained seemed
to be in all the right places...

Following chapel, April changed into a white skirt with a colorful orange and black border with a matching short sleeve blouse. She slipped on a pair of white flats, picked up her cane, walked carefully down the steps, and outside. Halfway down the walkway, she saw Monty pull into the parking lot. Instead of coming to meet her as he usually did, he stayed inside the car. He didn't move as she approached the vehicle. One arm rested over the steering wheel and he silently studied her.

At the look on his face her welcoming smile dissolved into a frown. "What's wrong?" she asked, slipping into the seat beside him.

"I had a look at my calendar. In five weeks I will be leaving Ft. McClellan."

"You should be happy to be getting out of the Army. You've often said that the military life wasn't for you."

"I am glad to complete my duty, but I'll be leaving you here. It gives me a bad feeling. Let's get married now." He gave her no chance to reply, but he bent his head and kissed her passionately.

Shock waves rippled through her. He laid claim to her mouth with a fierceness that would have terrified her in the past. She clung to him, her fingers gripping his shirt, giving herself up to the pleasure he offered her— a pleasure she might never experience again.

"We can't—there's too much red tape. And there is still the approval of your father. Have you heard from him since you translated and mailed my letter to him?"

"No," he said simply. "It's our custom to seek our parents approval in my country."

"And what happens if he is not agreeable. Then what?"

"I am hopeful that my father would be favorable, but I will marry you with or without his blessings. I don't want to think about that now. I just want to be with you. How I hate it when I have to leave you every night when that blasted horn blows."

331

"Me, too," she whispered.

"Look," he said, fishing a card from his shirt pocket. "Because of our excellent Command Inspection, my whole squad was given a pass for next Saturday. Do you think you could get one? We could go somewhere in my car."

"I don't know if that's a good idea."

"I promise that I won't pressure you. I just want to be alone with you and not have to leave you when I kiss you good night."

"It's not you that concerns me. I don't know if I can trust myself," she confessed.

"Do you mean that?" he asked, a look of astonishment on his face.

April nodded, her eyes avoiding his and heat warming her face. "Girls have feelings and desires, too. There has been many nights that I've wished you didn't have to leave me."

He grinned, shaking his head.

> Friday, 13 June 1958
> Dear Dreamcatcher,
> This is my first Duty NCO since returning to full duty. Tonight, I was working in the Orderly Room catching up on paperwork when a call came in for me. Richard Sheets called to tell me that Cordero would be leaving the post in a week, and he wants to see me. I took the opportunity to ask him why they had followed me all over the post. He laughed and said it was Montoya that they followed because they knew that he was going to see me. When I asked him *why*, he said it was because of the incident with Angel Conde. Cordero wanted to make sure no one else bothered me, and it was the only way Cordero could see me.
> Richard apologized for what happened at the lake with Cordero. He felt that he was at fault because he had goaded Cordero into acting the way he did by telling him that he was going to take me away from him. I said to forget it that I never blamed him.
> All this time I had thought Cordero stalked me to be annoying until the hospital occurrence.
> I told Richard that I would speak to Cordero and I got off the phone with a headache and feeling ill…

Before going into the building, April took off her raincoat and shook it, vigorously.

"Retreat is cancelled," said Sgt. Levy, as April entered the Orderly Room.

"I know. This rains not going to let up. By the way, how are you feeling?" she asked, peeling off her wet gloves.

"About the same. Thanks for taking my class. You had a call from Cordero." Sgt. Levy pursed her lips and handed her a pink slip. "I don't know why he thinks you would speak to him after all this time."

"I didn't tell you that his friend, Richard called me Saturday night while I was on duty. He said Cordero was leaving the post and wanted to see me. I agreed to speak to him." She glanced at the message in her hand. "I'll call you later," beneath Cordero's name.

"Do you think that is wise?" Sgt Levy frowned.

"He can't hurt me anymore."

"But what about him?"

"I never forgave him for destroying our friendship. It has bothered me all this time. I think it's time I faced him and let it go." While she had tried diligently for over a year to put all thoughts of Cordero out of her mind, she had never succeeded nor forgiven him.

"I hope you don't regret it," said Sgt. Levy, the frown still creasing her forehead.

"So do I."

On Monday evening, April waved to Monty as he left her company's parking lot. She started to turn away as a blue '57 Chevy pulled along side. The driver leaned across the seat and opened the passenger door.

"Chica, get in," said Cordero.

"I'm not going anywhere with you. I still recall what happened the last time. Park in the lot."

Cordero backed the car into an empty space and got out. He came around and lounged against the fender of the Bel Air, his posture deceptively lazy with his feet crossed at the ankles. His mode of dress, his usual all black clothing. He reached into the breast pocket of his shirt, removed a pack of cigarettes and methodically tapped one against his thumbnail.

"When did you start smoking again?" she asked.

"When you stopped seeing me." His dark eyes were shadowed with regret. He produced a silver lighter, lit up, and dropped it back into the pocket of his black pants. He took a long draw from the cigarette and blew out a cloud of smoke.

"I didn't think you would want the car seen here. Isn't that why you met me in the lot?"

"You're mistaken, I wasn't waiting for you. Montoya came by to see me on his way to college. I would wager that you drove behind him on your way here. Besides, my first sergeant has a car just like this one," she said, indicating the blue and white automobile.

"So that's who the Chevy belongs to that I've seen you driving. I wondered about it. Does Montoya know you are meeting me tonight?" Cordero asked, with a careless smile. He raised his smoking cigarette to his mouth, drew on it, allowing his gaze to move over her length.

"He does. We don't keep secrets from one another." She looked up at him with those unusual turquoise eyes that matched the color of her blouse.

"And he didn't object?" He took a final drag of his smoke, raised his foot and tapped the butt on the sole of his shoe before ripping off the paper and scattering the remains on the ground. The small paper, he rolled between his thumb and forefinger into a tiny ball and pocketed it.

"We trust each other," she said.

He noticed she kept her distance from him as if she was afraid of him. Certainly her gaze never met his.

"What are you afraid of?" he asked, quietly.

"Nothing," she replied.

"Everyone's afraid of something."

"What are you afraid of?"

"More than I care to admit." He shrugged, pushing away from the automobile. "C'mon, let's sit in the car. How is your ankle? Should you be standing?"

"It's okay. I have been dancing several times."

"Yeah. I know. I recently saw you at the service club. Ah, c'mon, get in the car. I promise not to touch you. We'll just sit and talk." Without looking directly at her, he whipped open the passenger door and held it for her, easing it shut when she was safely inside. Walking around, he opened the driver's door and slid behind the wheel. He stuck the key into the ignition but he didn't start the engine.

"You came to see me at the hospital. Didn't you?" she asked.

Resting his hands on the steering wheel, he stared straight ahead for several long seconds.

"How do you know? You never saw me."

"No, but Bryza, the nurse did. I asked her to tell you to come talk to me when I was awake. But you never came back again."

"I wish I would have known. Why did you change your mind about talking to me?"

"While I was in the hospital, I had a lot of time to think, and because you came to see me. Do you know how close you came to running into Montoya that one Sunday?"

"I spoke to him in the corridor of the hospital. We had both just returned from a week in the field. I went back for another week. After that you went to therapy and I never went back to the hospital again."

"You were in the field at the same time as Montoya? How was it possible that you came the day of my surgery?"

"I went on sick call. My platoon sergeant and I are drinking buddies. He let me go on sick call for the rest of the week."

"What excuse did you give?"

"None. I told him the truth, that someone close to me was in the hospital and I wanted to go see her."

"There's something that I've been curious about. Tell me what Montoya said when you returned Reinaldo's ring?"

"Nothing. I walked up to him and said, 'Montoya, I have something that belongs to you.' I handed him the ring and walked away. Did he ever say anything to you about my giving him back the ring?"

"No. After that incident he forbid me to mention your name. Richard told me why the two of you followed me. I couldn't believe you would waste your free time like that."

"The thought of never seeing you again hurt like hell. I didn't know how much a part of me you had became until you walked out of my life. I apologize for the lies I told about us. It was wrong. I'd give anything to be able to go back and make things right between us. Words can't possible erase what I've done to you. Yet they are all I have to offer. I need to have your forgiveness," he said, in soft tones.

"Enough," she said, quickly putting up her hand. "I accept your apology, and I do forgive you. But…nothing has changed."

"I still love you, Chica."

"I'm sorry, there's nothing else I can say." She raised her face slowly, her gaze meeting his across the short distance. Her heart ached for the regret she read in his eyes. She recalled what her mama had told her. People cannot be held accountable for love others give them unasked. They cannot prevent or alleviate the pain it causes. She had not encouraged him, but in some way, she felt responsible for hurting him.

"I would sell my soul not to love you. I want you more than my next breath. I know you don't love me, but I can't seem to stop loving you. You are so deep inside me, and no matter what I do I can't get you out. I don't know how in hell I'm going to cope with not being able to see you after I leave here. I do love you. Don't ever doubt that."

"I did care for you once, Cordero, but we were never destined to be together. Nothing happens without a reason. Montoya and I actually got together because of you. He was a friend that comforted me when I cried because of you. As a result, my relationship with Montoya developed into something deeper.

"I can look back over the months and see it all. His loneliness—my hurting. We healed each other and fell in love. It was that simple. Oh, we had our problems, and you were at the center of most of them. I learned that love doesn't happen overnight. It is built on trust, honesty and respect. Do you understand what I'm trying to tell you?"

"I guess I do. But you don't know what it's like to have the one you want, the only one you'll ever want, reject your love. I hope you never do." He paused and turned away from her and glanced out the windshield. "Are the two of you getting married before Montoya leaves next month?"

"No. I'm meeting him in New York in October after my ETS."

"What if he returns to New York, finds someone else and forgets about you?"

"I have to go. It's getting late." She grabbed the door handle.

"Wait. I have something of yours." Cordero lifted his hand to the beaded chain around his neck and pulled it up. His fingers grasped his cross and the small silver heart with a tiny bird attached. "I thought you might want this returned."

"No." She shook her head. "You keep it."

"Thanks," he said. He watched her for a moment, and then his lips curved in a half smile before he captured her hand and placed a warm kiss in the center of her palm, folded her fingers over the spot and slowly released her hand.

She rubbed her hand as if it pained her.

"Did I hurt you?" he asked.

"No, it's just…no." She dropped her hands into her lap, staring at him oddly. "I better go."

"I'll walk you to your door," he said. He got out, rounded the car, and opened her door.

"No. I'd rather you didn't. Good-bye, Cordero, I wish you all the happiness." She held out her hand to him, her small, soft hand. The hardest thing he'd ever done was clasping it and let it go.

"*Via con Dios*, Chica," he said. He turned, getting in the car, then looked back at her. "I want you to know in my heart, I'll always love you." His eyes burned, his throat choked up, but he hadn't felt like bawling since he was a kid. He damn sure felt like it now. All his symptoms pointed to it with an ache in his chest and his stomach all tied up in a knot. And he wasn't close to being hung over. He sure as hell knew what that felt like.

And this wasn't it.

To cheat oneself out of love,
Is a terrible deception.
It is an eternal loss,
For which there is no restitution.

Chapter 37

April turned away, proud of herself for sounding so light and calm, pleased that she hadn't broken down and cried in front of him.

It was only when she reached the steps at the bottom of the walk that she allowed herself to stop and turn around, vowing not to cry. But the tears came anyway blurring her vision as Cordero drove out of the lot. She unlocked the double doors and waited for the sound of the Chevy to fade away. She entered the building and hurried up the steps to her room. Dry sobs tore from her throat while she sank onto her bunk crying for something she could not name.

During the night, April awoke with a gasp, perspiring. She sat up in bed disoriented for a moment in the dark room. Then she remembered where she was and why she had become so rudely awakened.

Her nightmare had been so vivid, so real. In the dream it was just as Cordero suggested. After Monty returned to New York he called, informing her that he'd made a mistake and asked to be released from his promise of marriage.

The following morning she greeted Sgt. Levy in the Orderly Room dropped her cap on her desktop and moved to the coffee stand.

"You're awfully quiet this morning," said Sgt. Levy. "How did it go last night?"

"Rough. But I didn't cry in front of him. In fact, when he said good-bye, he sounded on the verge of tears." She deftly measured the coffee and filled the container from the water cooler.

"I guess he really loved you, huh?"

"He said as much."

"It's good that you didn't cry in front of him, but I bet you did later. Your eyes are still red."

"You're right, I did. I didn't make him love me, and I couldn't make him stop. I can't describe the hurt in my heart at his obvious pain. I felt so guilty and helpless. There was nothing I could do or say to make it less."

"When does he clear post?"

"Friday morning. Monty will be leaving in twenty-three days. The time is going so rapidly."

"I just made next month's duty roster and you are the unlucky one to have to work on the 4th."

"I had already figured it out. Monty and I planned a picnic at the lake on the 5th. Why don't you join us?"

"I wouldn't want to intrude on your last days together."

"We aren't going alone. Monty invited a friend that he worked with when he was assigned to Headquarters last summer. We'll make a foursome. How about it?"

Sgt. Levy hesitated for a moment. "Sure—why not. I don't have any plans."

April hadn't told Sgt. Levy about her dream last night. It must have been brought on by what Cordero had said about Monty going to New York and forgetting about her.

On Thursday morning she marched into the CO's office and asked for an overnight pass. Her dream had occurred for the third time in as many nights. Only this time in her dream Monty had told her he had changed his mind about marrying her because he wanted a Spanish wife.

The following Friday afternoon she covered her typewriter and straightened her desk. The phone rang. From habit she looked at the clock. It was 1630 hours, but she didn't hesitate to answer now that Cordero was no longer on the post.

"Hi, it's Monty. How about going to the Flick after chow to see my favorite team, Dean and Jerry in *Hollywood or Bust?*"

"Okay with me." She hesitated for a moment. "Do you still have that overnight pass?"

"Yes, I do."

"I've got one, too. I thought it would be nice to go somewhere to be alone." There was a long pause on Monty's end of the line.

"Forget what I said. It was a bad idea," she said.

"April, I don't know if I can behave the way you expect me too."

"Why don't you let me worry about that?"

"Whatever you say. I looked at my *short timer* calendar this morning. Only nineteen more days until I leave for New York."

"I know," she said quietly.

In the restaurant, Monty sat watching her, a teasing glint in his chocolate brown eyes. His hand raised a corner of the damask table cover.

"We don't have a brown bag under our table," he announced.

"Are we supposed to have one?" April asked.

"Look at all the tables around us."

She followed the direction of Monty's eyes. On the floor just at the edge of the table covers sat brown paper bags of different sizes and shapes.

"You're right. We don't," she said, looking beneath their table. "What are they for?"

"This is a dry town. You can't buy liquor for miles except on the post. People bring their own bottles and the restaurant supplies the rest. It's called a *set up*. You probably didn't notice when the waiter took our order, he asked me if we needed one."

She glanced at the table on either side of them. Each held an assortment of glasses, buckets of ice, bottles of club soda and ginger ale.

"My hometown is dry too. But you can't get this kind of service at any of our restaurants. How did you know about it?"

"While you were on TDY, I came here to celebrate CQ's going away party. That's why I picked this place. They have good food."

"Were there girls at the party?" she asked, not quite meeting his eyes.

"Just a bunch of us guys. Are you going to be a jealous wife?" He gave her a teasing grin.

"Now that you've brought the subject up, I've been wanting to make something clear to you. I've been told that it is common for the men of South America to have other women after they are married. You may as well know now that I'll never share your affections with any other woman. I'm rather selfish that way, and I would not tolerate it."

"Does that mean I'll have to give up all my girlfriends in New York and Ecuador," he said, still grinning.

Her mouth suddenly felt dry and she licked her lip nibbling on the lower one out of habit when she was troubled to relieve some of her tension.

April's feelings must have reflected on her face for Monty was quick to say, "Peachy, don't look so serious. I was only kidding."

"This is not a joking matter. If it's on your mind to follow that custom then I think it's best that we end our relationship now. I meant what I said, I will never share my husband."

"By now you should know that I'm not like other men. Since we met I haven't so much as looked at another woman," he assured her.

"Really? What about the WAC you met at the Hilltop Club dance while I was on TDY?"

"I told you about her in my letter. She come up to me and started a conversation saying she was from Company D, and she knew that you and I were friends. She asked about you. And I told her of your part in the Third Army Show, and then I asked her to dance. That was all it was to it. I never saw her again. Don't tell me you were jealous?"

"I might have been," she acknowledged.

The waiter brought their food and they ate quietly commenting about the delicious food. But all through dinner, neither seemed hungry, though their eyes devoured each other.

When they had finished the dessert his hand rested over hers on the table. His long fingers absently caressed the back of her hand while they talked.

"Are you ready?" he asked, pushing back his chair.

"I am if you are," she said. She folded her napkin neatly, placing it beside her half full plate.

A short time later he pulled in under a *vacancy* sign at the Anniston Arm's Motel.

"Wait in the car," he said, and got out, then he disappeared into the well-illuminated office.

Monty unlocked the door and stepped back to allow her to enter the dimly lighted room.

"It's nice," she said, glancing around at the modern furnishings. In front of the floral curtained windows, two matched overstuffed chairs sat next to a round table. She walked to the window and pulled the drapes part way and gazed out into the dark. She looked over her shoulder at him where he leaned against the open door watching her.

"Is there something wrong?" she asked, turning about to face him.

"No. I just enjoy looking at you. Especially knowing that I don't have to leave you at midnight." Monty shut the door and connected the chain guard before pressing the lock on the knob. Then he crossed the narrow room to where she stood next to the window. He reached past her and closed the half-open panels.

"April,' he said, softly. "Look at me."

When she wouldn't, he put a finger beneath her chin and raised it.

"Are you sure about this? I came here with honorable intentions."

For an instant she felt a pang of fear. She had sworn that she would never do this, without a wedding ceremony first. Yet here she was, and she had been the one to insist they spend the night together. It was too late to back out. She was about to abandon everything she'd been taught, and she didn't care. For once she was going to go with her heart. She wanted this night to be special, to show Monty how she felt about him. What she was just beginning to understand herself.

"I know what I want. Perhaps you're not sure?" she said.

His answer was to pull her against him with an eagerness that forced the breath out of her body on impact. His breath caressed her cheek and she caught the spicy scent of cinnamon and mint. His lips brushed hers with the softness of a shedding dandelion. Then he kissed her again. This time his mouth did not skim lightly over hers, but covered it, warm and moist, and so utterly delicious. A moan escaped, unbidden, from deep within her. He urged her lips apart and when she felt his tongue tasting her mouth, her bones seemed to melt. Her knees buckled, and she clung to him, her fingers gripping the fabric of his shirt.

"When you kiss me like that you make me want to touch and kiss you all over. Do my kisses affect you that way, too?" Heat began to rise in her upper body and she continued without giving him a chance to answer. "You must think I'm terrible...so bold and unladylike," she said, and was rewarded by his deep chuckle.

"I think you are beautiful. When was the first time you felt like touching and kissing me like that?" He grinned, a mischievous twinkle gleamed in his eyes as he lowered his head and gazed deep into her eyes.

"That time you picked me up in the pool and let me slide down your body. I became aware that not *all* your muscles were in your arms and chest. And when the tops of your ears turned red, I knew you had been affected by it, too."

"Yeah, I was more touched by it than I can explain. I was afraid of frightening you after what had happened to you at the lake," he acknowledged with a boyish grin.

"I was never afraid of you but I was concerned because of my feelings—things I hadn't felt about any other guy. You awakened a desire in me that I never knew existed."

His lips split into a smile and he chuckled softly as he gathered her back into his arms. She trembled and he held her away.

"Are you afraid?"

Fear wasn't the word she would have used. Scared stiff and excited at the same time better described her emotions at that moment.

"Yes—no, it's just that I've never done this before." Her heart pounded loudly in her ears. Warmth blossomed within her and more heat burned her cheeks.

"I know," he answered, huskily.

April tried to tell herself how wicked this was even as her body yearned to get closer to him.

His eyes held hers as she unfastened the buttons on his shirt. She pushed it off his shoulders to reveal the triangle of dark hair she remembered from the pool. Next she removed his shoes and socks. She fumbled with his belt and his fingers took over to help her. The metal clasp slid free, then the zipper of his trousers. She caught her bottom lip between her teeth and looked away as he stepped out of his pants. He wore nothing but white BVDs. Quickly, she gathered up his clothing and laid it in the nearby chair.

His hands went to her waist and up her back. The touch of his fingers against her skin was electric, and she swallowed convulsively as he slowly slid down the zipper. He turned her in his arms and pushed aside the bodice. With his thumbs he slid the dress and slip down her body and let it settle at her feet. He picked up her clothing and tossed them on the chair to join his discarded things. She stood before him in her stockings and heels with a white, one-piece garment that the sales girl had referred to as a *teddy*.

"Do you know what seeing you like this does to me?" asked Monty. He pulled the pins from her hair and let it cascade around her shoulders. "You can't begin to imagine how much I've longed to see you, touch you. Just the thought of it has driven me almost loco. You smell so sweet and feel so wonderful in my arms." She was more than he hoped for and everything he wanted.

He wished she understood Spanish. There were better words to express the depth of his passion in his native language.

"*Te adoro mi amor.* I adore you my love."

He rose to his full height looking her up and down. "Your are so lovely."

"Thank you," She blushed a pretty shade of pink. "You make me feel as if I really am."

"I speak only the truth."

His arms embraced her; his hands came around to caress her breasts through the sheer lace as his mouth placed warm kisses from her nape to her waist where the garment plunged into a V.

343

"April, if you want me to stop, say so now, for if I kiss you again, I won't be able to quit."

"I trust you," she said. "I think I've always trusted you."

She lifted her arms and looped them around his neck, drawing his head to her and angling her face to offer her mouth to him.

That was all the invitation he needed. He pushed the last covering off her shoulders and with his thumbs skimmed the sheer garment over her hips to pool at her feet. His underwear joined hers on the floor.

His whole body shuddered at the first contact of their naked skin. He kissed her hungrily, letting her know how much he desired her. In her innocence, April held herself a little stiffly against him, but as his lips moved over hers with arousing intensity, she softened and relaxed when their nude bodies came together again. This was how it was supposed to be. Two people in love holding each other with nothing but feelings between them.

"Do you want me?" he whispered, unsteadily.

"Yes, but…" she faltered, drawing back.

"It's all right if we know intimate things about each other and touch each others bodies like this. We are going to be married," he said, softly.

"There's something I have to tell you."

"I'm listening." He grinned down at her.

"You were in the 30th Chemical barracks when Cordero told almost the entire platoon that he had been intimate with me."

"Yes." He couldn't imagine why she would bring that up now.

"It wasn't true," she said, quietly. "He never touched me. No man has."

His smile was filled with tenderness. She was telling him she was still a virgin and blushing like she considered it to be terribly embarrassing.

He kissed the tip of her nose. "I already knew," he whispered back. He had known from the first time that he'd kissed her that she was untutored, sweet and innocent.

His arms wrapped around her holding her close, feeling her breasts like satin against him, loving the nakedness of her skin and the sweet smell of her. The contact of her naked body against his almost shattered his control. It was the most wonderful feeling he'd ever experienced.

"I like feeling you next to me like this," she said, her voice faintly surprised. She had mirrored his exact thoughts.

He watched her with fascination, taking pleasure from her joy.

The initial touch of his body against hers overwhelmed her. Her body tingled everywhere Monty touched her with his lips until April thought she would burst from the delicious feelings. His mouth was like fire, a searing heat that made her blood run faster and her heart speed up in her chest. The fear she'd felt only moments ago was now becoming excitement. Her arms slowly lifted to curve around his neck. There was no thought of resistance or stopping now. Her hands clung to his shoulders, she arched into him until her breasts, and thighs were pressed full-length against him. He kissed her; she gave herself up to the pleasure and heard his moan as he took the kiss deeper. And all she could think was that she loved him, and she wanted to belong to him heart, soul, and body. Beneath her thighs and along her back she could feel the hard muscles of his arms flex. She was hardly conscious of the soft sounds emerging from her throat as she reacted with instinctive ease and of him laying her down on the bed. Her body seemed to have a will of its own as she matched each and every one of his movements.

She expected some guilt of remorse for having this sinful lust. There was none. Her only regret was that it might be the only time they'd share this pleasure.

Stolen fruit tastes the sweetest,
But beware of the bitter after taste.

Chapter 38

Monty cautioned himself to slow down. He wanted this moment to last, to give her pleasure. He pulled back from her long enough to reach for the night table drawer and withdraw a single, foil packet. After he ripped it open, a few moments later his body settled between her thighs.

"Let it happen. Let yourself go," he tenderly whispered, encouragingly caressing her with gentle hands and kisses.

Slowly, he brought her to a wild shuttering completion, and they came together in an explosion of passion.

His eyes opened in time to catch her expression. Her eyes squeezed shut, the cringe of pain crossed her face as she clutched his shoulder and buried her nose in his neck.

Monty cradled her face with his hands and brushed his thumbs over her cheeks wiping away the moisture. With tender words, he soothed her until she relaxed.

"Did I hurt you?"

"A little," she whispered.

"I'm sorry it couldn't be helped. I wouldn't hurt you for the world. You know that, don't you? I love you more than my life."

"I know." She swallowed and sniffed.

"Shhh," he said, absently stroking her hair. "Don't cry."

"I'm not crying," she sniffed loudly into his shoulder.

"April, look at me." He placed a finger beneath her chin and tilted it upwards. "Are you sorry?"

"No. I'm deliriously pleased. These are my happy tears."

He covered her lips and her body in a touching of souls. And afterwards, they slept blissfully together.

The beginnings of a beard darkened Monty's jaw, and his hair was boyishly tousled in a most appealing manner. April could welcome to wake to this picture every morning. His slow even breathing told her he was still deep in slumber. Sensuous lips slightly parted were too strong a temptation for her to resist.

She lifted his heavy arm and moved slowly so as not to awaken him. Quietly, she raised and leaned over to place a soft kiss on his mouth.

He snuggled against her, throwing his arm across her waist again as he buried his nose in her neck.

"Mm—hmm," he sighed, "your kiss sure beats that horn all to pieces that wakes us in the men's barracks every morning."

Monty lay quietly studying the young woman next to him. On her side facing him, she had one arm flung above her head; the other draped over his chest. She had fulfilled every dream that he'd ever had of her. April had been like fire and lightning in his arms, and he had found himself burning in her embrace. He loved her with all his heart and soul. She had given him a most precious gift, that of her innocence. And he felt incredible satisfaction that he was the first to love her, and he would be the last.

He silently recalled the first time he'd seen her and how he desperately wanted to touch and be touched by her. Now he could touch, and taste her to his heart's content. He was thrilled to have been the one to take her to a place that she'd never been before. This was his woman—his *mujer*. Only his.

Monty watched her face as his hands caressed her gently, kneading her breasts, as they lay full in his hands. With the least persuasion, her nipples beaded as he rolled them gently between his fingers.

April's eyes snapped wide open.

"Does that feel as good to you as it does to me?" he asked, huskily.

"Monty?" she murmured.

"Were you expecting someone else?"

"No." She smiled, her eyes glowing mischievously.

"Good. Because I intend to be the only man you ever awake to find in your bed."

"I never knew," she whispered, softly. "I never had any idea."

"About what?"

"That making love could be so beautiful—so marvelous."

"I have wanted to be with you like this for so long that it is hard to believe that you are really here in my arms and not just another of my dreams."

"I'm very real. Is it always like this?" she asked.

"No. I don't think so. It's never been like this before for me. But then I've not had much experience."

"I find that difficult to believe," she said, quickly.

"It's true. I have always been shy around women."

"Pray tell me who was the guy that undressed me last night?"

"That was different. It seems I had waited for a lifetime just to love you like that." His fingers brushed back the hair at her temple. "Do you have any idea what you do to me?"

She shook her head and smiled at him.

"You're the love of my heart. *Te amor mi corazon.*"

That part of a man's body that could be so soft and light grew thick and heavy. Monty let it prod against her belly. His breathing became ragged and short as she snuggled into his muscular frame.

"Monty, I want to make love with you again," she whispered in a voice filled with embarrassment. A becoming flush spread over her skin rising past her throat covering her face.

"I can't—I can't make love to you. I don't have any way of protecting you."

"I don't understand—you did last night."

"I had protection then. I don't have any more. What I used was a gift from my platoon sergeant in basic training. He gave them to all the guys. He said it was a part of our equipment that we should never be without. I'd carried it in my wallet for almost two years."

It took only seconds for her to comprehend what he was trying to tell her, and when she did she denied the caution he was trying to instill in her.

Monty gathered his clothes and sat on the bed. She grabbed his arm as he started to dress.

"Where are you going?" She didn't let go of his arm.

"To buy more protection."

"It's okay. We are getting married."

"Are you sure?"

"Well, you did propose to me, and I said yes," she teased.

"You know I don't mean that. I don't want to make love to you without protecting you. I could make you pregnant."

"I don't care that you can't protect me...it doesn't matter. We are practically married. We will be in a few months."

The corners of his mouth turned up in a bemused smile. He dropped his clothing on the floor and he gently cradled her face between his hands. Slowly, he brought his mouth down to cover hers. He kissed her tenderly then he kissed her with an intensity that caused April's heart to race and her body to tremble.

Swiftly, he moved under her, naked, and pulled her gently on top of him, her body came alive in his arms. Goose bumps skittered up her arms as her heart accelerated.

Powerless to stop the riotous sensations Monty aroused in her, April strained shamelessly against him, her breasts pressing the solid walls of his chest. His hands slid down her back to grip her bottom, guiding her hips in synchronization with his.

"Oooh," she sighed.

He chuckled, the sound deep and warm, curling around her like an embrace.

She was almost there poised on the rink, one final thrust and she exploded, and the throbbing pleasure carried her to the stars. The splendor overwhelmed her. April wasn't afraid, even when she felt as though her mind had become separated from her body. She hadn't thought she could feel anything more intense than what she had experienced last night. But she was wrong. This time, Monty's loving her was more than she dreamed—never imagined possible. She settled back down to earth, all her weight resting on him.

No matter what happened tomorrow, next week or in the months to come, she would always have this memory of him.

When she opened her eyes, he was smiling at her. His dark eyes held an amused gleam.

"How do you feel?" he asked, quietly.

"Incredibly wonderful. Better than last night. There was no pain."

"Didn't you know a woman only feels pain the first time?"

She shook her head. No, she hadn't known about the *pain* or the *blood*.

"Will it always be like this?" Tilting her head, she looked into the dark depths of his eyes and her heart thrummed wildly.

"Oh, yes." He nodded with a bashful grin. "Each time will be better than the last."

Inclining his head he covered her lips with delicate slowness. As his mouth became more demanding, she eased her arms about his neck, letting her fingers run through his wavy hair.

349

In no time they were lost in a world of tender caresses and gentle sighs. A place where only lovers can go.

Later when she slipped out of bed to shower and get dressed, the tenderness between her thighs drew her attention. But no amount of discomfort could blemish the memory of last night and this morning. Nothing could ever mar the beauty of her and Monty's lovemaking.

Before noon, they returned to the post. He dropped her off at Company D and later in the afternoon he picked her up and drove to the WAC pool.

Monty's friend, Gaitan, from Post Headquarters was there with his girl friend, Peggy. A dark eyed girl of Italian decent who would be returning to her hometown of Brooklyn, New York in less than a week after her discharge.

April sat under the umbrella table and Peggy sunbathed on a nearby lounge. Her eyes were drawn to a turquoise '57 Chevy parked by the fence at the end of the pool. She scanned the pool area. Richard appeared on the high diving board above the deep end where Monty and Gaitan swam. His dive was perfect. He swam like he danced, with precision and grace. After a couple of laps he got out on her side of the deck. Wet, sandy brown hair glinted a bronze shade, catching the sun as he strode jauntily over to the table and sat down uninvited. He inclined his head toward her with a rueful grin.

"Hello, Richard." She greeted him, handed him a towel, and introduced him to Peggy, who said, "hello" closed her eyes and continued to sun bathe.

"Nice dive," she commented. "I've never seen you swim before."

"Cordero didn't like to come to the pool because of the ugly scar on his chest. Did you see him before he left?"

"Yes, I did. Since he was driving your car, I'm sure you already knew he came to my barracks to say good-bye."

"I wasn't sure. Cordero doesn't have the best track record for telling the truth. He said he talked to you, but he wouldn't comment about it."

"You're leaving in a few days, aren't you?" She casually changed the course of the conversation. "What are you going to do when get home?"

"First, I'm going to take a nice, long vacation."

"I thought that was what you've been doing these past two years." She laughed and said, on a more serious note, "And then what?"

"I'm thinking about registering for some classes in the fall." Richard folded the towel neatly and placed it on the table.

"You never did tell me what you were studying other than *girls*."

He laughed. "I was enrolled in law school. My father wanted me to follow in his footsteps."

"So, you're going to be a lawyer like your dad?"

"That's not for me." He shook his head. "My plan is to get into the field of electronics. It's destined to be the thing of the future."

"As long as you like what you're doing. I think that's the most important aspect of a person's job."

"What about you? Are you really marrying Montoya?" He gazed down at her bare finger. "I still don't see you wearing an engagement ring."

"Unless Montoya changes his mind. And it was my choice not to have a ring."

He picked up her left hand and stroked his thumb down her ring finger.

"If it was me, I'd put a wedding band on this finger before leaving you on the post." He squeezed her hand before placing it back on the tabletop. "If Montoya doesn't make you happy or for some reason things don't work out— look me up in Trenton, New Jersey," he responded with a quick laugh.

"Always the kidder, aren't you, Richard?"

"April, do you recall what I once told you about my teasing you," he said, seriously.

"Yes. I do," she said, becoming serious, too.

"I meant it then, and I still do." He glanced in the direction of the pool. "I'd better say good-bye. Montoya is looking daggers at me," he said, making another short laugh.

"With you and Montoya leaving, there won't be any of the guys left at the 30th Chemical Company that I know. Jerry and Larson told me so long at the dance last week before they left. I wish you a happy life and good luck in your new career."

Richard stood and executed his British half salute. "Be happy, Chica."

She rose and returned his salute with one of her own before walking over to where he stood, putting her hand out to be engulfed by his. "Thanks. You, too."

Without looking back, he strode toward the dressing rooms. Shortly, she caught sight of him as he exited the pool complex. Her eyes followed him to where his Chevy was parked. He looked in her direction just before getting in his car and waved.

She lifted her hand and returned the gesture. She and Richard did have some good times together, and she would miss her best dancing partner.

The following days seemed to speed by. She wished she could make them slow down. All hers and Monty's off duty hours were spent together. They had so little time left, it was important not to waste a precious moment. Most evenings they just sat in his car and he held her. Leave taking became a painful ordeal. She clung to him desperately not wanting the night to end. But Monty didn't make and sexual overtures beyond warm kisses and close embraces. He showed her every respect when they were alone. Yet all the time she was aware of his restraint. Occasionally, she glimpsed evidence of his passion in the darkening of his eyes and his ragged breathing as he kissed her. It was as though he wanted to show her that their sexual compatibility wasn't the only reason he wanted to marry her.

> Monday, 30 June 1958
> Dear Dreamcatcher,
> This morning my friend, Girad called to tell me she just cut my orders that I was being promoted to SP 4th Class. It will officially come out on orders tomorrow.
> In the evening I called Monty to give him the news. He said we would have to celebrate. But to tell you the truth, I don't feel like any celebration. He leaves in ten more days. I told him since I get a pay raise that it is customarily for me to treat...

On Saturday after their dinner in Anniston at a Chinese restaurant, Young China, Monty drove back to park in Company D's lot.

"You realize that you outrank me now. Does that mean that I have to obey you?

"Mmmm what do you think?"

"I think I'm going to like being your slave." Monty turned to face her. "I need you. It's an ache that never leaves me. Do you know what fear is?"

She searched his handsome face and shook her head bewildered by his sudden change of conversation.

"Fear is knowing that I am not good enough for you. It's dreading the moment when you come to New York and see the tiny apartment and you decide that you don't love me enough to live there."

"Monty, you mustn't think like that," she pleaded. "Don't you know where ever you are I will be happy to be with you?"

"Fear is lying awake at night," he continued, "wondering how I'll bear the pain. I am so afraid of losing you it makes me physically ill."

"That's nonsense. I don't wish to hear you talk like this. The day you lose me will be because you don't want me."

"Don't mind me." He cradled her head against his heart. "It's just that we have so little time left until I leave."

"Remember what I told you before I went on TDY? Before you know it—we will be together—this time for good and always."

"Do you promise?" he asked and smiled at her.

"I promise." April said the words, but like him she had begun to have her own worries and doubts, as the time grew short. She could only hope and pray all their plans and dreams would come true.

Following their picnic lunch at Reilly Lake with Sgt. Levy and Monty's friend Gaitan, Monty spread his Army blanket beneath a shade tree. Gaitan and Edie remained at the table talking.

She sat with her back against the trunk and Monty lowered himself until he was sitting on the ground beside her. He stretched out and laid his head in her lap. She took a bite of a peach and offered the rest to him.

"I couldn't eat another mouthful after all that fried chicken, potato salad, watermelon, and cake. Besides you're the only *Peachy* I want to taste. I would almost think you are trying to tempt me. Shouldn't you use an apple instead? I must say you've changed since we spent the night together."

"Shhh—they'll hear you," she whispered. "You promised not to talk about that." The heat rose in her neck and face. "I still am not comfortable about preempting our wedding night."

"Are you sorry?" he asked, quietly.

"Of course not. How could I be sorry about something as wonderful as what we shared?"

She had seen Monty numerous times without a shirt before at the pool. She had never really understood why girls went goofy over guy's muscles but gazing at Monty, she discovered she wasn't exactly immune to them either. And now, suddenly she was thinking all sorts of things that she shouldn't be thinking. It was hard to keep her thoughts in line when confronted by six feet of warm muscles and bronzed skin. A triangle of black, curling hair spanned his broad chest before tapering down to a narrow line that disappeared beneath his military Khaki shorts. She found herself wanting to run her hands over his body, feel the rippling muscles under her fingers.

What would he say if he could read her thoughts? Would he think her outrageously bold?

Memories are the most beautiful pictures our minds can paint,
And nothing can ever erase them.

Chapter 39

Ever since he had been drafted Monty had disliked the Army. Taking orders and being told what to do and when—but with April at his side the post had become a special place.

"I use to hate this miserable Army and this post. Now I don't mind it so much because you are here with me. Seeing the post with you, I think it is very beautiful, and it's not a bad place to be after all."

"That's very sweet. I'm happy you feel that way."

His fingers found hers in the grass behind them and braided them with his own.

The first gentle drops of rain spangled through the leaves of the tree above. Thunder distinctly rumbled low in the distance.

"That doesn't sound good," he said, sitting up and slipping on his shirt. He glanced at the car where Gaitan and Sgt. Levy busily loaded the left over food and picnic items. He extended his hand and pulled April to her feet then he shook out the blanket and stuck it under his arm. Together, they sprinted to the car.

Raindrops clung to April's eyelashes and he used his thumbs to wipe them away. Outside the gray sky opened up and rain came down like bullets, pounding the roof of the automobile.

"That was close," he said, sliding the key in the ignition and starting the Plymouth.

As he drove the rain turned to a light summer shower—the kind that appears suddenly—then goes almost as quickly as it came. By the time the car reached Company D, it had stopped raining. The water in the trees and grass sparkled as the sun came out to dry up the crystal-like tears.

Time was slipping away faster each day. Precious time that belonged to them. He would soon be leaving the post. And he didn't want to think about being alone in New York without her.

Sunday, 06 July 1958
Dear Dreamcatcher,
This was the last day I could spend with Monty before he leaves. I can barely write because my tears keep splattering on the pages of my journal.
After dinner this evening, we went to the Hilltop Service Club where we first met. Monty played the piano until I started to cry. Then we walked out to sit in the car and he held me for a long time until he drove   me back to my barracks and it was a tearful good night with extremely salty tears...

Early Thursday morning, April waved to Blackledge sitting in the front seat as Monty backed the green coupe into Company D's parking lot. Monty got out and came around to the rear of the car where she waited.

Barely had she spoken a greeting and he opened his arms. She went into them hugging him fiercely, willing herself to remember this moment, every touch, sound and word to cherish when he was far away.

"I see you got your new patch sewed on," he said, stepping back from her and running his hand down her shoulder to touch the insignia. "You really look sharp in your uniform. I don't know whether to salute or kiss you."

"Two of our platoons are graduating today. Our Command Inspection is after breakfast followed by the ceremony and a parade."

"You are not marching, are you?"

"No, but I wish I could."

"April,' he said, and cupped her face, tilting it up. "Leaving you is the hardest thing I've ever done in my life. I love you. You know that, don't you?"

"Yes," she whispered. "I know you do." She blinked back the tears that threatened to spill from her eyes.

"I want you to remember that while we are apart. Trust me, sweetheart, when I say everything will be all right. We'll be together again soon. I promise it."

"Yes, Monty." She drew one more jerky breath. "I love you, too," she managed to say, her voice cracking. "I love you so much."

"I know—think how happy we are going to be together. I want you to remember that when you are lonely and I'm not here. I love you, Peachy, only you."

355

She was crying. Not sobbing, just the tears silently rolling down her cheeks. She nodded, biting her lips.

"Shhh…" He pulled her close, kissed her, stroking her back. "Don't cry or I'm going to cry, too." He kissed her again with loving tenderness.

"Monty…oh, Monty…" She held tighter grabbing every moment possible in his embrace. "I love you s-so m-much," she choked, clutching his cotton shirt in her fist.

All too soon, he set her from him, and then stared into her eyes with his tortured gaze.

"I'll be counting the days until we are together again," he said.

She touched his bronzed cheek with her palm and blinked back the moisture in her eyes. "And so will I."

Again, he embraced her and hugged her close for another moment, then stepped back. "I better go…I wouldn't want you to be late for inspection."

She walked with him to the driver's side of the vehicle. He reached into the back seat and brought out a folded shirt.

"Here is the shirt you wanted," he said, and he handed her a red and blue plaid cotton shirt.

"Thanks," she said clasping it to her breast. "I'm going wear it to sleep in."

He gave her a quick, hard kiss that felt strangely like the last time he would ever kiss her and entered the car.

Before she closed his door, she said good-bye to Blackledge.

"Drive safely," she said, stepping away from the car. It was like having her insides torn from her to let him go as she stood in the bright sun, the rays beating down on her. She hugged Monty's shirt as he drove out of the lot. Moments later, she stood in the parking lot and waved until the green Plymouth disappeared out of sight. Now she knew what it meant to be truly alone. She stared at the empty street, and she wept salty tears onto Monty's shirt.

From her pocket, she took her CQ handkerchief and dried her face. Carefully, she folded Monty's shirt, before she walked slowly back to the building. She climbed the stairs to her room and placed the shirt beneath her pillow. If only she could stay there and curl up on her bunk and weep. With the inspection at 0900 hours she couldn't mess up her bed or her uniform. Instead, she went to the latrine and splashed cold water on her face and applied fresh lip-gloss.

Down in the Orderly Room, she waited for the inspecting officer feeling like her mind was not in step with her body.

That night after Monty's departure, April woke from a troubled sleep with wet cheeks. She sat up, put on the lamp beside her bed, and glanced at the wall clock. She sighed. It would be several hours yet before reveille sounded. With her arms around her middle, she clutched the fabric of Monty's shirt close and wept.

Saturday, 12 July 1958
Dear Dreamcatcher,
Pvt. Axel has been transferred, and I am once again temporally in charge of the mail. When I went to pick up the mail in the afternoon, I was relieved to learn that Sgt. Bannon had been replaced.

After mail call I drove to the hospital to take mail to a trainee who got bit by a squirrel. They are keeping Pvt. Wade for observation. This was the first time I had been back since my therapy ended. Bryza and Don married and left the post.

It seems all the people I know are gone...

Monday, 14 July 1958
We had a bad storm last night with a lot of thunder and lightning. The rain didn't stop until morning.

I got my first letter from Monty. I was so happy that I cried. Only a few short days have past since he left, but they seemed like weeks. He arrived okay in spite of some minor problem with the brakes of his car. I carried his letter around with me reading it at every opportunity...

Thursday, 17 July 1958
It was so hot here today that I came back to the mailroom. It's much cooler than in my room. It feels like we are going to get another storm.

I had a dear letter from Monty. I read it over and over. In reply I wrote him a six-page letter. While I was writing I heard *Taps* sounding. I mentioned it in my letter how it reminded me of him. When we were together and he would say *shut up* to the horn as it meant it was time for us to say good night and go to our respective barracks...

Wednesday, 23 July 1958

After I picked up the mail I had to go to Battalion HQ to watch a "Re-up" film. Also I listened to a speech from Capt. Fraser telling me if I re-enlisted for three years I could go to Officers Training School and graduate a 2nd lieutenant. Somehow, I don't think Monty would approve of that…

Friday, 25 July 1958

This morning I had a pleasant surprise. Company A has not graduated their platoons and is temporarily housing their in-coming trainees in our third floor bay. Joan Cunningham, the sister of one of my high school classmates from Kentucky is one of the recruits. It was nice to see someone from my home state.

I had a wonderful letter from Monty. He sent me a *short timer* calendar…

Friday, 01 August 1958

Our new mail clerk, Geraldine Foster arrived today. Pvt. Foster just graduated from Clerical School and she's still wet behind the ears. She is tiny with short brown hair that curls around her face. I look like a giant next to her. Her nickname is Pixie and it sure suits her with her big brown eyes. As I am writing, she is here in my room playing my Elvis records. Like myself, she is an Elvis fan. "Treat Me Nice" is playing. Some of the words say *don't kiss me once, kiss me twice*. That was what Monty always told me after we saw the movie in which Elvis sang that song. I had not played my records since he left because they make me too sad…

Saturday, 02 August 1958

I had a nice surprise this morning; Robert Cunningham came from Ft. McPherson to see his sister, Joan. He is as good looking as ever and he drew a lot of attention when the three of us dined together in the mess hall. In the evening he asked me to go with him to the NCO Club. It was my first time there. I guess it's nice but noisy and smoky.

I mentioned Robert and going to the NCO Club in my letter to Monty tonight. I hope he won't disapprove...

Wednesday, 06 August 1958

This has been a pleasant day. Our only platoon is in the field. Tonight I'm the Duty NCO and Sgt. Levy is CQ and Runner. Our building is almost empty except for a few cadre and Company A's Platoon on the third floor.

My friend Carmen from the HQ Mess has been after me to go with her to a Flamenco Show at the NCO Club. Her boyfriend, Frank, is attending a Retirement and Awards dinner and she wants me to sit with her to hold a table, as he will be arriving late. I am giving it some thought, as my room is getting pretty boring.

Today's sweet letter from Monty told me he had been baby-sitting for his sister. I jokingly replied that it was good that he was getting some experience. I might need him to baby-sit for me sometime in the future...

You shouldn't even be going; a small voice nagged April as the dream like nylon taffeta dress floated around her legs. Her shoulders were bare except for the tiny spaghetti straps. She slipped on the cuffed long-sleeved matching jacket and buttoned it at the waist.

Quickly she fastened a glittering turquoise blue flower in her hair behind one ear. The color was the same as her dress reflecting the uniqueness of the shade in her eyes.

April got out of the car and thanked Sp. Walters for the lift to the NCO Club. Inside she allowed her eyes to wander and search the nearly empty room. It was smaller than the Hilltop Club ballroom with two thirds occupied with round tables of different sizes leaving only a small dance floor. In the middle of the ceiling a large cut glass mirrored ball, spun very slowly projecting colored lights in patterns on the walls, ceiling, and the floor.

Carmen waved from a table near the dance floor in front of the raised stage. April returned the gesture and cut a direct path through the middle of the room. She greeted Carmen and took a seat next to her facing the entrance.

"I wasn't sure that you would show up when I sent you the ticket. Is this your first time here?"

"My second. I was here with a friend from back home last Saturday. But we didn't need a ticket."

"The club only charges a fee when they have special entertainment like tonight. Oh, there's Frank. The dinner must have ended sooner than he expected," Carmen said, lifting her hand.

She looked toward the entrance in time to see Frank return Carmen's wave. A long line had formed that disappeared on the other side of the glass doors and around the corridor. As she watched, Frank turned his head to speak to the tall guy behind him. When he turned around they were both smiling and looking directly at her. Without a doubt they were talking about her. April wished that she had the ability to read lips as she stared back at the good-looking, dark complexioned soldier in dress uniform.

"Is that guy with Frank?" she asked

"Oh, that's his boss, Staff Sgt. Vinluan. Frank probably gave him a lift to the club. From the way he is looking at you and smiling, I thought maybe the two of you knew each other."

"I don't know him or why he is smiling so much. But I wonder why I suddenly feel like I'm on a blind date," she accused her friend.

"Don't look at me like that. Honestly, I didn't know he was coming," Carmen denied.

As the two guys crossed the floor, her gaze returned to the taller of the men who moved with a sureness of purpose, completely at ease. She noted several chevrons on the sergeant's jacket along with a number of medals and ribbons.

The band began to play as Frank introduced her as PFC Terry to Staff Sgt. Benjamin Vinluan.

"It's Specialist Terry now," Carmen corrected, "she got promoted since you last saw her."

The tall dark haired sergeant, who'd claimed her attention as he crossed the room a few moments before, extended his hand.

She offered her own in return. His grip was firm and sure.

"Your name is Elaine, is it not?" he asked.

Beneath the intensity of his gaze, her own wavered. She found herself focusing on his powerful build—his sooty-black lashes and generous, uneven mouth.

There was no reason she could think of why the sound of her name on his lips had the effect of a feather skittering along bare skin. She shivered.

"Yes, but everyone calls me April. Have we met before?"

"I spoke to you once, but we've never officially been introduced."

Frank whisked Carmen onto the dance floor leaving her alone with the sergeant.

"Were you expecting someone?" he asked, indicating her purse in the vacant seat next to her.

"No, I'm not." She didn't move her purse and he took the seat opposite her.

"Do you like Spanish music?" asked the sergeant.

"Very much. My fiancée is Spanish."

"Is he here at the club?" The sergeant's eyes roamed slowly around the immediate area before returning to focus on her face

"No. He's in New York."

"A civilian?"

"He finished his tour of duty a month ago and he is working in New York."

"Oh, I see," he said, nodding his head.

"You may know him, Alberto Montoya. He worked at Headquarters last summer with Capt. Putman in the Circulation Department."

"No," he answered, his voice dropping lower as he leaned closer. There was nothing overly suggestive in his manner of speaking…but when he spoke softly as he was doing at that moment, there was a husky depth in his voice that caused her to blush. "I only arrived on post six months ago. My assignment to HQ is temporary. Actually, I am awaiting orders for a tour of duty in Germany. Have you any inclination to go over seas?"

"Had I planned to re-up I would have liked to go out of the states. I truly love the service but since I'm getting married at the end of my ETS…" She shrugged letting her words trail away.

"Naturally," he lingered over the word drawing out the syllables. "I understand."

The silky quality that caused her to blush was back in his words again.

Vinluan came around the table and stood behind her as the musicians began their rendition of "Mona Lisa." She could almost feel the warmth of his body against her shoulders.

"May I please have the pleasure of this dance?" his voice vibrated with charged emotion near her ear.

She turned to face him and with a quickening heartbeat she found herself pinned beneath a pair of intriguing, dark eyes like liquid velvet.

"May I?" He whispered in that low warm sensual drawl as he extended his hand.

"Yes, I'd love to," she heard herself murmur to her surprise. She placed her hand in his bronzed hand.

"What lovely hands, especially the one without a ring," he said, and chuckled softly as he gathered the slender fingers within his grasp. "Perhaps it is not a serious engagement." He raised one black eyebrow.

"I am most serious about it," she assured him. "It was my choice not to have an engagement ring."

She followed him through the crowd of dancers to a small cleared area of the floor. His hand slid gently to her waist and brought her into the circle of his arms. It was then she felt his body tense, and a faint tremor rippled through him.

"Is something wrong?" she asked at his reaction.

"Let's just say you affect me strangely." He said with a bashful grin, shaking his head.

He swept her into the midst of the couples beneath the glimmering mirrored ball. She moved easily in the sergeant's arms gliding effortlessly. He was an excellent dance partner. She felt light and graceful as she followed his fluid movements about the floor. The music ended and she moved as swiftly as possible out of his arms. She stumbled on unsteady legs as she stepped away from him. Instantly, he was at her side, an arm circling the back of her waist as he escorted her from the dance floor. They returned to the table, and Frank led her out for the next number.

"Frank Rojas, just what in the *Sam Hill* is going on?"

"Not you too. I'm already in the doghouse with Carmen for bringing the sergeant. When he saw you while we waited in line he said you were the girl he had been looking for. All he knew was your name, Elaine. I never made the connection as Carmen always referred to you as Terry or April."

"April is my nickname. You should have told him that I was engaged." She glanced at their table where Vinluan sat watching her and Frank dancing.

"The guy was so happy that he found you, I hadn't the heart to tell him." He blinked and a quirky, humorous grin spread across his face.

Vinluan was standing when they returned to the table and he took her hand before Frank could seat her.

Another tremor raced through his body when he brought her within his arms.

"That must happen because it's been a long time since I held such a lovely lady in my arms." He grinned, his teeth flashing whitely in his teak brown face.

She found his words disturbing. Her cheeks warmed, and she was conscious of the strength in the arm circling her waist, of the firm clasp of his fingers on hers.

The tune ended and they returned to the table. Before she could take her seat Carmen rushed her off to the powder room. Inside the restroom, they joined the line waiting to use the facilities.

"What did you do to Sgt. Vinluan?" Carmen asked. "He appears to be hypnotized or something as he has not taken his eyes off you since he arrived."

"Nothing. I merely danced with him so as not to appear rude, since he is sitting at our table."

"He asked me a lot of questions about you while you danced with Frank."

"What kind of questions?" she asked, moving forward in the line behind Carmen.

"Your age, what company you were with and if you really were engaged. Things like that. Don't worry. I only told him that you were engaged—nothing more," said Carmen, entering an empty stall.

Sgt. Vinluan and Frank were conversing in Spanish when she and Carmen returned to the table. They quickly switched to English and the sergeant rose to seat her. He had flawless manners, rising when she came or left the table and helping to seat her. Except she didn't think anyone ever told him it was rude to stare the way he had been gazing at her.

The lights dimmed, the noise quieted in the room and the floorshow started.

The Flamenco presentation was spectacular, much better than anything she had seen on TV or in the movies. However, she wasn't able to lose herself in the colorful dances—she was too acutely aware of the man sitting across from her who made her uncomfortable with his attentions and kept her constantly blushing.

"Terry, I'm sorry I have to leave so soon," announced Carmen, after the show. "I have to be at the mess hall at 0430 hours, but you and Sgt. Vinluan could stay and enjoy the music."

"I can't stay," she said, quickly, shooting a stern look at her friend.

"I better be going, too," agreed Sgt. Vinluan. "Mind if I catch a ride with you, Frank?"

"Not at all," said Frank. He stood and assisted Carmen in getting up.

The Staff Sergeant's presence unnerved her. What she wasn't willing to admit was why?

A short while later, Frank pulled into Company D's parking lot.

"Thank you for inviting me, Carmen. I had a wonderful time. The show was marvelous, like nothing I have ever seen. And thanks for the ride, Frank. Good night everyone," she said with her hand on the door handle.

363

Before she could open the door, Sgt. Vinluan got out and held the door. He grasped her hand and helped her from the back seat. He clasped it securely as they stood outside the vehicle, and he would not allow her to remove it from his hand. A warm flush spread upward from her neck to her face.

"Elaine, do you believe in love at first sight?" he asked. The tone of his velvet voice caused her to blush again.

"I'm a little too old for fairy tales."

"Actually time has little to do with love. Some people meet and fall in love in the space of hours. Love doesn't have a timetable nor does it discriminate against age. It can happen to anyone at any time." His eyes held hers captive while he spoke and she couldn't look anywhere except at him.

Before she knew what he intended, in one smooth movement, he raised her left hand and brushed his lips across her fingers. Her heart quickened at his touch sending a chill up her back.

Heat rushed to her cheeks as she jerked her hand from his grasp. Without a word she turned and hurried down the walk leaving him standing beside the car.

He had to have one of the smoothest lines she had ever heard, not that there had been many, but she had heard a few. But none that could have compared with his.

She reached the front door with her heart beating a little faster than it should have been.

Life always offers choices,
Sometimes it's difficult to choose the right one.

Chapter 40

April scooped up her ditty bag and checked her reflection in the mirrored latrine door before flicking off the lights. Midway down the hall, a recruit in a PT dress knocked on her door.

"Are you looking for me, Private?" she called.

The trainee turned and came toward her. "Pvt. Bristol. Yes, Sp. Terry. You're wanted on the phone."

"Do you know if the call is long distance?"

"No, I don't. The CQ, Pvt. Nance took the call."

"I'll be right down as soon as I put away my things."

It must be Monty. Who else would call her so early on a Sunday morning?

"It's a guy," whispered Pvt. Bristol, as she handed April the phone.

"Hello, Monty?"

"Sorry—if I've disappointed you. It's Benjamin Vinluan. We met at the NCO Club last night. Do you have any plans for this evening? I would like to see you."

"Sgt. Vinluan, I was serious when I told you that I am engaged. You're wasting your time and mine. Please don't call me again." She quickly hung up, hurried up to her room, and finished dressing for church.

After returning from chapel, when she arrived back at her barracks the CQ handed her two pink slips. Both messages were from Sgt. Vinluan.

April disposed of the messages in her waste can before changing her clothes. She had just finished tying her sneakers when the Runner, Pvt. Bristol knocked at her door.

"Sp. Terry, you have a telephone call. I got his name this time. It's from a Sgt. Vinluan."

"Please take a message," she called from behind the closed door.

Just when she was getting accustomed to answering the phone without being afraid, this had to happen. Why was she so unlucky?

She picked up her keys and went out locking her door. A few minutes later she knocked at Sgt. Levy's door.

"What am I going to do?" she asked, after she told Levy about what resulted in her going to the NCO Club. "Now I'm afraid to answer the phone again. And what will I tell Monty. When I told him about going to the club with my classmate's brother last week he got upset and said that he didn't want me in places like that. Now he will be angry with me for going there again."

"I think it best that you not mention it to Monty."

"But I always tell him everything. We don't have any secrets from each other. I told him about the things I did while on TDY."

"This is a whole new ball game. You weren't engaged then. Don't tell him anything. That's my advice."

The following morning she read a letter from Monty that gave her a real guilt trip. He remarked how sweet, sincere, and true she was and if there were more girls like her, then there wouldn't be many single men left in the universe.

> Tuesday, 12 August 1958
> Dear Dreamcatcher,
> No letter from Monty today. By now he must have my letter telling him about my going to the NCO Club again. I should have listened to Sgt. Levy.
> In the afternoon, Carmen called. She apologized for Frank's friend getting so carried away with his attentions toward me. I told her that I thought the whole episode was a joke. And he had one of the smoothest lines I had ever heard. She didn't agree with me. She said Sgt. Vinluan is a serious person and she thinks he is sincere about his interest in me...

April covered the typewriter on the desk in the mailroom, and picked her cap off the peg by the mailroom door.

"Duty calls," she said.

"That's right," said Pvt. Foster, as she placed the last of the re-direct letters in the bag and locked it. "You're got Retreat tonight."

"I'll see you at the mess hall," she said, going out and up the basement steps.

At the top of the stairs, April smoothed down the skirt of her tan uniform and she proceeded down the corridor to the CQ area. Behind the counter stood two nervous trainees.

After giving them their instructions for the evening, she asked them a few questions. Satisfied they knew their Runner and CQ duties; she walked over to the plate glass doors. Using one as a mirror, she set the garrison cap on her head at an angle.

The phone on the CQ counter jangled loudly in the silent foyer.

"Company D, Pvt. Rusk speaking. One moment please."

"Excuse me Sp. Terry, this call is for you."

"Take a message, Private, it's almost time to fall out the troops."

"It's long distance," replied the recruit.

She stepped up to the desk and Pvt. Rusk handed her the receiver. "SP. Terry speaking."

"April?" said a familiar voice.

"Monty?" she said, hesitantly.

"Were you expecting someone else?"

"No. I'm surprised that you called in the middle of the week."

"I just got home from work—read your letter and called."

"Did you translate my previous letter and send it to your father?"

"Unfortunately, yes. The letter I received today really shocked me. I never knew you were that kind of woman."

"What are you talking about?"

"I would never have believed that you would take up with a man after the first meeting."

"I never wrote anything like that in my letter to you."

"You didn't have to. It is clear to me that you are not the woman I want for my wife. Consider our engagement over."

"What did you say?"

"I said our engagement is ended—finished." He raised his voice.

"If this is a joke. I don't find it amusing. Or have you been drinking?"

"It's not joke. As for drinking, that's not a bad idea." He snorted a short bitter laugh.

"Monty, I don't understand…" Why couldn't she manage more than that husky whisper?

"I don't want a wife who can't be obedient." He continued as if she hadn't said a word. "I specifically told you that I did not agree with you going to the NCO Club."

"I am an adult. I think I'm capable of making my own decisions."

"The one you made was a mistake—just like our engagement—a mistake on my part—I trusted you. Now I find that I never knew you."

"Aren't you lucky, you found out in time? Well, there is one good thing," she said, angrily glancing down at her bare ring finger.

"What?"

"I don't have a ring to return."

"That was your decision," he said. His voice was clipped and impersonal, certainly nothing like it had been the night they made love. For some reason his lack of emotion stung. Heartbreaking disappointment ran through her. Obviously, when Monty had made love to her, it hadn't meant as much to him as it had to her.

"I'm on duty. I have to fall out the troops for Retreat. Have a nice life, Montoya," she said in a flat little voice, forcing the words past trembling lips. Suddenly she desperately wanted to cry.

"Wait. You owe me an explanation."

"There's nothing to discuss. I'm sorry our relationship ended like this."

"Damn it, we've been intimate."

"I must have been a great disappointment," she said, and slammed the receiver down onto the base.

She reached across the counter and flipped the PA switches on the squawk box.

"Privates—fall out for Retreat—on the double." She whirled and broke into a run blowing her whistle as she shoved through the twin doors to the outside.

Following Retreat, April barely remembered dismissing the trainees to their platoon sergeants. She took a deep breath and walked slowly back inside the building.

"Pvt. Woods, you go to chow first, and then you go when she returns," she said, turning to the other girl. "I'll be down the hall in the Orderly Room until you both have eaten. Then I'll be in my quarters."

An hour later in her room, she turned on her radio. Anything to take her mind off the conversation with Monty.

She slipped out of her starched uniform and hung it on a hanger placing it on the outside of her military locker. With her knees pulled up to her chest and her arms wrapped around them, she curled up on her bunk. She laid her cheek against one knee, closed her eyes, and wished she could close her mind, as easily. But it kept playing over and over Monty's phone call like a scratched record. When was she ever going to learn? A body would think that even a poor, dumb girl from the hills would know better than to make the exact same mistake twice. Trusting her heart to the wrong guy.

Tears found their way down her cheeks in fat wet droplets that veered down her jaw and dampened the tendrils of hair slipping out of the bun on her neck.

All her dreams of love and marriage completely shattered. They had all been an illusion created by her naïve romantic heart. It was hard for her to accept the bitter truth. Life did not come with a guarantee, where the love you felt for someone would be returned and you lived happily ever after.

Before going to bed, she took Monty's shirt from beneath her pillow and put it in the bottom of the bureau. Then she removed the cherished ID bracelet, dropping it on top of the shirt, and closed the drawer. She wrote only one line in her journal. *Monty broke our engagement and my heart.*

The following morning she entered the Orderly Room and greeted Sgt. Levy solemnly. She took her seat behind the desk and routinely shoved a blank Morning Report in the typewriter. She began typing as if her heart wasn't broken and her world hadn't fallen apart.

Methodically, she finished the report, surprisingly without any errors. She flipped the form in the captain's in box and sat back down.

"You're mighty quiet this morning. I take it, you had a routine evening...no problems?" asked Sgt. Levy as she glanced across the room over her black rimmed reading glasses.

"Nothing out of the ordinary." She glanced up at the large wall clock above the entrance. "I guess I better make some coffee, the captain should be here soon," she said, getting up and going over to the corner stand next to the water cooler.

"They didn't serve muffins in the mess hall this morning?" asked Sgt. Levy, indicating the empty tray beside the coffee machine.

"I didn't make it to chow."

Sgt. Levy opened and closed the lower, metal desk drawer.

"Here," she held out a small box of cookies. Give her a couple of these. They should satisfy her sweet tooth."

"Thanks. What would I do without you? I think you must have a small grocery store stashed in that bottom drawer." She shook out three-square cookies on a napkin and popped it on the tray before handing the box back to the sergeant. April picked up the tray and hesitated in front of Sgt. Levy's desk. "I need to talk to you."

"Sure," Sgt. Levy said, glancing from her papers. "Put that on the captain's desk and pull up a chair."

"Not now. I meant privately. If you're not busy after chow tonight, could I come up to your room?"

"You sound serious," Levy said, peering over the rim of her glasses.

"It is," she affirmed.

The Orderly Room door opened and Capt. Fraser strolled in followed by Lt. Sousa.

After exchanging greetings, the two officers went into the captain's office.

"I'm not doing anything tonight," informed Sgt. Levy.

The intercom buzzed.

"Yes, Ma'am?" she said, holding down the button.

"Please bring in a delicious cup of that coffee for Lt. Sousa."

"Right away, Ma'am." she answered, and smiled.

Following the evening chow, April stood outside Edie's door and rapped. On her off duty hours, she affectionately referred to the sergeant as Edie.

"It's unlocked."

She had been in Edie's room numerous times, but she had always been in a rush, just stopping long enough to show off a new dress or an outfit. Pretty blue-checkered curtains framed the double windows that matched the bedspread on the bunk. A long blue shag rug ran the length of the space beside the bed. In one corner, a desk held a small TV set. Along one wall, a vanity with a mirror above just like the one in her room sat next to a small refrigerator.

Edie dropped her book down on the desk, picked up the chair and moved it over next to the vanity and she sat down on the bench.

"Sit here and tell me what has robbed you of your usual sunny disposition?"

"It's Monty," she blurted, dropping onto the chair. "Yesterday he called just before Retreat and broke our engagement."

"What reason did he give?" Edie's eyes widened.

"I don't think it was any one reason. He said that I wasn't the kind of woman he wanted for his wife."

"I bet you told him about going to the NCO Club and meeting that Hawaiian that's been calling you ever since. Am I right?"

"I had nothing to hide. I only told him what a nuisance the guy made of himself at the club. I didn't do anything wrong."

"Knowing you, I can believe that. But if you look at it from Montoya's point of view...he's up there in New York. You're alone down here and he

370

doesn't know what's going on. You shouldn't have told him about the guy coming onto you."

"I've always told him everything that happens to me. Like when I was on TDY."

"This is a different situation. You weren't engaged then. You have a lot to learn about men."

"I was trying to be honest because I don't want to keep secrets from him."

"In this instance, I think you were a little too honest for your own good. And what about the guy you met? Maybe he is serious. It all sounds so romantic to me. A man falling in love at first sight."

"Oh, come on, Edie. Even at my age, I know when I'm being handed a line. He was smooth, a real charmer, I grant you that."

"If you say so. You're taking this very calmly. At least, you're not crying."

"I guess I'm still in shock, waiting for reality to sit in. Ever since Monty left, I have been expecting something like this to happen. You might say I'm relieved that it's finally over."

"What brought on this kind of thinking?"

"Cordero."

"Cordero?" she repeated, frowning.

"The evening he came to say good-bye, he suggested that Monty would forget me when he returned to New York. I've been bothered with bad dreams and now it's happened. My dreams have become my worst nightmare."

"I'm so sorry. Truly, I thought you and Monty were made for each other."

"So did I. This morning I just wanted to stay in bed so I wouldn't have to face anyone. Life is so unfair." To her embarrassment two big tears silently rolled down her cheeks.

"Here." Edie leaned forward and picked up a box of tissues from the vanity. "I know you are hurting. I was once disappointed in love myself." The sergeant got up and crossed to the refrigerator. "How about a soda? I've got orange and grape."

"No, thanks."

Edie nudged the door closed and returned to sit on the bench next to her.

"Time is a great healer and getting interested in another man can help." Edie gave her an encouraging wink. "Perhaps, you should consider answering the sergeant's calls. What was his name?"

"Staff Sergeant Benjamin Vinluan," she answered, and sniffed. "I can't. I don't want to get involved with another guy. It hurts too much."

"Pain always leaves a lesson. If we learn from that, we will not have to suffer from the same mistake again."

"My biggest *mistake* was falling in love with the wrong guy."

"I've learned you don't choose who you love. You can hide your feelings but they are always there, no matter how much you wished them to disappear."

"My solution is never to fall in love again. That way I won't be hurt," she declared.

"Very true. A heart not given is a heart never broken, nor ever fulfilled. My advice to you is to reach out and grab happiness with both hands because it may never come your way again."

"Why, Sgt. Levy, I never knew you were a philosopher."

"I was speaking from experience," said Edie. She picked up a cut glass bottle and sniffed it.

"You must have been terribly hurt."

"It was a long time ago," Levy said, placing the perfume back on the vanity. "I try not to think about it."

"Thanks a lot for listening to me. I feel much better." She stood and returned the chair beneath the desk and moved toward the door.

Edie followed her. "Anytime you want to talk, just knock on my door. And don't forget what I said about the sergeant. Another man is the best medicine for a broken heart."

She closed the door softly and went down one floor to her room. In her bunk she curled into a tight ball and cried herself to sleep.

The following Friday afternoon at 1630 hours, Sgt. Levy handed her the phone when she entered the Orderly Room.

"Phone call for you, Sp. Terry."

In the office with other cadre present Sgt. Levy used April's rank and name, never calling her April, or Little-Bit as she did on their off duty hours. However, she did give her a conspirator's wink before she left the room.

"Sp. Terry speaking."

"I bet you thought I had given up on persuading you to go out with me?" A voice came over the line not altogether unfamiliar to her. "I hope I haven't caught you at an inopportune time calling during duty hours, but you never returned any of my calls," said Sgt. Vinluan.

"It's never been my policy to call men on the phone. I wasn't being rude. It's just not the way I was brought up."

"I understand and I respect you for it. I've been away at Ft. Bragg. That is why I haven't called. Elaine, how about having dinner with me?"

"Really, I don't think—"

"They are serving prime rib at the NCO Club tonight. I can vouch for the quality."

"I'm not much of a red meat person."

"There are other choices on the menu. Why not come along and watch me indulge. I was going to say pig out, but that would be insulting the beef."

April smiled.

"You're smiling, that's a start."

"How did you know I was smiling?"

"I felt the warmth of it through the phone line. What else?"

"You're teasing me, now."

"I rather thought I was flirting—it was my idea to make you smile. Most of the time I succeed in what I set out to do."

"Is it also your goal to turn the head of every girl you meet?"

"Only yours," he said, huskily. "What about it? Will you be my guest and watch me put away fourteen ounces of prime rib in nothing flat?"

"I'm afraid I left my stop watch in Kentucky," she said, in a light tone.

"I'll bring mine. The club begins serving at 1800 hours. What time can I pick you up?"

"I haven't agreed to go."

"Surely, you won't make me eat alone?" he cajoled.

She glanced at the clock above the Orderly Room door.

"In an hour," she said, and quickly, replaced the receiver onto its cradle before she could change her mind.

Out in the foyer, she found Sgt. Levy lounging by the CQ desk.

"Well, are you going to dinner with him?"

"Were you listening?"

"No, just curious. He did ask, didn't he?"

"Why don't you come with us? The club is serving prime rib. That's not something you'll ever find on our mess hall menu."

"It's tempting, but no thanks. Two is company—three is a crowd. You go and have a good time."

"I'd better go change."

After her shower, April sat down at the vanity to arrange her hair. Next she smoothed on a pink lip-gloss before opening her civilian locker. Her hand snagged the hanger of a crisp pink and white-stripped dress with a white lace crinoline. She stepped into the half-slip and eased it up over her hips. After pulling the dress over her head, she smoothed it down over the flared slip and zipped up the low back. From the bottom of the locker, she selected a pair of strappy white sandals. Recalling how cool the air conditioning was at the club the last time, she took a heavy lace shoulder wrap from her footlocker. Before leaving the room she clipped on a pair of white floral design earrings, took one last look in the mirror, and picked up a small white purse from the vanity.

She went up to the third floor and knocked at Edie's door.

"It's open." Edie was sitting in front of the TV. She turned and gave a low whistle. "I want to caution you about drinking. You know nothing about this guy. It's best you keep a clear head."

"Sgt. Vinluan doesn't drink, and I won't either. Although it sounds like something I might start doing."

"Don't you dare!"

"I was just kidding. But I'm not going to sit in my room and mope like the first time I got my heart broken."

"Good for you."

"I better get going, and I promise not to drink."

"If it's not too late, come up to see me when you get back."

"Okay," she said, going out the door.

Downstairs, she stopped at the CQ desk and signed out. April glanced at the white clock above the counter, 1730 hours. She went to the double doors, gazed out at the parking lot as Sgt. Vinluan got out of a military vehicle and started towards the building.

She glanced back at the CQ behind the counter. "My ride is here. Good evening, Private."

Before stepping out into the early evening, she draped the white wrap over her left arm.

Halfway down the cement walk, Sgt. Vinluan met her. He smiled broadly. "Does this mean you were anxious to see me or—"

"I just didn't want you to miss out on the prime rib," she finished for him and laughed.

The sergeant was handsomely dressed in a light gray jacket with contrasting darker slacks. He wore a white, silk shirt opened at the neck.

"You look lovely." His black eyes swept her from her head to her sandals and back to hold her gaze. He grasped her left hand and brought it up to his lips, placing a warm kiss across her knuckles.

"Still no ring—that's a good sign," he commented.

If only he knew.

He continued to hold her hand as they walked to where the vehicle was parked.

It was then that she noticed the driver in a khaki uniform behind the wheel. The PFC got out and held the door while she and the sergeant entered the automobile.

"I thought you would be more comfortable with someone else in the car," he said, quietly.

"That was very thoughtful," she whispered back.

"Thank you for accepting my invitation to dine with me this evening," he said, in a normal tone.

"Thank you for inviting me," she returned sincerely, smiling at him.

The sergeant reached into his jacket pocket and brought out an object covered by his fingers.

"Here," he said, holding out his fist to her.

She automatically opened her hand beneath his, palm up.

A round heavy, shinny object dropped into her open hand.

"What are you doing with a stopwatch?" she asked, after examining the object.

"Oh, I always carry one of these in case I meet a girl from Kentucky." A broad grin spread across his bronzed face.

"Sure," she said, handing him the watch.

Their driver started the engine and backed out of the lot. Soothing music emitted from the speaker behind her. She closed her eyes as the car eased smoothly down Galloway Road. Momentarily, the auto came to a complete stop then moved forward into a left turn on Baltzell Gate Road. Even with her eyes closed she knew precisely where they were. She had traveled the road so often with Monty, going to the movies and various other places around the post. What was he doing tonight?

"You're awfully quiet," the sergeant interrupted her thoughts. "The music is not that great. You must have been a thousand miles away."

"Something like that."

They arrived at the NCO Club and Sgt. Vinluan helped her out of the car after advising the driver to return for them in two hours.

Inside the club she sat with Sgt. Vinluan at a small table for two. Chatting with him, she learned several interesting aspects of his life while waiting to be served. He was a career soldier with sixteen years of service, presently assigned to HQ S-2 Intelligence Division. Vinluan was a Japanese name, and his father was a mixture of Japanese and Hawaiian with Spanish and Indian on his mother's side. He said that made him a *hapa* the word for half-breed in Hawaiian.

Their meal arrived and she gazed down at her plate of succulent prime rib, baked potato smothered in butter and sour cream.

"Wait," she said as Ben picked up his knife and fork and started to cut off a forkful of meat. "Aren't you forgetting to set your stop watch?"

"I was only joking about using the watch." Humor rippled through his voice. "A good cut of meat is like fine wine. It should be savored, never hurried. The same holds for the appreciation of a beautiful woman." He winked broadly at her.

The food was delicious, but she ate very little of hers while, Ben, as he asked her to call him, cleaned his plate leaving a lone sprig of green parsley.

"Dessert? They bake a mouth watering apple pie."

"I'm not much for sweets except for a love of ice cream. It's my weakness."

After dessert they wandered into the lounge as the band that played for the diners had taken a break.

"Would you like a drink?" Ben asked, sitting down next to her.

"Ginger ale."

"Make that two," he said to the bartender. "I owe you an apology for the other night," he said, turning to her. "I know it was rude of me to stare the way I did. I had searched this post for you, I walked into the club, and there you were sitting next to my friend, Frank's, girlfriend. I wasn't sure that I hadn't dreamed you. After meeting you, I knew instantly that you were the girl I wanted to marry. I know I must sound crazy to you. And I hope you don't think that I've lost my mind. It's my heart that I've lost to you. The problem is I'll soon be leaving for a tour of duty in Germany. I don't have time for a proper courtship."

"Ben, I'm very flattered, but I'm not available. I'm in love with someone else."

"If I only had the time I'm sure you'd come to feel the same way I do about you."

The first notes of a song blared from the band.

"Why don't we dance," she suggested.

Ben stood, held out his hand and she moved into his arms to the band's rendition of "Young Love." He began singing the words to the hit tune.

She tilted her head and smiled when the music ended. "That was nice. You have a pleasant voice," she complimented him, as they walked back to their table.

"Lots of practice. I played the guitar and sang with my high school group in Hilo." He helped seat her and sat down. "I have a house there. Nothing fancy but large enough for a wife and a couple of kids."

She glanced nervously around, uncomfortable with Ben's remarks about a wife and kids. Across the room she caught the movement of Cpl. Velez rising from his table and moving in their direction.

"Could we please leave? There is a guy on his way to our table that I had rather not see." She looked down at her hands in her lap trying to hide the heat in her face.

"Of course," said Ben, glancing at his watch. He helped her rise and draped her wrap around her shoulders.

They were silent on the return to her barracks. The driver held the door and Ben offered his arm as she exited the vehicle. He walked her to the door of her building, kissed the tips of his fingers, and brushed them lightly across one side of her cheek.

"I'll call you," he said, walking away.

April signed in and went up to her room feeling as though the evening had happened to someone else and not her.

After exchanging her clothes for a T-shirt and shorts, she went down to the mailroom. Pvt. Foster had cleaned and there was nothing to do there. She returned to her room and she was unlocking her door as the Runner, Pvt. Cook approached and said there was a phone call for her.

Her heart began to pound as she hurried down to the foyer. Who could be calling her at 2200 hours? Had Monty changed his mind?

"I'm sorry to call so late, but I was thinking about you. I didn't want to wait until tomorrow. I had a most pleasant evening and I hope you did, too," said Ben.

"Yes, I had a nice time, and you were right about the food."

"I hope I didn't say or do anything to upset you. Your eyes didn't have the sparkle I noticed the night we were introduced."

"You truly do your job well. I guess I wasn't successful at hiding my feelings from the world." She paused and took a deep breath. "My fiancée recently broke our engagement."

There was a notable silence before Ben spoke.

"I can't honestly say that I'm sorry, but I do have compassion for you. If there's anything I can do to cheer you up, please let me know."

"Thanks. It's not the first time that I've been hurt. As an adult I should be able to gather up the pieces of my disappointment with dignity and deal with it."

"What are you doing tomorrow?"

"After our company inspection in the morning, I planned to go to the WAC pool and lay in the sun. I don't swim," she confessed.

"Why don't I pick you up?"

"I'd rather you didn't. There are a few things I have to do first. Why don't I meet you at the pool?"

Edie was the only one who knew of her broken engagement, and she didn't feel up to answering any questions from curious cadre that might see her with Ben.

"I'll see you about 1330 hours. Good night and pleasant dreams," said the sergeant.

She listened to the dial tone for a full minute before she returned the phone to the base.

Following the inspection and lunch on Saturday she went to her room and exchanged her uniform for a black bathing suit. She covered it with a sleeveless white blouse and a black skirt. Before leaving her room, she placed sun tan lotion and a large towel in her red beach bag.

Instead of waiting at the bus stop, she set out walking. A car horn honked as she reached the WAC Chapel. She swung her bag over her shoulder and increased her strides.

Up ahead, an unfamiliar black and white Buick pulled over to the curb. Ben got out and stood beside the vehicle, a big grin spread across his face.

"Would the beautiful lady like a lift?"

"What? No staff car?"

"This belongs to a friend of mine who recently left the post. He had some offers but nothing definite. I'm going to try to close a deal for him. Until then I have the use of it."

He held the door for her and she got in. Stuck in the back window was a hand written *for sale* sign followed by a phone number.

Inside the pool complex, Ben went to the locker room, and she walked out to the patio. April put her things on a table beneath a red and blue umbrella. She slipped off her blouse and stepped out of her skirt, folded them and placed the clothes inside her large, beach bag.

A diver slicing into the water drew her attention to the deep end of the pool. Several moments passed before she recognized the black haired swimmer surfacing in the middle of the pool. Darkly bronzed arms cleaved the water with the expert strokes of an accomplished swimmer. After swimming several lengths of the pool, Ben halted at the side nearest her. His teeth flashed in a wide smile as he hauled himself onto the cement edge and stood. The sun glinted off his wet skin making him appear to be a highly polished statue. Six foot of splendid masculinity, wide shouldered and narrow hipped, with the firm rippling muscles of an athlete. His chest was smooth, without a single hair, perhaps the results of his Indian heritage.

Ben jumped back in the pool and motioned for her to join him.

"*Komo mai,*" he said. "That's Hawaiian for come into the water."

"Okay, but don't splash my hair," she warned.

Ben played like a child walking on the bottom of the pool on his hands letting his feet stick out above the water. And then he swam across the pool imitating a dolphin coming out of the water at intervals and disappearing beneath the surface.

She laughed at his antics.

They both got out and he stretched out on a large beach towel while she blotted herself with another towel and sat under the umbrella.

"I'm glad I can make you laugh. It makes me unhappy to see you sad. Do you want to tell me about it?"

"I'd rather talk about you."

"What do you want to know?" He got up and sat next to her.

"Everything."

"I thought I told you all about myself last night."

"I meant your hobbies—what you like to do when you are not working—things like that? Do you have any brothers or sisters?"

"I'm an only child, I'll be thirty-four on the seventeenth of October. I read a lot, mostly mystery stories—history interests me, too. I love to play chess, sing and play the guitar and the mandolin."

"I know you like Spanish music, what other music do you like?" she asked.

"Classical music and opera. I would like to play for you but my guitar was packed for shipping to Germany. If you like I will borrow one from one of my friends."

"That would be nice. You haven't asked anything about me?"

"I know everything I need to know about you."

"How could you? Except for what Carmen told you, I haven't said anything about myself."

"I've read your 201 File. What would you like to know about yourself? I know where you have a birthmark like a six pointed star." His lips spread into a wide grin.

"That information is confidential. How—"

"I told you I work in S-2. With my security clearance, I have access to all the 201 Files."

"Just what kind of job do you have?" she asked.

"I am an investigator. I work with Board Cases, and I find persons who don't want to be found."

"In other words, you are like a Military FBI?"

"Something like that." Ben laughed. "Enough about me. How about coming back to eat at the club with me or we could go to a nice restaurant in Anniston."

"No, but if you invite me to your mess hall, I'll eat with you."

"Are you sure you want to eat there. It would be a treat for the guys to have you dine with them, but I warn you, they will show their appreciation by whistling."

"That's okay. I've been whistled at a few times in my life," she said, laughing.

"I'm sure you have," said Ben, laughing along with her. "Don't forget that I warned you."

After a warm shower, she dressed in her favorite yellow dress and sat down at the vanity. She brushed her hair back and pinned it with a cluster of yellow silk flowers on the left side. Before leaving her room she put her dog tags and keys in a small clutch purse. Downstairs, she signed out and walked outside and down the wide sidewalk to where a black and white Buick was backing into a vacant space.

Ben got out of the car and he gave her a loud whistle and grinned.

"What was that for?"

"To prepare you for when we walk into my mess hall."

The headquarters mess was small compared to hers. Less than seventy-five men were seated around the room and she counted a total of nine girls.

Ben's whistle did not prepare her for the reception she received. It sounded like all the guys whistled at the same time.

"I told you so," Ben said, grinning from ear to ear.

The men continued to whistle sporadically until they reached their table and sat down.

"Did you know that it is a Spanish and Hawaiian custom for a girl to wear flowers behind her ear on that side of her face to let people know she is promised. I feel like I'm seven foot tall."

"Maybe I should go to the ladies room and change the flowers to the other side." She teased him.

"Absolutely not. I'm enjoying myself. They think you belong to me." Ben picked up his cup and sipped the black coffee.

Ten minutes later he finished the last of his applesauce and placed his utensils on a napkin.

"Would you care for seconds?" he asked. He stood and picked up his tray.

"Oh, no. I haven't finished with my tray."

Ben went through the mess line again returning with two loin chops, a mound of potatoes smothered in gravy and more applesauce, minus any steamed veggies.

April observed Ben busily devouring a pork chop, and she picked up her knife and cut herself a small bite of meat. She wished for his stopwatch to find out how fast it took him to finish off his second tray of food.

"Would you like to go to the club for awhile? Although, you will probably find it dull in comparison to my mess hall."

They laughed together as they exited the building.

Later at the NCO Club, she sat with Ben at a small table at the edge of the dance floor and sipped soft drinks.

From the bandstand, the three-piece combo struck up a lilting tune.

She looked at the couples already on the dance floor and cast him a wistful smile.

"Would you care to dance?" he asked.

She inclined her head in silent acquiescence. After his initial tremor as he put his arms around her, his movements were sure and fluid. They swayed to the sensuous beat of a slow ballad, one she had often danced to with Monty. To her surprise her steps didn't falter. She didn't have to think about her movements—they flowed naturally with his as she instinctively followed the shifts of his muscles.

The music ended. Ben immediately loosened his hold, allowing one arm to curve lightly around her back as he led her from the floor. Instead of returning to their table they stayed near the floor and waited for the next number.

At the end of the dance they walked out to the parking lot. A white Ford blocked Ben's car.

"I'll get the license number and have it announced over the PA for the owner to move it."

"Don't bother. Let's just sit in the car and talk. I feel the need of a shoulder to lean on." She got in and sat quietly for a few moments her hands folded in her lap.

"I'd like to hear what took the sunshine out of your smile," he said, softly.

"Just the same old story—girl meets boy—falls in love and gets disappointed when he betrays her. Only in my case it happened twice. I must have been born a loser."

"Tell me about it and let me be the judge of that."

April began pouring out the sordid incident with Cordero and the reason she wasn't wearing a ring when they met. She concluded with the plans she made with Monty before he went to New York and his recent telephone call that informed her that she was not the woman he wanted to marry. With her eyes closed against the pain, she rested her head against Ben's shoulder, tears slipping down her cheeks.

"I'm sorry," she apologized, opening her eyes. "I never meant to turn into a water fountain."

"Elaine, it's all right to cry, to wish for things to be different."

She nodded, her sobs quieting to deep, cleansing breaths.

Ben gently pressed a folded handkerchief in her hands, and then leaned over and kissed her softly on the cheek. It was meant as a token of his affection—a kiss of comfort.

The motor of a car starting in front of them startled her as she wiped at the moisture on her face. She opened her eyes in time to see the vehicle blocking Ben's car drive away.

Ben moved over and turned the key in the ignition of the Buick. Ten minutes later, they pulled into Company D's parking lot and he cut the motor. He turned to her and cupped her face in his hands. The hands holding her trembled and a slight shudder seemed to pass through his body.

"You must know that I want to kiss you good night."

She nodded, her eyes avoiding his.

Angling his head to one side, he traced the curve of her mouth. His lips were warm and velvet-soft as they brushed a chaste kiss across her mouth. He deepened the kiss and teased her lips open against his, just the tip of his tongue slipping into her mouth. He kissed her like Cordero had but unlike him not savagely but very tenderly and she was surprised to find it most pleasurable and comforting. She waited for a spark of something— anything—to encourage her to accept the love he offered. But she felt only guilt and bewilderment at her own behavior as she struggled to understand why she had allowed Ben to kiss her. She should have protested and pushed him away. Instead she had sat there in a mindless daze while he took advantage of her.

"Why did you kiss me like that?"

Ben rested his forehead against hers.

"Elaine, I meant you no disrespect," he murmured. "I've never kissed a woman like that. None have made me feel like I do toward you. Neither have I trembled when dancing or touching a woman before. I was embarrassed the first time it happened but now I'm getting used to it." He laughed good-naturedly and got out of the car.

He held her hand as they walked to the door of her building.

"Thanks for a pleasant evening, especially the fun time at your mess hall."

"We'll do it again soon. I'll call you tomorrow," he promised.

Ben brought her hand to his lips, and softly caressed her fingers. His expressive eyes held hers in a sensual spell as he deliberately moved her hand across his chest and laid it over his heart before squeezing it and letting it go. It was an intimate, tantalizing gesture that left her still feeling its effects long after he had said goodnight and left her at the entrance of Company D.

The human heart breaks piece by piece.
When mended it often leaves a gaping hole,
That can never be filled.

Chapter 41

Sunday morning, April signed out for the chapel. Ten minutes into the sermon, Ben moved into the pew next to her and took hold of her hymnbook.

"Good morning," he said, once the hymn finished. He didn't speak again until the service terminated.

"How did you find me?" she asked as they walked out to the parking lot and got in the car.

"I phoned and your CQ was kind enough to tell me you went to church." He headed the vehicle in the direction of Galloway Gate.

"Ben, my barracks is in the other direction."

"I know. I missed chow and unless I get something to eat, I might be tempted to take a bite out of you, *nani maka lau.*"

"You'll have to explain that to me."

"Simple," he said. "The color of your dress makes your eyes appear green, that's *maka lau*—green eyes. And *nani* is—"

"Beautiful—beautiful green eyes," she finished for him. "*Mahalo,*" she replied. Thank you.

"You are a fast learner. Let's see if you can guess this word. *Kilu?*" he asked, with a question in his voice.

"I don't know that word." She shook her head.

"It's a very important word to a Hawaiian male." He leaned over and kissed her.

Now she knew *kilu* meant kiss.

They went out the check gate, heading for the drive-in restaurant across the street.

"Could we go some place else?" she asked quickly. That particular place held too many sad memories for her.

Ben turned and drove down the street to the Waffle House.

He ordered a breakfast of eggs, bacon and pecan waffles while she ordered a chicken sandwich.

"How is it you stay so trim with the large amount of food you consume?"

"I try to work out an hour each morning. I lift weights and I swim when I'm near water, also *hee-nalu*, surfing."

Their food arrived and Ben gave it his undivided attention, finishing before she could eat all of her lunch.

She looked up to catch him staring at her. "You make me blush when you look at me like that."

"I love everything about you. Especially when you blush. You are *maikai, anoi kauwa*. Which means that you are pretty and healthy when you blush and I desire to be your slave."

"I think it's time to leave."

After a few blocks, Ben stopped the car in front of an ice cream shop. The bell above the door jangled announcing their entrance to the store.

"What flavor do you prefer?" he asked.

"Strawberry."

"That's my favorite, too," he said. He stepped over to the counter and placed their order. Moments later, he laughed as he handed her a single cone and bit into his triple scoop.

She licked at the soft pink swirl of strawberry getting some of the ice cream on her lips.

Ben leaned down and kissed her mouth. "I just discovered a flavor that I like even more than strawberry."

"Really?" she asked. "What's it called?"

"Second hand ice cream," he said, teasingly licking his lips. "Very tasty."

"I think it's pretty nice, too," she replied, smothering a giggle.

They left the shop and he turned her in the other direction when she started toward his parked car.

"I want to show you something down the street," he said, linking her arm through his as their footsteps echoed on the cement walk. He stopped in front of a jewelry store with a sign stuck in the door. 'Closed on Sunday.'

"Elaine, I realize you don't love me but I have enough for both of us. This is not the way I planned to propose. But I don't have time for a proper courtship. I am not complete—you are my other half that will make me whole. Will you marry me?"

"What am I going to do with you?" she asked, smiling and shaking her head.

"Simple—marry me." He pointed to a display of engagement and wedding rings in the shop window.

"Which one do you like?"

"Ben, I can't accept a ring from you. I'm still in love with Monty. I've been thinking about calling him. I want to hear him tell me that he doesn't love me anymore."

"I wish I could ask you not to call him. I'm sure that the two of you will patch things up. He'd be a fool if he didn't."

They walked back to the car and he drove to Company D. He trembled when he kissed her good night. Quickly, she opened the Buick's door and ran to the front entrance and she didn't stop until she reached her room.

The following evening, she went to the Orderly Room after chow. Inside, she leaned against the door without turning on the light. Slowly, she moved through the half darkness around the filing cabinet and switched on the wall light. Her eyes focused on the telephone on the desktop as she took off her hat. Never taking her eyes off the black object, she walked around and seated herself behind the green, metal desk. She reached for the phone and placed it down in front of her. She would face the truth of their relationship—no more avoiding or guessing. No more assuming. After staring at it for a few moments, she picked up the handset and carefully dialed Monty's number in New York. The telephone receiver in her hand seemed to be made of lead. She had difficulty keeping it to her ear as she waited for him to answer. It rang four times before his sister Maria answered. "I'm glad you called. My brother has had a difficult week." She sounded encouraging.

A short heavy silence followed while April waited for Monty to come to the phone.

"Monty," she said in a rush not giving him a chance to hang up on her. "I realized that in all the talking you did—there was one thing you never did say."

"I've nothing more to say to you."

"Oh, but there is. You never said I *don't love you.*"

"I don't have to—"

"Just say it. *I don't love you any more.* That way I'll know once and for all. I'll understand why you're doing this to us and I won't bother you again."

Seconds passed, as the line was silent. She waited, almost afraid to breathe, for his answer. Forcing her tone to be calm, she took several deep, ragged breaths. "The way I see it, the decision is yours now."

"You win, April. I can't say it. I don't know what got into me. I've been miserable ever since I called and said those cruel things to you. These past weeks, I've tried to write you, but I keep throwing the letters away. I don't know what to say to erase the hurtful things I said on the phone. I've acted like a fool, and I'm so sorry. Please forgive me."

His words were like a soothing balm to her bruised heart.

"Monty, there is something you should know. I haven't sat in my room crying. I've been seeing someone."

"It doesn't matter. All I want to know is that you still love me and that you can forgive me for being crazy jealous."

"Monty, you know I do."

"If it wasn't for my job, I would leave right now and drive down there so we could get married."

"I understand, and it won't be long until we'll be together."

Too soon they were saying good-bye and after he hung up, she felt a total positive sense of joy and optimism about their future. She and Monty were right for each other. In spite of all the obstacles they had encountered, they had found solutions. And because of that she wasn't afraid anymore. She never felt happier than she did at that moment. Nothing—absolutely nothing in the whole world—could spoil the glorious future she visioned for them together.

> Tuesday, 19 August 1958
> Dear Dreamcatcher,
> Ben called me this morning. I told him that he had been right that Monty and I made up. He said that he didn't regret falling in love with me and he could still hope as long as I was single. And the time he had spent with me had been the happiest in his life. I didn't know what to say to him. It hurts me and I feel sad that I let him console me and I can't comfort him in return...

> Thursday, 21 August 1958
> We are getting ready to graduate a platoon. Our company is planning a picnic and pool party on Saturday. The trainees will entertain the cadre in the evening with songs and skits.
> In the afternoon mail, I got the cutest Teddy bear from Monty. I will sleep with it tonight and pretend it is Monty...

Saturday, 23 August 1958

Today I received the most beautiful engagement ring. It was packed in three different sized containers. Pvt. Foster brought the package to the Orderly Room and the cadre could hardly wait for me to open the box. The diamond is set in white gold flanked by two smaller stones on each side. I still can't believe it. I keep gazing at my left hand. My ring is a perfect fit, too. A beautiful note came with it asking me to marry him and share his life. I only wanted a wedding band, but I love my ring. I called Monty a little while ago to tell him how happy he had made me, but I scolded him for spending the money. He said that he wanted the whole world to know that I belonged to him.

I was so excited about my ring that I almost forgot about our party. It was a huge success...

Monday, 01 September 1958

I had to work today even though it is a holiday. We are short one platoon sergeant and I am filling in to march the troops to and from classes. In the afternoon I took them for inoculations. I'm glad they got them and not me.

Monty wrote me a sweet letter telling me that he was going to the beach with his sister's family to celebrate Labor Day...

One week later April looked up as Pvt. Foster entered the Orderly Room and hung the jeep keys on the pegboard.

"Sorry, no mail for you."

She nodded her head and returned to the stack of certificates on her desk. It didn't help that she was starting to feel nauseous again. These mysterious sicknesses were beginning to become a nuisance. Earlier that morning she'd had to rush to the latrine as soon as she got out of bed.

Nauseating bile rose in her throat.

Just then, Sgt. Levy looked up from her desk. "My goodness. What's wrong? You're white as a sheet."

"Excuse me, I'm going to the latrine," she said on a note of desperation and hurried from the office. Oh, God, she was going to be sick. She fought down another wave of nausea.

Minutes after losing her lunch in the toilet, she went to the sink, splashing cool water on her face and rinsed her mouth. She stared at her reflection above the washbasin, her eyes wide with shock. How could she have been so dumb? The signs had been there for days but she had been so caught up in preparing the work for the graduating platoon and fretting over the absence of mail from Monty, she had been blind to the facts.

Could she be pregnant? It was the only explanation for the nausea and increasing bouts of sickness in the mornings. When had she last had her period? She was as regular as clockwork, every twenty-nine days.

She left the latrine and walked rapidly to her room. According to her calendar her last period was the fourteenth of June, a week before she spent the night with Monty.

> Thursday, 04 September 1958
> Dear Dreamcatcher,
> This morning, I made a shocking discovery. I am almost certain that I am pregnant. It has been over two months since my last period. I made an appointment for Saturday with a Dr. Nesbitt that I found in the Anniston phone directory.
> Still no word from Monty—I don't know what to think.
> Why doesn't he answer my letters…

On Saturday afternoon, April borrowed Sgt. Vinson's car and drove to Anniston to keep her appointment with Dr. Nesbitt.

She arrived a half-hour early as instructed. In the cool waiting room, she sat down with a clipboard filling out an information sheet for the receptionist. Minutes later, she stood taking the completed form to the desk and her knees suddenly turned to liquid. She wavered, lifting a hand to her forehead. Her skin was moist.

"Mrs. Terry? Are you all right?" asked the girl behind the counter.

"Yes, just a dizzy spell," she said, clutching the edge of the desk.

"Dr. Nesbitt is ready to see you now. Can I get you a cool drink? A cup of tea?"

"No, thanks. I'm fine."

Twenty minutes later she sat in a deep cushioned chair facing a thin middle aged man who viewed her over half moon spectacles resting partway down his long nose.

"Your suspicion was correct. You are expecting," said the doctor. He studied her folder. "From the information you've given, your baby should arrive the latter part of March."

He closed the file and reached for a yellow prescription pad. He wrote briefly on it, then tore off the page and handed it to her.

"This is for prenatal vitamins. Do you have any questions?"

"I'm ill each morning. Can you give me something for the nausea?"

"That's very common. It's known as morning sickness. Normally, it only lasts a few weeks, but some expectant mothers are bothered with it throughout their pregnancy. There is a drug I could prescribe to elevate it. But since this is your first pregnancy, the less medication you consume, the better for your baby. Try ginger tea in the mornings. Most women find it helpful. Also nibble on dry crackers before your breakfast."

"Thank you, Dr. Nesbitt. I'll do that."

"I want to see you again in four weeks." The doctor rose from his chair and held the door for her. "My receptionist will make your next appointment. If you think of any other questions, don't hesitate to call my office. Congratulations, Mrs. Terry."

April left the cool office in a daze and stepped out into the simmering heat of the afternoon.

Unbidden her fingers traced a light path across her narrow waist, and then paused in an unconsciously protective gesture over her stomach.

She was pregnant. It was one thing suspecting that she might be and quite another having it confirmed.

Inside the car, she rolled down the windows and leaned back against the cushioned leather seat. She slid the controls into drive and moved out into the flow of traffic.

What would Monty say when she told him about the baby? Would he be pleased? True, they had talked about having a family, but not this soon.

And what of the WAC. If anyone found out she would be discharged in disgrace. If Pvt. Wells hid her pregnancy for seven months, she should be able to conceal hers for another month. She just didn't like being dishonest.

The light changed, and her attention returned to the road ahead.

It was mid afternoon when she swung the car into the back lot behind Company D.

After returning the keys to Sgt. Vinson and thanking her for the use of the car, she went directly down to the mailroom. Pvt. Foster handed her a single envelope. Her heart accelerated, but it was not from Monty. It was a letter from her brother, Eugene, giving her his new address in Fairbanks, Alaska.

Today made an entire week since Monty's last letter. Could he be ill or working overtime?

She slowly climbed the stairs to her room, sat at her desk, and wrote to Monty. She didn't mention anything about the baby. She would wait and tell him the news when they spoke on the phone. How would he react to becoming an expectant father?

Sunday morning, she awoke earlier than usual. Something had disturbed her sleep. Perhaps it was the baby or knowing for certain she was pregnant. She recalled what she had written in her journal before going to bed. She'd had that strange feeling like when Monty left to go to New York that she was never to see him again. Could it be true? She shook her head. Permitting her thoughts to travel such a path was both detrimental and useless. It served no purpose.

She reached for the cracker box beside her bunk and munched a few squares. So far she had been fortunate, for although she experienced a slight queasiness on waking it had not developed into morning sickness, yet.

Grabbing her robe from the foot of her bed and picking up her ditty bag, she headed for the kitchen. She made a cup of ginger tea and sipped it before going to the latrine.

In the evening after chow, she returned to the Orderly Room to check over the forms for the captain's signature on Monday.

She sat at her desk thinking about the morning and how guilty she felt when she attended church. A child conceived outside marriage was a sin in God's eyes. The price she paid for loving Monty, she paid silently with her heart. Yet, it was impossible not to ponder what her future might hold, and that of her unborn child.

The sharp ring of the phone on her desk made her jump. Automatically, she picked up the receiver. "Company D, Sp. Terry speaking."

"April?"

"Monty. It's so good to hear your voice. I've been concerned—you haven't answered my last four letters. Have you been ill?"

"No—yes. I've been heartsick."

"Me, too. Darling, I've been so worried when you didn't write. Have you heard from your father?"

"Yes," he said his voice barely audible.

"Well, what did he say?"

"He gave his blessings." There was a heavy inflection in his low voice, which gave the words, accented tones.

"Oh, darling, that's wonderful—see, you were anxious for nothing. I knew when he received my letter and learned how much we loved each other, he wouldn't object to our marriage. I'm so happy you called. There is something important I have to tell you."

There was a long silence that stretched into moments.

"April," her name came out hoarsely, torn from some place deep inside him. "I can't marry you." Monty's voice grated harshly, the smooth tones roughened. She had never heard him sound like that before.

"What do you mean? You just said your father gave his approval."

"It's not my father—"

"Then you don't love me," she said, interrupting him. "What have I done wrong?"

"I love you with all my heart and soul. *Todo mi alma, mi vida.*"

"I don't understand—why are you telling me this?"

"It's Esther—she is here in New York—I have a son," he said hesitantly.

"But how—"

"She found out that she was pregnant after I left Ecuador to come to the states."

"But why did she wait so long to tell you? You told me that you wrote to each other for a while after you came to New York. I don't understand."

"It is complicated. I would rather not go into details. I wish I could see you—explain it to you in person. But it is not possible for me to leave my job right now. I have been trying to write to you. I start a letter and the paper ends up in the wastebasket. It is killing me—I couldn't write—I didn't know how to tell you all this."

"Do you love her?"

"I don't think I ever did. At least, not the way I love you." His voice sounded muffled and broken.

With an effort she pulled her shattered thoughts together, trying to think of something to say.

"Does she love you? Of course, she does—she had your son. How old is he? He must be about a year and a half. Is he handsome? If he looks like you, he must be adorable." She was blabbing incessantly, but she couldn't seem to get control over her tongue or her emotions.

"He will be two next March—look I don't want to talk about it. I want to know if you are going to be all right. I know this has come as a great shock to you—for me, too. I want you to understand that I will never love any woman but you. No one but you will ever have my heart."

She couldn't reply. In the emotional state she was in right now, she couldn't have spoken a word if she'd tried and her soul shriveled with each of his words. The heart breaking catch in her voice must have been audible over the static on the line.

"Please say something—tell me you understand and forgive me." The hoarse desperate note in his voice brought tears to her eyes. It was difficult to sit here while every sweet dream she had imagined crumbled into dust. She was shaking so hard her chest was in danger of caving in around her heart. It hurt to draw sufficient air, and she could barely speak.

"You are marrying Esther?" She forced the words out. A fresh jolt of pain shot through her.

"Yes," he whispered. "A child deserves two parents. Please understand that I must take responsibility for what I've done. I can't walk away from my obligation. You must know that I never intended this."

What about their baby? Didn't it matter? Didn't it need parents, too? What good would it do to tell him she was expecting his child? She couldn't bring herself to force him into a decision—he could only marry one of them. And she was here far way while the other woman was there in New York with him and his son. It was a tragedy with no possible happy ending for her.

"I do," she returned, softly. "I would expect no less of you. I will be returning your ring by parcel post. How much should I insure the package f—"

"Don't," he cut in. "I want you to have it."

"Under the circumstances, I couldn't possibly keep it. Give it to Esther. You told me you had never given her a ring. She wouldn't have to know it was bought for another woman."

"I would know. Please keep it."

"I can't," she whispered, brokenly catching her breath determined to maintain her composure. "It would only be a reminder of our lost love." She tried to stifle her sobs.

"What will you tell your family and the cadre in your company about your broken engagement?"

"To Sgt. Levy, I'll tell the truth. I'm not in the habit of discussing my personal life with the other personnel."

"You could say that you changed your mind about marrying me," he suggested.

"I couldn't lie about it."

"It would make me sound less of a heel if you did."

"Sgt. Levy is not like that. She will understand as I do."

"And your mother?"

"I can't tell her the truth right now. I don't want her to share my pain."

"Thank you for that."

"It's not for you. I don't want her to be hurt like I'm hurting at this moment."

"I know. I am grieving, too. I thanked you because I am troubled at not being able to keep my promise to your mother. I am concerned for her feelings and at the same time, I do not wish her to think bad of me."

"When the time comes, I'll say that I was at fault and spare her being hurt."

"What are your plans after your ETS?"

"I don't know." All the plans they had made together had been an illusion. Her romantic heart had reached for moonbeams and wished on stars. Now in the space of a few minutes her whole world had crashed, and her life would never be the same again.

"You said that you had something important to tell me. What es it?" The trace of his Spanish accent seeped into his words.

Her hand tightened around the receiver. She started to speak but of what use would her words be? How could she tell him that he would have another child born in March? How ironic—both his children sharing the same birth month, but different mothers.

"Uh—" she swallowed past the sudden constriction in her throat trying to think of something to say. "Sgt. Levy is being transferred to Ft. Knox, Kentucky. Is-isn't that something?" she stammered.

"Yes. I know—you wrote me about it in one of your letters that I couldn't answer."

"I guess I forgot. I wrote you so much." She cradled the receiver against her ear with an uplifted shoulder while she reached across the desk to snag a box of tissues.

This was the last time she would ever hear Monty's voice, and she didn't know how she was going to bear it. She brushed helplessly at the tears leaking from her eyes and let the sound of his Spanish accent wash over, she would remember it forever. Her heart was shattering, but she was doing the right thing by not telling him about the baby.

"You are so beautiful and sweet. In no time you'll find another guy to marry," he whispered, hoarsely, his voice sounding on the verge of tears.

"How could I ever be happy with someone else loving you the way that I do? What would I tell my husband on our wedding night? I'm no longer innocent." No, she could never marry. She would raise their child alone. All hope was gone for the two of them, but she would do everything in her power to keep the truth from him—to make sure he had what he wanted in his life—his son.

"Peachy, don't say that. You don't know what your words do to me. I would never have taken your innocence had I not thought we were as good as married. I want your happiness more than anything else, but more than that I want your forgiveness." His tone took on a rasping sound.

"Monty, there is nothing to forgive. You didn't do anything that I was not willing for you to do. I am more at fault for I wanted you to make me feel the things of a woman. I begged for your loving, and I thank you for those memories."

She felt ill. It was not due to her condition. Those symptoms had ceased in the past weeks. Nevertheless, she had to put down the nausea that rose in her throat as she gripped the receiver so tightly her knuckles streaked white.

The tears that peppered Monty's voice welled up in her own eyes as a sharp piercing pain speared through her heart.

"Monty, I wish…" Her voice wavered but she recovered swiftly. "I wish you all the happiness." Her throat closed and she was incapable of speech. Before she could regain her voice, there was an audible click and then a dial tone. The line was dead. And just as soundly, her heart broke.

She clasped the phone to her breast and placed her other hand on her belly where her child was growing beneath her heart. Slowly, she replaced the receiver gently on the base. Her hand remained on it a short time as if she could prolong her contact with Monty.

Life was so unfair. She loved a man she couldn't have. The pain spread out in waves, first her throat and then her chest, working its way down to her stomach. She thought she might be sick. The roaring in her head was deafening, and the whole room seemed to fade.

A low, agonized moan broke from her lips. April's hands came up to cover her face, she rested her head on her crossed arms on the desktop, while silent sobs racked her body. How could she ever get through the rest of her life without Monty?

She didn't regret loving Monty. She would make the same choice should she be able to go back and relive that night with him when she became a woman in his arms. But the results of it weighed heavy on her as she contemplated raising her child alone.

April straightened her desk, locked the Orderly Room and wearily climbed the flight of steps to her quarters.

Inside her dark room, she sat staring through the window, her throat aching with more tears, letting her mind turn in endless circles. Every thrilling moment with Monty replayed across her memory as she considered everything that had happened since they'd met. When he'd curled himself around her—held her close—given her pleasure beyond her dreams. Beautiful memories she would treasure forever.

Her baby would never have a father to tease, love, cherish and protect it. The child would be entirely hers. Monty must never know about it. He was doing the noble thing by marrying his child's mother. In a short time, Monty would forget she'd ever been a part of his life.

It was evident that her pregnancy could not be kept a secret from everyone, nor did she expect it to be…but Monty's role as her baby's father would be her secret.

Exhausted, she got up and readied herself for bed—to her only place of solace.

Do not wish for something you cannot have.
Accept what you do have,
And make the most of it.

Chapter 42

The instant April opened her eyes she sensed something was wrong. But it was minutes before her mind allowed her to recall the pain of the night before. Monty was marrying Esther. A cold knot bunched in her stomach as she recalled their phone conversation. Her heart lurched with such force she found it difficult to breathe. It was all she could do to stop herself from being sick.

Suddenly the truth of the situation hit her. She was pregnant—without a home or a place to go—and no one to love and care for her or her child. From now on her only concern had to be for her child's well being. In spite of her brave thoughts, ahead of her lay some of the loneliest and most desolate days of her entire life.

She would have liked to remain in bed with the covers pulled over her. But what scrap of honor that still remained wouldn't allow her to take the coward's path. Pride made her get out of bed, shower and dress and go down stairs with her head held high and every line of her body stiff and straight.

As soon as she entered the Orderly Room, Sgt. Levy took one look and asked, "Little Bit, what's wrong? You look like you just lost your best friend and spent the night crying?"

"I guess you could say that, only it's much worse," she allowed, quietly.

"Want to talk about it?" Sgt. Levy invited.

"Later, in private," she replied, seating herself at her desk. She picked up the phone and dialed the mailroom extension.

"This is Sp. Terry, I need a carton—about the size of a shoe box. Thanks," she said, and hung up the phone.

"Aren't you going to chow this morning?" asked Sgt. Levy.

"I don't feel like eating."

"Hold down the fort," said Sgt. Levy, rising from her desk. "I'll bring you something back from the mess hall."

"No, thanks I couldn't eat a thing."

At the end of the day, she picked up the cardboard box from her desk, and she followed Sgt. Levy out of the office.

Behind the closed door of Sgt. Levy's room, she tearfully told her about her broken engagement and the baby. When she finished speaking, Edie opened her arms. "You poor child," she said, sadness cracking the older woman's voice.

April went into her outstretched arms, fighting to hold back her tears. She rested her forehead on Edie's shoulder, drawing comfort from the human touch of someone that cared for her and would make everything right if it were in her power. But not even God could change the past.

Sgt. Levy held her loosely; moving her hand in little circles down the back of her neck and quietly stroked her shoulders. Eventually, her tears stopped and she moved back. She inhaled raggedly and wiped her face with the tissue Edie handed her.

"Feel better?"

She nodded, in a numbed affirmative gesture. "I don't know what's gotten into me. I don't usually cry like that. I thought I could handle this. Guess that was really a stupid assumption from someone who's never been in this situation before."

"It's probably the baby. Hormones—I've heard that pregnancy makes a woman cry at the drop of a handkerchief. Here, sit down." Edie pulled out the bench from beneath the vanity for her while she sat at the desk.

Her hand rubbed over the engagement ring on her finger and slipped it off. From her shirtwaist pocket, she fished a tiny white satin covered box. She placed the ring gently inside the velvet-lined container, snapping it closed. With her head lowered, she studied her bare ring finger, where once there'd been a sparkling engagement ring, now only a pale mark encircled her finger. April felt odd without the ring. But nothing she'd done lately had been very ordinary.

"So that's what the box is for. Your are returning your engagement ring?"

"Uh-huh," she said and sniffed.

"I'm so sorry," said Edie, moisture welling in her black eyes. "How do you feel about the baby?"

"I want this baby." She smoothed her hand across her still flat stomach and brought it to rest against her heart. "It hurts to think of him with another woman. It's agony to imagine spending my life without him and knowing that he'll never see our child."

Moments of silence passed between them before Edie began to speak.

"I don't think I've ever told you that I was adopted."

"No, I didn't know." April shook her head.

The sergeant moved across the floor and opened the small refrigerator. "How about a cold drink?"

"No thanks."

Edie took out an orange soda and used the bottle opener attached on the side of the fridge. From a box on top of the appliance, she took a straw and stuck it in the neck of the bottle before returning to her seat.

"The earliest photo I have of myself was taken at the age of three with my adoptive parents, a Jewish couple in Philadelphia. They couldn't have any children of their own, so I never had any brothers or sisters that I know of. Or if my parents died or they just plain didn't want me.

"In junior high, I fell in love with the son of a wealthy Jewish land developer. James was a grade ahead of me, the popular star quarterback, and drop dead handsome. After he graduated from high school, he didn't go on to college but went to work for his father."

Leaning forward slightly on the bench, April encouraged Edie to continue.

"My parents planned for me to attend college, but all I wanted was to marry James and have some kids. Make a family of our own. They never refused me anything. Finally, I persuaded them to let me marry James. My wedding was planned for June, right after my high school graduation. A beautiful gown was custom made along with the dresses for six bridesmaids. The two hundred invitations were mailed. Our reception was to be held at James' father's country club."

Edie paused and took a sip from the straw in the bottle of her orange drink.

"Three days," she continued, "before our wedding, a young girl I knew in school, a junior when I was a senior, came to my home. She was about six months pregnant, and she said that James was the father. She was in tears, telling me how sorry she was and that she hadn't known he was engaged until she read the announcement of the reception to be held at the Golden Hills Country Club."

"Oh, Edie, how awful. What did you do?"

"I took the coward's way out. I ran away and joined the Women's Army Auxiliary Corps."

"She could have lied about who fathered her baby."

"No." Edie sighed. "I knew it was true. James had been pressuring me to be intimate all through my junior and senior years. I've often wondered if I had given in to him if we would be married today."

Edie picked up the bottle and took another long drink of soda.

"I haven't told you the real kick in the teeth. Later my adoptive mother wrote me that they got married on the wedding date that James and I had chosen. And their reception was held at his father's club. Over the years my mother kept me informed about people I knew back home. The last I heard, James had half a dozen kids. The family we had planned together."

"Oh, Edie, I'm so sorry."

"Don't be." Edie sighed. "It was a long time ago. It wasn't the end of the world, it only felt like it."

"You never went back?"

"No. I couldn't. The Army became my home."

"So that's why you've never married."

"Maybe. I think for me, James was the only man. Sure, over the years, I've met other guys and dated, but none of them ever measured up to him." Edie took a deep breath and exhaled. "I once read some where, that for every woman born—there is that inevitable encounter with one man and the woman's life is never the same, regardless of how many times she may fall in love afterwards. The tender joys of first love live in the heart forever."

"Mine won't be the same, that's for sure. I'm left with a reminder and a heart full of pain." Her hand slid down to her flat stomach. It didn't seem real. A tiny life was growing inside her. The child she and Monty created in that brief moment of love. Her life, her future, now seemed like a jigsaw puzzle that someone had dropped and there were pieces missing, so it could never again be reconstructed to form the same picture. Unlike Edie, who was left with nothing, she would always have a part of Alberto Montoya.

"The pain never quite goes away. Like I said, it wasn't the end of the world. That's just the way things are sometimes. I had to accept it and get on with my life. The question is, what are you going to do?" asked Edie.

"I can't go home. I don't have one to go to, and I already ran away once—there is no place for me to run to."

"What about your grandmother?"

"Granny lives way up in the hills. In winter the roads are impassable. She usually comes into town to stay with my mother because you can't reach her place except on horseback. I can't see myself with a big belly bouncing around on a horse. Can you?"

Edie started to laugh, and April joined her, laughing, too, until the tears rolled down their cheeks.

"I'm sorry to laugh like this," Edie handed her a tissue. "It does present a funny picture."

"I needed that," she said, dabbing at the wetness on her cheeks.

"You know if anyone finds out about your condition, you'll immediately be given a medical discharge."

"Like Pvt. Wells—I know. Please help me keep my secret so I can stay until my ETS?"

"You know I will—no need to ask," Edie assured her.

"I have some money saved. Maybe I could get a room in town, find some kind of work." She continued, "I'm strong and healthy. I figure I could work up until the time my child is born."

"And after the baby comes?"

"I'd put him or her in a nursery. A lot of women who have children work. I'd be no different."

"Have you considered getting married?"

"Who'd want to marry a girl that was pregnant with another man's kid?" She gestured to herself with an open hand.

"What about that sergeant that keeps calling you?"

"Sgt. Vinluan?" She shook her head negatively.

"Didn't you tell me that he had proposed to you?"

"But that was before I learned I was pregnant." She rested her hand momentarily on her flat stomach.

"If he really loved you—it might not make a difference."

"That's out of the question."

"Why not tell him and let him decide?"

"My pride for one thing. It's about all I have left." She gestured to herself with an open hand.

"He might surprise you."

"It wouldn't matter. I don't love him."

"You learned to love Montoya when you loved—"

"Don't say his name. That's one of the pains I've learned to live with. I hurt him so much—this must be my punishment."

"That's nonsense," said Edie as she got up and put the empty soda bottle on top of the squat refrigerator.

"I guess I deserved to be hurt, too."

"No one deserves what has happened to you." Edie moved to stand behind her placing a caring hand on her shoulder. "I wish I was staying here so I could keep an eye on you. But I don't have a choice. I go where the Army sends me." Edie squeezed her shoulder and went to the vanity. She pulled out the lower drawer, removed a small-yellowed box, and handed it to her.

"What's this?"

"A replacement for your finger. It looks naked without your engagement ring."

She flipped the box open. Nestled inside on black velvet rested a sparkling diamond engagement ring.

"Oh, this is gorgeous," she said, moving it back and forth in the light.

"Somehow, I never got around to returning it to James," she shrugged. "Try it on—my hands use to be tiny like yours."

"Oh, no, I couldn't wear this. What if I lost it?" She stared at the dazzling ring in her hand.

"You'd be doing me a favor. I don't know why I haven't gotten rid of it." Edie made a useless gesture with her hand.

She slipped it on. It fit perfectly. "It almost looks like my ring except the stone is much larger."

"It's one karat."

"Wow! It must be worth a lot."

"I expect so—more than when it was given to me."

"No," she said, removing the sparkling ring. "I couldn't wear it. It would be dishonest." April handed the box with the ring to Edie.

"You don't have to say anything—just wear the ring. If you don't—there will be questions asked about your bare finger."

"Well, I suppose you're right. I don't have to explain to anyone what happened. Although, I imagine that Pvt. Foster is already wondering why Monty's letters have stopped."

"You don't need to be concerned about her for awhile. She just put in for a ten-day leave. Her sister is getting married. You'll be in charge of the mailroom until she returns."

"She mentioned it but I didn't know she was taking time off to attend the wedding. Have you heard anything more on my replacement for company clerk?"

"Uh-huh, I don't expect Sgt. Vinson's going to be pleased after the problem with the last one. Her name is Pvt. Centers, a former MP who got busted for drinking on duty. That's all I know about her."

"Golly—jeez," she said, unconsciously using Sgt. Levy's favorite expression.

"My sentiments, exactly," Edie agreed.

"I best let you get some sleep," she said, standing and scooting the bench under the vanity. "Thanks for listening to me."

"I wish I had a solution for you. I do suggest you mail that ring from the main post office facility."

"I'll do that," she said, moving toward the door.

"Here, don't forget your ring," said Edie, holding out the box that contained James' ring.

"Okay," she said, accepting the tiny container. "I'll only wear it when I'm on duty."

"If you need to talk, just knock on my door."

"Thanks again. I don't know what I'd do without you."

"You'd manage—you are a survivor like me. I just wish I could help you more. Good night, sleep well."

Closing the door behind her, she went straight to her room, wanting nothing more than to sleep. To escape from her thoughts and her aching heart.

Within moments, she knew sleep was impossible. All she could do was stare at the ceiling and wipe at the dampness on her cheeks.

The following morning all the training she'd received paid off because she did her job without pause, but her mind was several hundred miles away in New York.

In the evening she retired to her room, dreading the time she would have to close her eyes and sleep. For then the real battle began. Unhampered by her conscious will, her love and regret fought the nightmarish truth, leaving her crushed when she awoke with a jolt to find hot tears streaming down her face. Muffling sobs in her pillow, she waited for the arrival of 0500 hours.

Sunday, 07 September 1958
Dear Dreamcatcher,
One week has passed since I confided in Edie. A week in which I have cried myself to sleep each night.
Sgt. Vinson returns from her vacation tomorrow so I will be just plain Specialist Terry again.
Tonight, I am the Duty NCO and so far it has been a peaceful evening. I doubt that I'll sleep any because I have to

go for my physical tomorrow afternoon. I am so afraid the doctor will discover that I'm pregnant when he does the internal exam. Sgt. Levy doesn't think so. I hope she is right. She told me that several years ago she re-upped and the day she went for her exam she got her period. When she asked the doctor to reschedule the exam, he said that the primary reason for the internal was to determine if an EW was pregnant. "Obviously you're not," he'd said and stamped her papers complete. She told me to wear a sanitary napkin and say that my period was early. I had to borrow a belt from Edie as I use tampons. And she gave me a pad to go with it. I don't like the deception but it appears that I have no other choice...

The following, afternoon she entered the Orderly Room wearing a big smile and waved a medical paper in front of Sgt. Levy.

"I don't believe it," she said, and collapsed on her chair. "I passed the physical without an internal exam. I still can't believe it."

"I told you it would work," said Sgt. Levy, a wide grin spread across her face.

Late in the afternoon, she placed the last of the graduating certificates in the captain's in box along with the letter to accompany the fifty-nine WAC Form 51 Competition Certificates to WAC HQ for Lt. Col. Lathrope's signature.

She closed the door to the captain's office and stopped in front of Sgt. Levy's desk.

"Are you going to chow or do you want me to bring back a tray for you?"

Sgt. Levy covered her typewriter and stood. "I'll get my hat and walk over with you." She opened her lower drawer and took out her garrison cap.

The phone rang, as Edie set the hat on her short, black curls. The direct line button lit up red.

"You want to answer that?" Sgt. Levy arched a black brow.

"Uh-uh—it's after quitting time. The last time I answered that line off duty, it was bad news."

"Company D, Sgt. Levy speaking. One moment, please." She pressed the hold button. "It's for you. It's him." Her eyes widened.

"Monty?" She asked. Her heart started to race, thundering in her ears.

"No. Sgt. Vinluan," the sergeant said, pushing the handset into her hands. "Be nice to him."

April pressed the flashing button, and a crafty smile curved Edie's lips as she scooted out the door.

"Hello, Elaine. I was pleasantly surprised and delighted that you finally decided to return my calls. I apologize that I wasn't here to take your call in person. I was unexpectedly called to Ft. McPherson."

"Sgt. Vinluan—"

"Ben—you promised to call me Ben."

"Ben, there has been some mistake. I haven't returned any of your calls."

"That's strange. I'm holding a message call sheet in my hand with Sp. Terry's name and phone number 8142 at Company D. Isn't that your company's telephone number?"

"Well—yes, but I didn't make…oh forget it. It was someone's idea of a bad joke. I'm sorry you got caught in the middle."

"Why not take advantage of it and have dinner with me?"

"I can't. Right now I'm going through a difficult time and I just wouldn't be good company."

"Why not let me be the judge of that. I've been told that I'm a very good listener and I have tolerably broad shoulders."

"This is something I'll have to deal with alone."

"I take it that things haven't worked out between you and your boyfriend like you anticipated?"

"You could say that."

"My offer still stands. I have two good shoulders just going to waste."

She smiled.

"I felt your smile."

"How is it, you know me so well?"

"I'll explain it when I pick you up at 1800 hours."

The dial tone told her he had hung up. She drew the phone from her ear and hugged it to her for a moment. With her eyes squeezed shut, she struggled to make sense of her feelings. She went out, closed the office door and locked it.

"Are you going to see him?" In the CQ area, Sgt. Levy leaned against the counter her lips pursed in a knowing manner.

"You—you called him and gave my name," she accused, pointing a finger at Sgt. Levy.

"Guilty as charged." The sergeant executed a little half salute, British style. "You haven't been out of this building except on company business in weeks. Even I go to the beauty parlor and attend an occasional movie." She fisted her hands on her hips looking ready to do battle. "Tell me, what did he say?"

"Ben wouldn't take no for an answer. He's picking me up at 1800 hours."

"Good." Sgt. Levy grinned and winked.

The NCO Club was not yet filled. They were seated at a table away from the air conditioning vents. At the edge of the parquet dance floor, a guy sat at the piano playing soft music.

The waiter appeared, Ben ordered for her, and suggested a glass of red wine.

She declined, asking for a glass of lemonade. Dr. Nesbitt had said alcohol was not good for the baby. Much later, she finished the last of the Caesar salad and took a sip from her glass. A goblet of wine sat untouched in front of Ben.

Their waiter approached with a large tray and deftly slid a plate in front of her and one for Ben. After asking if she wanted more lemonade, he removed the empty salad bowls and withdrew.

"Elaine." Ben leaned forward. "I believe the gentleman two tables away on your left is trying to get your attention. He has been staring at you ever since we sat down." He took a forkful of food and chewed with enthusiasm.

She glanced over to the specified table where two men sat. One had his back to her and the second guy facing her wore a summer dress uniform with corporal stripes. He was handsome with black hair and dark complexion, most assuredly of Spanish origin.

He smiled warmly and inclined his head in recognition. She let her mouth curl up in a half smile and returned her gaze to Ben.

"I don't place him, but he appears to recognize me. Probably, sometime I danced with him at the service club." She returned her attention to her plate. "How is this dish called? I've never eaten it before."

"Tortellini. It's made with ham and spinach, that's what gives it the green color."

"It's delicious," she said, putting a generous fork of the pasta in her mouth.

"Coffee?" Ben queried after they finished eating and the plates were taken away.

"A glass of ice water with lemon, please."

He ordered black coffee for himself and she sipped the contents of her glass thoughtfully. Should she tell him about her broken engagement? Could she bring herself to speak to him about the baby?

"How much?"

The sound of his voice startled her, and she turned towards him in silent query.

"Your thoughts, how much for your thoughts?" Ben elaborated, leaning toward her.

Dear heaven had he guessed? What would he say if she told him she was pregnant?

A figure clad in a khaki uniform suddenly filled the space between them. She gazed into the dark eyes of the mysterious man from the table across the aisle.

He smiled. "Sgt. Terry?"

"Specialist Terry," she corrected.

"Specialist Terry," he repeated. "Emilio De la Fuente. I use to play chess with PFC Montoya. The best opponent I ever had. Do you remember me?"

"Yes, of course. May I present Staff Sgt. Vinluan, Cpl. De la Fuente."

Ben stood, extended his hand. "Would you join us for a drink?"

"No, thanks. I'm sorry to intrude. I just wanted to inquire about Montoya." His gaze slid back to her.

"Montoya was recently married. He's living in New York," she said, calmly.

De la Fuente's eyes widened, as did Ben's.

"Sergeant, would you mind if I danced with Sp. Terry?"

"That's up to her," replied Ben.

She nodded her acceptance.

The corporal moved her chair back as she rose from her seat. They circled the floor before he spoke.

"You took me by surprise when you said Montoya was married. I always presumed the two of you..." his voice trailed off.

"Yes—so did I. He married a girl from his country. They had been engaged prior to Montoya entering the Army."

"I'm sorry," he said, simply.

"Me, too."

"Could I call you sometime?"

"I'm afraid I'm not good company right now."

"Is that why I haven't seen you at any of the recent dances at the Hilltop Club?"

"I suppose so. I haven't felt like going out."

"Vinluan?"

"We're just friends."

"I see," said De la Fuente.

The music ended and he escorted her back to the table. She couldn't quite meet Ben's eyes as Emilio held her chair. After issuing a polite good night to her and Ben, the corporal took his leave.

Ben remained standing, leaning forward, and placing his hands on the table, palms down.

"Would you mind explaining that statement you just made to the corporal about Montoya being married?"

"I rather not discuss it."

"Is that why you danced with De la Fuente, to set him straight about Montoya?"

"If you are referring to him staring at me with eyes that accused me of—"

"Betraying Montoya," he finished for her.

"I had a different word in mind."

"Cheating?" he suggested.

"Something like that."

"Are you going to go out with De la Fuente?"

"Of course not. Not that it's any concern of yours."

"Oh, but it is. I meant what I told you the last time I saw you. My intentions toward you haven't changed. They are still quite honorable."

"If you knew the truth you wouldn't think so highly of me."

"Try me. I can be very understanding." He elevated his voice above the music and noise.

She looked away at the packed room, and then turned back to him.

"It's much to crowded and I don't feel up to airing my troubles in public. Please excuse me. I want to use the ladies room before we leave."

"I'll meet you out front with the car." Ben scooted her chair back for her to rise.

They were silent in the ten-minute trip to her barracks. Ben backed the Buick into the lot, avoiding the shining of the large spotlight on the end of the building in their faces. He cut the engine, braced his right knee in the seat between them and clasped it with both bands. "I'm listening—tell me what happened. You won't shock me. I have found that there is always a solution to every problem if only a person has the courage to search for it."

"You don't understand...there is no solution for my problem."

"Let me be the judge of that."

"Shortly after Montoya and I patched things up between us, his ex-fiancée showed up with his son." The words broke from her in a half sob.

"Of all the…" Ben exhaled loudly and straightened, picking up her hand in his.

"Naturally, he felt obligated to marry her," she continued.

"You poor kid." His strong fingers curled more tightly around her hand.

"I'm not asking for your pity. Please do not offer or even feel it for me. But that's not the worst of it. Before he left, I-we" She stuttered. "…we were intimate, anticipating our wedding night. Now I find that I am pregnant."

"Elaine." Saying her name as if he cherished it, he gently lifted her hand and pressed it against his cheek, an endearing gesture that made her suddenly feel dizzy and it had nothing to do with her condition.

"Does he know about the baby?"

"He has his life in New York" She shook her head. "I'll never see him again."

"Are you sorry?"

"No." She swallowed. "No," she repeated. "I'm not sorry. I want the baby. I'm just sorry it will never know its father and he will never see his child."

"You don't intend to tell him?" His eyes widened in disbelief.

"I couldn't." She shuddered and very slowly shook her head again. "It wouldn't have been fair to force him to choose."

"You're pregnant by him and worried about being fair?" Ben raised his voice a notch.

"You don't know all the circumstances."

"Don't you think he has a right to know? If it were me I would want to be told."

"What possible good could it do? He already has a wife and son. It would only cause him grief that he couldn't give our child his name. No—it's better that he never finds out about the baby."

"You're still in love with him, aren't you?" Tipping his head to one side, Ben looked at her, smiling in gentle understanding.

"I wish to heaven I didn't love him, but I still do. I can't have Monty or his love. My baby is all I'll ever have of him."

He stared at her for a long moment then opened his arms, and gathered her into his embrace. The hard arms about her squeezed gently, holding her as if he could make it all better. And for a few minutes, it felt almost as if he could. He comforted her with his hands, smoothing her hair, rubbing her back, and murmuring words of solace. She clung to him grateful for his presence and buried her face in his chest. Unable to hold her tears, she sobbed on his shirtfront. He continued to stroke her hair, holding her close, letting her weep.

"Ssssh," he said, soothing her. "You're not alone. I'm here. My offer still stands. Marry me. By the time you give birth the baby will be ours, regardless of how it came to be conceived."

She stared up at him in obvious surprise at Ben's casual acceptance of such an important undertaking.

Gratefully, she took the handkerchief that he pressed in her hand, dried her face, and leaned back in the seat.

"Will you marry me, and let me give your child my name?"

"Ben, please. You are a wonderful guy, but what you're offering is too generous even to consider. I do care for you. But I couldn't do that to you. What I feel for you is not the kind of love a marriage is built on."

"Let me worry about that. I'm not asking you to love me," he said, "only that you allow me to love you."

Could she do it? He was such an incredible guy. She liked him, cared for him, and had the highest respect for him. Maybe it bordered on love. She sensed in Ben so many of the fine qualities that had made her fall in love with Monty. They both were sweet—gentle—caring and the list just went on. What more could a woman ask for in a man?

"Don't you know that there are no rules for the length of time that it takes to lose one's heart to someone? People often fall in love on a first meeting—after a few days. I've been in love with you for over six months and I didn't even know your last name. Why can't you just accept that I love you enough for the both of us? And I'll love your baby, too."

"Oh, Ben I wish it were that simple. I'm so ashamed that I have no love to give you." She raised her head to look into his tormented eyes. She wanted to offer comfort, but she couldn't even give him that.

"Elaine, a gentleman's adoration need never embarrass you even if you cannot return it." He kissed his finger and pressed it to the tip of her nose. "I want to marry you and take care of you," he said gently. He added, "And your baby. You don't have to give me an answer today. But I'd be the happiest of men if you'd say yes right now."

His words had a devastating effect on her. She wished she could accept his proposal. For a little while she longed for her battered and bruised spirit to be pampered. Life had thrown her a cruel curve—she was tired of fighting it. She yearned for a strong shoulder to lean on, a firm hand to hold. But she cared too much for him to take the chance of ruining his life along with her own. Ben deserved a woman who would love him wholly and completely, the way she loved Monty.

"I thank you from the bottom of my heart for your generous offer. I hope someday that you'll find a woman worthy of your love."

Ben leaned his head on his crossed arms around the steering wheel and was quiet. It was as if he pondered the things she had told him. Then he straightened and turned to her.

"What will you do?"

"I don't know." She took a deep breath and sighed.

"You do understand if your superior officers learn of your condition, you'll immediately be discharged."

"I know—I'm hoping that I can stay until my ETS at the end of this month."

"There is something I haven't told you. My orders came through for Germany. I leave early Monday morning."

"Is that why you proposed again?"

"Partly, if we married now you could follow me to Germany after your ETS."

"It's probably for the best that you are leaving. I don't want to see you hurt."

"At least, let me be your friend until I go." He held out his hand palm up. His voice was low and velvety as he continued, "Please—it would mean a lot to me."

"All right, Ben," she said, and placed her hand in his. "If that's what you want. Friends." In an odd way, she felt some of the pain easing, as if talking with Ben had made it less.

"Dear friends," he said, and he gently squeezed her hand before letting it go.

Her steps faltered as she climbed the stairs to her room. But when she lay down and tried to sleep images from the past and present pulled and tore at her.

What was Monty doing? Was he enjoying his son? Was he making love to his wife tonight?

Stop! She couldn't think of that. If she thought about Monty, she would go crazy. And if she didn't think about him, she would die.

She wrapped her arms around herself, trying to hold herself together. Again, she closed her eyes and tried to force her working brain to relax. What would happen if her condition were discovered?

Love cannot be measured and weighed,
And it should never be compared.

Chapter 43

The following morning April told Sgt. Levy about her conversation with Ben. And then she had to explain all the reasons why she couldn't marry him. It would be easy to imagine herself in love with the handsome sergeant. But she could not wrong Ben by marrying him when she would always love another. Monty was the person who owned her heart, and he was the guy she couldn't have. The one man who wasn't free to return her love.

In the afternoon, she closed the lid of the large gift box on her desktop. "I still feel rotten about taking the gown and robe," she said, indicating the white carton.

"Just think of it as a going away present. Be glad I was able to select a serviceable outfit instead of the filmy, sexy thing the cadre wanted to give you."

"If you hadn't warned me about the surprise bridal shower, I might have gone to pieces in front of everyone. Thanks, Edie."

"Well you might have returned the favor and hinted to me that they were giving me a surprise going away party at the same time."

"What? And spoil their fun. While you thought you were planning a party for me it was actually for the two of us."

"I was real surprised when Lt. Col. Lathrope dropped by to wish me luck at my new post."

"I thought it was very grand of her. But after all, you've been around for a long time."

"Yeah, I'm about as old as dirt," Edie said. She wrinkled her nose and rolled her eyes toward the ceiling.

April giggled and picked up the box from her desk. "I better put this in my room before I go to chow. Are you leaving the office now?"

"As soon as I put the left over cake in my fridge upstairs. There was no room in this one," Edie said, waving at the pink and white confection on top of the tiny tabletop refrigerator. "Why don't you stop by after bed check for a late night snack? I've got ice cream, too."

"I don't think so, I'm watching my weight." She patted her rounding stomach.

They left the office laughing together.

Later in the evening while on Duty NCO she sat alone in the dark Orderly Room. Tears nearly blinded her as she stared at the telephone.

What would happen if she had the courage to tell Monty about the baby? What would he say if she simply picked up the phone, called him, and said, "I'm pregnant?" Demanding nothing, expecting nothing? Didn't he have the right to know? Then she imagined his eyes with pity in them. No. She couldn't bear that.

"Oh, Monty..." Sobbing uncontrollably, she collapsed across the desk, her right arm outstretched toward the telephone.

She had given him her heart and soul and reached for a dream of life and love she'd never thought existed for her. Now to have that love stripped from her seemed all the crueler for the loveless years ahead. Those passionate hours spent in Monty's arms would remain in her heart forever. She curved her arms around her stomach, cradling her unborn child.

A knock interrupted her soul-searching. Quickly, she straightened, composed her features and swiped at the moisture on her face.

"Come in."

Pvt. Hudson, the CQ on duty entered, carrying a flashlight.

"Sp. Terry, it's almost 2200 hours. You said I was to let you know when it was time for bed check."

Immediately following the checking of the last platoon, she went to her room and curled up on her bunk without removing her clothing. With her face turned into her pillow, she wept.

She must have cried herself to sleep for the next time she opened her eyes the sun was streaming in her window that she had forgotten to close the shade. Wearily, she pushed herself up and swung her legs over the side of the bunk in anticipation of another day of duty. Today was the Third Platoon's graduation, and she would be attending the parade as a spectator.

Next to her on the parade ground, bright Alabama sunlight glinted on the gold US and the Pallas Athene insignia pinned to Sgt. Levy's lapels. April squared her summer garrison cap and then tugged it precisely to the right angle over her brow.

A distant drumbeat carried on the morning air. She titled her head as the sound took on a familiar rhythm. She hadn't marched to that tune in months, but she identified it immediately. Sousa's march, "The Stars and Stripes Forever." Proud young women in starched summer dresses marched onto the parade field adjacent to the WAC Band in preparation for their graduation ceremony.

As was the custom for all WAC Basic Military Training at Ft. McClellan, WAC Battalion Headquarters conducted a formal parade every eight weeks marking the trainees graduation. She had marched in numerous of these parades as cadre and as a member of the WAC Color Guard. The color and pageantry of the event stirred something deep within giving her a feeling of patriotism, duty, and loyalty to her country.

The tempo of the drum now called to her—drew her like a magnet.

Across the field, rows of bleachers were filled with proud parents—excited children—invited guests and the uniformed training instructors who'd worked diligently these past eight weeks to turn raw recruits into disciplined members of the Women's Army Corps.

Massed troops waited patiently in front of the reviewing stand for the parade to begin. The Stars and Stripes waved in the breeze next to the WAC colors.

She pulled her gaze from the flags and let it drift down from A, B, and C Company to her own Company D. Freshly starched and ironed beige uniformed women standing at parade rest, hands clasped loosely behind their backs.

Goodness. They looked so young. Had it really been only twenty-two months since she had stood on the same field anticipating her own graduation? She felt a tug of envy for the future that stretched so limitlessly before them. What honors would they bring to the uniforms they wore so proudly?

An officer quick stepped to the center of the field and faced the lined troops at parade rest.

The WAC Band belted out a few short chords, alerting the trainees, officers, and the visitors the commencement of the ceremonies.

"Bring your troops to at—tenn—shun!"

One after another, the company commanders echoed the Adjutant's bellowed commands. Three hundred chins lifted, shoulders squared. Guidons whipped up, and the green and gold pennants snapped in the breeze.

Unconsciously, April pulled back her shoulders and dropped her hands loosely at her sides. Her pulse accelerated in a quick, steady cadence. She gave her undivided attention to the ritual announcements that preceded the ceremonies.

The reviewing party arrived and the colors marched forward. She came to rigid attention. At the first note of the national anthem, her right arm snapped up in sync with all the others on the field. Palm blade straight, fingers just touching her brow, she stood proud and erect. The emotions that comrades-in-arm rarely, if ever, admitted coursed through her body.

Pride—Patriotism—Duty—Loyalty—Honor—Camaraderie. A sense of belonging to a higher group. A compelling need to return some measure of service to the nation that nourished them.

Throughout the ceremonies, she stood at the end of the field. She barely heard the introduction of the reviewing party. She watched with abstract interest when the officers massed in the center and marched forward, then returned to lead their troops. Only a part of her listened to the stirring remarks by Lt. Colonel Lathrope. Her thoughts stayed focused entirely on the troops. With eyes right, the women's arms whipped up, saluting the reviewing officer as she marched past. April stood next to Sgt. Levy and together they proudly saluted the graduates.

As one platoon after another filed by, she recalled how she'd stepped out some twenty months ago. Like these eager young women, she'd marched off the field straight into months of routine, incredible challenges, excitement, and occasional frustrations. She'd made some unwise decisions during those months that she regretted. There had been instances she'd give anything to turn back the clock and make the right choice. And then there were the many wonderful, exciting good times, too.

April waited with Sgt. Levy until the last platoon had passed in review. They walked side by side away from the parade ground and got in the jeep. In silence, she drove back to the parking lot of Company D.

> Saturday, 13 September 1958
> Dear Dreamcatcher,
> This morning our Third Platoon graduated. As I stood watching the young women, I vividly recalled the past two years with mixed sentiments. The incredible challenges, excitement and occasional frustrations, which I've dealt with both military and in my private life. I am remorseful for the pain that I caused to another, and for the heartache that never leaves me. And then there were all the triumphant

wonderful times, too. My achievement of becoming WAC of the Month, and a member of the WAC Color Guard not to mention the great attainment of becoming the youngest Acting First Sergeant in the history of a Training Battalion.

Although I lowered my principles, I have not lost my loyalty, pride and honor for my uniform and my country. I am so privileged to be able to complete my tour of service with dignity and self-esteem. I credit my extensive training as member of the WAC that gave me the courage and self-worth to attain my goal.

I am so fortunate to have found a position as the receptionist of my doctor where I can remain before and after the birth of my baby. That alone was a miracle, and I have located a small-furnished room near by where I can walk to my job.

In less than two weeks I will be leaving Ft. McClellan to meet a new challenge. There will be many difficult times ahead, but I look forward to the birth of my baby with breathless anticipation. My military education has given me the confidence needed to handle each situation as it occurs to the best of my ability.

My love for Monty continues to cause my heart to ache. How long will it hurt before the pain finally fades and becomes more bearable...

Ben closed the Buick's door, locked it and pocketed the key. A woman on the other side of the Hilltop Service Club parking lot wearing a white dress caught his attention. She was walking rapidly with her arms crossed tightly over her chest, her head down and her shoulders slightly hunched. It was obvious from her uneven stride that she was upset.

"Elaine. Stop," he called as he sprinted across the pavement.

She kept walking.

When he caught up with her, he took her arm, halting her in mid stride.

Her shoulders jerked, and her head came up as she turned slowly to face him. All he saw were her eyes; the anguish in them was immense. His first instinct was to take her into his arms and hold her until the pain went away. To assure her that everything would be all right. He could read the clear signs in her eyes and body language that told him not to trespass, and he quickly ignored her signals.

416

"Don't cry," he said, brushing at the wetness on her cheeks.

She swallowed a sob and tried to turn away, but he reached for her pulling her gently into his arms. She struggled to get free, but he knew she needed comforting. Her thoughts were so easily read, her every expression so refreshingly honest and transparent.

"Settle down. Just let me hold you." He urged her face into the hollow of his throat and held her as she sobbed into his shirtfront, feeling her pain.

"I'm getting your shirt all wet," she mumbled, her hand swiping at the damp material.

"That's okay. I have plenty of others."

She raised her head. Bleak eyes looked at him, and the sight sent an aching shaft through his heart.

"Do you want to tell me what turned on your waterworks?" he teased, winking down at her.

"The Spanish Band is playing in the club." She sniffed. Her even white teeth mashed her lower lip. He could see she was fighting her tears.

"They must be pretty awful to make you cry," he said, a grin hovered around his mouth.

"No," she said. "They played beautifully. It was the song that made me cry. Memories are sometimes a terrible thing."

"Yes, I know. What are you doing here alone?"

"I was feeling sorry for myself, and Sgt. Levy chased me out of the building."

"You should have called me. That's what friends are for. I know—you don't phone men," he said, holding up his hand.

"Why are you here?"

"I was looking for you. I called your company and the CQ told me you had signed out, and she thought you were coming to the Hilltop Club. I borrowed a camera to take some pictures around the post. There's a place over by Post Headquarters that reminds me of Japan. Why not come take a drive with me?"

"I thought you sold the car."

"I did, but I arranged to keep it until I leave on Monday."

Across from the Post HQ was a small creek spotted with sunshine and a half dozen ducks swam in circles. An intricate stone bridge arched over the lazy steam with weeping willow trees lining the sides. Rose of Shannon and hibiscus bushes intermingled around the edges. From the center of the bridge could be seen a colorful flurry of varied gold fish in reflected shades of orange and gold.

"This bridge was built in 1944, and it is known as Rock Bridge," Ben informed her as he focused the camera where she was posed standing at the entrance of the structure.

They spent the rest of the evening together until it was time for her to return to her quarters.

"Tomorrow is the last time I can see you before I leave. My time is so short. I wish there was someplace I could take you where I don't have to share you with anyone."

"Come over after chow tomorrow night, and we could just sit in the car," she suggested, extending her hand. "Thank you for a pleasant and unusual afternoon."

He took her hand and held it; he smiled at her slightly, patted and released her hand.

The following evening Ben's eyes widened appreciatively as she walked out to meet him in Company D's parking lot. His whistle was long, low and too exaggerated to be offensive, his eyes danced with mischief.

He opened the door and held it until she was seated. He closed it quietly, rounded the car, and slid behind the wheel beside her.

She told Ben about her decision to remain in nearby Anniston until the baby was born. And she gave him the sad news about Sgt. Levy being transferred to Ft. Knox at the end of the month.

"Are you going to be all right?" he asked with tender concern, and in his eyes she glimpsed the love that he couldn't quite hide.

"I'm fine. We both are," she said, laying a hand over the gentle swell of her stomach. "I've already found a job and a place to stay in Anniston."

"That's good news." Ben paused for a moment. "Are you sure you don't want me to take you to the NCO Club?" He gave her hand a reassuring squeeze.

"You were the one that said you didn't want to share me with anyone. Otherwise I would have suggested that we go to your mess hall."

His head dipped, his mouth coming against her shoulder—not a kiss, a mere resting of his lips against her, and even through the fabric she could feel his smile.

"Not on your life."

They laughed together, and then he said in a serious tone, "How about going for an ice-cream cone?"

"Are you insinuating that I need fattening up?"

418

"Not at all. I consider ice-cream a happy food, and you need cheering up."

Ten minutes later he parked in front of a shop, and he helped her from the car.

"Strawberry?" he asked.

"That sounds marvelous."

As he promised, Ben bought them each huge ice-cream cones. They sat at one of the small tables inside the store eating their delicious frozen treats.

She took a long, slow lick of the cool dessert and smiled when she caught him watching her. "I told you ice cream was my weakness."

After finishing their delectable concoctions, they went back to where Ben had parked his car and returned to her parking lot at Company D.

Later, he held her hand when he walked her to the door. They stood wordless, Ben continuing to clasp her hand. April allowed the physical contact, taking encouragement from the sensual pleasure that flowed from his hand. She took a calming breath, slowly withdrawing her hand from the comfort of his.

"Are you sure you'll be okay?" he asked for the second time.

Unable to answer, she nodded her head. *No, she was never going to be the same with the awful hurt inside her heart.*

"There's something I want you to promise me." He draped a protective arm around her shoulders, pulling her close to him.

"What?"

"If your financial situation gets to the point where you can't handle it, you'll let me know. I had a copy of my orders sent to you and if you ever need anything, anything at all," he repeated. "I want to help, if you'll allow me."

His offer touched her heart and she took a minute to swallow, tears burning the back of her eyes at his generosity.

"Thank you, Ben. That means a lot to me. I'll be fine. Really."

"I want your promise."

She nodded against his chest.

"Good, girl."

"Dear, sweet Ben, I'll never forget you or your kindness. You were here for me when I so desperately needed someone to lean on. I'm going to miss you."

"I'll miss you, too. I'll be thinking of you every time I eat strawberry ice cream."

"Maybe you should switch to another flavor?"

"Gladly, if it would be your second hand kind."

She couldn't help smiling at his reply.

"You're smiling."

"Only you know how to make me smile these days."

"I'm happy I can still do that."

His hands moved in small circular movements over her shoulders and back. He caressed her as if she belonged to him, as if she were precious to him, cherished by him. She shivered and clung to him grateful for his presence.

"You're cold. You'd better get inside."

"Alright," she said, stepping back from his embrace. But she wasn't cold. Except maybe deep down inside, where she didn't think she would ever be warm.

Ben touched his fingers to his brow in a mocking salute. "It has been my pleasure, *aloha*," he said. He left with his shoulders square, his gait steady, but she knew what the effort cost him. Her vision blurred as she watched him walking to his car. In moments, the brightness of the Buick's taillights disappeared into the night shadows leaving her alone in the darkness.

On Monday morning the phone was ringing when she entered the Orderly Room.

"Good morning, Company D, Sp. Terry speaking."

"Elaine? It's me, Ben. I haven't got much time. I have a flight to catch. I just wanted to call and say good-bye. These past days have been the happiest for me. I cannot imagine my life without you in it. I'll see you in two years," he said, then the phone clicked in her ear.

Minutes later, she was still holding the receiver when Sgt. Levy entered the Orderly Room.

"That was Sgt. Vinluan. He called to say good-bye, and that he would see me in two years. I don't even know where I'll be in that length of time." She frowned, gently replacing the receiver on the cradle.

"You never can tell," replied Sgt. Levy, shaking her head.

Ten days later April sat in the Orderly Room talking with Lt. Sanchez.

"You did a good job instructing Pvt. Olsen with the guidon. Too bad you had to miss the parade."

"Thank you, Ma'am. Like Pvt. Olsen, I had the same fears the first time that I carried it, too. I prayed all the way across the field that I wouldn't stumble or worse fall on my face before I reached the post position. I'll see her in this coming Saturday's parade."

"Did Capt. Fraser leave yet?" asked the lieutenant, pausing with her hand on the doorknob.

"Yes, Ma'am, just a few minutes ago."

"I'll see you later this evening." Lt. Sanchez exited the room, closing the door behind her.

Almost immediately the door opened again and Sgt. Levy entered the Orderly Room.

"I just passed Lt. Sanchez in the hall," said Sgt. Levy, removing her hat and plopping down in her chair. "Have the rest of the officers left?"

"All gone for the day. Lt. Sanchez will be back—she's the DO tonight."

"Are you all packed?" asked Sgt. Levy.

"Yes, what about you?"

"I've still got plenty of time. How are you moving your possessions to your efficiency?"

"Sgt. Vinson is loaning me her car after the parade Saturday. She thinks I'm taking my footlocker and luggage to the train depot."

"If I wasn't on duty, I'd go and help you. You shouldn't be lifting anything heavy."

"That's okay. The building has an attendant, he'll assist me."

"You missed a great parade. You can be proud of Pvt. Olsen. She did good."

"Lt. Sanchez said as much. I'm staying for Saturday's parade. Where is Pvt. Foster?"

"She went down to the mailroom. She's holding mail call out on the walk when the troops return from the parade field."

"I heard from Sgt. Vinluan."

"What did he have to say?" Sgt. Levy stood and walked across the room.

"Not much." She picked up a picture post card from her desk and handed it to the sergeant.

Sgt. Levy looked at the colorful photo of Munich before turning the card. She read aloud the single line on the back. "Thinking of you and wishing you were here. Ben."

"It says a lot," said Edie, handing the card back to her. "Are you going to write to him?"

She glanced at the card in her hand and shook her head. "I've already hurt him enough."

"I still think you should have married him. From what you've told me about Ben, he would have made a wonderful father for your baby."

"He's a marvelous, terrific guy, and I do care for him, but I have no love to give him except as a friend."

"I understand. It's just that with me leaving I would be more at ease knowing someone was looking out for you. I don't like to think of you alone in Anniston."

"I know. It want be for long, soon I'll have my baby." She sighed, and brushed her hand over her rounding stomach.

April opened her top desk drawer, removed a tiny box, got up, and handed it to the sergeant.

"Thanks for the loan of this. I won't need it any more. Tonight is my last official duty. Only three more days before my ETS."

"And seven days until I leave for Ft. Knox," commented Sgt. Levy, pocketing the ring. She opened the door and held it for her to pass.

"Are you excited?" she asked, as they walked down the hall toward the CQ area.

"Somewhat. Say, who is that man talking to your CQ?" asked Sgt. Levy, pausing, tilting her head to one side.

April's brain was playing tricks on her, confusing her. It couldn't be true. The voice sounded so familiar. She felt sick again. Perspiration broke out all over her. The hallway began to fade. She found it hard to breathe with a loud buzzing inside her head like a swarm of bees.

"Monty." Her voice sounded strange and far away even the roaring that filled her brain subsided. Her knees turned to spaghetti, her vision clouded and she became weightless as if she were floating. Suddenly, there was only darkness, and she slowly fell forward into it.

To live in love is life's greatest challenge.

Chapter 44

Monty heard April call his name from the foyer where he leaned on the counter speaking with the company's CQ. Quickly, he dashed around the corner and down the hall toward where she and Sgt. Levy stood.

He caught April as she slowly slipped to the floor.

"Take her to the Day Room," instructed Sgt. Levy, hurrying ahead of him and opening the door.

He gently laid her on the couch and turned to Sgt. Levy.

"Call a doctor—an ambulance!"

"Monty, calm down. There's no need for a doctor. April's not ill. She's pregnant."

"Pregnant," he repeated. "But how?"

"I expect you'd know more about that than me," responded Sgt. Levy. "I'll get a cold cloth for her head." She walked to the door, opening and closing it quietly on her way out.

Monty lifted her soft hand to his lips, tenderly kissing each fingertip before enfolding her hand in his. He'd had twelve hundred miles to prepare for this. Probably, he'd thought of at least that many different ways to say what he needed to tell her. Clever, romantic ways. Every one of them flew right out of his head with her lying there so pale and still.

Sgt. Levy entered and handed him a cold, wet handkerchief.

"Here. It's about time you took care of her." The sergeant's grin softened her words as she left them alone closing the door behind her.

He smoothed back her hair, leaned down, and kissed her before he placed the white cloth across her forehead.

April moaned softly, tears staining her cheeks.

"Monty…" She opened her eyes.

"Hello," he said gently, smiling down at her. "How do you feel?"

"What?" her eyes widened as she looked up at him. "I fainted?"

"Yes, you did." There was so much more he ought to say but no words would come out.

April closed her eyes. When she opened them, the Day Room was still as it had been before. Monty had not vanished. He was now looking at her with deep concern.

"I didn't mean for anything like this to happen," she said, trying to get up.

"Just rest," said Monty. He pushed her gently down and placed the cloth back on her forehead.

"I'm sorry for all the trouble." She relaxed but clung to his arm and glanced away from him. "I wasn't consciously planning to get pregnant. You needn't concern yourself that either I or my baby will make any claims or demands on you," she told him tensely. "It wasn't your fault—"

"Of course, it's my fault."

"No. You don't owe me anything. I don't blame you in any way. You did try to warn me..."

"I should have guessed when I phoned and you said that you had something important to tell me. I should have known. You knew that you were pregnant when I called—didn't you?"

"Yes," she whispered. "I didn't want you to know."

"I know now," he said quietly. "Don't you think a man has the right to know he is going to be a father? Peachy, why didn't you tell me?"

"Don't you think I wanted to? How could I tell you when you suddenly called and told me that you had a son and you were obligated to marry his mother?" She brushed angrily at her eyes misting with tears.

"Were you just going to have my baby and never let me know about it? Why?"

She couldn't answer him.

"Don't you have anything to say?"

"I'm sorry. I'm so sorry."

"You're sorry about the baby?"

"Oh, no. I love my baby," she said, placing a protective hand on her stomach. "I'm sorry you found out. I never meant to cause you any trouble." A sob tore her throat. "Why have you come back?" she asked in a broken whisper.

"To return this." Monty reached into his breast pocket, removed a small jeweler's box and placed it in her hand.

Her hand shook. She had trouble opening the lid. Inside, she found the engagement ring she had returned to him. Only now beside it rested a matching wedding band.

He lifted the diamond engagement ring from its velvet nest. Without any conscious thought, she held out her left hand, and Monty tenderly slid the ring on her finger.

"There," he said, and smiled. "It's back where it belongs. The other ring will join this one as soon as we can get a license. We're getting married." He said as if he expected an argument.

"I don't understand." She buried her face against his neck.

"I know you don't. I've come to take you to New York with me. Please forgive me. I wanted to tell you with different words. I even practiced what I would say while I drove down from—"

"What about your son? Didn't you get married?" she interrupted him, raising her head to gaze bewilderedly up at him.

"There never was a child. Esther lied. She tried to trick me into marriage so she could remain in New York."

"But how—"

"I refused to marry her until she could produce proof of my son. I demanded that she send for him. She kept putting me off. Finally, I called my father when she couldn't even show me a picture. From my father, I learned she married a guy in Ecuador, and he was killed in an automobile accident. Esther came to New York and when her money and visa ran out, she devised this scheme to get me to marry her."

"Are you really here?" She stared wonderingly into his eyes unable to believe what she was seeing and hearing. "I haven't imagined you, have I?"

"Believe it. There were times I doubted that these past weeks were real. Life lost all meaning for me, except where you are concerned. I didn't fully realize this until I almost lost you. I've never known what lonely was until I was forced to live without seeing you. But you were always in my thoughts. I'd go to sleep with the image of your lovely face in my mind. And I'd wake with it still there. I've heard your laughter and seen your smile in my dreams." He paused before continuing, "Peachy, you are my heart, my soul, and the air I breathe. I never lived until I loved you. I've missed you so." He slipped his arm around her middle and drew her next to him.

With closed eyes, she pressed her face against his shirtfront. She was acutely aware of the warm scent of his skin beneath the fabric, the comforting rhythm of his heartbeat below her cheek. And she recalled the hundreds of images she suffered of not ever seeing him again. Never had his arm's felt so wonderful. To love and be loved was such a fabulous feeling. A light, airy joy, she wanted to laugh and dance about the room.

"Are we really going to have a baby?" He had used *we* and there was a delirious look of wonderment in his eyes as he waited for her to confirm his question. "Are you sure?"

"Yes." She placed her hand over her slightly rounded stomach and gently massaged. "I've seen a doctor in Anniston."

"Are you okay?" he asked, in a concerned tone.

"I am," she sighed, "now that you are here. Are you glad?"

"More than that, I'm the happiest man on earth," he murmured. His head lowered raining kisses over her face. "Peachy, I'm sorry—so sorry I put you through all that. I love you so much. Will you forgive me?"

The husky raggedness of his voice as he whispered his love to her sent ripples of exquisite pleasure racing through her veins. She clung to him reveling in his passionate embrace.

"There is nothing to forgive," she said softly. "I don't blame you. It wasn't your fault." She turned his hand and pressed a kiss into his open palm. She had not thought she could love him any more, but she did. Much more.

Monty's throat grew tight with a powerful mixture of love, emotion and un-measurable joy. A delightful smile swept over April's face. She touched a hand to his cheek in a gesture so endearing, he felt his heart overflow with love. He reached out a hand and she laid hers in it, loving feelings pouring between their linked fingers.

"Oh, Monty, my ring's so beautiful." She moved her hand, wiggling her fingers. "See how it sparkles."

"Not half as beautiful as you are." He meant it with all his heart. Her eyes sparkled, and her skin seemed to glow.

As the tears slipped from her eyes, he lightly reached out a brown masculine finger and gently wiped them away.

"Sweetheart, don't cry. I'm here." Tortured by her tears, he clasped her tighter holding her face pressed to his chest, imaging all the nights he'd made her weep like this, despising himself with a vengeance.

"These are my *happy tears,*" she sniffed.

"I want us to get married right away. Tomorrow if we can arrange it."

"No. I'd have to go through proper channels. Other than, Sgt. Levy, no one knows I'm pregnant. I don't want a medical discharge when I'm so close to my ETS."

"So this is about your honor?"

"You might say that. It's the way I want it."

"I want whatever pleases you," he said, gazing into the lovely face of the woman who was promising him all that he had never had. He gathered her close; amazed at the feelings he had for this one small female. Because of her he'd found happiness and his heart's desire.

And here in his arms was *everything* he ever wanted.

The End

Printed in the United States
50927LVS00004BA/43-69

9 781424 123452